THE HORDE

Guy Cousins

To Wendy
Best wishes
Guy
2/6/08

Salvatore Publishing

Copyright 2008
© 2008

www.salvatorepublishing.com

ISBN 978-1-4092-3121-9

For Rowena, Matthew
Becky, and Hannah

With Love...

Prologue

Above the squall, she heard the juggernaut thundering towards the house. Lights flashed into the bedroom, crafting ghostly shadows across the walls as the lorry screeched into the hairpin outside.

'Alan for God's sake wake up!' Janet threw off the covers and leapt out of bed.

A deep rumble and the house erupted in an explosion of sound. The foundations quaked, ornaments crashed to the floor, and the ceiling cracked above her head.

Now she screamed.

Alan woke up and sat bolt upright, eyes glazed, face dusted with plaster. 'What the hell's going on?' he yelled.

Janet couldn't answer.

The bedside lamp flickered and died. She steadied herself against the wardrobe, terrified the floorboards would crack beneath her as Alan groped for the door handle, telling her to stay put.

'No, don't leave me.' She ran to him, pressed herself against his chest, and hooked her fingers into the flesh of his back.

He held her for a brief moment, then turned and snatched the door open. 'Come on, we need to found out what the fuck's going on.'

A waft of hot rubber ascended from the hall. The clunk of a dislodged brick.

Alan tried the landing lights - nothing.

Janet peered into the darkness, and realization struck. The stairs were gone. She stumbled into the bedroom and found her cell phone lodged behind the bedside cabinet. Alan fished a torch from the drawer and seized the phone from her.

'Jesus Alan!'

'I know what I'm doing.'

He dialed 999, and relayed the details to the operator as Janet stood in the doorway shivering. When he'd finished, he snapped the phone shut and handed it back.

They stepped onto the landing as the wind whistled through the house. Alan played the torchlight into the room below, and Janet scanned the wreckage, fighting the urge to belt out her terror in one unrelenting scream.

A huge articulated trailer lay on its side in her living room, surrounded by mounds of rubble. The TV, armchairs, and Chesterfield sofa had all gone.

'A bloody artic',' Alan said, 'it's come right through the front of the house.'

Janet followed the torchlight across the prostrate trailer. The back doors were unhinged, partially obscured by rubble. No identification marks, but she noticed a blue shipping container buried inside.

A faint scratching sound emerged.

The light faded.

Alan smacked the torch on the heel of his hand and homed in on the twisted doors.

'Look! Something's trying to get out.'

Janet froze.

Bricks tumbled away and a huge black shape surfaced into the light, broad and heavy like a bull. A plume of hot breath wafted through the haze as the creature clawed through the rubble.

Alan gripped Janet's arm and pulled her back from the precipice.

The creature's gaze shifted upward, yellow eyes pierced the gloom, and its jaws snapped open to unleash a sickening roar.

Janet caught its foul breath, dropped the phone, and watched it clatter to the floor below. She screamed.

Alan yanked her back into the bedroom, slammed the door, and braced himself against it. She joined him in a huddled vigil, wanted to speak but her lips were numb.

'A bear,' Alan said. 'It must be a grizzly.'

She heard the creature shuffling amongst the wreckage downstairs.

A bear? No, she had already erased that possibility. It didn't fit.

A thunderous roar came up through the boards. Janet squeezed her husband's arm and buried her head into his chest.

He stiffened and pushed his ear to the door. 'Oh Jesus.'

'What is it?'

'I think there's more than one of them.'

Sirens wailed in the distance. Janet squeezed her eyes shut and prayed they would arrive in time.

1

Sunday April 25

One mile outside Zarcom Research Facility,

Devon, England

THE CREATURE'S EYES BULGED behind a mesh of surgical sutures, stitched in a criss-cross pattern over the orbs to stop them popping out of its skull. Beneath the emaciated face, a slogan scrawled in blood: *Stop Animal Testing Now!*

Matthew Hunter rested the placard against the car door and a shudder of revulsion went through him. 'It's bloody disgusting, what the hell is it?'

Nina Siketi slammed the boot and eyed him over the roof of the car. 'A monkey of some sort, who knows? It's up to us to get the message out there and get the cruelty stopped.'

Hunter stared back at her in disbelief. *Like you give a shit,* he thought. He still hadn't figured out what they were doing here. 'Rumour has it Zarcom are closing this place down so we're probably wasting our time.'

Nina sighed. 'You'll see for yourself when we break in. Come on. We're moving out.'

'What do you mean *break in*? That's a joke, right?'

No reply. She grabbed the placard, and fell into step with the other protesters streaming out the woodland car park. The main procession, up to a thousand strong, surged down the narrow thoroughfare towards the Zarcom Research facility. Hunter caught up as she disappeared into the sea of green jackets and woollen hats. He had no choice but to follow. Back in London, Jeremy Bryant had made his feelings clear: 'One more week Hunter, get me a story, or you're out!' The editor-in-chief of The Daily News wasn't renowned for his patience.

Among the host of banners he noticed another placard identical to Nina's. The woman beneath it screamed the universal war cry; 'Get Zarcom out. Stop the testing now!' Her face contorted in a bloodlust glare, she looked capable of tearing a man apart.

Overhead, black clouds streaked the grey sky and the chants became more frenzied, almost malevolent. A sharp tug on his sleeve diverted his attention. Nina pulled him close and shouted what sounded like: 'Joy neen.'

'What?'

'Join... in!'

Her transformation from journalist to animal rights activist was startling, but when Hunter tried to imitate the others he felt like a fraud. Not an advocate of animal testing, he didn't oppose it either - he'd never given the subject much thought.

The demonstrators funneled down the narrow thoroughfare, urged on by a monotonous drumbeat. Their numbers appeared to swell; people fell into ditches and cried out in alarm. Hunter's legs were no longer his own, his chest tightened and he gasped for air as people surged back and forth as if caught in a riptide. He figured they must have hit the police cordon up ahead. Synchronized chants soon dissolved into an avalanche of screams. Hunter heard something snap and hoped it wasn't bone... it didn't sound good.

He craned his neck, desperate to find Nina, but only saw a blur of seething faces. Caught in the whirlpool of camouflage jackets and banners, he squirmed to free his arms as a grim realization swept over him. His only chance to break free was to clamber over the top of the crowd - an idea his conscience had to wrestle with.

No choice. He had to save Nina.

Hunter sucked in a deep breath and began to climb, using legs, knees and clothes - anything he could grapple to hoist himself up. A punch smacked into the back of his head but he managed to clamber free. People stared up at him, enraged as he stomped across the cobbled heads and shoulders, swerving to avoid the hands that tried to drag him down.

Thirty yards to his right, the spearhead of the protest battled against a wall of riot police, and on the other side of the hedge, a handful of fugitives were being chased across a muddy field. He saw a youth on his back, shielding his face as a swarm of uniforms dragged him through the mud. The kid's arm was torn away and Hunter realized his mistake – he was looking at Nina.

He shouted to her, lost his balance and plunged down amongst the tangle of limbs as the crowd engulfed him with wretched intent. Hunter lashed out and forced himself up towards the blotches of sky. With a final effort, he scrambled to the summit, and launched himself at the hedgerow. Pain shot through his hands and face as he landed on the nest of thorns and rolled into the field behind.

Back on his feet, Hunter staggered across the sodden earth, searching for Nina's black beanie hat and green combat jacket, but so many of the protestors fitted her description. One ran towards him, a tall lean guy with gelled-up hair.

'Go back man, you're gonna get hurt!' The accent took Hunter by surprise – American. 'Hey! Are you listening?' They've got dogs for Christ's sake. They'll rip you to pieces.'

Hunter brushed past him, eyes fixed dead ahead. When he reached the fence separating the two fields, he stopped and scraped his soles on the wire as he surveyed the area. The police had their hands full, carting dozens of protesters back to the vans. In the distance he saw a high metal fence, partially obscured by a cluster of trees - the boundary of the Zarcom Research facility.

A voice at his shoulder, the American again. 'Dude. You gotta come with me.'

Hunter turned and glared. 'Look mate, I don't know what you want but...'

'You're Nina's friend right?'

'What?'

'I'm Tom Swain. Nina sent me to find you.' The American offered his hand and Hunter shook it tentatively. 'Look behind you, we need to get outa here.'

Hunter spun, and saw two Alsatians tow their handlers across the second field towards him. *Shit!*

Swain urged him to make a run for it and Hunter didn't argue. The two men turned back and jogged along the edge of the field until Hunter's lungs began screaming for a break.

'Keep going buddy, they're slowing up,' Swain yelled from the rear.

Hunter pushed on a few yards and finally stopped, hands on hips, chest heaving.

Swain trotted up, and put a hand on his shoulder. 'Okay, you can rest easy. They've turned back… You alright bud? You look kinda shaky.'

Hunter sucked in deep breaths. He noticed a silver canister in Swain's hand but was too tired to ask questions. Eventually, he coughed out the words. 'I saw Nina being arrested.'

'Don't worry, she got free. She's a little prickly, but that's Nina for you.' The American slipped the canister into his jacket pocket and buttoned down the flap.

Hunter wiped sweat from his face, inspected the blood smeared across his hand. 'Who are you exactly?'

'I told you, I'm a friend. The name's Tom Swain. C'mon, let's join the others.'

'Others? No thanks, I've had enough of this shit.' Hunter turned and started for the road. 'The local fucking police,' he called over his shoulder, 'bastards all of them.'

'But Nina's waiting for us at the meet point. You can check her out for yourself.'

Hunter searched for a gap in the hedge but Swain wouldn't let it go.

'I swear she's okay. The girl's a tough cookie, maybe tougher than you think.'

Swain was right - Nina wouldn't give up so easily. Hunter stopped, and looked back, face bloodied, hair meshed with dirt.

'Take me to her.'

2

THE DEMONSTRATORS RETREATED FROM the police cordon, a broken army, bedraggled and fatigued. Blankets and first aid kits appeared from rucksacks and carrier bags, people tended wounds and passed around bottled water. Hunter weaved through the stragglers, a step behind Swain.

'So you're a reporter,' Swain said.

Hunter was mortified. 'Who the hell told you that?'

The American smirked. 'Don't worry, you're safe with me. We need your help to expose these bastards and once we're inside the facility, you're gonna have a hell of a story to tell.'

Who is this guy - some kind of eco-warrior, all whiskers and piercings?

Hunter changed the subject. 'So what did Nina say about me exactly?'

'Only that you two work together. The Daily News right? She reckons you're gonna help us.'

Great, she'd dropped him right in the shit this time. What was she thinking?

Swain seemed to register Hunter's anxiety. 'What's the big deal? You're part of the team dude. You should be proud.'

Team? The idea was to infiltrate the extremists, not join their bloody crusade. Hunter tried to remain calm. 'Tom, you're not making sense.'

Swain raised his hands, a concilliatory gesture. 'Dude, I'm just the messenger sent to get you. All I know is you've got clearance to join us, the rest you'll have to find out from the lady herself.'

Hunter sighed and touched his face with his fingertips. *More blood.* He had to figure this thing out before he got any deeper. These people were highly motivated and he didn't want to cross them. 'Sounds like Nina's a member of your group - Animal Rights I mean.'

Swain laughed. 'Let's just say she planned the break-in and wants you with us. She sent me to save your sorry ass.' Swain's brow arched quizzically. 'What were you doing climbing all over those people back there anyway?'

Hunter flinched with unease but ignored the question.

Minutes later they reached a dirt track leading to a small coppice set back from the road. Nina stood next to a beat up minibus, huddled in conversation with three men dressed in army surplus.

'What did I tell you?' Swain said. 'One tough lady.'

Muted cheers and congratulatory handshakes awaited their arrival. Hunter wanted to thank them all for nearly getting him killed, but didn't. He saw his chance to pull Nina aside, and steered her away from the others.

She snatched away from him. 'What the hell are you doing?'

He scrutinized her bruises. No blood, but her left cheek was swollen. 'You set this whole thing up.'

'Is that all the thanks I get for helping you?' She wound back her hair and fixed a ponytail.

Hunter lowered his voice to a whisper. 'Why didn't you tell me you were involved with these people? That American knows I'm a reporter.'

'There's no time to explain Matt. We're about to execute the plan. You're here to write the story but if you don't want it, I can cope without you.'

'You'll be arrested before you get across the first field.'

Nina rolled her eyes. 'What's wrong with you? All that shit about fearing for your job. I'm handing you a scoop, no strings. Trust me, this will make headlines and you'll be writing them. Do you want it or not?'

She was right. If he didn't take a risk, he was toast anyway. 'Okay so I need a story, but I'm not a charity case.'

'No, you're a damn good reporter. But it's time to rough it up a little Matthew, time to get your hands dirty.'

'Yeah – okay. But who are these guys?' Hunter jerked his thumb at the others.

'Friends.'

'I deserve more than that. At least tell me who I'll be sharing a cell with once we get arrested.'

'No one's getting arrested Matt, not if you stay close and follow my lead. Come on, I'll introduce you.'

Nina called everybody to attention. Besides Tom Swain, there was Phoenix, Amazon and Turk, bizarre names that transpired to be self-appointed call-signs.

Amazon and Turk resembled chilled out hippies. The type you might find on street corners, disheveled dogs in tow. Both had tousled, unwashed hair, fuse wire goatees, and eyebrows sprouting thin metal spikes. Turk had dark skin and black hair, but Amazon was a red-head. They seemed harmless enough.

Phoenix was altogether different - a muscle-bound black guy from south London, whose face was marked with scars. The longest wound was on the nape of his neck, a three inch pink line scored into his black flesh. Hunter sensed a whiff of violence about him and decided to steer clear.

Nina explained the strategy. The first assault on the barricade had been a ruse to test police strength. Some protesters had deliberately got themselves arrested in order to keep the police vans busy. Now they were regrouping, preparing to make another surge at the blockade and create a further distraction. With the police overwhelmed, Nina's unit could assail the eastern perimeter, and sneak into the Zarcom complex unopposed.

'We know Zarcom has made cut-backs on security. There's only skeleton cover at the weekend, so our main concern is the law.' She glanced at Hunter and tossed him a silver canister, identical to Swain's. 'You'll need this. Don't be afraid to use it.'

He caught it one-handed 'What is it?'

'Mace. In case you get cornered.'

Before he could object, she ordered the group to move out as Swain distributed gloves, ski-masks and backpacks of equipment. The whole plan seemed terrifyingly akin to a terrorist plot and these men undoubtedly belonged behind prison bars. And yet, as Hunter lined up to board the minibus, he felt a curious mixture of excitement and dread.

Phoenix started the engine, and the bus rattled down the track leaving a cloud of exhaust in its wake. They turned left onto the road, and circumnavigated the fields to the far side of the facility. Moments later, Phoenix pulled into a circle of trees five hundred yards from the outer perimeter.

From the front of the bus, Nina made a brief address. 'This is the assembly point. If anything goes wrong then we meet back here. The facility is protected by two fences, the second is electrified. I've arranged for the power to be isolated, but don't go charging in until we've double-checked. Any questions?'

Hunter said nothing, and as the group filed out of the bus he clenched his fists and closed his eyes. *Just go Matt. You need the damn story.*

3

Helmand Province, Afghanistan

10.14 am local time

RASHEED SAJADI GAZED AT the ash fluttering across the town square, a curtain of black and grey flakes, some tipped with an orange glow. He snatched one from the air and a searing pain shot through his palm. He winced, and brushed it away in disgust.

Why am I still here, in this stinking town?

His father had joined the Taliban revolt a year ago and hadn't returned since. Every few months a messenger arrived with a little money, and sometimes a letter, but it was never enough.

Tiny fingers groped Rasheed's hand. He closed his eyes and smiled. 'Jamila?'

The little girl giggled and pointed across the deserted street. 'Fire!' she yelled excitedly.

Rasheed nodded. 'Yes... fire.' Two blocks away the government offices were ablaze, belching black smoke and soot into the sky. 'Quick. Get inside little one.' He took his sister's hand, but she stamped her foot and returned a defiant glare.

'Don't make me tell Mama,' he warned her. He knelt and rested his hands upon her shoulders. What if the chaos and destruction became normal to her? What would his father say, and more to the point his sick mother?

Rasheed couldn't let her down.

He remembered how things used to be. The vibrant marketplace stacked with fresh produce - figs, dates, and olives as well as the smell of freshly baked naan wafting from the tandoor bakery.

All gone.

Qatif had become a neighborhood of battle-scarred buildings where only bandits and thieves found refuge.

Jamila squealed, 'Look - big fire.'

Flames leapt high above the buildings, and smoke billowed into the square as the sky darkened in the acrid haze. Rasheed felt the earth tremor beneath his feet and heard a distant rumble.

Tanks!

He hoisted Jamila to his chest. Her dress darkened and a warm fluid trickled through his fingers as her bladder emptied. Rasheed stepped back and kicked the front door with his heel. Jamila clung to him, fingers like barbs in his neck as he stumbled into the house. He tried closing the door, but it had warped long ago and wouldn't shut. He put his sister down, and regarded her tear stained face. 'You must wash. Can you manage that?'

She nodded.

'Good girl. There's a pail of water beside Mama's bed.'

Jamila peeled off her soiled dress, let it fall to her ankles, and toddled down the hall. Rasheed watched her disappear, then picked up the garment and took it into the front room where he dropped it into a bucket of water.

Tentatively, he peered through the window. A column of black smoke spiralled above the town, forming a T-shape in the sky. The trouble had erupted an hour ago, and most of the locals had fled. But with a bedridden mother to care for, Rasheed could not run. Now, as the minutes ticked by, he noticed the flames were dying down.

Small feet pattered up the hall and stopped at the doorway behind him, but his gaze remained fixed on the skyline. 'That was quick. Did you wash everything?' he said absently.

No reply.

He turned and saw Jamila draped in an oversized dress, the hem bunched on the floor, the front splashed with water.

'Mama's friend let me have it,' she said. 'The girl who wore it before isn't here any more.'

The story sounded grim, and probably was. Rasheed had always wondered about the dark blotches on the garment, guessed they were blood stains, but couldn't be sure.

Water dripped from Jamila's hair, her fringe pressed flat across her forehead in a comical fashion.

'You forgot to dry yourself didn't you?'

But her eyes were now fixed on the tiny puddle shuddering at her feet. The shelves at the back of the room trembled, pots rattled, and smashed to the floor, but Rasheed was more concerned about his sister. She ran to him, grabbed his legs and buried her head into his knees. He squeezed her tight and stroked her hair as he gazed outside.

The first tank emerged from the smokescreen like a great beast, turret swiveling to survey the buildings across the street, and a second followed close behind. Not the biggest tanks the British had unleashed on Qatif, but terrifying nonetheless. 'Warriors,' the foreigners called them.

A flash of light sparkled from a building across the street as the first tank drew level with the house. Rasheed ducked to form a protective shield over his sister. She screamed as the missile exploded. The ground quaked,and the window shattered above their heads.

A chatter of machine gun fire.

Rasheed knew he couldn't stay any longer. His priority was Jamila, but where could he take her?

Heat gusted through the broken window. He peeked out and saw the first tank ablaze. A human torch stumbled from the wreckage.

Another explosion.

Rasheed dropped to his haunches but Jamila squirmed from his grasp. 'Mama Mama!' She ran out of the room, and vanished down the hall.

He called after her, but as the stench of burnt flesh wafted into the house, a morbid curiosity gripped him, and he peered outside once more.

The second tank shifted its cannon to the right, and fired at a derelict house across the square. The shell smashed into the upstairs window, and blasted away the entire upper floor. Machine-guns returned fire from the rooftops. Rasheed covered his ears, terrified, but unable to tear himself away.

Muzzle flashes leapt from the roof opposite and two rockets streaked down towards the tank. The first missile sent up a huge explosion in the road. The second scored a direct hit and split the machine apart, sending chunks of twisted metal clattering across the street.

Rasheed pulled back from the window. Hunched low, he ran to his mother's room and found Jamila under her bed. His mother lay on the mattress, her eyes firmly shut.

He stooped and grabbed his sister's hand. 'Come Jamila.'

Her face quivered, tears rolled down her cheeks. 'What about Mama?'

'She will come later.' He pulled her up.

'But we can wake her,' Jamila said.

Rasheed examined his mother's lined features as he gently shook her. 'Mama can you hear me?'

No response and her breathing was shallow. He turned to Jamila. 'Come... we must go.'

Her eyes searched his face as she twisted a finger through her wet hair and struggled to comprehend.

Rasheed knelt, and pulled her close. 'Please understand. We must go now. God will keep Mama safe until we return.'

The little girl stepped back and regarded him with a considering look beyond her years. 'I will wake Mama, and then we will all go together.'

A crash echoed in the hallway – the sound of a door slamming against a wall. Rasheed sprang to his feet and told Jamila to crawl under the bed. He crept into the smoky hall, and through the haze saw the front door swinging on its hinges.

A body slumped across the threshold.

A British soldier.

Rasheed edged closer. The man's face was bloodied, his uniform charred and torn. His upper body was flopped inside the house, and his legs splayed out into the street.

Flames crackled outside. Rasheed looked out but the intense heat and sight of burnt human remains forced him to retreat. Briefly, as he ducked into the hall, he glimpsed a figure in a black turban and white dish-dash, stalk through the debris. A single gunshot cracked from somewhere across the street. More militia appeared, picking through the charred bodies, pumping bullets into each and every one.

Taliban?

'Rasheed quick, bring him inside!' The voice sounded weak but authoritative. Rasheed spun and saw his mother, propped against the wall, Jamila at her feet, arms wrapped around her legs. The little girl's eyes were now free of tears, and her lips curled into a smile.

'Quickly Rasheed. Take him to my room and lay him on the bed.'

'Yes Mother.'

'Quick Rasheed, quick!' Jamila shrieked.

He hooked his arms around the soldier's chest, and heaved him into the hallway as the sound of sporadic gunfire filtered through the gloom. Rasheed grunted and wheezed under the strain but didn't like the idea of using his mother's bed. 'Mother you are sick, you need...'

'God will take care of me. He has granted me the strength to stand, and now we must help the soldier.'

Rasheed dragged the man next to the bed, but couldn't lift him up. 'I can't do this on my own,' he gasped. The front of his shirt was smeared with blood.

'Put the mattress on the floor,' his mother said. She turned and spoke gently to Jamila. 'Run and get a towel my darling.'

'Yes Mama.' The little girl ran across the hall into the room opposite, wet hair bouncing between her shoulders.

Rasheed slid the mattress to the floor and rolled the soldier onto it.

'Good Rasheed. Now run and close the front door. We must keep out the smoke.'

For that, he needed something heavy to wedge the front door shut. He ran into the back yard and picked up a large stone, staggered back inside and shoved it against the door. But Rasheed couldn't help himself, and curiosity got the better of him once more. He glanced into the street and saw one of the militia prod a blackened corpse with the muzzle of his gun. Beneath the man's turban, his features were concealed by a scarf, loosely wrapped around his face. As the stranger bent down to inspect the body, his scarf slipped and Rasheed glimpsed the colour of his flesh - *white*.

He closed the door, pushed the stone up against it, and scurried back to his mother's room. He found her knelt at the soldier's side, unwinding a roll of tattered bandage. Jamila watched from the corner, looking pleased with herself, her anxiety now gone.

'Is the soldier still alive?' Rasheed asked.

'His heart is weak, but he lives.'

He watched her dab the man's bloody neck with a damp cloth and then smear a green paste over the lacerations with her fingers. Finally she bandaged the soldier's neck. She didn't notice the tiny glistening orb snagged in the wet cloth. But Rasheed did.

He said nothing. He wanted to tell her about the men outside, but it didn't matter who had attacked the British troops, or why, the local Taliban chieftain would expect to be told.

'Mother, Salim will want us to turn the soldier over to him.'

'That man is a butcher, Rasheed. I will not have his name mentioned in this house. Is he responsible for this?'

'I don't think...'

A rap at the front door. A rock scraped against the stone floor – the rock Rasheed had placed there to keep it shut.

Jamila snatched his hand and squeezed it tight.

Rasheed stared at his Mother. 'If they find us helping the soldier, they will kill us all!'

4

HUNTER STUMBLED AT THE rear of the group as they charged across the open field. The heavy rucksack thudded between his shoulders, and his hair was sodden inside the mask.

They reached the perimeter fence, a twelve feet barrier of steel bars topped with spikes. Twenty yards beyond, two cameras gazed down from high-mounted pylons. On Nina's signal everyone hit the dirt, all eyes fixed on the pods. Seconds ticked by but the cameras didn't move.

Amazon and Turk delved into their backpacks and extracted paintball rifles. The two men knelt down and fired through the bars. Paint pellets zipped through the air like swarms of maybugs that splattered the cameras in green goo. Paint oozed down the pylons, and dripped from the mountings.

Swain slipped on a pair of protective goggles and started up the metal grinder. The petrol motor rasped and sparks showered the ground as the blade sliced through the bars. Birds took flight and rabbits zig-zagged across the field in panic. Hunter covered his ears, expecting to see a posse of security guards come tearing out of the complex, but no one came. The American crafted a perfect square at the base of the fence and stepped aside to allow everyone through. One-by-one, the group members slithered through the gap and sprinted across the open ground to the inner boundary.

A sign read: HIGH VOLTAGE DANGER OF DEATH.

Swain was last to arrive. He picked a wrench from his rucksack, tossed it at the wire and watched it rebound without a spark. An air of expectancy spread through the group as he took a set of bolt-cutters to the mesh.

Hunter heard the distant uproar of protestors attacking the police once again on the other side of the facility.

Swain finished the job and Hunter helped him heave the wire netting aside. Nina instructed Turk to guard the escape route and spare kit. Only Swain and Phoenix took their packs this time.

The squad ran across open grassland and reached the first building, a flat roof construction complete with windows of reflective glass. Nina stopped at the corner, waited a few seconds, and then waved them on.

Strung out in single file, the group dashed across the empty car-park, past a cluster of small out-buildings, towards the main entrance. Hunter's senses nagged him with questions. Everything appeared deserted, no cars, people, or signs of security.

At the entrance, stone steps led to a door marked: *Block E Reception.* Swain dropped his pack to the floor and extracted a small plastic box which he popped open. He peered into the keyhole and selected a picking tool from the box which he wormed inside the lock.

Hunter felt sure animal research wasn't the original purpose of the facility, more like a Victorian hospital. The tall chimney was undoubtedly an incinerator stack, ideal for disposing of animal remains, and Hunter noticed a trace of smoke drifting from the top.

Someone's got something to burn.

The click of the lock forced him out of his reverie. Swain twisted the door handle and pushed it open. 'Easy as pie,' he muttered.

'Wait!' Nina looked up at a red light pulsing above the door. 'Shit, they know we're here. Follow me.'

She burst into the building, and the squad bundled in behind her. They shot past the reception desk, through a set of doors into a long corridor. The smell of cleaning fluid clung to the floor and walls. Overhead, tubes flickered like Morse-Code. Science labs lined the passage. Each door housed a glass panel affording a view inside. All locked and empty.

Hunter became conscious of his trainers squeaking on the polished floor, and the trail of mud left in his wake. He flagged behind the others, feeling his heart pound against his ribs like a boxer working a speedball. When he finally caught up, Swain had already started work on the doors to a room marked: 'Mammalian Testing.'

'This is it,' Nina said. 'This is why we're here.'

'You realize it's probably empty?'

If she was concerned she didn't show it, and merely turned to watch Swain agonize over the lock. Hunter glanced down the passage and spotted a red light in the ceiling. He tugged Nina's sleeve and pointed. She nodded and instructed Phoenix to stand guard at the end of the corridor.

'You know what do to if you see anyone?' she said.

The big man gave a thumbs-up and lumbered to his post.

Hunter fingered the outline of the Mace canister in his pocket. Sweat streamed down his neck and arms. He was desperate to rip the damn mask off and dry his hair.

Swain switched instruments several times, before attacking the door with a chisel. Nina peeled back her sleeve, and checked her watch, while Amazon struck a languid pose against the wall.

Swain jammed the chisel into the centre of the doors, raised his foot and kicked hard. The wood splintered and the lock broke.

'Thank you sweet Jesus. I hope this is worth it.' He dumped his tools in the bag, pulled open the doors and led them inside.

The room was the size of a large hospital ward. Dead tubes sparked overhead, creating a strobe effect. The smell of bleach couldn't hide the underlying stench that emanated from the floor and walls, urine and excrement - unmistakably animal.

Hunter buried his face into the pit of his elbow, but the smell clawed at his throat. His mouth filled with water and he gagged.

He recalled the tortured face of the monkey on Nina's poster and imagined the frail creature in this room, along with thousands of others - cages crammed with mice, rats, and monkeys, all of them agitated and fearful. In his mind, the flickering tubes exaggerated their fraught expressions.

'Empty!' Swain yelled. 'Fucking great!' He slammed his pack on the ground and began pacing like a caged tiger, bad-tempered and brooding. 'All this for nothing. Somebody must have squealed on us.'

Nina pulled a camera from her jacket and tossed it to him. 'We need photos. Get as many shots as you can.'

Swain began dutifully taking snapshots, and now Hunter understood why Nina was in charge. She'd given Swain a simple task - a little responsibility, and got him to focus. She'd retaken control, and the American seemed unaware of it.

Hunter spoke to her quietly. 'They're burning something in the next building - I saw smoke. This place might be abandoned but the incinerator is definitely still in use.'

Swain overheard. 'Bullshit. I didn't see any smoke.'

Suddenly Phoenix burst through the doors. 'Everyone out! They're coming.'

5

JAMILA SLID UNDER THE bed, and poked her head out, face upside down, eyes full of questions. Rasheed ushered her into hiding, and continued his vigil, fists clenched, every muscle tensed and ready to snap. Smoke ghosted into the room and he uttered a quiet prayer, his mouth trembled as the words trickled out.

Footsteps and whispers in the hall. A woman called out his mother's name. 'Nura? Nura are you there?'

Two figures cloaked in burkas appeared in the doorway, and Rasheed immediately sighed with relief. It was Rabia, and her daughter Aisha. The two women shuffled into the room like grief stricken wraiths, dark eyes peered fearfully through the slits in their head covers.

'Nura? What's... oh no. ' Rabia's hands flew to her face as if to swallow a scream.

Rasheed turned and gasped with horror. His mother was on her knees, holding the soldier's pistol in her frail hands. The muzzle drooped, her grip loosened and the gun hit the floor with a dull clunk. She picked up a towel and blotted her eyes. 'Please forgive me. I don't know what I was thinking.'

Rasheed noticed the empty holster strapped to the soldier's thigh. How terrified had his mother been to contemplate taking the gun, to even consider using it?

'Mother, you should be in bed.'

'No Rasheed please. Don't worry.'

'Praise God we arrived in time,' Rabia said. 'Aisha saw Rasheed drag the soldier into the house. There is blood on your doorstep and along the hall. We managed to sneak past the gunmen outside but they will come. I know they will come.'

'Who did this?' Nura asked her.

Rabia shrugged. 'Taliban I think.'

'Not that it matters, they're all the same. Now where can we go? We have nowhere to hide this man.'

'I know a place,' Rasheed said. 'An empty building about half a mile outside town, it will be safe for now.'

His mother sounded unconvinced. 'But all the houses on the outskirts have been blasted into the desert.'

'Not this one. It's Waheed's old house. Only one room, but it will do.'

'Who else knows about it?'

'Nobody. Waheed went to live with his sister in Herat'

'I've been there,' Aisha said.

Rasheed shot her a look of surprise. 'When?'

'I go there sometimes to be alone.' Her eyes bore into him. 'Who do you think keeps it clean?'

Rasheed tried to restrain his annoyance. He didn't need a girl to tidy up after him, or share his hideout.

Rabia insisted they make haste - get the soldier out of the house and across to the hideout without delay. She told her daughter to help.

'We need strong sheets to make a stretcher,' Aisha said. She smiled at Rasheed. 'We can carry him together.'

He grunted and turned away from her. Jamila poked her head out from under the bed. 'I can carry as well,' she chirped.

Rasheed wondered how much his sister understood. Her eyes full of their usual eagerness peeked through the wet strands scrawled across her face. She seemed unaffected by the ordeal. Aisha asked her to help find some fresh sheets and the little girl could not hide her enthusiasm.

'I can do that easy-easy-easy,' she squealed as she rolled from under the bed. She snatched Aisha's hand and pulled her out of the room.

Rasheed sighed and turned his attention to his mother. He didn't know her exact age, but since his father's departure she had become old beyond her years. He gazed down at the soldier. The man twitched and moaned as if in the midst of a nightmare, his uniform, torn and stained with blood. But the horror was not his alone. Rasheed had watched his family lose all sense of hope as foreign governments and local warlords continued to use his hometown as a battleground.

His father once told him, 'A man without hope lends himself to Satan.'

Rasheed tried to remain positive. Jamila was his special gift, and the only visible proof that God still presided over this hellish place.

He watched the two girls unfurl a bed sheet outside in the hall. In Aisha, he saw what lay ahead for his sister, a life of servitude hidden behind a veil - no education, no voice. He wanted more for Jamila, much more.

Nura pleaded with Rabia. 'The soldier might still have pieces of metal in his skin. I must clean his wounds.'

'Let me,' Rasheed said.

Nura sighed, and slumped back against the cushions.

Rasheed squatted next to the soldier and checked the bandage his mother had wrapped around the man's neck. A glimmer of colour caught his eye and he saw the tiny piece of shrapnel snagged on the bandage - a perfect sphere the size of a pinhead. For an instant the orb was metallic, but it quickly changed to red, and then green. Rasheed pressed his index finger onto the sphere and it stuck to the dough of his skin. The object sparkled in front of his eyes, and mesmerized him.

'Rasheed you're needed,' his mother said abruptly. 'The girls are struggling to make a stretcher and we're running out of time.'

Before he could answer, a deafening explosion shook the foundations. Dust fell from the ceiling, and everyone cowered as debris clattered onto the roof above their heads. Jamila started to wail, and Rasheed dashed into the hall to comfort her.

Aisha urged him to hurry. 'We need two poles to make the stretcher.'

Rasheed shook his head. 'No time. We'll roll the soldier up in the sheet and take one end each. He's heavy but we'll have to manage.'

6

HUNTER FORCED HIMSELF THROUGH the pain, his limbs ragged and greased with sweat. The sound of gunfire echoed behind him and he fell against the wall covering his ears.

Jesus they've got guns!

Four men in black uniforms turned the corner at the bottom of the corridor. Swain, Amazon and Phoenix immediately turned into the next passage, but Hunter remained hunkered against the wall, unable to move.

'Shit Hunter, come on!' Nina seized the front of his jacket and tried to pull him up. 'For Christ's sake snap out of it!'

More gunfire. Bullets shattered the light above his head, and sprayed the floor with glass fragments.

Nina twisted his face to meet hers. 'Come on for Christ's sake, they'll kill you.'

Finally, Hunter's internal motor rebooted. He sprang to his feet and told her to run. Twenty yards back, the guards started to gain. Nina sprinted hard, and for once Hunter matched her stride-for-stride. They joined up with the others at the next intersection. Nina took the lead and headed right.

Another shot. Amazon feel to his knees, clutching his thigh, eyes clamped shut in agony. Hunter pulled up to give him a hand, and saw blood smeared across the tiles.

Phoenix grabbed Hunter's shoulder. 'Go. Leave this to me.' The big man dipped into his pack and extracted an Uzi machine-gun. He checked the weapon and aimed at the oncoming guards.

Hunter staggered back in disbelief.

'I said *go!*' Phoenix yelled.

Hunter turned and sprinted after Nina and Swain, leaving behind the discord of gunshots and moans of pain. Halfway down the passage he glanced back and saw Phoenix standing over Amazon's prostrate body, spraying bullets into the passageway.

Ahead, Nina waited at the corner, half hidden in shadow.

'Why have you stopped?' Hunter said, gasping for breath. 'We need to keep running.'

She looked over her shoulder into the passage behind. 'It's a dead end.'

'What!'

He shoved her aside and peered into the next corridor. Six rooms – three on either side and at the far end, a blank wall. Swain was kneeling at one of the doors, frantically working the lock.

Hunter glared at Nina. 'I thought you knew the layout of this place. You said nothing about guards with machine-guns.'

'Our information was wrong.'

'What about Phoenix? Since when did Animal Rights carry automatic weapons? This is bullshit Nina.'

Phoenix charged up the passageway to meet them. 'Amazon's dead. I couldn't save him.'

Nina and Hunter pulled back behind the wall as Phoenix turned and unleashed another volley at their pursuers.

Tom Swain finally broke the door open and the group dived inside. Hunter fell through the doorway and collapsed in a corner. Swain bolted the door top and bottom. Seconds later, footsteps ran past outside.

Hunter surveyed the empty room. The door looked solid enough, reinforced with steel kick-panels, but the windows were blacked-out and appeared to be made of toughened glass. In the corner opposite, Phoenix slotted a fresh magazine into the Uzi. Swain sat against the door, and Nina stood beside him, ear pressed flat against the wood.

Voices filtered through the walls. The door handle rattled. Footsteps clicked on the tiled floor and faded away.

Swain had bought them some time, but what next?

Hunter studied the masked faces around him, their eyes wide with fear. His clothes were soaked and the stench of animal excrement lingered in his nostrils.

Suddenly, the shrill sound of a ring-tone pierced the silence. Hunter sat up and fumbled through his pockets. 'Shit!'

Nina glared at him. 'Jesus! What's wrong with you?'

'You've got to be fucking kidding!' Swain growled.

Shouts erupted in the corridor. A boot smashed into the door, as the ring-tone continued to chirp. Finally Hunter turned it off, but the damage was done.

Swain wedged himself against the door and slid his pack across the floor.

'Get the windows!'

Hunter rifled through the contents of the bag but found nothing to break the glass with. Meanwhile, the door began to split under the constant barrage.

'Will someone get that fucking window!' Swain screamed.

Phoenix took a couple of paces back, raised his gun, and released a short burst of fire. Bullets deflected and zipped around the room. Everyone ducked and yelled at him to stop. The slugs punctured the glass but the pane remained intact.

The door buckled and the bolts snapped away. Hunter ran across and added his weight, alongside Swain and Nina. From the window came a loud thud followed by the sound of glass splintering. Hunter turned and saw the middle pane billow like a sail. The rasp of a petrol motor ripped through the air, and sparks showered the room as the metal grinder powered through the tangle of glass and wire.

Turk – thank god!

Within seconds an opening appeared, big enough to climb through. Nina went first, and Phoenix followed.

'On a count of three,' Hunter yelled at Swain.

They counted, and on three, both men sprang away from the door. Phoenix thrust his gun through the window and cut down the first two guards as they burst into the room. Hunter scrambled through the hole and landed on the spongy grass outside, but Swain caught his foot on the glass. Blood spurted from his trailing leg as Hunter and Turk grabbed the American and hauled him out.

'Where's Amazon?' Turk said.

Swain rested a hand on his shoulder. 'I'm sorry man, Phoenix tried to save him but…'

No time to contemplate the loss. Nina told Phoenix to hold off the guards, and ordered everyone else across to the incinerator block. The chimney stack towered above them – wisps of smoke now clearly visible at the top.

Klaxons barked like seals from every corner of the facility.

Hunter barely noticed the roar of the protesters at first, but as the shouting grew louder, he glanced along the main thoroughfare and saw hundreds of people run past the security huts, ransacking everything in their path.

'This is our chance,' Nina said. 'The guards wouldn't dare open fire now.'

Phoenix came bounding across the grass. 'We're clear!' The guards pulled back.'

The group huddled around the building entrance. Phoenix took aim, and blasted away the lock. Nina kicked the door, and the squad moved inside.

Swain and Turk guarded the exit, while Nina led Hunter and Phoenix along the main corridor and through a set of swing doors into a brightly lit room littered with medical equipment. Three figures dressed in bio-hazard suits stood around a steel table. Their heads jerked up as the doors burst open.

'Raise your hands and back up against the wall,' Phoenix bellowed.

No response.

'Do it!'

In unison, the three suits lifted their hands and shuffled back. One glanced fleetingly at a steel trolley draped in a white sheet. The object concealed beneath was shaped like a specimen jar.

Hunter took a step closer to investigate, but Nina got there first, and yanked away the sheet to expose a glass tank filled with cloudy liquid. Sloshing around inside was a fleshy pod, the size of a football.

Hunter inched closer. The pod was punctured with tiny holes that hissed air. A network of capillaries extended through the object and embedded within the translucent flesh, a living form about twelve inches long, curled in a perfect circle.

A baby in a womb.

The thing twitched and jerked inside its protective sac as if an electric current was shooting through it. The mouth appeared disproportionately large. When the jaw snapped open, Hunter saw rows of tiny razor white teeth.

'Grab it,' Nina said, 'We need the evidence.'

Hunter backed away. 'You've got to be joking?'

One of the bio-suits spoke up. 'Please. Let us destroy it.' The man removed his respiratory mask. A guy in his fifties, thin face and sparse gray hair.

His two colleagues also removed their hoods - a guy in his twenties and a woman not much older. They all looked terrified.

'Keep your hands up,' Phoenix snarled.

The older scientist eyed Hunter. 'Please understand. You've no idea what you're dealing with. I'm begging you. Let us finish our work.'

'We'll kill it,' Nina said, 'once we've exposed your little experiments. Where are the rest of them?'

'That's the last one.'

'Not the embryos, I'm talking about the adults.'

The klaxon reverberated through the walls, and Hunter noticed a second alarm chiming alongside.

Turk burst into the room. 'We need to go, the place is being torched.'

Nina grabbed the trolley and began wheeling it towards the exit, but Hunter put a hand out to stop her. 'Enough. Let it go Nina, we've got the story.'

'But we need the proof.'

'No. We need to get out of here.'

She cursed, thrust her hand into the tank and tried to grab the creature. The thing squirmed like an eel, but she managed to seize on it.

Hunter backed away. 'Leave the damn thing alone. It might be diseased for God's sake.'

The embryo wrapped itself tight around Nina's hand until her fingers reddened. She held it up in front of her face and scowled. 'I've got you now you aggressive little shit.'

Suddenly blood spurted from her hand and she yelped as the creature sank its teeth into her flesh. She tried to shake the thing loose. 'Help me for god's sake!'

Hunter got behind her, slid his arms around her waist, and pulled the canister of Mace from his jacket. He took aim and sprayed. The creature went into a twisting frenzy before it flipped onto the floor and scurried under a row of trolleys.

Nina yanked herself free from Hunter's grasp. 'Without the evidence there's no story. We can't prove a damn thing.'

'The place is on fire, and everyone's leaving. I'm not getting burned alive or caught by the police. Let's go.'

7

WHEN HUNTER AWOKE, HE found himself sprawled on the floor of his apartment, fully clothed and soaked in sweat. His head pounded and his guts bubbled like a drum of acid. Peering into the grey light, he rubbed the back of his neck. The room looked like a wheelie-bin had been upturned and the contents kicked around for good measure - beer bottles, leftover pizza, and items of clothing strewn in every corner. The air reeked of stale sweat.

His senses recovered, and the nightmare unfolded.

Yesterday.

The Zarcom Research facility.

People were dead.

What had Nina got him into? He should have followed his instincts and returned home before the protest march had even started, but of course he hadn't. Now he was up to his neck in something he didn't understand.

He climbed gingerly to his feet and switched on the TV. The same old routine - check the latest news from Afghanistan and then hit the shower. His brother's unit was stationed in Helmand but that's all he knew. They hadn't spoken for two years. Hunter needed time to work through some personal issues, and that's how he played it - alone. Today he had the added pressure of finding out if the debacle at Zarcom had made the headlines.

BBC News flashed up on the screen, more violence in Iraq. Four coffins draped in the Stars and Stripes were being loaded into a large military aircraft. Hunter felt nauseas. Four US troops killed in a car bomb explosion in Baghdad. More young lives lost in a hostile country, and any one of them could have been his brother.

The phone rang and he answered with a bleary 'hello.'

'Matt…?' *Nina's voice.*

'Oh, it's you.' He picked up the remote and muted the TV.

'You sound bloody awful,' she said.

'Hardly surprising all things considered.' What did she expect? She'd dragged him into this nightmare with her convincing sales pitch.

Help us break-in Matt. Think about the animals. Think about your career. You can have all the plaudits.

She'd boxed it up, detailed the benefits and overcome his objections. She'd sold him the idea, and he'd bought it without considering the cost. There was always a cost.

'Why are you still home? You should have left by now.'

Hunter sighed. 'What do you want from me Nina?'

'I called to tell you everything's okay.'

He pushed his fingers through his hair, and raised his eyes to the ceiling. 'Yeah right – and you expect me to believe that?'

'The whole thing has been hushed up; Zarcom didn't even make local news.'

She sounded pleased with herself. Had she forgotten about the guards, her dead friend, and the abomination floating in the glass tank?

'What are you mixed up in Nina and why the bloody hell did you get me involved?'

'I can't talk on the phone. We need to meet up.'

'And I suppose you'll tell me everything?'

'Of course. I would have explained yesterday but you couldn't wait to speed off on that dreadful motorbike of yours.'

'Yes, I decided to cut and run, and I'm still running Nina, but there's nowhere to hide is there? What about the shootings?'

'The men Phoenix killed were Zarcom security - Mercenaries. The company won't press charges and the government doesn't want the police involved. No one wants an investigation.'

'Of course not, why would they? Only a few people dead.'

'Just give me a chance to explain Matt, before you start confessing to things and stirring up trouble.'

'Nina, I trusted you and you've let me down big time.'

'Just come and find me when you arrive at the office. I'll explain everything, but move yourself, it's already past nine.'

Before he could reply the line went dead and she was gone.

Hunter leaned back against the wall, cradled the phone to his chest and breathed a sigh. Once he'd resolved this, he promised himself never to get involved with the woman again. Ever.

The offices of The Daily News were located inside the INP building, a towering obelisk of glass and grey marble that stood on the south bank of the Thames not far from the London Eye. The INP group - Independent News and Periodicals – boasted a wide portfolio of publications, all owned by media tycoon Sir Edward Lang.

Hunter snaked through the London traffic on his Triumph motorbike. When he arrived outside the building, he shifted to the centre of the road, waited for a break in the traffic, and then arced across the street before plunging into the murk of the underground car park. He locked up the bike and headed for the elevator. On the fifth floor, he pushed through the double doors into an open expanse of desks, computer monitors and droning office noise.

A stagnant pool of boredom.

Hunter couldn't be bothered to engineer an excuse for his lateness, he'd probably used up his last one some time ago anyway. He dumped his bike helmet on the desk, sat down and powered up his laptop.

A booming voice spoke behind him. 'Hey man, I was thinking about sending the boys out to find you.'

Hunter swivelled round in his chair as Tony Vichelli waddled towards him. Tony was Croydon born, Italian descent, and modelled himself on Al Pacino. Weighing in at over twenty stone meant he never quite pulled it off.

'Jesus Matt, you look like you've been attacked with mustard gas and a pick-axe. What happened to your face?' Tony's chins sloshed like water pillows as he spoke.

Hunter grimaced. 'Rugger match. Listen - have you seen Bryant this morning?'

'Oh yeah, and he's more anal than usual. I'd keep your head down if I were you. The word is he's already blasted Siketi today.'

'Is she okay?' Hunter glanced across at Nina's empty desk, her coat draped over the back of her chair.

'Is Miss 'hard-nose' okay? She's got skin like rubber that woman. You can throw what you like at her and it'll come back at you, twice as fast and twice as hard. You know her better than most.'

Tony was right. Hunter was the only person in the office who bothered with her. To everyone else, Nina Siketi was a tough bitch you didn't mess with. But why was Bryant on the warpath? Surely he didn't know about Zarcom - please say he didn't because that would be game over for both of them.

On cue the office doors gusted open and Nina charged through looking pale and flustered.

'I'll leave you guys to it,' Tony said. He slapped Hunter's shoulder and shuffled back to his seat.

Nina grabbed her coat and scurried over to him. 'Call me later. It's urgent.' Her green eyes flashed, wide and searching. She looked somehow vulnerable, although not defenceless. More like a wild animal backed into a corner; scared but ready to fight.

'Okay, but where are you off to?'

'You'll find out soon enough.' She forced a smile, spun on her heel and started for the exit.

Hunter watched the empty space long after she had gone. Keyboards clacked and phones rang, but the noise did nothing to distract him. Something was very wrong and he sensed it was to do with Zarcom.

A finger tapped him on the shoulder, the abrupt and bad-tempered Jeremy Bryant, editor-in-chief of The Daily News.

'My office in five minutes Hunter.'

Hands in pockets, Hunter glanced over his shoulder. 'Not bad news I hope?'

'It's always bad news where you're concerned. Five minutes, and don't keep me waiting.'

Bryant's office was a partitioned affair set along one side of the main office with windows that looked out across the entire work area. The door was ajar when Hunter arrived, he knocked and stepped inside.

Bryant sat behind his desk, huddled over a myriad of papers. 'Take a seat,' he said without looking up.

Hunter obeyed.

Bryant scooped up his paperwork and squinted across the desk. 'I've got a situation and I need your help.'

'I'll do my best.'

Bryant leaned back and tucked his hands behind his head, exposing islands of sweat under his arms. 'Zarcom research facility.'

Hunter shrugged. 'What about it?' He had to bluff his way through this.

'Don't bullshit me. I want to know what you and Siketi got up to down there.'

'What have you heard?'

Bryant's face reddened and veins surfaced on his neck. He pushed a sheet of paper across the desk. 'That's a hard copy of the e-mail I received this morning while you were sleeping off your hangover.'

What's the slippery bastard up to?

Hunter picked up the note and noticed his hands were trembling. The author's name meant nothing to him at first. Foreign - Arabic perhaps. Then it struck him. The name was Cyrus Modjarrad, Iranian billionaire and owner of Zarcom Research. The e-mail had originally been addressed to Sir Edward Lang, who in turn had forwarded it to Bryant with a further note attached. Hunter felt sick as he read Lang's comments:

The following employees must be interviewed as soon as they arrive in the building today. Miss Planchard has prepared documents on both of these individuals and you must take the appropriate action as described in the accompanying report.'

Hunter read the names: 'M Hunter' and 'N Siketi.'

Oh God, they knew. He scanned further down the page and read Modjarrad's complaint - something about, a 'journalistic intrusion' into his company's affairs.

Hunter slid the paper back across the desk and slouched in his chair. He had to remain cool. 'What's it all about?'

'You tell me.' Bryant bared his teeth. 'What the fuck have you two been up to? I send you on a simple job and the next day the shit hits the fan. I trusted Siketi to watch you, make sure there were no fuck-ups. Looks like I was wrong.'

'What's in the reports?'

'Siketi's been fired.'

Hunter stared in disbelief. 'You've sacked Nina?'

'Have I got your attention now?'

'But why... what's going on? What has Modjarrad's got to do with Sir Edward Lang?'

Bryant let the question hang, the corners of his thin lips upturned in a half-smile clearly enjoying the moment. He placed his elbows on the desk and leaned forward, regarding Hunter over the top of his spectacles.

'You were supposed to report on the activities of these New Age thugs. Instead, you and Siketi decided to join up with them and break into a high security facility. Not only that, but you trashed the place and terrified the staff. The problem is, although Zarcom Research is owned by this Cyrus Modjarrad guy, Sir Edward Lang is actually major shareholder in his company. You stitched up the guy who pays your wages... and mine.'

'Jesus. So why didn't you warn us before you sent us down there?'

'You weren't supposed to break-in to the place you moron. What were you thinking?'

Hunter shrugged. He genuinely didn't know, even now. 'So what are you going to do? Fire me?'

'Oh I wish Hunter, because that would be sweet. Unfortunately I have other instructions. I pleaded your case of course, told Lang what a stupid half-wit you were and that the paper would be much better off without you, but it seems he has a soft spot for you. Fuck knows why.'

'I don't understand... Why sack Nina but not me?'

'You'll find out soon enough - everything will be made clear. I have a little job for you, a request from Sir Edward himself. Get a pen ready, you'll be making some notes.'

8

LANCE MURDOCH PAID THE driver, collected his case from the back of the cab, and strolled up to the glass office block. A sign above the entrance read: 'Zarcom Research. London Headquarters.'

He flashed his pass at the receptionist and stepped into the elevator. The lift glided up to the top floor, and Murdoch walked into a spacious corridor. He'd been here many times, but still marvelled at the height of the ceilings and the marble interior lined with tropical plants - some over twenty feet high. He turned left through a set of glass doors and walked into a circular atrium.

Cyrus Modjarrad's secretary glanced up from the large oval desk. 'Go straight in Lance, Mr. Modjarrad is expecting you.'

He thanked her, crossed the room to Modjarrad's office and knocked, determined to remain assertive. He guessed what was coming. As head of Zarcom security, the problems were stacking up and his neck was on the block, not for the first time.

Modjarrad's voice boomed from the office. 'Come in.'

Murdoch opened the door and entered. The room was spacious, a polished teak desk in the centre and floor-to-ceiling cabinets set along the back wall. To his left, a glass coffee table set low to the ground encircled by leather chairs.

Modjarrad stood at the window, his back to the door. 'Take a seat Lance.'

Murdoch walked to the table and sank into a chair. Modjarrad maintained his rigid stance, hands tucked behind his back. When he finally spoke, there was a hostile edge to his voice.

'We've got problems Lance, and it seems they all lead back to you.' The Iranian billionaire turned and glared.

Murdoch, stared at the floor and said nothing. Modjarrad's anger usually burned out after the initial rant.

'First, we lose a valuable shipment, then we suffer break-in at our Devon facility. *Now* I learn your men screwed up in Afghanistan. The target you were supposed to kill is apparently still alive. Tell me I'm wrong.'

Murdoch cleared his throat.

'We're doing everything to find him, but there's a Taliban unit in the area and the British are tracking them. Even if the target did survive, he won't get far, and the locals won't help him.'

'May I remind you, if this man talks to the security services, we're finished? Everything I've worked for - my entire business - will go up in smoke, not to mention the damage to my reputation. People depend on me Lance and in turn I depend on you. Up to now you've let me down.'

'We're monitoring the situation closely. I guarantee we'll find him.'

'And the missing livestock?'

'The animals are proving elusive. Somehow they're avoiding detection, and we can't source their signals. I've got six teams operating in Kent, but we're chasing shadows.'

Modjarrad's eyes narrowed. 'That's not what I want to hear Lance.'

'We've scoured a wide area, and all resources are being utilized, but I need more men.'

'You need more resources? *Fine*, you can have them, but you've got forty-eight hours to locate and destroy every animal. Understood?'

Murdoch nodded.

'Okay. Let's move on. Tell me what happened in Devon.'

Shit. The one thing Murdoch didn't want to discuss. He shifted nervously in his seat. 'We were twenty minutes from total shut down… They took us by surprise. It's all in my report.'

Modjarrad approached the table and lowered himself into a chair. 'Yes, but your report doesn't explain how these people infiltrated the facility without being challenged.'

'We had already shipped out all the labs and anything left was being burned. Security measures were in place and we had a strong police presence at the gate. We didn't expect a bunch of demonstrators to cut the power to the fence, and we still don't know how they managed it. The alarms went off when they got inside the main building, and we intercepted them in the corridors.'

Modjarrad leaned back in his chair. 'What makes you think these people were ordinary protestors? Perhaps they were spies sent by another company or even the British government. For a start, one of them was armed.'

'No. They couldn't be.'

'Why not? The attack was well planned. Like you said, how could a bunch of protesters pull that off, and what were they doing with automatic weapons? You tell me you're short of men and yet four of your guards were killed in a single exchange. You can see my problem Lance. What am I supposed to think when you can't even grasp what's going on under your nose?'

'It won't happen again.'

'No, I'm sure it won't. I'm a reasonable man Lance. People make mistakes, but I always give second chances. However, I think it's fair to say yours are all used up now. Do I make myself clear?'

Murdoch nodded.

'Good. From now on, we have to assume MI5 are onto us, but I won't be able to hold them off indefinitely. We must transfer all operations to the new facility, including the data and systems from these offices. We have to avoid the security services until I find a new buyer for the technology.'

Murdoch couldn't believe what he was hearing. They couldn't hide from MI5 - not for long.

Modjarrad seemed to read his thoughts. 'Lance, I will not sacrifice a lifetime's work, and this is our only option. Eliminate the target in Afghanistan and destroy the rogue chimeras, then the authorities have nothing. Can I trust you to follow this through?'

But Murdoch's thoughts were elsewhere. The incident in Devon still bothered him. 'I sent you the video footage of the break-in. Have you gleaned any information I should know about?'

A sardonic smile. 'I'm still making enquiries. You just concentrate on clearing up the other issues and I'll deal with these so-called protesters. No excuses this time Lance.'

9

AFTER HIS MEETING WITH Bryant, Hunter felt numb and needed some air. More importantly, he needed to speak to Nina. He leaned against the wall of the elevator and watched the numbers descend. The woman in the opposite corner bit her lip and stared at the ceiling. Next to her, a beefy guy in a suede jacket whispered in her ear, something about 'calling security.' The woman said nothing, just kept her eyes fixed on the invisible object above her head.

Hunter's right hand throbbed, and he noticed his knuckles were scuffed and bruised. When he looked up, he locked eyes with the guy in the suede jacket.

'Just calm down fella, you're scaring the lady.'

Hunter was taken aback. 'What the hell are talking about?'

'Punching the wall like that. What's your problem?'

'My problem?' Realization struck. 'Oh God. I just hit the... I... I didn't realize.'

The elevator juddered to a halt, the doors slid open, and the woman hurried out.

Hunter speed-tapped the button for the ground floor.

'You look like you need help.' The man's tone sounded calmer now, more confident.

The doors closed and the car renewed its descent.

Hunter took a deep breath. 'A friend of mine got some bad news. It must have got to me more than I thought.'

'I'll say. Look at the wall panel. I'm surprised you didn't break your hand.'

A dent in the aluminum plate distorted Hunter's reflection into a grotesque blur. A sense of giddiness overcame him and he began to sweat.

The elevator reached the ground floor. Hunter stepped into the lobby and checked his watch – 11:15. He bustled through the revolving doors and ran down the steps into the street, checking his speed dial for Nina's number.

She answered on the second ring.

'Matt, thank God. Where are you?'

A police siren erupted in the street. A squad car nosed through the slow-moving traffic.

Hunter put a finger to his ear and shouted, 'I'm in the shit, same as you.'

'Bryant fired you?'

'No, but I don't trust the bastard. He's up to something.'

'Matt I'm struggling to hear you. Get a cab and meet me at Lucio's.'

'That shit hole?'

'It's quiet and we can't risk being seen together. Not until we've had the chance to talk.'

'Okay, but this had better be good.'

Hunter closed down the phone and hailed a cab.

Lucio's was Nina's favourite haunt, a poky little cafe tucked down a narrow street, just off Tottenham Court Road. Hunter climbed out of the taxi and spotted her at a window seat, talking into her phone. He sauntered in and ordered a bottle of water at the service counter. At a nearby table, workmen tucked into greasy plates of eggs and bacon, and an old man pored over his newspaper as he sipped tea from a chipped mug.

Hunter paid for his drink, wandered over to Nina and pulled up a seat as she finished her call.

She slipped the phone into her bag. 'There's not much time, we need to get through this quickly. Let's start with the embryo.'

Hunter grinned. 'The one that tried to snap your hand off before I saved you?' He unscrewed the bottle and took a long swig.

'Glad you find it funny. If you haven't already guessed Zarcom is conducting illegal animal experiments.'

He eyed her wearily. 'Okay, I can understand why you wanted me in on the story, but I have a couple of questions. First, why didn't you say anything about the guards having weapons?'

'They took us by surprise Matt. We weren't told about the armed security.'

'Phoenix had a pretty good idea. Why the hell was he packing a machine-gun, and more to the point, where did he get it from?'

Nina sighed. 'I didn't come here to talk about that. I want you to understand what we're involved in here.'

'I understand that I'm a witness... no an accessory to multiple murders. How many guards did your friend kill? Three? Four?'

'Trust me Matthew, you're in the clear. Zarcom can't afford the publicity. The company is owned by a dangerous man and he has to be stopped.'

'Yes, Cyrus Modjarrad. Bryant took great delight in telling me that one, and he took even more pleasure in telling me Sir Edward Lang has shares in Zarcom. I don't need to remind you he pays our wages. Which comes to my next question, why didn't you tell me all this before we went charging in there?'

'The truth?'

'Yes the truth, of course the bloody truth, that's why I'm here.'

'Because you wouldn't have come.'

'So you lied to me? Jesus Nina.'

'Not a lie Matthew. You didn't ask.'

'So you manipulated the situation, which makes it worse. You promised me a story, one that you knew could never be printed because we were screwing the guy who owns the Daily News.'

Nina rolled her eyes. 'You're jumping to conclusions Matt. I did give you a story, but I never said you'd be making headlines for The Daily News. This will go global and you can sell to the highest bidder.'

Hunter rested back in his chair and took another swig while he mulled it over.

Leave his job, and put himself on the line?

No. He didn't take risks.

Nina interrupted his thoughts. 'So what does Bryant want from you?'

'As penance, I've been given a shit story to write, something about a horse sanctuary in Kent funded by Zarcom. Makes up for torturing little creatures in their labs. Quite sweet really. My remit is to write an article, describing Zarcom Research as a caring company.'

'They're using you Matt.'

'I know. That's why I need you to tell me everything, so I understand what I'm getting into.'

Nina leaned in. 'Zarcom evacuated the Devon site recently, but we don't know where they moved their operation to. Our sources told us there was still activity over there last week. I've searched for leads, anything unusual in press reports that might indicate their movements. I mean, how many lorries would it take to relocate an entire research facility?'

'But they were burning stuff Nina. Perhaps they didn't move anything at all.'

'No, we got lucky. We caught them destroying defective embryos. I think I've discovered something. I made notes from a news report I found on the internet this morning.' Nina opened her bag and plucked out a note which she passed to Hunter.

He unfolded the sheet and read the scrawled handwriting.

Saturday - midnight. Articulated lorry lost control in wet conditions and jackknifed into a house near Tunbridge Wells, Kent. Residents escaped unhurt, but reported seeing several large creatures escape from the trailer. Police confirmed that four black bears, en route to a local zoo, were quickly recaptured at no risk to public safety.

'Bears… what's the link?'

Nina snatched back the note and stuffed it into her bag.

'Think about it Matt. An articulated lorry transporting bears in the middle of the night - at the weekend? In the last hour I phoned three zoos, two in Kent and one in East Sussex, but came up with nothing. Then I called the Tunbridge Wells Gazette and spoke to a local reporter who proved very helpful. He knows the owners of the property and promised to pass on my details. Before you arrived, I got a call from a lady named Janet Carter. It was her house that was destroyed. I've got an appointment to see her on Wednesday at the accountancy firm where she works.'

'What else did she tell you?'

'Nothing on the phone, but she sounded scared stiff.'

'But Nina we're talking about bears here, not nasty little reptilian creatures. There's a big difference.'

Nina's leaned closer, her voice barely a whisper. 'I believe they're linked. We don't know how big these things grow and what we saw wasn't a reptile, it was mammalian.'

'What sort of mammal?'

'I can't tell you that.'

'You're holding out on me.'

'No, I'm protecting you. I need your help, but I can't tell what I'm not sure about.'

'Why me? You've got all the help you need with your aggressive hippie friends.'

Nina's mouth twisted into a half-smile. 'Because I trust you.'

Hunter eyed her suspiciously, drained the plastic bottle and crushed it in his left hand. His right hand was still as sore as hell.

'You've crossed the line with this Nina. I'm not convinced the police won't follow up on the shootings.'

She shook her head. 'They can't. Zarcom hushed the whole thing up, and don't forget their guards started the shooting. That alone would make headline news and finish the company altogether. I want to expose these bastards Matt, sod the shitty newspaper. I'll go freelance and crucify them. I need you with me.'

'That easy?'

'Of course. Who are you indebted to? Listen, I'll pick you up in the morning and we'll travel down to Kent together. You can speak to this Janet Carter and see if I'm onto something. I know a place where we can stay overnight. We'll check out this horse sanctuary tomorrow, then drive over to Tunbridge Wells on Wednesday.'

'And your Rambo friends?'

'I won't involve them.'

'Okay, you've got one more shot Nina, but any more bullshit and I'm out. Clear?'

She grinned. 'I'll pick you up in the morning at eight.'

10

THE ROAD DISSECTING THE town square in Qatif was scorched black and the smell of death hung in the air. The seven dead soldiers had been removed, but the shells of the burnt-out tanks remained. Rasheed felt uneasy. No response from the British. No search parties, helicopters, or planes. Yesterday, he and Aisha had carried the only survivor of the attack across to a small building on the outskirts of town. The man was barely conscious, but remained alive.

The militia had left town shortly after the ambush, but Rasheed and his family had sought refuge overnight at Rabia's house.

Nowhere felt safe.

Now, as the afternoon sun faded, he ventured out into the desolate town square. The acrid stench of burnt remains filled his nostrils, forcing him to cover his face. He crossed the street to his house; a single storey building of dry mud and straw, the façade now riddled with bullet holes. Inside were four simple rooms, and located in the yard an outhouse and a well, the family's only source of water

Rasheed pushed the door and stepped inside. Streaks of blood trailed up the hall, smudged with boot prints. Rasheed checked every room. All ransacked. Beds upturned, clothes and utensils scattered on the floor. He searched his mother's room, and found the tiny metal sphere on the floor, but this time the colour remained a dormant grey - any sparks of colour or energy now gone.

He couldn't bring his family back here. The militia might return.

But who were they? Not Taliban, at least not Afghan.

Worried the bandits might have poisoned the water, Rasheed checked the well outside. He lowered a metal pail down into the black opening until the rope slackened and a splash echoed up from the bottom. Once it was full, he worked furiously to haul the bucket to the surface, lifted it out and tasted the water. Satisfied it was clean; he splashed his face and filled the pitcher.

Time to give his mother the news.

Aisha was waiting for him at the front door when he returned. 'Are you going to check on the soldier again?'

'Yes, when I've found some clean bandages.'

'Can I come with you this time?'

Rasheed shook his head. 'No, it's too dangerous, and Jamila might follow us. She worships you Aisha.'

On cue, the little girl ran into the hall. 'Aisha did my hair,' she said gleefully.

Rasheed stepped back and admired her freshly spruced curls. 'Very pretty. Now go and play little one, Aisha will be along in a minute.'

'We can play dressing up again,' Jamila shrieked and darted back into the front room.

Once she was out of earshot, Rasheed spoke to Aisha in a low voice.

'My house has been wrecked. The bandits must be looking for the soldier. They're not Taliban though. I saw one of them in the square yesterday. His face was the colour of milk.'

The girl's eyes widened. 'Then you must stay with us until this is resolved.'

'I know. Will you explain everything to your mother?'

'Of course.'

'And say nothing to Jamila. In the meantime, have you got some fresh bandages I can take with me?'

Aisha nodded and hurried upstairs.

This particular house was one of the larger properties in Qatif, a two-storey building, like several others on this side of the square. Rabia had made up a cot for Rasheed's mother on the ground floor. He sat beside her and gently relayed the bad news.

'You are a good boy Rasheed. It is brave of you to help the Englishman. Hopefully the other soldiers will look kindly on us and send more men to protect our town. I am sick of all this fighting.'

'Me too Mother. Me too.'

Ten minutes later, armed with bandages and the pitcher of water, Rasheed left the house. He had intimate knowledge of the backstreets and chose his route carefully.

The hideout was half a mile outside town, hidden amongst dunes of sand. A squat building made of dried mud, no windows and a sheet of corrugated metal for a door. A perished Soviet tank sat rusting nearby, a relic from a previous war.

Rasheed pulled the metal sheet aside, and stepped into the dim room. The soldier lay in the corner, still unconscious. Rasheed got to work. Checked the man's pulse, and unwound the bandage from his neck.

Clear liquid seeped from the wound, but the blood around it had coagulated. Rasheed washed the cut, fixed a clean dressing, and drizzled water over the soldier's cracked lips. The man shuddered and groaned, his eyelids fluttered and he murmured words that Rasheed could not comprehend. He knew a little English – hello, goodbye, welcome. The man repeated the same word, over and over.

'Mat.'

Rasheed had heard this word spoken by an Englishman before. A few weeks ago, on his way to the mosque, he had been stopped by a British patrol. One of the soldiers smiled and pointed to the prayer rug under Rasheed's arm. He said the same thing several times, and fortunately Mullah Ahmed was on hand to interpret.

'He's interested in your prayer mat Rasheed,' the old man said.

'Why?'

Mullah Ahmed shrugged. 'Perhaps he wants to pray.'

Rasheed remembered the word clearly. 'Mat.' *Yes of course.*

He sprang to his feet. 'Yes my friend. I will get you a mat. Every man should pray. I will bring one tomorrow.'

The soldier did not respond. His head flopped, and he drifted back into unconsciousness.

In the meantime, I will pray for you.

11

Tuesday 27th April

10:47 a.m.

Kent, England

NINA TURNED OFF THE main road onto a pot-holed track signposted, 'Faraday Horse Sanctuary.' The car bounced along, jolting Hunter and Nina in their seats as they approached the farmhouse. The paddocks on either side were vacant, and it wasn't until Nina pulled up outside the house that Hunter saw the stables in the backyard.

He got out the car, and sucked in a gulp of fresh air. Beyond the fields, the sanctuary was enclosed by dense woodland, and the smell of wet pine wafted on the breeze.

A man in his late sixties shuffled up to the car, white hair streaked yellow, and a face grizzled with stubble. He introduced himself as Jim Faraday and when he spoke; his voice had a distinctive smoker's rasp.

'I hope you had a good journey Mr. Hunter. Please come in.'

Hunter exchanged pleasantries and strolled into the house with Nina. The living room was dusty, crammed with ornaments and knick-knacks and smelled of dog. The old man offered them seats but his cheery demeanor quickly turned sour. 'I'm sorry if I seem a little distracted, but one of our horses escaped last night. My wife is leading the search and won't be able to join us.'

Hunter saw his chance to cut the interview short. 'If it's a difficult time, we'll get through this quickly and...'

Faraday shook his head. 'No need. Please, make yourselves comfortable. I'll make some tea.'

Hunter sighed, and dropped into the sofa beside Nina. She pointed to a soiled armchair next to the fireplace. Underneath, a disheveled mongrel watched them suspiciously, until Faraday returned. Hunter hoped Nina wouldn't mention any of her wild conspiracy theories about Zarcom, and Faraday seemed to register his anxiety.

'Don't worry Mr. Hunter, I know why you're here. I want to help Mr. Modjarrad. This sanctuary relies solely on donations from his company, and there are six other animal shelters dotted around the country, all supported by Zarcom.'

Hunter exchanged puzzled glances with Nina, and then turned his attention back to Faraday as the old man stood over the table and poured tea.

'You know Zarcom is involved with animal experiments?' he said.

Faraday added milk to the three cups. 'Yes, but their work is essential - for the good of mankind so to speak. Mr. Modjarrad is putting something back, that's the important thing.' He handed them each a cup, and shuffled across to his armchair.

Suddenly, the dog sat bolt upright, whimpered, and circled round to his master's feet.

Faraday bent down and ruffled the mutt's head. 'What is it Hamish?'

But Hunter had already heard the sound coming through the walls.

A woman's scream.

Faraday dropped his cup, splashing tea all over the carpet.

Hunter made a bolt for the front door, and ran outside, closely followed by Nina and then the old man. In the stables, the horses bucked and whinnied.

Faraday staggered to his Land Rover. 'Get in the car!'

'No time,' Hunter replied. 'Take Nina. I'll catch you up.' He vaulted the fence into the paddock, and ran towards the wood.

Two women emerged from the trees in a tight huddle. To Hunter's left, Faraday bore down in the Land Rover, streaked past and skidded to a halt near the group. The old man sprang out of the vehicle with the agility of someone half his age, Hamish scampering behind him. Hunter caught up, just as Nina clambered out the passenger door.

Faraday held his wife's tear stained face in his craggy hands. 'Fran, thank god you're safe. What happened?'

'In the woods. It's horrible. Don't go in there Jim please.'

'Is it Pru?'

'I think so.' She bowed her head and wiped tears from her eyes. 'I can't tell.'

Faraday's expression darkened and he turned to the girl standing next to his wife. 'Gemma, are you fit to drive the car back to the house?'

Gemma nodded. Faraday strode back to the Land Rover, dived in the back and emerged with a shotgun.

His wife looked horrified. 'Please Jim. Let the police handle this.'

'Just a precaution. I'll meet you back at the house.' He loaded two cartridges into the gun, snapped the barrel shut, and started for the trees.

'Wait,' Hunter said, 'we're coming with you.'

He and Nina ducked under the fence and entered the wood, a step behind Faraday. Hunter took long strides to avoid the water-filled ruts, his feet slipping on the slick surface. They ventured deeper and soon the scent of wet earth gave way to the putrid smell of decay. Faraday swatted through a cloud of flies and then stopped and stared at the woodland floor. Suddenly his legs buckled. Hunter grabbed the old man's arm to steady him and pulled his jacket across his face to block out the smell. No sign of the body, only the head of the animal remained. A sculpture of modern art nestling in a patch of open ground, crawling with flies. The horse's cheeks had been gauged out, and the eyes bulged as if the lids had been stapled back. The surrounding flora was hosed with blood and tissue. Nina stood transfixed, face hidden behind a handkerchief, eyes moist and bloodshot. Hunter, heard footsteps crunch through foliage nearby, and urged everyone to stay quiet.

A figure leapt between the trees to their left, and Faraday raised his gun.

'Gotcha.'

He fired before Hunter could stop him.

The gun bucked as the shot echoed through the treetops. A murder of crows squawked and took flight. The bullet whizzed through the branches, leaving a trail of twigs and leaves fluttering like confetti in its wake. Thirty yards away, a branch shattered and crashed to the ground.

'Whoa don't shoot!' a voice yelled from behind the blanket of ferns.

'Christ Jim, that's a person out there.'

Hunter reached out to disarm him, but Faraday snatched the shotgun away.

'Probably the same person that killed my horse.'

'You don't know that.'

The voice called out again. 'I'm coming out... I'm unarmed.'

Two hands appeared, raised in surrender. The figure stood up and stepped out of the undergrowth, a small man wearing spectacles and dressed in camouflage.

Faraday growled at him. 'What do you think you're playing at? Who the bloody hell are you?'

'My name's Richard Monkton. I'm following a trail from Walker's farm. Oh dear, is something dead around here?'

'What trail?' Nina said.

The guy wasn't listening. He edged towards the horse remains, adjusting his glasses as he peered at the ground.

'The lady asked you what trail you were following,' Faraday snarled.

Monkton snapped to attention. 'I'm not exactly sure... a heavy quadruped. Two of them in fact.'

'Quadruped? Speak English man. Why are you following trails in my wood?'

'Your wood?' Monkton stepped closer. 'I was invited here by Mr. Walker the farmer... god that stinks. I must take a sample.' Monkton slipped his pack from his shoulder and extracted a small plastic box of surgical items.

Faraday glared at him. 'I'll shoot you before you start slicing bits off my horse. We'll wait for police forensics.'

Hunter tried to calm the situation. 'For god's sake Jim, he's got the message. Put your gun down.'

'This is the work of gypsies,' Faraday continued. 'They're always stealing sheep and chickens from the local farms. This is a matter for the law.' He turned to Hunter. 'Would you mind waiting here while I go back to the house? I sense you can be trusted Mr. Hunter. People need to show respect for Prudence. I won't be long.' Faraday glared at Monkton and then sloped off into the trees.

'What exactly are you doing here Mr. Monkton?' Hunter said.

'Call me Richard please. I'm a cryptozoologist. I investigate reports of unidentified animals.'

'A monster hunter? The search for Nessie and all that?'

'Not quite, although that would be a fantastic find. I approach things from a scientific angle, not the fairytale stuff you hear about. I try to disprove these sightings as much as anything. Everyone loves a good monster story don't they?'

Hunter laughed. 'Nina and I are journalists. We're used to hearing strange things.'

'Journos eh? Well you've certainly found something to write about here, because despite what the old man wants to think I can assure you this attack was carried out by animals, not gypsies. I could do with a saliva sample though. Whatever killed this horse basically ripped its head off with a single bite. The DNA deposits would tell us a lot.'

Nina agreed. 'He's right Matt, we need a sample.'

Hunter didn't want betray the old man's trust but... 'Okay, make it quick.'

Monkton retrieved his tools and began scraping away pieces of flesh from the head, placing each sample into a separate plastic tube, the size of a test-tube. When he'd finished he stood up, coughed, and spat into the dirt. Hunter watched with interest. He was curious about this trail Monkton had followed.

'Can you show us what you're talking about Richard? I think I need to see this with my own eyes.'

'I'd be delighted.' Monkton scooped up his rucksack and beckoned them deeper into the trees. Soon, he began pointing at the ground. 'Here we are. This is fairly representative of what I found right through the wood.'

Hunter scratched his chin, and stared at the floor. All he saw was random indents in the mud. 'Holes?' he said, trying not to sound sarcastic.

'No they're definitely footprints. From these tracks I can estimate the size and weight of the creatures. I'd say at least eight hundred pounds, probably ten to twelve feet in length excluding the tail.'

Hunter snorted dismissively. 'Come on Richard, we need more than this. These aren't animal prints.' He glanced at Nina for collaboration, but she was bent over the tracks like a kid engrossed on a nature project.

'Oh, I forgot to mention,' Monkton replied, 'these animals are highly intelligent. The prints have been deliberately smudged.'

'Which suggests people did this. The gypsies Faraday was talking about.'

'Sadly not. We're talking about two large predators. They came through here in single file and if I'm right, you'll find more evidence around the spot where the horse was abducted. This trail leads to the farm on the other side of the trees. The creatures carried the horse through the wood.'

'Excuse me? You're suggesting two animals - which you fail to identify - *carried* a horse!'

'There are no abrasion marks in the soil to indicate the creature was dragged, and I doubt it came of its own free will. They brought the poor thing into the clearing and tore it apart, probably in a feeding frenzy I would imagine. Afterwards, one of them must have taken the carcass deeper into the trees, while its friend took care of the tracks. Made a damn good job of it too.'

Overhead, the crows returned to the canopy, and for a moment Hunter felt like he was being watched. He shrugged it off.

'Richard, the only creatures that could pull that kind of stunt are homo-sapiens. I don't buy into this intelligent animal crap. Sorry.' He looked at Nina, 'Time to go.'

'Where are you off to?' Monkton asked.

'For a beer at the Kings Arms about three miles from here. We're booked in overnight. You're welcome to join us if...'

Hunter froze. A sound erupted only yards away - a loud guttural roar of pure aggression. It triggered a primeval, instinctive fear inside him. Every hair bristled, every vein pumped with adrenalin. His mind conjured images of a big cat - a lion maybe - but how? He registered the terror on Nina's face and noticed his own hands start to tremble. Something moved through the undergrowth. Hunter pulled Nina close and scanned the trees.

'This sounds exactly what we're looking for,' Monkton said.

Hunter was incredulous. *What we're looking for?* More like this thing was looking for them... He heard not one, but two of them, prowling through the vegetation. Something big crouched behind the ferns to his left.

Hunter took a step forward.

Nina shook her head at him. 'For Christ's sake back off.'

No. He had to see.

Another step.

The ferns erupted, and a huge black shape crashed through the undergrowth.

'Run!' Nina screamed.

Hunter spun and grabbed Monkton's arm. 'Go!'

In a flash the beast was on his heels, Hunter heard the thing grunting and splashing through the wet earth behind him. To his right, the second creature tore through the brush, angling in to cut him off.

He leapt over a dead trunk, slipped, managed to stay on his feet and continued to run - he wouldn't be caught, just wouldn't.

Monkton and Nina broke clear to his left, both ahead of him now.

A low-flying jet screamed overhead, and the air shuddered. Hunter lost his footing, and the world became a tumbling mass of wet leaves and vines. He rolled over and over, down a muddy slope.

When he came to rest, he heard a loud gunshot. Hunter curled into a ball, and put his hands over his face.

A second shot. The bullet whistled past and cannoned off a nearby tree.

Nina called out to him. 'Matt, its okay they've gone.'

Hunter peeked through his fingers and gingerly got to his feet. 'Holy Christ. What were those things?'

Faraday emerged into the clearing, the shotgun cradled across his chest.

'I told you the gypsies were rough around here. You're best leaving them alone in future.' Faraday fed two fresh cartridges into his gun, and snapped the barrel shut. 'I'd like you to leave now.'

Hunter didn't need telling twice and noticed Faraday's finger on the trigger. 'Okay Jim, we're leaving.'

The old man grimaced. 'Good. The police will be here soon. It's best you're not here when they arrive.'

'You mean your friends from Zarcom,' Nina snapped. 'And that silly gun of yours did nothing to scare those creatures away, so don't kid yourself.'

Hunter glared at her. She was probably right, but did she have to be so damned antagonistic? He opted for diplomacy. 'All right Jim we're off.' He grabbed Nina by the elbow and steered her away. 'Joining us Richard?'

12

RASHEED SPOKE QUIETLY AT his mother's bedside. 'The soldier's health is improving Mother, I think he will live.'

Her expression darkened. 'Be careful Rasheed. We don't know who attacked these men. This is the Devil's work.'

'God will protect me.' He squeezed her hand as she laid back and closed her eyes. Her life seemed to be fading before him, but what could he do? Only show her that he was strong, even if it wasn't true.

Aisha walked in. Her face glowed, and her smile radiated warmth. 'I'm coming with you,' she said.

Rasheed's mouth dropped open. 'Why?'

'Because I can help. I made food for the Englishman. And I have this.' From behind her back she produced a dog-eared book.

'What good is that?'

'It contains English words, translated into Pashto. I got it from Mullah Ahmed. If the soldier speaks and we don't understand, we can look the words up.' She opened the book and showed him the text.

Rasheed was unconvinced. 'But it's too dark outside and there are no lights in the hideout. Besides, the writing is too tiny to read.'

'We are not peasants Rasheed. I have a torch and the batteries are still good.'

Rasheed stiffened. An attractive girl, confident and resourceful - he didn't need Mullah Ahmed to tell him that this was a dangerous mix.

'Well? Am I coming or not?'

His mother chuckled and lifted her head. 'She is a strong girl Rasheed. Let her go with you.'

He turned to Aisha. 'All right, but you must do as I say and stay out of sight.'

Her eyes sparkled and she returned a beaming smile.

Rasheed tried to ignore the tingle in his stomach as he led her outside into the sultry night air. A dog howled in the distance, and the twang of a mandolin drifted from a nearby window. They crept through the gloomy backstreets to the edge of town, and then out across the desert until they reached the hideout.

Rasheed slid the makeshift door aside, and instructed Aisha to wait for him.

'Take the torch with you,' she whispered.

'No. The light might give us away.' He put his finger to his lips, gave her a reassuring smile, and then stepped inside, groping his way in the dark. He tripped on the blankets. Searched the floor but couldn't find the soldier.

A shriek went up outside. *Aisha!*

He ran back to the entrance, bumped into the wall, found the doorway and ducked through. To his left, Aisha stumbled backwards, hands over her face with shock. Slumped against the wall to his right, the British soldier groaned and stared back at him. The man made various gestures with his hands and then dropped to his knees, murmuring something unintelligible. 'Mat... ma...'

Rasheed rushed to him. 'Yes, I have it for you, but you must go inside. It is dangerous out here. Dangerous for all of us.'

The man's eyes fluttered and his head sagged against the wall.

'Give him water,' Aisha said.

Rasheed scooped a handful of water into the soldier's mouth. Aisha held out the bowl of rice and the soldier accepted the food with a trembling hand. After two mouthfuls, he looked up and stuttered a few words. Aisha switched on the torch and opened the dictionary. When the man spoke again, Rasheed told her not to bother - he understood perfectly.

'Thank you.'

Rasheed managed to reply in his best English. 'You welcome.' Pleased with his efforts, he unfurled the prayer mat. 'For you.'

The soldier prodded his chest with his forefinger. 'Christian.' He repeated the word slowly. 'Chris-chian.'

Rasheed felt a surge of excitement. 'Yes, you Chreezchen.' He grinned and placed his palm flat on his chest. 'Muslim.' Pointed at Aisha, 'Muslim. Pashtun.'

The soldier's eyes rolled, and he slumped forward into the dirt.

'Quick Aisha, we must get him inside.'

The girl wedged the torch between her teeth and grabbed the man's legs, Rasheed took his arms, and together they struggled through the narrow doorway, and dumped him on the blankets.

Aisha played the torchlight over the soldier's scarred face. 'We must get help. He needs more than we can give him.'

Rasheed had not considered this. Who could they ask, indeed, who could they trust? 'We'll have to wait until morning and see if his strength returns. Then perhaps he can tell us who to contact. For now we must leave him to sleep. Come, we must go.'

They trudged back across the dunes. The town was discernable in the distance by the scatter of faded yellow lights. Aisha insisted on using the torch to guide them, and this time Rasheed did not argue.

'When is your father coming back?' she said abruptly.

He shot her an indignant look of surprise.

'I'm sorry Rasheed. I didn't mean to offend you.'

'My father is Talib. He does as he pleases. But he wouldn't be happy about us helping the soldier.'

'He would be angry with you?'

'Very.'

'I can't imagine it. He seems such a kind man and your mother loves him dearly.'

'He hates all foreigners Aisha. He is only happy around his own people.'

'My father is much the same. He cannot make a living here, so he returns every few weeks with money and food, but only if a bus is available from Kandahar. We're lucky to see him once a month.'

'Does he still repair cars?'

'I suppose. I don't ask.'

They reached the main road into town and Aisha stopped at the roadside. Her willowy figure cut a sleek outline against the jagged mountains in the background. She shivered and stared into the darkness, directing her torch into the empty void of the desert.

'What's wrong Aisha?'

No reply.

Rasheed raised his voice to disguise his anxiety. 'This is no time for games. Come, let's go.'

She spun around and glared at him, thrust the torch under her chin, and contorted her face into a ferocious scowl. Rasheed yelped and jumped back with shock. Anxious and confused, he stared in dismay as she fell into a fit of giggles.

'You are the Devil!' he yelled. He glared at her in disgust, turned, and marched back towards town.

She called after him. 'I'm sorry Rasheed. I couldn't resist.'

'The Devil's daughter!' he yelled over his shoulder.

A strange sound echoed across the mountains - the roar of a large and powerful animal.

What kind of creature would make such a sound?

The sky lit up and the air crackled with the sound of gunfire. Rasheed spun around and saw lights flash over the mountain tops.

The animal boomed another ferocious roar that ripped across the dunes.

Aisha ran up to him, and together the two Afghans ran home. This time their terror was real.

13

RICHARD MONKTON BREEZED INTO the bar of the King's Arms at around seven-thirty, ordered a Coke and wandered over to Hunter's table. 'Where's Nina?' he said, pulling out a chair.

'Making notes in her room. She'll be down soon enough.'

'Good. Gives us a chance to discuss things in private. What are your thoughts about these creatures?'

Hunter swooped for his beer, drained the glass, and slammed it down. 'Nina's got her own theory but I think the whole thing's a hoax.'

'What? I know we didn't get a clear view of the beasts, but we'll know more once I've got the test results. One thing for sure – they *were* real.'

'Sshh. Not so loud. My career's under threat as it is.'

'What do you mean?'

Hunter glanced at the three pensioners playing cards at a nearby table and then at Cissy the barmaid, whistling Abba tunes as she refilled the optics.

Satisfied he couldn't be overheard, he leaned in. 'Richard, I'm a serious journalist, and this story is way out there with alien abductions, and the Yeti. We must be careful what we say. Those card players are locals, and local people gossip. One word out of place will start as a ripple and could end up being a bloody tsunami.'

Monkton nodded and dutifully lowered his voice. 'What happened this morning was weird.'

'Weird? I'd say terrifying.'

'Quite. I got the impression Faraday would have shot us right there in the woods if we hadn't walked away. He seemed upset about his horse at first, and half an hour later he was a lunatic with a gun.'

'That's because someone got to him.'

'Like who?'

'Faraday's sanctuary is sponsored by Zarcom Research, but it's all a publicity stunt. In reality the company is involved in animal research, genetics and inter-breeding. Nasty business. It's possible there's a link between Zarcom and these creatures, but until we find concrete evidence, I'm treating the whole thing with a degree of skepticism.'

'I've got some ideas Matthew.' Monkton's eyes blinked excitedly behind his thick lenses. 'Have you heard of the Beast of Gevaudan? Unlike other monster stories, this one has strong foundations in truth.'

'Monster stories?' Hunter shook his head and groaned.

'No listen.' Monkton's voice sank to a whisper. 'In 1764, the beast roamed a region of France known as Gevaudan…'

'Yeah, just give me the bones Richard, not the whole thing.'

'Sorry. This beast was reportedly the size of a cow but resembled a wolf. It was responsible for more than a hundred deaths, mainly women and children. I believe there are parallels between this legend and the creatures we saw today.' Monkton lifted his rucksack from under the chair, fished out a heavy book and laid it on the table.

A cheer went up from the card table. One of the players scooped a nest of coins to his chest while another yelled, 'You cheating bastard Peterson!' A fit of laughter ensued before the group settled for the next hand.

Monkton leafed through the pages. 'Here we are.' He twisted the book so Hunter could see the drawing.

'Looks like a dog,' Hunter said, unimpressed.

'Don't be so hasty to dismiss the idea Matt. I'll get you another drink while you read through the chapter.' Monkton stood up and headed for the bar.

Hunter sighed, and reluctantly scanned the text.

The beast hunted early in the morning or at night, and attacked without hesitation or apparent reason. Corpses were mutilated, throats torn out, and their bodies ripped apart, sometimes eaten. Often, the beast left only the head of the victim behind.

He flipped the cover and read the title: 'Creatures of Myth and Mystery.' The author: R. M. Monkton. Hunter smiled and flicked through the rest of the book.

Monkton finally returned with a fresh pint. 'What do you think?'

'It's hardly conclusive.'

The little guy looked crestfallen. 'I thought it would be a good place to start.'

Hunter hadn't read all the text, but there was no need - this creature wasn't even close. 'It's just a bit thin Richard, that's all.' He stopped at the next page and studied a photograph of a strange-looking statue. The caption read: *Etruscan bronze of a Chimaera.* 'If I had to guess,' Hunter said, spinning the book and jabbing his finger at the picture. 'I'd say that creature was more likely. Something more feline.'

Monkton bent over the page until his glasses were inches from the text. 'Matthew, I owe you an apology. I was focusing on the animal's behaviour. I never considered this possibility. This creature is a chimera - a mix of different species - in this case, a lion, a goat and a serpent.'

'I didn't say that's exactly what it was Richard - just my impression. The shape of the body and the head, its lionesque, but it ain't lion... if that makes sense?'

Monkton's face lit up. 'It fits!'

'For Christ's sake Richard, what did I say about keeping your voice down? Sure it fits, if you believe in mythology. We might even run into a couple of Gorgons or a Minotaur if we search hard enough.'

'I'm not talking about mythological creatures Matthew, but hybrids - animals with mixed DNA, two or more genomes.'

'How's that possible?'

'Its advanced technology, but scientists are experimenting with this stuff all over the world.'

Hunter sighed. 'Genetic engineering? You're starting to sound like Nina.'

'She thinks so too?' Monkton's eyes widened with obvious delight. The little guy had some back-up.

Great, Hunter thought, *now I'll never hear the end of it.* He changed the subject. 'Let's talk about this book of yours. I see your name's on the cover.'

'It was actually written by my uncle Robin, now sadly deceased. He raised me after my father died and my mother abandoned me at birth. You could say I'm his protégé.'

Hunter had never heard a grim story delivered with such a cheerful and unaffected tone. 'So it's fair to say you're an expert on crypto... whatever?'

'*Zoology.* Yes, I've researched more than most. Uncle Robin taught me everything. He was a journalist just like you.'

'Newspapers?'

'Radio. He worked for the BBC World Service in London.'

'I know it, Bush House on the Strand.'

Monkton nodded but his face sagged. Maybe Hunter had touched a nerve after all.

The room fell silent. All eyes turned as the door swung open and Nina walked in. She ordered vodka and ice at the bar.

'Listen, I don't think we should discuss this with her,' Monkton whispered. 'There's something about her I don't trust.'

'Yeah, she has that affect on people.' Hunter smiled and sipped his beer. 'When are you going up to London to deliver those samples?'

'Thursday, first thing.'

'Good, I'll come with you. In the meantime let's just see what Nina comes up with. Okay?'

'Okay.'

Cissy loaded Nina's drink with ice and slid the glass across the bar. 'Two-fifty love please. Terrible business about all these sheep attacks isn't it?'

Hunter swept his gaze across the room and listened in.

'I know what's been doing the killing,' Cissy continued. 'I saw them. Loud they were, roared like lions.'

Nina handed her the exact money and turned away, drink in hand.

'Just a stray dog,' one of the card players piped up. Sniggers circulated the table.

Cissy reddened. 'You might laugh Harold Turner, but I'm telling the truth.'

Hunter decided to buy the woman a drink and call her over to listen to what she had to say. Cissy smiled at the invitation, puffed out her ample chest and poured herself a scotch.

'Are you mad?' Nina said through clenched teeth. She pulled out a seat and eyed Monkton's book. 'So that's what you two have been up to.' She viewed the cover and tutted. 'You guys need to get out more.'

Cissy waddled across the room, her girth straining beneath a dress at least two sizes too small. She parked herself at the end of the table, three feet back to give her stomach room. The chair groaned beneath her.

'Tell us what you saw Cissy.'

She glanced furtively around the room, slugged her scotch and started to speak. 'Two nights ago, I heard something snuffling around the bins out back. I thought it was a fox, so I got out of bed and went to scare the stinking thing away. We don't want scraps of food littering the yard do we? I got to the window, and the noise stopped. Complete silence. I couldn't see anything in the dark, but I opened the window just in case. As soon as I pulled the latch, one of the dustbins went over and a huge black shape leapt over the fence into the back field. The animal was at least the size of a horse but more powerfully built.'

She raised her voice for the benefit of the card players. 'Much bigger than any dog.'

She returned her attention to her immediate audience. 'The thing streaked away quicker than a greyhound. I've never seen anything like it. I screamed out the window, woke up the landlord, and he was miserable bugger the whole next day. That's when the bloody thing roared back at me - and not just one, there were two of them. I shut the window, jumped into bed and dived under the covers. I called the police but they weren't interested.'

'Can you describe the animal?'

'I only got a glimpse but I got good idea of its shape.'

'And...?'

Cissy jabbed a finger at the photograph in Monkton's book - the bronze chimera. 'The animals looked something like that.'

'You're sure?'

'Oh yes. Like nothing I've ever seen before. What is it anyway?'

Hunter took a deep breath. 'Something that really shouldn't exist.'

14

AT FIRST LIGHT RASHEED wrapped a disc of Naan in a cloth sheet and crept through the house as the women slept. He checked on his mother, and thanked God she was still alive. Jamila dozed at her feet, thumb planted in her mouth. Rasheed smiled to himself and padded barefoot to the front door, opened it without a sound, and stepped outside, clutching the roll of cloth.

Halfway across the street, Aisha called out to him. He turned and groaned as she hurried up to him.

'I couldn't sleep Rasheed.'

'You shouldn't have come. It's far too dangerous for you now.'

'I have the dictionary.'

'Good, give it to me and go home.'

He held out his hand, but she hid the book behind her back. 'No. I am the interpreter.'

'Aisha, I don't want to argue. There's no time.'

'Good. So let's go.'

He saw determination in her eyes, her chin jutted in defiance.

Just like Jamila.

Just like his mother.

'Come then,' he said softly, 'we must be quick.'

Christian Hunter sat up, stretched his arms, and winced as his bones creaked. The pain had dulled since yesterday, but his neck was still tender.

He tried to recount the recent events but his perceptions were fogged. He knew an Afghan boy had helped him, but struggled to recall what had happened. What about his unit?

The mission... the chimeras didn't return as they should have done.

Images flashed through his mind. A trail of mutilated bodies - women and children. The animals were chipped and should have been easy to follow, yet their signals kept fading. Air reconnaissance wasn't a viable option, the creatures shied away from planes and helicopters.

Of course - the assignment...

Conduct a ground search and destroy the creatures on sight. The convoy had finally established a clear signal. They were two miles from contact, and then... the ambush. The Warrior had burst into flames, and he remembered climbing out...

The memory faded.

He struggled to his feet, and shifted the corrugated metal away from the doorway, stepped out into the baking sun, and his eyes contracted in the glare. He heard what sounded like a gasp of shock. Shielding his eyes he identified the silhouettes of the two young Afghans standing before him.

Christian raised his palms. 'Friend. Friend.'

The boy held out a parcel wrapped in cloth and Christian accepted the offering. He unfolded it carefully. Inside was a thick disc of naan bread, still warm. 'Thank you.' The skin around his eyes and mouth stung when he smiled.

The boy grinned and beckoned him into the building. 'Come. Come.'

Inside, the kid pointed to a rug lying in a triangle of daylight in the centre of the room. 'Mat... look... mat.'

Christian was baffled. 'Okay, it's a mat. So what?'

The boy jabbed a finger at Christian's chest. 'Chreez-chen.' Then at himself, 'Mus-lim.'

Slowly, the boy's face began to register disappointment. He cast a bemused glance at the girl standing in the doorway. Her brow furrowed and she shrugged.

I haven't got time for this, Christian thought, I have to make them understand.

He put his thumb to his ear, pinkie stretched to his mouth, indicating he needed a phone. The boy returned another puzzled expression, while the girl frantically leafed through a small book.

Christian made a scribbling motion over the palm of his hand. 'Pen. I need a pen.'

The girl lost patience, snapped the book shut and thrust it into the boy's hand, jabbering words that sounded like a rebuke. She folded her arms and turned away. As she stared into the desert, her expression changed from anger to despair. She screamed and ran outside. The boy cried out to her, and then gave chase.

Christian hobbled to the doorway, but could only watch the two Afghans dash across the desert towards the town. Then he saw her - the tiny figure of a little girl crouched at the base of a sand dune.

Aisha stooped and grabbed the little girls shoulders. 'Jamila! What are you doing here?'

'I saw a big bear,' she replied.

Rasheed caught up and knelt before his sister. 'Jamila look at me. How did you get all the way out here?'

'I ran and ran.'

'Did you follow us?'

She shoved her fingers into her mouth and nodded. 'I wanted to see the bear.'

Rasheed gripped her hand. 'Where did you see it?'

She pointed to the mountains in the north and then to the town itself. 'It goes over there, and then goes back that way.'

Rasheed stared at Aisha. 'We must get her home.'

But the little protested loudly and stiffened when Rasheed lifted her into his arms. 'Come Jamila, we must go home.'

15

NINA WAS UPTIGHT.

HER driving was reckless, and Hunter lost count of the near misses they encountered on their ten mile journey to Tunbridge Wells. When they finally arrived in the town's multi-storey he wanted to empty his stomach. He clambered shakily from the car, and tried to muster an excuse to take the afternoon train back to London rather than risk his life again.

The multi-storey was part of the Victoria Place shopping centre located in the centre of town. They took the lift down into the mall and walked outside into the chill morning air. Minutes later they arrived in Tamworth Street, home of accountancy firm, Donald & Watson.

Hunter reckoned this meeting with Janet Carter was a waste of time. The lorry crash had already been covered by a couple of national papers as well as regional television.

Screw it. If this didn't prove newsworthy, he'd just make something up, a strategy that seemed to work for everyone else at The News.

Janet Carter greeted them in reception. She was mid-to-late thirties, freckled skin stretched over hollow cheekbones and red hair like coiled wire. She immediately apologized. 'I told everybody you're here to discuss my insurance claim. I don't want these people to know I'm talking to the press.'

They followed her through the building to a room at the back. Hunter thought the office environment at the News was dull but this place was different class. Grey carpets, church refectory furniture and dour faces with starched expressions watched suspiciously from behind heavy desks. Everyone spoke in hushed monotone voices.

Polite to the point of rudeness.

Janet ushered them into a large annex and offered them seats at a conference table. She poured a cup of water from the dispenser, and sat down.

Her face tightened as she started to speak. 'My husband wants to brush everything aside and pretend it didn't happen, but I can't do that. I need to tell people what I saw in my house that night – demonic creatures… huge, evil things.' She glanced down at her manicured hands resting on the desktop like a pianist about to start a recital.

Hunter readied his pen and notepad. 'Press reports suggest the animals were black bears. In fact they've quoted your husband as saying…'

'Alan hasn't spoken to anyone, let alone the press. He's in the force you see. It wouldn't look good if he spoke to the newspapers.'

'Are you saying all the media reports are false?'

'I'm telling you it wasn't a bear.' She bit her lip and closed her eyes. 'The thing was massive and roared like a lion. It had piercing yellow eyes and a huge mouth full of sharp teeth. You won't find one at your local zoo, that's for sure.' She glanced first at Nina, and then Hunter. 'Please believe me. We must expose the truth.'

Hunter remembered the two beasts that had chased him at Faraday's place the day before but still thought it might be a hoax. He gazed through the dust motes and studied Janet's face for a sign of deception. She avoided eye contact and fidgeted with her hands. There was a tremor in her voice, but she seemed truly afraid.

Eventually, he said, 'Can you tell us exactly what happened?'

'I was in bed reading when I heard a lorry speeding through the rain towards the hairpin bend just outside our house. I told myself the driver would slow down, but he didn't.' She paused while she took a sip of water and dabbed her eyes with a handkerchief. 'The house erupted like a bomb had detonated beneath us. Everything disappeared - the stairs, furniture, the TV - everything. The driver steered into the hairpin but his trailer jackknifed and smashed right into our living room.'

'You're very brave to be back at work so soon,' Hunter said.

'Hobson's choice. A day at the office or a day with Alan's mother - no contest really.' She managed a weary smile. 'We were lucky to escape with our lives. The lorry was massive, one of those articulated things.'

'Did you see a logo on the side, or any other identification marks?'

'One of the doors had sheared off exposing a blue metal container inside the cargo hold. That's where the animals escaped from, and that's all I saw.'

'Can you describe the creature in more detail?'

The muscles in Janet's face stiffened. She took a breath. 'Alan flashed a torch over the wreckage, pointing and saying "there Janet, there." I noticed movement under the mound of bricks. They started to fall away - hesitant at first, but then the scrabbling became more frantic. More purposeful. A shape emerged from the shadows like a...' She dabbed her cheeks. 'As I said before, it was like a lion, but much bigger. I'd say the length of a family saloon, longer maybe, and about five feet high - easily as big as a horse.' She swallowed and closed her eyes. 'It looked up at me, lips peeled back exposing its teeth, and two bloody great fangs at the front. It smelled like rotting meat and...' She buried her face in her hands and began to sob.

Hunter glanced at Nina who pulled two fingers across her lips, telling him to keep his mouth zipped. Probably the right thing to do but Hunter didn't like it.

Janet jerked her head up. 'It wasn't a bear. It damn well wasn't.'

'I believe you,' Hunter said. He'd tried to blank out the truth, but now everything was falling into place - the embryo at Zarcom, the creatures at the horse sanctuary, and now this.

'A demonic beast,' Janet said, 'there's no other way to describe it. I know they're still out there. People are going to die unless we go public.'

'But we need proof, preferably something on film.'

'There'll be evidence soon enough - when the bodies start piling up.'

Hunter's phone rang. He stood up and took the call.

'Matt, it's Richard Monkton. Where are you?'

'Tunbridge Wells. You sound a bit shaky, is everything okay?'

'I'm not sure. I'm on the outskirts of town, a street called Garnet Road. Can you get over here?'

'What's going on?'

Monkton hesitated. 'Our four-legged friends I'm afraid.'

'Oh Christ. Richard, we're on our way.'

Hunter closed down the phone and saw the alarmed expressions of the two women. 'Nothing to worry about,' he lied, 'just a stray bull roaming around a housing estate. I'd better check it out.'

He knew his excuse sounded lame, but inside he felt a sense of urgency, bordering on panic.

If these creatures get amongst the populace...

It didn't bear thinking about. Hunter gave Janet his card and thanked her, grabbed Nina's arm and made for the exit.

16

NINA SLAMMED THE CAR into reverse, swung out of the parking bay, and drove down towards the exit. She followed the GPS north, and minutes later they arrived in Garnet Street, right in the heart of a large housing estate. Nina stopped opposite a small crowd huddled at the roadside, and Hunter got out to take a look. The object appeared to be a grey fleshy mass sprawled across the pavement.

Richard Monkton hurried across the street, scarf flapping at his throat. 'Matt! Thank god you're here.'

'What the hell's going on Richard?'

'Come on, I'll show you.'

They crossed the road and mingled with the onlookers. Hunter nudged his way through until he got a clear view. Nina pushed in from the other side, camera in hand.

Hunter's first thought was a decomposing octopus with tentacles splayed like bicycle spokes. But the smell wasn't fishy and he realized the tendrils were in fact shredded internal organs. Blood from the entrails seeped into the gutter and trailed down the street.

Hunter pulled Monkton aside. 'Animal intestines right?'

'Yes, a horse I think.'

'Could it be a practical joke?'

Monkton shook his head. 'I've got something else to show you. It's in the car, but...' He glanced back over his shoulder. 'I don't want Nina anywhere near.'

'I know. You don't trust her, right?'

'She's trouble Matt, I know it.'

Hunter didn't argue. He noticed she was already jostling people aside to get her photos, hardly endearing herself to the locals. Typical.

'Okay Richard, we'll keep your findings quiet for now.'

His attention was diverted by a high-pitched squeal from the crowd. He turned and saw a young girl vomit in the gutter. A kid in shorts was laughing at her, holding aloft a twig with a scrap of intestine skewered at the tip.

'Vernon, stop that!' A man wearing a faded white t-shirt, yellow stains under the arms, grabbed the youngster and lifted him off the ground.

The boy kicked and hollered. 'Get off me you bastard, you're not my real dad.'

Curtains twitched, and people scuttled out of their homes to join the gathering, but no one moved to stop the guy raising his hand to the kid.

Dark and disturbing images flashed through Hunter's mind, distant memories from his own childhood. Without thinking, he stepped forward and snatched the man's wrist in mid-air. 'That's not how to teach him,' he said.

The man scowled and let go of the boy's shirt, dropping him in a heap on the ground. Anticipation rippled through the crowd. The man's eyes flashed with anger. 'Do you want some?'

Hunter released the guy's wrist and felt a stinging pain in his shin. He looked down as the boy aimed another kick at his leg. 'Leave him alone you wanker.'

'All right kid, I was trying to help you out.'

Egged on by the mob, Frank raised his fists and curled his upper lip into a snarl. The boy ran to his father-guardian. 'Have him Frank.'

Hunter threw up his hands in exasperation. 'What's the point?'

Before Frank could throw a punch, Nina sidled in between the two men. 'For Christ's sake, calm down the pair of you.'

The boy arched his back and launched a gobbet of spit that looped inches past her ear.

Nina stared back in disbelief. 'You dirty little shit!'

Monkton tugged Hunter's arm. 'Back off Matt. We don't want to get involved. Let's go.'

'Yeah, you run and hide,' Frank said. The man wore a permanent sneer that made Hunter want to smash his teeth in.

The rabble closed in, goading Frank into a full-bloodied fight. To Hunter's relief, the whoop of a police siren pierced the air and a patrol car slunk around the corner.

Monkton took Hunter's arm. 'Quick, I'm parked in the next road. You need to see what I've found.'

Hunter turned, and followed him out of Garnet Street, leaving Nina engaged in a heated debate with Frank and the brat.

Monkton tossed his scarf over his shoulder. 'Right, let me explain. I got a call from a woman this morning saying she'd lost her dog. I asked her why she thought I could help, and do you know what she said?'

Hunter shrugged. 'I've got a feeling you're gonna tell me.'

'Apparently she thought I was hunting for escaped bears, god knows what she was talking about. She said her dog had gone missing and she was scared the poor thing might have been attacked. She got my number from John Wilson, the farmer I went to see yesterday.'

'You haven't got a mutilated dog in your boot have you Richard? I wouldn't put it past you.'

'Of course not. I got here an hour ago, saw the mess back there and continued searching. On the other side of the estate, just past the football field, I noticed movement in the hedgerow, pulled over to take a closer look and witnessed what I'm just about to show you.'

They approached Monkton's Jeep, an ex-US military vehicle complete with the white stars and canvas top.

'Christ Richard, it's only the mud that's holding this rust-bucket together.'

'Yes well my line of work doesn't pay too well.' Monkton unlocked the door, rummaged in the glove compartment, and emerged with a digital camera. 'I kept it locked away for safe-keeping after I took the film.'

'Film?'

Monkton pressed the play button and passed the camera to Hunter.

The picture was shaky at first but Hunter identified what looked like a large animal hidden behind a clump of bushes. The sound was poor, mostly the rustling of Monkton's jacket as he fidgeted to hold the camera steady. The branches shook violently. Monkton gained better control at this point and both sound and picture settled. Hunter heard a grunt and twigs snap but the animal itself remained obscured.

He willed the thing to show itself. 'Come on baby, let's see you.'

A large black head pushed through the leaves but the image lost focus. One thing for sure: it wasn't a bear.

Monkton peeked over his arm. 'This is the good bit.'

The creature's head turned slowly towards the lens.

'Here she comes,' Monkton said.

'Christ!' Hunter nearly dropped the camera. The beast turned full on and poked its head clear of the branches. Yellow eyes glared. A deep growl and the jaws shot apart, exposing two sabre-like fangs and rows of razor-teeth.

Hunter's skin turned to goose-flesh. 'Jesus. What the hell is it?'

'Sshh... keep watching.'

The creature stretched its mouth disproportionately like a snake - wider than any mammal Hunter had ever seen. It roared and he got a view deep inside its gullet. The picture wobbled as the animal turned and dragged itself from the bushes. Another roar and it tore through the undergrowth into the field behind. Hunter struggled to get a true impression of the creature's size but figured Janet Carter was right, the length of a car and about five feet high. Despite its bulk, the beast seemed extremely agile.

'Richard this is incredible. There's no chance of it being a hoax?'

Monkton snorted. 'Even Spielberg couldn't pull that off Matt; it's a real animal all right. The thing bolted but I didn't have the guts to follow it.'

Hunter handed back the camera. 'What's on the other side of the playing field?'

'An industrial park – no houses.'

'We must warn people Richard, there's no room for secrecy now. Everyone needs to know about this.'

Monkton blinked twice. 'There'll be panic.'

'We must inform the authorities, the police, military - anyone with guns. You know I'm right.'

'And what about Nina?'

'She probably knows more than we do, and I want to find out why. There might be more of these things running loose, and we can't wait until someone gets killed. Like you said Richard - they're predators, and from what I've seen, they have no fear of us. None whatsoever.'

17

THE HIDEOUT WAS HOT and infested with flies, but Christian dared not venture outside for fear of being seen. He kept a watchful eye through the crack in the corrugated door, praying for help to arrive. His strength had returned but his body was still wracked with pain. He thought of his comrades and knew they were dead.

The immediate problem was the rogue chimeras. They should have homed in on his position by now. Unless... his neck injury.

Christian unraveled the bandages from his neck. The skin was tender at the top of his spine and sticky with blood. He touched the wound with his fingertips. The laceration had completely eradicated the previous scar.

The implant must have become dislodged.

But with no signal emitting from the implant, his chances of rescue were slim. The chimeras wouldn't find him, but neither would a search and rescue team.

Yesterday his unit had left for Sangin to provide fire support for a covert operation. That was the story. In truth, they had set out to locate and destroy the two creatures.

But someone else must have known.

His unit had been attacked with powerful weaponry, anti-tank missiles and heavy calibre machine-guns. The ambush had been precise, and well planned. Christian guessed who was behind it. They wanted him dead, and would continue to hunt him down.

He wrapped the bandages loosely back around his neck, allowing the injury to breathe. Through the crack in the door he saw the Afghan boy running across the dunes towards the shelter - alone this time. Christian observed the look of anguish on boy's face and heard him cry a single word that sent a chill through his spine.

'Taliban!'

Christian fumbled for the gun in his thigh-holster and kicked the corrugated sheet away from the doorway.

'Taliban come! Taliban come!'

Christian shielded his eyes from the sun. 'Where?'

The boy pointed to the north-east horizon, a faint dust-trail heading towards Qatif. Christian holstered his gun and patted him on the back. 'Thank you.'

This time the youthful face did not register excitement at hearing him speak. His eyes were wide with dread. He beckoned Christian to follow as he turned and ran back towards town.

Christian did his best to keep up, weaving between the sand dunes. The vehicles were closing in, two pick-up trucks, and a posse of mopeds.

The kid changed tack and accelerated diagonally to the left. From here, the houses of Qatif looked like rows of broken teeth smashed and crumbling with decay. They made it safely across the wasteland and found refuge amongst the ruins of a bomb-damaged house on the outskirts of town. There was no roof on the building but the walls offered some sanctuary.

Christian sat on a concrete slab and caught his breath, his chest heaved, and his body was crippled with pain. The boy looked at him with a pitiful smile, gabbled something in Pashto which Christian took to mean, 'wait here,' and then scrambled back across the piles of stone before disappearing into a nearby street.

The noise buzzing around the town square was alien to Rasheed. Men with rifles strapped to their backs raced through the streets on spluttering mopeds. People appeared from their houses and waved at the Taliban soldiers with welcoming smiles just as they would if a British patrol arrived, although the crowds consisted mostly of men.

Two Taliban pickup trucks parked next to the burnt-out British tanks. Clusters of armed men spilled out, barking orders as they set up defensive positions around the street.

Rasheed got to Rabia's house, slipped inside and closed the door.

Aisha appeared from the back room and ran up the hall to greet him. 'Thank God you are here.' She touched his arm but did not throw her arms around his neck, nor kiss his face as he secretly wished.

'Your burka. You must put it on,' Rasheed said.

'But I'm not going outside.'

'Do it Aisha, please.'

She lowered her head and turned away but Rasheed put a hand on her shoulder to stop her. 'There's still blood at my house. I need to go back and clean the floor.'

Her cheeks reddened. 'No. Everything is scrubbed and tidy. You are safe now.'

'How...? You cleaned it for me?'

She nodded. 'Did I do a bad thing?'

'Of course not, you helped us all Aisha. Thank you.'

She beamed a disarming smile. 'There is food waiting for you. Come and eat while it is still warm.'

A fist hammered on the front door and they both jumped with shock. A man's voice bellowed. 'Rasheed are you in there? Rasheed!'

His Father's voice.

Rasheed waved Aisha away. 'Hide, and don't come out until I tell you.'

She scampered down the hall and disappeared into the back room. Rasheed cleared his throat and opened the door. At first he didn't recognize the man standing before him. A weather-beaten face half-hidden behind a scraggy beard and dark eyes lined with black kohl.

'Step aside then boy. Let me in.'

Rasheed couldn't speak. He had waited so long for this reunion, but now a sense of foreboding overcame him. A large canvas sack rested at his father's feet. The top was tied with a length of cord, and blood soaked through the bottom. He caught a whiff of the foul stench and knew it was something terrible.

His father picked up the bundle and struggled into the hall. Even with all his strength, the man needed two hands to lift the sack inside.

'Papa Papa.' Jamila charged into the hall and raced up to her father.

But Asad Sajadi ushered his daughter away with a wave of his hand. 'Go back child.'

Jamila ignored his command and dived between his knees squeezing her arms tightly around him, a look of sheer joy on her face. Asad fended her off, and regarded his son with a stern expression. 'Take Jamila to the women and tell them to stay in their rooms. You and I need to talk.'

Rasheed lifted Jamila into his arms. She wriggled and cried out in frustration as he carried her down the hall to the back room where Rabia and Aisha, sat next to his mother as she slept.

'Your father is here?' Rabia asked. 'Shall I wake Nura?'

'No, please don't. He seems troubled and I must hear what he has to say first.'

Rasheed left the room and closed the door to the sound of Jamila wailing inconsolably. He found Asad in the front room seated on a rug, the bloody sack lying at his feet. The smell was like rotten meat and Rasheed tried not to breathe it in.

Asad fixed him with a steely glare. 'Where is he?'

Rasheed sat down slowly. His mind whirled and he struggled to answer. 'Huh?'

'Don't mess with me boy. The British soldier. Where have you hidden him?'

'He, he… is badly injured and I swear he is no threat to us. We…'

'Just tell me Rasheed.'

'But mother said Salim would kill him Father.'

'Salim is dead. I lead these men now - I am their commander.'

Rasheed stared in disbelief. His stomach tightened, as his mind confronted this new nightmare. *What will become of us?*

'You have nothing to fear my Son. I am here to protect you.' Asad's expression darkened. 'I have witnessed terrible things. Many Afghans have been slaughtered by these men. Now tell me where the soldier is. Don't make me ask again.'

Rasheed couldn't form a reply. His eyes flashed over the bundle leaking blood over Rabia's clean floor.

Asad's patience snapped. 'You want to see it? Is that what you want – to see what these bastards have brought into our country?'

'There's blood coming from it Father.'

'Yes. And you are so curious that you cannot ignore it. Very well, I will show you, but make sure you spend the rest of the day praying for your own salvation, do you understand?'

Rasheed nodded. *He would do no such thing.*

Asad untied the cord and tipped the sack upside down, shook the object until a huge black fleshy mass dropped out and hit the ground, splattering blood across the stone floor. The thing rolled a few inches and came to rest.

Rasheed realized it was a severed head, and recoiled in horror. He'd never seen such a creature - such a grotesque image. Yellow eyes, black flesh and a huge mouth with so many teeth he couldn't begin to count them. Surely this wasn't real?

'Now listen carefully,' Asad said. 'This beast was brought here by the soldier and others like him. It has killed many people. Now for the last time, where is he?'

Rasheed looked up, swallowed, and told his father the whole story, starting from the beginning.

18

MONKTON WAS RELUCTANT TO share his discovery, but Hunter had to convince him.

'We'll work something out with Nina. I'll tell her about the film if she agrees to tell us everything she knows about these things. What do you think?'

Monkton thrust his hands in his pockets. 'Hmm... Okay, but I'm not handing my camera over to the authorities, I'll never see it again. I'll go into town and use the library computer to save a copy onto disc.'

'Sounds good, and we'll meet outside the police station in say... one hour?'

'Fine. But if that woman doesn't play ball, I don't want her anywhere near me or my film.'

'Oh she'll play all right Richard. She won't be able to help herself.'

Monkton tossed his scarf over his shoulder, climbed into the Jeep, and on the third attempt started the engine. Hunter gave him a thumbs-up as he drove away leaving behind a trail of black smoke.

Finding himself alone, he was overcome by the horror of it all. Images of the beast replayed in his mind, his sense of time and reality momentarily suspended. The world around him seemed somehow artificial, buildings and people no more than scenery and actors in a bizarre fabrication. He felt detached, couldn't cope or reason with the situation. Life had a rulebook, a kind of programming that could be relied upon - the laws of physics, biology, cause and effect. Now everything was confusing. This creature made no sense, it didn't fit. Not here in the South of England. Not anywhere.

An icy breeze whipped through his jacket, chilled his bones and brought him back into the present. *Come on Matt, pull yourself together. Focus.* He had to grab Nina and get some answers. He started to run.

Back in Garnet Street, the police were still on the scene. A female cop made notes while her disinterested partner spoke into his radio. No sign of Frank or the kid. That was a good thing. Hunter wanted to tell the cops about the animal right there and then, but didn't know how to explain. 'Officer, my friend saw a monster, and...'

No - that wouldn't work.

He saw Nina push through the crowd and make her way to the car while furtively stuffing something into a plastic bag. She glanced up and their eyes locked. To his amazement, she beamed a smile. 'Where's your funny little friend?' she said.

Hunter stood at the passenger door, and peered at her over the top of the car. 'We can talk on the way into town.'

'Intriguing.' She opened the back door and dumped the bag on the seat. Hunter climbed in the front, wondering how best to approach the subject.

Go easy, he thought.

She got in and started the engine, turned the car around and drove calmly away from the estate.

Hunter glanced over his shoulder at the bag. 'Samples?'

'You can smell it, huh?' She flashed him a grin, far too cheerful for his liking.

He hesitated before making his move 'Okay, I think you've been right all along,' he said. 'These creatures are definitely real, and I agree Zarcom is involved.'

No response, her gaze remained fixed on the road. Hunter watched her closely as he continued. 'They were in a hurry to evacuate the site in Devon, and must have travelled through Kent with the livestock. The destination might have been somewhere in the county itself.'

Still no reaction. His patience snapped. 'No more games Nina. I've figured out what's going on and we need to talk.'

'What the hell's got into you?'

'We had a deal to share information.'

'And you think I'm holding back?'

'A lot's happened in the last twenty-four hours. Nothing you've told me makes any sense. Why did you include me on the Zarcom story? And no more bullshit about trying to help me get a scoop because I'm not buying it.'

She shrugged. 'Please yourself. I don't know the whole story, only what I've been told.' She eased up on the accelerator as they approached a set of lights.

'Told by whom?'

'I can't reveal my sources Matt.'

'Well I've got some new information of my own. I wanted to share it with you but I can't if you insist on hiding stuff from me.'

'What are you talking about?'

Hunter smiled to himself. Nina's dogged curiosity would be her downfall. 'You first.'

The lights changed, Nina crunched the gears and pulled away, cursing.

Hunter watched her expression tighten, her face twitched as she wrestled to keep her cool. He waited for her to break and it didn't take long.

She shot him a look, 'For Christ's sake what do you want from me?'

Hunter settled back and folded his arms, reeling her in gently.

Nina slammed a fist into the steering wheel. 'Look I can't tell you, so don't ask. I don't want to fall out over this Matt.'

'Me neither, but Richard captured one of these things on film, so maybe its time we both came clean.'

She attempted to laugh it off. 'Nice try.'

But he saw her knuckles tight on the wheel, strangling the life out of it. Without warning she hit the brakes. The Focus screeched to a halt and Hunter jerked forward in his seat. A car horn blared behind them but Nina didn't seem to notice.

'You're serious aren't you? Her eyes narrowed and the veins in her neck tightened. 'That's what you and that weasel friend of yours were up to – sharing secrets.'

'Pull out of the traffic and we'll talk.'

She put the car into gear and pulled into the side of the road. The driver behind maneuvered round them and flicked an angry V-sign as he sped past.

'Bollocks to all of you!' Nina screamed. She switched off the engine and fixed Hunter with a spiteful glare, 'Do you have it on you?'

'No, Richard has it, but he's reluctant to share it with you. He wants some answers and so do I.'

'You won't be able to handle the truth.'

Hunter scraped his fingers through his hair. 'Are you kidding? What do you think is going on here, and just how pathetic do you think I am?'

Nina knew exactly which buttons to press. All she had to do was question his emotional stability, and of course he'd proved her right.

For Christ's sake calm down Hunter - control yourself. He felt like kicking the door open and storming off. *Don't do it. Keep reeling her in, she's just wriggling.*

He cleared his throat. 'We need to work together. For once I need *you* to trust me.'

Her eyes searched his face, as she weighed up the risk. Truth was he had no idea what he could cope with. Recent events had been so dramatic, so unbelievable, that bad news seemed almost normal. Taking the train home, buying a crate of beer and watching sport used to be normal - right now that would be heaven. But when Nina finally spoke, Hunter discovered he wasn't prepared at all.

'When was the last time you spoke to your brother?' Her tone was accusing, almost scornful.

As if living one nightmare wasn't enough, in one sentence she had disturbed something much deeper in Hunter's psyche - a spectre he'd spent years trying to run from.

'What's that got to do with anything?' He was shaking now.

'If you reckon you can handle the truth you need to answer the question.' Again unsympathetic. Was she deliberately trying to hurt him? He loved Christian, of course he did, but he couldn't talk about him without a whole load of other stuff flooding back into his head. He'd spent years building defences and shunning his brother was part of the strategy. He didn't want to let it all back in now.

'We haven't spoken for two years or so. We exchange cards at Christmas and birthdays - that's all.'

'Two years!'

'Come on Nina, this isn't about family get-togethers. What's your point?'

She eyed him warily as rain pattered on the car roof. When she spoke, there was a hint of sorrow in her voice. 'Christian told me about Zarcom.'

Hunter stared at her, expecting her to laugh or say, 'fooled you,' but she didn't. 'What's my brother got to do with this? He's in Afghanistan, and how the hell do you know him anyway?'

'We were lovers until a few months ago. When we separated, I returned to the UK and started work at the Daily News.'

The words came at him like arrows. Hunter closed his eyes, tried to make it all fit, tried to comprehend. His mind reeled, words stuttered from his lips. 'What were you doing in Afghanistan? I mean… what's Christian got to do with any of this?'

'I can't discuss my work in Afghanistan, not with you, or anyone else.'

'Can't or won't?'

'Both. Some things are personal Matthew, and I can't go into detail how I met Chris either, you'll have to ask him yourself. We were great together, but after a few months things changed. Chris became secretive. He urged me to return home, insisting that I was in danger, but wouldn't tell me why. Of course I wasn't going to accept such a lame excuse for a break-up. He promised to explain but only if I agreed to come back to the UK.'

'And he told you about a science research project in Devon? That doesn't add up.'

She shook her head. 'He was involved in a secret mission to search for and destroy Taliban units hiding in the mountains around Helmand Province. He had witnessed atrocities, terrible things that he found hard to live with. I sensed he wanted to go into detail but he insisted it would put both our lives at risk.' She stared at her fingers interlaced on her lap. 'I couldn't help myself. I kept on pushing until he told me more. He mentioned Zarcom and told me about a contract to supply military hardware to the MOD.'

'But Zarcom's into animal research, not weapons.'

'Exactly. I did some digging and the trail led to Devon. I told Bryant I wanted to cover the protest march, but I really wanted to discover the truth about this project.'

Hunter wiped his hands down his cheeks. 'So why include me in your little scheme?'

Nina reached out and gently took his hand, but he snatched it away from her.

She said, 'Chris told me to find you when I arrived in England and ensure your safety, but made me promise not to say anything. That's why I took the job at The News, to get closer to you.'

'What do you mean "ensure my safety?" You're not making sense.'

'I needed to tell you about Zarcom but couldn't just blurt it out. I fooled Bryant into sending you to Devon with me. I told him I needed a minder in case I got into trouble.'

'But you caused the trouble. And who were those fanatical friends of yours?'

'We all share the same idea. We want to expose this project.'

Hunter glared. 'You wheedled military secrets from my brother and then told a bunch of New Age activists everything. What kind of friend are you?'

'They're not activists. They're ex-military, and I didn't tell them anything they didn't already know.'

'Bullshit!'

'You said you could handle the truth. We need your help to expose Zarcom, for your brother's sake if nothing else. He's in danger Matthew.'

Hunter watched rivulets of water race down the windscreen, felt his pulse throb inside his head. He felt completely out of his depth. 'You're saying Zarcom has a contract to supply the MOD with what... genetically mutated animals?'

'Yes.'

'Animals bred specifically for combat?'

'Yes, but the project is still at an early stage. These creatures have only recently been introduced into Afghanistan.'

'And Chris is involved?'

'I'm afraid so.'

'But why? He's just a soldier serving his country.'

'Your father Matthew. The link between Chris, Zarcom and you, is your father.'

19

CHRISTIAN HEARD SOMEONE STEP through the rubble behind the wall to his right. A man wearing a black turban popped up from behind the demolished masonry, a Kalashnikov tucked against his shoulder, the muzzle aimed straight at Christian.

Another half-dozen armed men emerged from the piles of rock, and within moments he was surrounded. They tore at his clothes and grabbed his hair, pushed him to the floor and kicked him. Christian rolled to one side and managed to stagger to his feet, but a punch landed on his cheek and sent him stumbling sideways. More punches rained in, buffeting his head back and forth. His legs buckled and he collapsed to his knees.

Somewhere above him, a voice bellowed a command in Pashto and the attack petered out. A tall man, sun-darkened face and black beard, stepped forward. His clothes were soiled with dust, his eyes black as charcoal. He stood erect like a proud warrior, regarding Christian with repulsion and something else – curiosity perhaps.

Two of the Taliban grabbed Christian's arms, and one held a gun to the back of his head. They shoved him forward and marched him into town.

Rasheed stood in the doorway at Rabia's house watching the Taliban militia drag the soldier into the street, led by his father. Blood streaked the Englishman's face and he struggled to walk. They took him into Massoud's house on the opposite side of the square. Two armed men stood guard outside to keep the growing mob at bay.

Flushed with guilt at betraying the soldier to his father so easily, Rasheed felt he must help the Englishman. He hurried across the square and slipped down the backstreet behind Massoud's house but in the back yard saw two more armed men at the rear entrance.

Along the side of the house, Rasheed spotted an open window on the top floor, too high to reach, but accessible from the roof. The gaps between each building were about four feet wide – easy to jump across. He could climb to the top of the end house, and make his way across the rooftops, swing down through the window and get inside. Then he would find his father and plead with him to show leniency towards the soldier – maybe even let him go.

Hunched low, Rasheed retraced his steps to the last house on the block, kicked off his sandals, and started to climb. The walls were rough, punctuated with deep crevices – mostly due to erosion, but some were bullet holes. The fissures were deep enough to grip with his fingers and toes, and Rasheed was light on his feet. He grasped the lip of the roof, and hauled himself up on his belly.

Massoud's place was five buildings along. Rasheed leapt nimbly across the rooftops while the men in the square shouted for the prisoner to be sent out. When he reached Massoud's, he dropped to his stomach, and slithered to the edge of the roof to view the street below.

Men punched the air and chanted. 'God is great.' Suddenly a cheer went up. Someone – Rasheed could not see who – stepped out of the door directly beneath him. An uneasy silence followed. Nobody moved. Then, he heard his father's voice.

'Hear me brothers for I have terrible news. I now have proof that these foreign invaders intend to destroy us all.'

A chorus of jeers went up. Asad waited for them to subside before continuing. 'Western governments worship money and their doctrine is greed. We seek only to serve God and purify our souls. The foreigners are puzzled why we live without fear. They come here with weapons so our country is no longer a safe place to raise our children. But we will not yield. We will continue to fight.'

The crowd cheered, again Asad waited for silence before continuing. 'Now they have brought the ultimate evil. From the bowels of their unholy lands they send legions of demons to destroy us. But have no fear my friends, for we will slay these beasts. Behold, I have a gift.'

Asad tossed a large object out of the door. The bloody head of the creature spiralled into the air and dropped into the crowd. Rasheed gasped in horror. The men backed away, and stared at the thing lying on the ground. A brief standoff ensued before they regrouped and swarmed around the grisly object, a ring of astonished faces, gasping and muttering quiet prayers.

One man threw a handful of dirt at the beast and soon they were taking turns, kicking the head around, hitting it with sticks, and rocks.

A child screamed. Rasheed looked up and spotted her running back through the crowd towards Rabia's house. Jamila. Oh God, Jamila.

20

RICHARD MONKTON SUSPECTED THE police were mixed up with Zarcom on some level. Once he declared his involvement they might keep tabs on him, follow him and tap his phone. Perhaps they already were...

On the drive into town, he noticed a blacked-out 4X4 on his tail. The car followed him into the multi-storey and up through the first two levels. Monkton's anxiety heightened, he wiped sweat from his forehead and took a deep breath. A row of spaces appeared on level 3, ideal for the 4X4 to park up. He crawled past the bays and was relieved to see the car stop and reverse into a space.

Monkton spiraled up to the next level, but had to be sure. He stopped the Jeep, leapt out and walked back to the ramp to get a view of the level below. He saw the driver of the other car and chuckled to himself. A young mother struggled in the back seat with a child in a safety harness, and there, leaning against the door was a folded buggy. Embarrassed at his own foolishness, Monkton hurried back to the Jeep and parked up.

The camera safely buttoned in his breast pocket, he speed-walked to the elevators. An icy wind rifled through the concrete structure, blasting his face and ears.

A sign read: 'Lifts out of order. Please use the stairs.'

Typical. The stairwell exit was at the far side of the car park, and a sense of apprehension swept over him once more. His footsteps echoed in his ears as he made his way back. No sign of the woman and her child – indeed the 4X4 had vanished. Monkton resisted the urge to dive into the Jeep and high-tail it out of there. The woman had probably driven off rather than take the stairs with a kid in tow.

The stairwell reeked of urine. Monkton shoved open the door and descended at speed, holding his breath. Rotting corpses and animal excrement didn't bother him, but stale piss turned his stomach.

A tramp slumped against the wall, blocked his path. Monkton stepped around him cautiously, and out of fear rather than generosity, dug a handful of loose change from his pocket and tossed them into the tray at the man's feet.

The tramp stirred as the coins rattled in the dish. 'God bless you sir,' he murmured.

Monkton hurried down the final flight and felt the welcome rush of cold sweet air. Black clouds shifted overhead and from the east and he heard the distant roll of thunder. He stopped on the pavement and his heart almost stopped with him.

The blacked-out 4X4 was parked immediately in front of him.

Perhaps it was a different car? Maybe the woman had pulled over to answer a phone call?

Taking no chances, Monkton turned and ran back up the steps. Out of nowhere, a tall figure charged into him. Winded, Monkton collapsed against the wall, fumbled to keep his glasses in place as he gasped for breath.

A man leaned over him – *the tramp*. Powerful hands gripped Monkton's lapels and straightened him up against the wall. Monkton blinked, tried to focus, but his glasses slipped off his face and fell to the floor. He heard the crunch of lenses being crushed underfoot, put a protective hand over his breast pocket where the camera was hidden, but the man prized his fingers away.

'I'll take that.'

'No please don't.'

The tramp closed his hand around Monkton's throat, squeezed until the little guy choked and his eyes watered. 'I could easily hurt you if I wanted. Now do as you're told and give up the camera.'

Monkton squirmed, overwhelmed by the man's strength. Why hadn't he followed his instincts and waited for Matthew? He should have followed his own advice and taken the film home. Now it was gone. The tramp ripped the camera out of his pocket and laughed.

Without glasses Richard Monkton's world was smudged and blurred. 'Who... who are you?'

The man's face leered an inch from Monkton's nose. 'Someone you shouldn't be messing with. You need to watch yourself Dick. We know all about you, and if we find out you've been messing with things that don't concern you...' The tramp sneered. 'I'll leave you to work it out. In the meantime here's a little taster.'

Monkton flinched and his legs buckled. 'Please no.'

The tramp laughed and let go. He dived into the back of the 4X4, closed the door and the car sped away, leaving Monkton cowering against the wall.

21

HUNTER DECIDED NINA WAS lying. His father had been a labourer most of his life. He'd certainly never been involved with Zarcom Research, and Nina had offered no explanations why Christian might have told her this.

And as for their alleged relationship?

No, he couldn't believe that either. He wanted to find out more, but right now couldn't find the strength to utter another syllable.

Hunter remembered the good old days: his father's drunken rages, the beatings, the misery. The memories flooded back and engulfed him. Christian was the only person he could speak to now. The demons were on his heels and not just metaphorically this time. What could he do – run harder, run faster? They'd catch up sooner or later. No, he had to face his past and the memories that tortured him. He had to discover the truth.

Hunter slouched into his seat and closed his eyes. He felt mentally drained, and craved for peace but life wasn't letting up. He had no idea how long they had been sitting in silence. Glancing at Nina, he realized she wasn't attractive at all. If Christian had hooked up with this woman then what the hell was he thinking?

Two police cars screamed past at high speed.

'We should go,' Nina said. 'The whole thing's about to kick off.'

'Okay let's join up with Richard. I've heard all I need from you.'

Nina's expression turned sullen, she started the car and pulled out, as another squad car flared up, and bulldozed its way through the parting traffic.

Hunter's phone rang. It was Monkton. 'Richard we'll be with you in…'

'Matt, please listen. I've been...' Monkton drifted out.

'Richard are you okay?'

No reply.

Nina scowled. 'He's fucked up hasn't he?'

Hunter pressed the phone hard against his ear. 'Richard, what's happened? Where are you?'

'I'm sorry Matt. They took the camera, I couldn't stop them.'

'Tell me where you are, we're coming to get you.'

Monkton's stuttered a reply, barely audible above the sound of traffic.

'Richard, I need you to hold it together. Look for a road name, anything to help us find you. '

'I'm in town near the multi-storey.'

Nina cut from one side of the road to the other, overtaking everything in sight. Hunter managed to calm Monkton down and get his position. He relayed the information to Nina. 'Vellum Street, at the back of the multi-storey.'

Nina jumped a set of lights and screeched into a right turn. Moments later, they spotted Monkton stumbling in the gutter, arms outstretched, scarf trailing in the dirt. Nina swerved into a bus lane, and switched off the engine.

Without spectacles, Monkton could barely open his eyes. He raised his hands as Hunter approached.

'Okay Richard. It's me - Matthew.'

Monkton held up the bent frame of his glasses. 'I need new lenses Matt, I'm blind without them.'

Nina gave Monkton a withering glance. 'So you got jumped huh?'

The little guy nodded. 'They followed me and even called me "Dick." If they know my name, they probably know about you guys as well.'

'And the film?'

Monkton's head sagged.

Hunter rested a hand on his shoulder. 'You're safe now. Tell us what happened.'

Nina sounded agitated. 'We need to follow those sirens if we want to catch the story. We can talk on the way. Let's go.'

'I can't,' Monkton protested. 'Not without my specs.'

'Looks like you're on your own Nina,' Hunter said. 'I'll help Richard get his glasses fixed and call you when we're done.'

She cursed under her breath and stormed back to the car.

Nina raced north through the suburbs, and rage boiled up inside her. Hunter was so damn weak - nothing like his brother. The creatures were out hunting for food and humans were their prey.

She absently stroked the back of her neck, and her fingers ran down the three inch scar at the base of her skull, hidden beneath the hairline. No physical discomfort, but the memories cut deep. Modjarrad would get his comeuppance - she would see to it personally.

But what could she tell Matthew Hunter?

Not the truth. She'd have to keep playing him - sacrifice him if necessary. Hunter was the only person capable of helping her exact her revenge, even if he didn't know it. She pulled out her cell phone and dialed his number, but her call went straight to voicemail.

Sirens wailed in the distance. An expanse of parkland opened up on her right as she headed out of town. The car behind, a blacked-out 4X4, was driving way too close, and started to annoy her. She was about to floor the accelerator and leave the car behind, but something caught her eye.

A flash of movement in the park: a black silhouette.

Beyond the trees, two powerful animals streaked across the grass, one behind the other. They might have been racehorses such was their size and speed. But a closer inspection revealed the truth. The feline symmetry, the heads stooped low, ears back, and muscular limbs propelling the animals forward in long elastic strides.

Nina hit the brakes and veered into the kerb. The 4X4 overtook her, and blasted its horn.

Hands trembling, she twisted in her seat and looked back at the creatures as they hurtled down the hill, heading for town.

Broad daylight and kids were just finishing school. The beasts were following an impulse they couldn't ignore – a powerful signal.

She fumbled for the Colt automatic taped under the dash, found the gun and tore it away. Glanced over her shoulder. Shit, they were already out of sight.

Nina noticed the 4X4 a split second before it reversed into the front of her car. The impact jolted her violently in her seat, a loud crunch and a tinkle of glass. She dropped the gun. Two figures in ski masks appeared either side of her car, silenced pistols aimed at her head.

The guy to her right spoke. 'Get out and keep your hands where I can see them.' He yanked the door open and waved her out of the car.

Hands raised, she swung her legs out and tried to stand.

A screech of brakes. A Mondeo skidded and mounted the grass verge on the opposite side of the road. The driver glanced across in horror and accelerated away, wheels spinning on the turf.

Get the number plate - please get the damn number plate, Nina thought.

But the guy didn't look back. He sped away, and raced down the hill - the same direction the creatures had gone.

The gunmen seemed unfazed. One of them was suddenly behind her. She felt a blinding pain as the pistol cracked against her skull. Her legs gave way and she blacked out.

22

ASAD PACED THE FLOOR while the two guards grinned at Rasheed from the other side of the room. The men had spotted him on the roof earlier and dragged him inside to face his father's wrath. In the corner, the British soldier was on his knees, hands tied behind his back, head bowed. A string of red spit hung from one corner of his mouth.

'You disgrace me boy,' Asad said. 'I left you in charge of the family and what do you do?'

Rasheed stared at his feet.

'Well, what have you to say to me?'

'Sorry Father.'

'Sorry? Do you think that covers it – sorry?'

Rasheed lifted his eyes and stared at the Englishman.

'Look at me, not him.' Asad bared his yellow teeth. 'I trusted you and this is how you repay me, leaving your sister and mother.'

Rasheed bristled with anger. His father hadn't even hugged his daughter or greeted his wife after all this time.

'Answer me!'

'I did everything you asked of me Father.'

Asad raised his right hand high above his head, ready to swipe - held it for a moment and then dropped his arm back to his side. He snapped his fingers at the guards. 'Leave us!'

The men shuffled out of the room. Asad waited until the door was closed, and then ordered his son to sit. 'You have spent too much time around the English Rasheed. I will forgive you this once, but I cannot allow it to continue. Do you understand?'

'Yes Father.'

'Once we have finished here, we will leave Qatif and you will join us. I will train you to fight, so that you may serve the Jihad.'

Jihad? Rasheed gripped the edge of the seat. Suddenly, he couldn't speak – couldn't breathe.

'If you have questions, then now is the time to ask.'

Rasheed opened his mouth but there was only one question on his mind. 'Are you going to kill the soldier?'

Asad rolled his eyes. 'What would you have me do? Tell me boy, what would you have me do with him?'

'Release him. Show these foreigners we are not savages.'

'What! Are you judging me? *Me,* your father.'

'Mother has missed you, and Jamila is growing up fast. I want to learn from you, but not like this. You can teach me carpentry. I want to marry and have sons. In turn I will pass your knowledge onto them, so they may build futures of their own.'

Asad folded his arms across his chest. 'And in order to live that dream my Son, first we must cast out the foreign soldiers.'

'Do not kill him father please. It will be an execution. The soldier's blood will forever be on your hands.'

'And what about the demon? This is no ordinary man. He is an affront to God. We have killed only one of these creatures, but there is another. We must find the beast and destroy it before it kills again.'

Rasheed didn't know what was more frightening - the demonic monster, or his father becoming a fanatic like Salim.

Salim the butcher. That was the name bestowed upon the previous Taliban commander and Rasheed knew his mother would not survive seeing her husband follow the same path.

23

HUNTER WAITED FOR MONKTON on a bench outside the opticians while he mulled over his friend's story. He felt utterly lost and exhausted. The buildings around the precinct seemed to bear down on him as people drifted in and out of the shops, blissfully unaware of the horrors lurking on their doorstep.

Whoever attacked Monkton, must have been tracking him for some time. Indeed, Hunter felt he was being watched right now.

A guy in a business suit walked past and barged his way through a group of youths. One of the teenagers turned and hurled a volley of abuse, but the man continued his stride. Hunter guessed he was in his early thirties, a severe crew cut and military bearing - could be a spy.

No, too obvious.

The man selling Disney balloons at the mall entrance seemed more likely. Here was a guy with a reason to stand in one place for long periods and observe the town centre. He was powerfully built - a definite possibility. Hunter watched the balloon seller select a Goofy balloon from the bunch and pass it down to a small blond kid. The boy skipped away with a beaming smile while his mother paid the man.

Hunter dismissed the idea, and retreated back into his world of paranoia - vans with listening devices, spies on street corners, snipers on rooftops.

Wait… rewind that thought. He spotted movement above the coffee shop just across the street to his left. A head bobbed up from behind the parapet and then disappeared.

Hunter got to his feet and scanned every rooftop, every shop doorway. His cell phone rang, and Nina's number flashed up on the screen.

Not now, he thought, *I've had enough of your shit.*

He cancelled the call. Time to collect Richard Monkton and get back to London where he could lose himself again.

Suddenly, the air resonated with a heavy thud that quickly became a deafening crescendo. Pigeons erupted from the precinct in a blur of gun-metal grey. Hunter dropped to his haunches, hands clamped over his ears.

Two Chinook helicopters roared overhead, followed by two Apache gunships - the roar of their turbo engines rattled windows and set off car alarms.

What if Nina was right? What if the whole thing was about to kick off.

A chorus screams went up in the adjacent street. Goofy skipped towards him - a cartoon head attached to the body of a small boy. The kid's mother gave chase, yelling at her son to stop.

More screams pierced the air, this time to the west of the precinct. Four youths sprinted back across the street, away from the mall. An elderly woman tripped and fell, sending the contents of her grocery bags sprawling across the ground. Hunter watched the crazy scene unfold around him. People barged into one another, ran into shops, looking for places to hide. Cars collided, horns blared, and sirens wailed in the distance. Someone yelled, 'Lock the doors now!'

The opticians closed their doors, and other shops followed suit. Balloon kid stood next to his mother as she banged on the door of a music store, along with a dozen other people screaming to be let inside.

At the mall entrance the balloon seller had his back to Hunter, facing the adjacent street, arms at his sides, completely transfixed. His vast collection of Disney characters drifted slowly above his head.

The balloons suddenly split apart. Mickey, Donald, Simba, a whole cavalcade of cartoon faces violently punched aside as an enormous black creature burst through them and pounced on the man, knocking him flat.

Hunter couldn't grasp what he was witnessing - a silent scream caught in his throat.

Oh God, they're here.

The same creature Monkton had captured on film: the head of a demonic lion, a muscular tapered body, twelve feet long, and a broad tail that swished like a bull-whip. The creature's hide appeared rough, stretched tight over the animal's powerful frame. The beast extended its jaw and clamped its fangs over the balloon seller's head, crunching into the man's skull. Bone cracked, and blood squirted like juice from a punctured grapefruit. Hunter staggered back and retched at the sight of this foul creature tearing chunks out of a human body.

Balloon kid clutched his mother's skirt and sobbed as she hammered on the door of a clothes boutique. Terrified faces stared back at her through the glass, but no one came to her aid. Other shoppers gave up trying and began streaming out of the precinct. From the bookstore, the guy in the business suit marched towards the beast, slipped a gun from his jacket and fired four shots, each one a direct hit but the brute barely flinched.

Numb with shock, Hunter registered the terror on peoples' faces but could do nothing to help. Amid the incessant screams, a small crowd ran down the street to his right. On their heels, Hunter saw a second creature leap onto the back of a young woman.

Now he heard himself scream.

From the north-east corner of the precinct a third beast appeared, and then a fourth. Shots rang out from the roof of the coffee shop. A sniper.

They knew, Hunter thought. *The bastards knew.*

But who were 'they'? The police… the military? Hunter looked for the guy in the business suit, but he had already vanished.

The first creature spat out the remains of the balloon seller, blood dripped from its mouth as it gazed across at Goofy bobbing in the shop doorway.

Hunter had to get to the kid. People ran, tripped, and fell, but it was the boy who had his attention. The second creature sloped around the corner, and the two of them began pacing slowly towards the boutique, tongues slapping over their teeth.

Richard Monkton put on his new spectacles and the world made sense once more. He paid the assistant and phoned Hunter but the call went straight to voicemail. He heard a commotion outside in the precinct, people bustled past him and ran to the back of the store.

Monkton ducked behind a gondola, and waited until the rush had subsided before hurrying to the front entrance. A knot of customers stared through the glass as a male assistant bolted the doors. But there were people out there, banging on the glass, screaming to be let in…So why was this guy locking them out?

'Bloody terrorists,' said a man standing beside him.

Monkton shook his head in disbelief. 'Can't be.'

Outside, bodies littered the pedestrian zone. In the middle of it all Matthew Hunter spun in circles, terror etched on his face.

Monkton grabbed the shop assistant, 'For god's sake open these doors.'

'No way man, I've been ordered to lock the place up. Security are on their way.'

'But my friend's out there!'

'I'm sorry. If you want to get out, you'll have to go to the back of the store and through the mall.'

'Damn you!'

Monkton raced back through the shop, reached the main concourse, and joined the crowds streaming towards the exits. He got to the stairwell, wormed his way up to level 5.

Exhausted, he stumbled through the doors into the car park. It was quieter up here - less than half full. He staggered to the Jeep, unlocked it, and sank into the seat, taking a moment to catch his breath before starting the engine.

Queuing traffic blocked the exit lane all the way down to ground level, but the way up was clear. Monkton drove up to the roof where he could view the streets around the mall. He skidded to a halt near the east wall, jumped out, and peered down into the street.

The traffic was at a standstill. The pedestrian precinct wasn't visible from here, but Monkton saw the one thing he dreaded, scramble across the cars. He watched the hulking beast attack a man fallen at the kerbside.

Monkton recoiled in horror. He had to get Hunter out of the precinct. There was only one way he could think of, and Monkton prayed it would work.

24

CHRISTIAN STARED AT THE Taliban commander. His mouth was dehydrated but he managed to speak. 'I can help you.'

The Afghan snorted, but Christian noticed a glimmer of understanding in the man's eyes so he struggled on. 'More of these creatures will come but if you release me, I can stop them.'

The commander laughed, and grabbed Christian's face in one hand. He spoke in broken English. 'More will come, and more will die.'

'Please, you must listen...'

The Afghan's fingers squeezed Christian's face harder. 'You will speak only when I tell you.' With his free hand, he pulled a knife from his belt. 'I believe you English call this "spilling your guts".'

The blade dug into Christian's stomach. He tried to speak but the man's hand was clamped too tight. He muttered through his teeth, spit dribbled down his chin. The Afghan unleashed a stinging backhand across Christian's face that twisted his head to one side. Then the man leaned in, nose-to-nose. 'You can start by telling me exactly what these creatures are and how to destroy them.'

Christian stretched his jaw. 'I can stop them. I know about the project to create these monsters, and everyone involved. I can get the whole thing shut down, but not from here.'

'You are only a fool who does his master's bidding. There is nothing you can do. These beasts have killed innocent women and children.'

'My government doesn't know what happened. My unit was ambushed by mercenaries, sent by the company who made these beasts. Please, I need to get back to England and speak to the people I know I can trust.'

'You lie.'

'It's true. I wrote a report damning the project, but someone intercepted it. These animals are impossible to handle, and kill at random. If the British government finds out, they'll put a stop to it. The men sent to kill me were dressed as Taliban fighters. Do you understand? They want you to take the blame for killing my men. If you let me go, I can tell my government the truth.' Christian took a deep breath. 'We're not here to attack the Afghan people. We only want to stop the terrorists who seek refuge in your country. '

The Afghan commander slid a finger along the blade of his knife. 'The only terrorists in Afghanistan are Americans and their greedy friends. You undermined a legitimate government, interfered with our way of life. We did not invite you, and yet you came with guns and missiles... and now this.'

'Your leaders were providing sanctuary for terrorists. What does it take for you to understand?'

A heavy boot struck Christian's chest and forced him back against the wall.

Rasheed jumped up and grabbed his father's arm before he could strike the soldier again. 'Father, please stop. This is not the way.'

Asad brushed him aside. 'Enough Rasheed. This man brings death and destruction, and all you can do is beg for his release. I need to make a fighter of you'

'But he might be able to help us.'

'God give me strength, you are naïve boy. He cannot stop the British soldiers. He does not speak for them.'

'Shouldn't we give him a chance?'

'Go home, I've heard enough whimpering.' Asad called the guards back into the room. 'Tariq, see that my son goes back to his mother.'

Rasheed looked up in desperation. 'But Father...'

'Later I will return home, and put everything straight.'

Rasheed's eyes widened. 'Are you staying this time?'

Asad shook his head. 'I have a duty. Until it is done, I must stay with my men, and you will come with us. We must destroy the other demon.'

Rasheed pleaded with his father, but the guard Tariq snatched his arm and pulled him effortlessly out of the house.

In the square, the local men were standing around debating while children played and their mothers watched from the doorways. Rasheed struggled against Tariq's tight grasp. 'I can go on my own.'

'You are sick boy. 'You misunderstand our purpose.'

'And what purpose is that?'

The man grinned. 'To exterminate the foreigners.'

At Rabia's house, the front door flew open and Aisha appeared, dressed in her burka. 'Rasheed, is Jamila with you?'

'Of course not, she ran back to the house. I saw her cross the square.' Rasheed yanked his arm away, and finally broke free from the Tariq's grip.

'She's not here,' Aisha said.

'What?'

From a street nearby, came the sound of a woman's shriek, followed by a single gunshot. Silence fell over the square. People looked at one another, and then began running towards the source of the commotion. Rasheed sprinted hard, and found himself ahead of the crowd.

Two blocks from Rabia's house, he stumbled across a woman knelt at the roadside, weeping into her hands while she rocked herself.

Another gunshot. Mustafa the baker stood a little way down the avenue, pointing a revolver at the sky, aiming at nothing. He fired again.

'The Devil is in town,' the woman cried. God save us please.'

Rasheed called out to the baker. 'What happened Mustafa?'

The man ignored him. His face quivered, and the gun trembled in his hand. People flooded into the street. Armed militia fanned out between the buildings on both sides of the road. Women jabbered as the men went to investigate a small bundle in the middle of the road. Rasheed noticed a trail of blood, and a wave of terror surged through him.

25

MONKTON STARTED THE JEEP and headed down to the next level of the multi-storey. From level five, a queue of traffic snaked all the way down to the exit, but the right-hand lane remained clear. Monkton swerved past a black Toyota at the back of the line, and sped down the ramp in the wrong lane. Disgruntled drivers blasted their horns, but Monkton continued his journey, hunched over the wheel in grim determination.

He reached level 4 without incident. A couple of cars tried to block his path but couldn't maneuver out far enough to stop him. Undeterred, Monkton made it safely to ground level and accelerated at the entrance barrier. The Jeep smashed through the barrier-arm like it was made of balsa wood.

A wall of traffic blocked the road, many cars had been abandoned, but at least the creatures had gone. The nearside pavement was clear, protected from the road by a metal crash-barrier that stretched the length of the street. An eight foot gap between the wall and the barrier offered Monkton his chance of escape. He reversed into position, drove onto the pavement, and raced up the hill where he turned right into York Street on the south side of the multi-storey. The pedestrian precinct was on the west side of the mall, and no more than fifty yards away.

Monkton cruised along the pavement, watched by the multitude of terrified faces peering out of their cars and from the buildings overlooking the street. He only hoped he wasn't too late.

Hunkered in the doorway of the boutique, the boy clutched his Goofy balloon and buried his face into his mother's chest. She stroked his hair and rocked him, too afraid to look up at the two creatures skulking towards her.

Hunter found himself in no-man's land, caught between the beasts and their prey. He ran to the boutique and hammered on the glass. 'Open this fucking door.'

Blank expressions gazed back at him but no one came to their aid.

The two beasts crept low to the ground like lions intent on a kill. Their pitiless eyes lingered on the boy.

But why had the shooting stopped, and where were the snipers and the guy in the business suit?

Hunter spun in circles, looking for help. Suddenly, a searing pain pierced his skull. He cried out and sank to his knees, tears streamed down his face. His neck went into spasm and he struggled to breathe. He checked the back of his head for a wound, but found nothing. Instinctively, he crawled towards the kid in a vain attempt to protect him.

The creatures were only feet away when gunfire erupted from the rooftops once more. The two animals shouldered up to each other, and bore down on their quarry. Not far behind, the other two chimeras rooted through the dead bodies, crunching into flesh and bone, oblivious to the bullets grazing their tough hides.

A bullet ripped into the leg of the beast nearest Hunter, but it kept on coming. The animal took a head shot, its left eye popped and blood spurted from the wound. The beast groaned and rolled its head, while its partner belted out an angry roar. Behind them, the other two animals raised their blood-soaked snouts and stared across the precinct towards the boutique, shoulders working like pistons.

The one-eyed beast thrust its head forward, its nose only inches from Hunter's face. All four creatures closed in, packed tight, shoulder-to-shoulder in the doorway. Hunter closed his eyes, anticipating the strike. Hot, stale breath swept over his face. The final moment of his life and he was powerless to act.

Monkton parked up, and ran into the precinct where a gruesome scene awaited him - a battlefield of mauled bodies.

A child wailed, and a woman screamed. Monkton saw people huddled in a shop doorway halfway down the precinct to his right and heard a man cry out in distress. He instantly recognized the beige jacket. *Matthew Hunter*.

One of the creatures reared up at his friend, as if to attack. Not thinking, Monkton screamed and clapped his hands to distract the animals.

Rotor blades thudded in the distance, and an Apache helicopter hovered into position directly ahead, about half a mile out.

The four creatures turned and glared at Monkton.

Oh Christ!

He stopped shouting. To his horror, the beasts wheeled away from the shop door and began trotting towards him. Monkton turned and ran as hard as he could, but sensed the creatures gather speed behind him. A whoosh of air behind him was followed by a blinding flash of light. Monkton rounded the corner, and dived into the nearest shop doorway.

The ground shook and the buildings around him ruptured as the blast ripped through the precinct, hurling chunks of stone and debris into the air. Monkton stayed down, as the jangle of alarms was joined by a multitude of wailing screams. After a few seconds, he scrambled to his feet and staggered through the powdery air, calling out to Hunter but fearing the worst.

The strike point was situated thirty yards from the boutique, right in the centre of the pedestrian zone. Dust swirled and bricks tumbled from the structures on either side of the smoking pit. Small fires broke out inside the buildings. People shouted for extinguishers and first aid as they stumbled out of the shops, their clothes and faces dusted white.

Monkton looked on, dazed and bewildered. He picked his way across the rubble, past the four hulking shapes lying amongst the glass and stone. Bodies ripped apart, blood and bone fragments splattered everywhere - some human, some not.

The windows of the boutique had been obliterated, but all the women inside had survived. A young woman staggered through the framework of what used to be the front door, her face streaked red, eyes squinting as she emerged. Monkton offered her his hand.

In the dust haze, a man coughed, and a child whimpered. All Monkton could make out at first was a bundle of rags - limbs caked with powder, and sticky with blood. But the jacket was unmistakable.

Monkton stooped and nudged his friend's shoulder. Hunter flinched, opened his eyes, and slowly raised his head.

'Matthew its Richard. Thank God you're alive.'

26

'THE DEMON!' MUSTAFA CRIED. 'The demon. I saw it.'

Rasheed sank to his knees and buried his head in his hands. *Thank God it's not Jamila.*

A crowd gathered around the coiled mass of intestines heaped in the road. Nearby was the severed head of a goat. Asad pushed his way through the onlookers and nudged the remains with his foot. 'I have seen this many times. It is the work of the beast.'

Rasheed pulled him aside. 'Father, Jamila is missing.'

'What?'

'I saw her in the square earlier, but she didn't return to the house…'

'Enough. Go and find her Rasheed.' Asad shoved him aside and ordered his men back to the trucks.

Rasheed ran behind the band of militia as they marched back to the square. Aisha was waiting for him further up the road.

'Rasheed! Your mother wants to know what's happening. What shall I tell her?'

He stopped and drew breath. 'Tell her Jamila is all right.'

'And is she?'

'I don't know.'

Asad climbed behind the wheel of the first pickup and his men piled in the back. The vehicle pulled away, followed by the second truck – both crammed with angry Taliban fighters. Rasheed watched them disappear down the street, heading south out of town.

Aisha grabbed his hand. 'Try not to worry. You must trust in God and believe the men will find her.'

'No, they're not looking for my sister Aisha. My Father is only interested in tracking down the beast.'

'Then *we* must look for her. When did you see her last?'

Rasheed wiped his eyes and recounted the events. 'One of the Taliban guards caught me on Massoud's roof and ordered me down. Jamila was running to your house but I didn't see her go inside. I only assumed.'

'Did she see you?'

'I don't think so.'

'If she was frightened she would have gone looking for you. You protect her Rasheed. She's probably searching the streets for you right now.'

'No, not the streets – she'll try and find me at the hideout.'

'Yes, of course!'

Aisha pulled her burka over her head and dumped it in the road. Beneath she wore pale linen trousers and a purple blouse. 'Hurry Rasheed. I will keep up.'

He sprinted out of town with Aisha at his heels. They traversed the desert without stopping for breath and arrived at the hideout minutes later.

No sign of the little girl. Rasheed glanced inside the doorway, but the room was empty. He called out into the barren landscape, but got no reply. Aisha stood outside the entrance and sniffed the air. An anxious expression crossed her face.

'What's wrong?' Rasheed said.

'Can't you smell it?'

He caught a whiff of the stale odour drifting from the hideout. 'It's only sweat,' he replied.

'Not that.' She beckoned him closer. 'Here.'

He stepped towards her and sniffed the air. A chill raced down his spine - the stench of rotten flesh.

'You recognize it don't you?' Aisha said. 'If you know something, you must tell me.'

'It is the demon.'

Her anxiety turned to panic and she spoke breathlessly. 'We must go back. This is not safe.'

'But Jamila is in danger. We all are. My father might be right, killing the creature should be our priority. We must help him.'

'Help him how?'

'The British troops brought these demons to Afghanistan. The injured soldier will know more about it than anyone. He might tell us how to destroy it if we can free him. We must help him escape.'

27

HUNTER'S THROAT WAS PARCHED and his skin felt like sand. He got to his feet, ruffled dust from his hair, and surveyed the precinct. Clouds of dust swirled above the blast crater twenty yards away. The surrounding buildings were devastated, windows blown-out, some on fire.

Amid the jangling alarms, he heard the kid cry out from the doorway. The deflated Goofy balloon lay crumpled next to what looked like a flour-dusted shroud, the boy's cheeks were streaked pink where his tears had run.

Overhead helicopters circled the town.

Monkton put a hand on Hunter's shoulder. 'Matthew we need to get out of here. What if we weren't meant to survive this?'

Hunter knelt, and took the kid's hand. He glanced at the mother, her head twisted at an unnatural angle, eyes glazed and vacant. Next to her shoulder rested the slab of concrete that must have killed her.

Jesus, what about the kid?

One of the Apaches swooped in closer and kicked up a cloud of dust.

Hunter glared at the sky. 'You did this you bastards!'

Monkton tugged his sleeve. 'Matt, we need to get out of here while we still can.'

Hunter wiped a tired hand down his face, and stared at the boy hugging his mother's limp body. 'I can't do this any more Richard.'

'You must. Take a good look around you. Can't you see what's happened here? The Army just fired a missile into a populated area – a town centre for Christ's sake. This must be reported Matt. Like it or not, that's your job.'

'I guess you're right.' Hunter glanced at the bodies lying around him. He couldn't begin to count them.

'They'll blame terrorists,' Monkton said.

Hunter grimaced. 'Perhaps. So what's your plan?'

'To follow you. You're the tough guy.'

Tough guy? If you knew the truth, you wouldn't say that, Hunter thought.

A procession of ambulances and fire engines arrived in the adjacent street. Overhead another helicopter joined the surveillance.

'Okay, there's nothing more we can do here. Where's the Jeep?'

'Just around the corner. Let's go!'

A paramedic ran over and attended to the kid while another checked on his mother. Hunter forced himself away and followed Monkton out of the square.

The Jeep had survived the explosion unscathed, parked in the relative safety of the next street. Monkton gunned the engine and steered through the strewn wrecks of cars that had been exposed to the blast. They broke clear and headed out of town.

'We'll crash at my place for a while,' Monkton said. 'Its about ten miles south but we can avoid the highways. If they set up road blocks, they'll concentrate on the main routes first.' He careered into a narrow side street, and sped through the suburbs into the countryside.

Hunter couldn't stop thinking about the kid. He should have stayed with him. *Christ. What a fucking mess.*

Monkton sensed his distress. 'You couldn't do anything for the boy Matt. In fact you probably saved his life.'

Hunter squeezed his eyes shut and leaned back in his seat. His clothes were tattered and covered in dust. His neck was stiff, but he'd only suffered minor cuts and bruises.

'I don't understand Richard. Why didn't the creatures attack me? One minute they were closing in for the kill, the next, they simply turned away and sauntered off.'

Monkton shrugged. 'They were probably eyeing the kid and waiting for the right moment to strike. Predators always go for the weaker prey – easy pickings. But I'll tell you one thing. Those bastards were coming straight for *me* before the missile hit.'

'You're kidding? You mean you were there... in the precinct?'

Monkton nodded.

'Shit, then you must have saved my life.'

Monkton turned his head and smiled. 'I never thought of it like that. So what do we do next?'

Hunter stared at the road ahead. The headlights carved yellow cones through the late afternoon gloom. 'First I've got to contact my brother. Trouble is, I don't have his details, and approaching the MOD is out of the question.'

'Can't your parents help?'

'I don't want them involved if I can help it. Don't worry I'll think of something.'

Hunter's cell phone rang. He pulled it from his pocket and saw Bryant's number flash up on the screen. Reluctantly he answered.

'Where the fuck are you Hunter?' Bryant had lost none of his charm.

'Heading back to London,' Hunter lied.

'What do you mean, *heading back?* Haven't you heard the news?'

Hunter shifted in his seat, unsure what to tell the miserable bastard. 'What news?'

'Fuck me Hunter, you're priceless. The biggest story to hit since 7/7 and you're clueless as usual. Turn round, get yourself back to Tunbridge Wells.'

'Why? What's going on?'

'What's going on? Surely you're not that fucking stupid! A bomb has just exploded in Tunbridge Wells town centre. A terrorist attack. You're my man in the area. Get the damn story, do you hear me?'

'Yes I hear you.' *The whole county can hear you.*

'This is your chance to redeem yourself Hunter. Screw this up and you can kiss your pension goodbye. Understood?'

Hunter's anger boiled over. 'All lies!' he retorted. 'The army is responsible. Someone ordered a missile strike on the town. I was right there when it happened.'

'Have you been on the juice again Hunter?'

'No, listen. Zarcom Research is behind this...'

Bryant cut in. 'We've got extremists crawling out of the walls, killing innocent people and you're still sulking about your girlfriend getting the boot. I want a full report within the hour, or you'll be joining her at the employment centre.' And with that, he was gone, leaving Hunter staring at his phone.

'He sounds like a pratt,' Monkton said.

'He is, and I've finished with that rag of a newspaper. Nina was right all along. Its time to go it alone and sell the story to someone who will listen.'

28

THE TALIBAN FLED TOWN, leaving only one man behind to guard Massoud's house. Christian lay on his side, feigning unconsciousness, waiting for the guard to leave the room. The man paced the floor, and lit a cigarette. Minutes dragged by until finally he opened the door and walked out into the hall.

Christian repositioned himself close to a patch of blood and saliva pooled on the ground – *his blood and saliva.*

He dipped his fingers and rubbed the viscous fluid over his hands and wrists, all the time squirming to free them. At last he managed to pull one hand free. The rest was easy. He untied his feet and stood up.

There was movement outside. Suddenly the door swung open and Christian launched himself at the intruder, catching the man in the midriff as he stepped into the room. Both men toppled to the floor, but Christian managed to roll on top of the guard.

What happened next was utter confusion. Christian was about to throw a punch but a girl shrieked in his ear and began clawing at his face. Bewildered, he clawed up the wall, shielding himself from the onslaught.

'Okay okay. Enough.'

The girl backed off, and helped the guard to his feet. No, not the guard - the Afghan boy.

Shit, what have I done?

Christian stammered an apology but his words went unheard. He glanced through the doorway into the hall and noticed a body slumped on the floor. The guard. Blood seeped from the man's temple as he lay unconscious.

'Why did you hit him like that?' Aisha said. 'He is Taliban. You were supposed to lure him outside, not crack him over the head.'

Rasheed dropped the metal bar he'd found amongst the tank debris in the square, and it hit the ground with a loud clang. 'He wouldn't listen Aisha.

What else could I do?' Rasheed knelt over the guard and began to undress him.

Aisha looked horrified. 'What are you doing?'

'We have to disguise the Englishman.'

'May God forgive and protect us Rasheed. Anything but this.'

Rasheed removed the man's dish dash and handed it to the soldier. He pointed to the guard, and tried to explain. 'You Taliban.'

The Englishman nodded, and started to undress, much to Aisha's distress. She turned her back, and covered her eyes. 'This is not right,' she protested.

Rasheed helped the Englishman change into the guard's clothes, including the man's turban. The task completed, he looked the soldier up and down. His face was swollen, and covered in stubble, but hardly constituted a beard. Still, his skin wasn't too white, and there was no time to search for a scarf.

Rasheed made various gestures, shielding his face with his hand. 'Hide… face… hide.' He had no idea if the man understood but had to chance it. He told Aisha to check outside.

She opened the door a fraction and peeked out. 'All clear.'

The soldier stooped for the machine gun lying next to the guard.

'No, no.' Rasheed waved his arms across his chest. 'No gun.'

The Englishman stepped back from the weapon and Rasheed kicked it away.

'We must go now Aisha. We will take him to my house first.'

She opened the door, and beckoned them outside.

Despite the burning pain in his limbs, Christian made purposeful strides across the street, a step behind the two Afghans. The street was empty, save for an old woman hobbling across the road with a bag of laundry. No sign of the Taliban trucks.

They reached a single storey house, riddled with bullet holes. The front door was splintered, and creaked loudly when the girl pushed it open. On entering the hall, Christian knew he'd been here before. *The ambush.*

The boy closed the door behind him and buttressed it with a large stone. He motioned Christian to a room at the back of the house, and the three of them sat on the floor in a loose circle. The boy was all smiles, but the girl's eyes flashed nervously around the room, her jaw clenched tight.

The boy removed a stubby pencil from his shirt pocket and began making sketch on a wrinkled sheet of paper. His hand moved rapidly across the page, and a picture started to take shape - a head, a gaping mouth complete with razor sharp teeth. He added eyes, ears and nostrils, before shading a mane around the creature's neck. The drawing was concise and there was no question what the boy meant.

The chimera.

The kid made a separate sketch next to the animal's head - a stick drawing of a little girl, long hair and a triangle for a dress. He pushed the paper at Christian, jabbing his pencil at the beast. 'Devil.' He made a snatching motion with his hand, and then prodded a finger at the stick girl. 'Devil... take... girl.'

'No,' Christian said. 'The Devil would not take. The Devil would eat.' He stuffed an invisible object in his mouth and made an exaggerated chewing motion.

'Forget it Rasheed, he doesn't understand,' Aisha said.

'He must. No one else knows what this creature is. No one else can help us.'

'But what if he doesn't know? What if your father is right about him and he just wants to destroy us?'

Rasheed clenched his fists. 'Aisha, I don't even want to think like that.' He looked at the soldier and held up the drawing. 'Please sir. Please help us find my sister.'

29

MONKTON'S HOME WAS A rusty caravan parked in an empty field. Conditions inside were cramped – books and magazines piled on the floor, and dozens of tins stacked on the work surfaces. Hardly the Ritz, but Hunter was glad of some respite. Monkton took two cans of beer from a tiny fridge and passed one over. Hunter cracked the pull-ring and gulped half the contents in a single quaff. The cool liquid soothed his parched throat but did nothing to ease his anxiety.

'It's just after seven - the news must be on about now.' Monkton said, adjusting the aerial on the portable T.V. 'Only poor man's telly I'm afraid, but I get a decent picture on BBC.'

The screen hissed and flickered before a female reporter came into focus. She spoke to James Docherty, the anchor back in the studio.

'James, we're on a housing estate in Tunbridge Wells, a mile from where the terrorist bomb went off. Police have sealed off the town centre and are currently evacuating the area. Just after three-thirty this afternoon, a bomb went off outside the Victoria Place shopping centre. Search and rescue teams are still finding bodies in the rubble, and the casualty list is rising.'

Right of screen, a segment showed smoke pouring over the town. The caption read: *amateur footage*. Breaking news flashed up: *Bomb Terror in Kent*.

'Have you gleaned anything from eyewitnesses Charlotte?' Docherty asked.

The screen split into two, and the reporter appeared side-by-side with Docherty, the anchor.

'Strange reports James. Some say they heard sporadic gunfire before the explosion. One source told me the shooting continued for up to ten minutes. The security services are staying tight lipped, but there are suggestions the terrorists were cornered, and detonated the bomb in desperation. We understand all the suspects are dead.'

Hunter leapt out his seat. 'Jesus, who came up with this bullshit?'

Monkton's eyes didn't move from the screen. Both men gasped in disbelief at the anchor's next question.

'Charlotte, is there any truth to these sightings of wild beasts roaming the town?'

'Yes James, reports suggest a group of black Canadian bears escaped when the vehicle transporting them crashed into a house in nearby countryside. Police confirmed that four animals were quickly recaptured but several are still loose and the hunt is on to recapture them.'

'So there's no connection to the explosion?'

Charlotte shook her head. 'Definitely not. This was a terrorist attack. In a statement made earlier, Charles Fenwick, head of MI5, stated there was evidence of an Al-Qaeda cell operating in the vicinity. This is what he had to say about today's events.'

Charles Fenwick appeared on screen amid camera flashes and jostling photographers. He was in his early fifties, silver hair, and lean features. Hunter listened carefully as Fenwick delivered a surprisingly calm address.

'I can confirm the emergency services have recovered two bodies, believed to be the remains of the bombers responsible for this atrocity. This attack was cowardly and indiscriminate. Among the dead are women and children including members of the Muslim community. The death toll presently stands at twenty-two, but we are still removing bodies from the scene. Of course, we will keep you updated with news as we get it.'

Hunter yelled at the TV, 'You stupid bastards. You saw what you'd unleashed, and you panicked.'

Monkton slumped into a seat. 'If they cover this up Matthew, there's no telling where it will end. They will probably force people to lie.'

'They can't. The truth will come out one way or another.'

'But how high up does this thing go? The government must be involved. They might…'

'Ignore the movies Richard. The security services won't start bumping people off, even if the government is involved on some level.'

'If you don't mind me saying Matthew, you're being naïve. I've got a bad feeling about this. Have you figured out who attacked me at the multi-storey?'

Hunter finished his beer and placed the empty can on the table. He'd been a journalist for three years, and had come across just about every conspiracy theory going, but this time the cover-up was real.

'The security services would have arrested you Richard. This was something more sinister.'

'Well I say we tread carefully. We might need Nina's opinion. I don't like her, but at least she's on our side.'

'I tried calling her earlier but she's not picking up. I'll try again tomorrow; let's see where we go from there.'

'And in the meantime?'

'You've got an appointment to see this professor friend of yours?'

'Yes, Professor Grealish. We're meeting at the London Institute of Biology at ten tomorrow.'

'I suggest we get a few hours rest and make our way to London overnight. We'll head west and take a longer route into the city, I don't trust the roads heading north, they'll be crawling with security. I'll be very interested to hear what the Professor's got to say about those DNA samples.'

'He won't have the results yet.'

'I'd like to pick his brains anyway. I want to find out more about genetic engineering. If we still think it's a good idea to consult Nina then we can take it from there.'

'And after that?'

Hunter shrugged. 'I've got some personal business to attend to, family stuff that I can't go into right now. Let's get some sleep. We'll leave at midnight.'

30

NINA SIKETI AWOKE IN darkness, curled up on a cold stone floor, limbs bound, and her mouth gagged with tape. An earthy smell filled her nostrils as if she were somewhere underground – a cellar maybe?

She struggled to sit up against the wall and winced, feeling the pain in her wrists and ankles. A thin strip of light seeped under the door on the far side of the room, and she snapped her eyes shut. She remembered - God knows she didn't want to - but her mind replayed it now: the chimeras racing across the park, the 4X4 reversing into her car, and then the gunmen... A simple trap. How could she have been so stupid? Her head throbbed where she'd been hit, and she wondered who her captors might be.

Modjarrad's people, or perhaps MI5?

Both wanted her out of the picture. But if the beasts had ventured into town, the casualty count would be colossal, and the secret would already be out. She rested her head against the damp wall and thought about Matthew Hunter. Bringing up Christian's involvement was dumb - she should have kept her mouth shut.

The sound of footsteps filtered through the door, casting shadows in the cable of light. Keys rattled in the lock, and the door creaked open, illuminating the cell. Two tall silhouettes stepped through the doorway and lunged at her. One pinned her down while the other slipped a sack-cloth over her head. The men yanked her to her feet, but her legs gave way. They grabbed her sweater and hauled her up, ordered her to stand. Disorientated, she found her balance, and her circulation returned.

The guards dragged her out of the room, her toes skimmed the ground as they whisked her along, weaving left and right through the damp corridors. A door was kicked open, light streamed through the sackcloth as she entered a brighter room. A chair scraped across the stone floor. They spun her around, and pressed her into a seat.

The guards mumbled to one another. Another set of footsteps walked in, circled behind her, and paused momentarily. A hand brushed her shoulder, gentle yet menacing. She shuddered, wanted to yell, but her lips wouldn't move.

A voice whispered in her ear. 'Calm yourself little girl.'

Nina recognized the voice of Cyrus Modjarrad and a rush of fear went through her. She writhed and twisted to break free from her bonds. The chair rocked beneath her and she toppled over, crashed onto her back and smacked her head on the ground. Pain washed over her, and a muffled yell jettisoned from her lungs.

'Pick her up!' Modjarrad growled.

The men grappled with her clothes, and hauled her back onto the chair.

Modjarrad's voice swooped in close to her ear once more. 'Settle down Nina, you will hurt yourself.'

She sensed him back away, leaving a scent of expensive aftershave lingering under her nostrils. He spoke calmly to the two men. 'You may leave us now gentlemen. Nina and I have much to discuss.'

She fought to compose herself. The door slammed shut, footsteps faded, her pulse pounded in her ears. Deep within, a voice cried out, 'do as he says and you might live.' She shook the thought away, determined not to break.

Modjarrad yanked the sack away from her head. Blinding light forced her eyelids shut. *Don't panic. You're trained for this.*

She opened her eyes and observed her surroundings: a table in front of her, a light shining in her face. Red-brick walls covered in mildew and a puddle on the stone floor… a disused bunker perhaps, or maybe a dungeon? Definitely underground.

She watched Modjarrad circle the table, his shadow ghosted across the walls behind him. He stood at her shoulder, but said nothing, allowing her time to consider her situation. Eventually he broke the silence. 'Well Nina, what have you been up to?' His voice haughty and accusing.

She sucked in a deep breath. *Tell him nothing.*

'What's the matter Corporal Standwick, unable to speak?'

She hated that name. That was a previous life, a life of subordination, manipulation and lies. A life of killing.

'I guessed as much. Let me remind you of your situation.' He began pacing, talking loudly. 'Breaking and entering, fraud, not to mention desertion, accessory to murder…' He rounded the table to face her. 'You've been trying to undermine my work Nina. It will not do.'

This is how Modjarrad played it - threats first, the physical stuff later. His fingers brushed against her cheek and he pinched the corner of the tape covering her mouth. With a snap of his wrist, he tore it away. She yelped, and tasted blood on her lips.

Modjarad's laugh echoed around the walls. 'If you co-operate, no harm will come to you. Insist on defiance, and I will inflict pain. Simple. But despite what you might think, I'd rather not entertain a violent course of action.'

Nina stretched her jaw and blinked into the light.

He stepped - almost glided - towards her, twisted the lamp aside, and stared into her eyes, his face etched with curiosity. He placed his hands on the table, and leaned forward. His jacket sleeves rode up to reveal a gold watch and diamond studded cufflinks. The suit was blue pinstripe, the shirt open at the neck as was his trademark.

'You betrayed your country Nina. Now you want to destroy my business, and my reputation. What should I do with you?'

Her stomach quivered as their eyes locked. Then it occurred to her. Modjarrad was unshaven – two days stubble at least. She noticed a slight odour beneath the aftershave, a trace of stale sweat. The lines under his eyes suggested sleepless nights. Strange, because the arrogant bastard was usually immaculate.

'Long hours at the office Cyrus? No time to shower?'

His face twisted with rage, and he slapped her hard across the face.

Nina's head snapped sideways, and she spat out the blood. The pain didn't bother her, not this time.

'I won't tolerate rudeness Standwick. Now tell me where your friends are.'

She glared back in defiance. Another open-handed slap struck her cheek, and her head began to sing.

'Fuck you!' Blood sprayed from her mouth. 'Your project has destroyed innocent lives. You need to be stopped.'

Modjarrad's eyes narrowed, and he lowered himself into the chair opposite. 'Innocent lives?'

'Afghanistan. I was there remember.'

A smile formed across his thin lips. 'Is that what this is all about? You think I'm some kind of monster because of events in Afghanistan?'

'It's a start.'

Modjarrad raised his hands, a show of deluded innocence. 'Those deaths were not my fault. We installed strict safety measures. If people were killed, then the responsibility lies with the handlers. Give a soldier a gun, and if he kills an innocent man, you cannot blame the weapon. You blame the operator. This is no different.'

'And do your paymasters see it that way?' Nina tensed, anticipating the blow, but it didn't come.

Modjarrad seemed distracted, anxious even. His paymaster was the MOD. She knew that because she'd been involved from the start. But what was Modjarrad doing in this stinking underground pit? This wasn't his style. Then the truth hit her, and she blurted it out.

'The MOD doesn't want you anymore. They want to shut you down. That's why you moved your operation, that's why you're here. You're hiding, waiting for another buyer to bail you out. The British have washed their hands of the project just like the Americans.'

Modjarrad leapt from his seat. This time the blow was a punch to the jaw. The chair disappeared from under her, and she hit the ground with a heavy thud. Her sight faded, and she drifted out of consciousness. The last thing she heard was her own satisfied laugh.

31

RASHEED COULDN'T MAKE SENSE of the soldier's words. 'He speaks so fast Aisha, I can't possibly keep up.'

'I know, and it's impossible to translate. Maybe this wasn't such a good idea.'

A vehicle screeched to a halt in the street outside.

Rasheed got to his feet. 'My father!' he yelled. Without thinking, he dashed out of the room, and ran up the hallway to the front of the house, where he peered out of the front room window.

In the square, Asad jumped out of his truck, and shouted for help as he ran to the back of the vehicle. He dropped the tail-gate and Rasheed felt a surge of nausea. *Oh God, no.* Piled in the back he saw a bloody mass of tangled bodies. The second vehicle pulled up, but the men in this truck were thankfully all alive.

Rasheed turned away, and dashed back to tell Aisha.

'Something terrible has happened. You must go home.'

'What is it?'

'My father has returned but some of the men are dead. Their bodies have been mutilated.'

Aisha's hand flew to her face. 'May God protect us. I can't go outside without my burka. You must go find out what happened, but use the back door. We don't want to raise suspicion.'

Hasan hurried out into the yard, and ran down the backstreet, circled the block and entered the square from the main road.

The dead were being laid out in the street by their comrades. Rasheed watched, praying that Jamila was not among them. Asad hauled another body onto his shoulder. The dead man's left arm hung from the torso, but the right limb was missing. All the bodies had been mutilated beyond recognition. Not bullets - their clothes and flesh had been shredded. This had to be the work of the beast. Rasheed closed his eyes and swallowed his guilt. He had betrayed his father.

But what of Jamila?

He turned and ran, wanting to let out one almighty scream. He followed the same route back to the house and stumbled through the yard door. 'Aisha, I think Jamila might be dead.'

'What!' Her voice was practically a shriek.

'The men must have been killed by the demon. They've been torn apart.'

'And Jamila is with them?'

Rasheed slumped to the floor with his head in his hands. 'No, but I know she is dead.'

'How can you be sure?'

'I'm telling you. The beast took Jamila and killed her. I know it.'

'Please stop it.' She turned and glared at the soldier, and then looked back at Rasheed. 'What if your father is right? What if this man is evil? The foreigners brought these creatures to our land and this man is involved.'

He shook his head in despair but knew she had a point. The war had split his family and broken their lives.

'I must tell my father what I've done. He will slaughter me, but I deserve it. I should never have helped this man. Don't worry, I will tell him nothing about you.'

'Be careful,' Aisha said, lowering her voice. 'The soldier might guess something is wrong. He might kill us if we try to run.'

Rasheed imagined the Englishman's hands around Aisha's throat, strangling the life out of her. He had to protect her. 'You go. Use the front door this time, and don't worry about your burka. Find my father and tell him the soldier is here. Go quickly.'

As she stood up to leave, Rasheed whispered: 'Wait. Smile at the Englishman. Make him think nothing is wrong.

Christian listened to the two young Afghans chatter, their voices rose and fell in obvious distress. They both looked terrified. Perhaps the uproar outside had spooked them? He picked up the sketch and pointed to the drawing of the stick-girl, but got no response.

The girl got up, and flashed him an awkward smile as she headed for the hallway. She scampered to the front of the house and Christian heard the heavy stone scrape across the floor followed by a creak as the door opened.

Strange. When the boy left the house earlier, he'd gone out the back.

The boy nodded and smiled uneasily, but Christian sensed he was no longer trusted. Now what? He couldn't allow himself to be recaptured, the Taliban would kill him. He had to make a move, and do it now.

The boy seemed to read his thoughts and stood up, jabbering rapid-fire sentences.

Don't waste any more time Chris. Get the hell out.

But his movements were restricted and he was slow to rise to his feet. The boy backed off. Christian reached out to him. 'Please... I don't know what happened, but I want to help.'

He heard people shouting outside. He stumbled forward, but the boy turned and ran after the girl.

Shit, not much time.

He hobbled out of the house into the yard. The backstreet was quiet, and there were plenty of empty buildings to make for. If he could just lie low until dark, he might stand a chance.

The light had dimmed outside as evening closed in. Rasheed ran into the square, but saw neither Aisha nor his father. The dead were being wrapped in blankets by a group of local men, and loaded onto a wooden cart. No sign of the women and children, and the two Taliban pickup trucks had gone.

Rasheed spotted Massoud standing outside his house, waving flies away from his face. The old man wasn't a Taliban sympathizer, but appeared supportive to their cause when they arrived in town. Rasheed ran to him, and asked where his father had gone.

Massoud sighed. 'He's taken his men back into the desert to catch the demon. When he returns, he will undoubtedly hunt down the soldier. A Taliban guard was attacked here at my house. The man had a nasty cut on his head where someone hit him and apparently his clothes were missing. You wouldn't know anything about that I suppose?' The old man smirked and his eyes glistened with amusement. 'What are we to do with you Rasheed? Such a confused young man.'

The boy smiled nervously. Before he could reply, he heard Aisha call to him.

'Rasheed, come quickly.'

He turned around but couldn't see her.

'Look, I'm up here.' She waved from the top window of her house.

Rasheed thanked Massoud and hurried back across the square. She greeted him at the door and pulled him inside. Suddenly her arms were around his neck, squeezing him. He gently pushed her away so he could breathe, held her face, and wiped the wet streaks from her cheeks.

'Did you tell my father about the Englishman?'

She shook her head. 'I didn't get a chance. My mother spotted me without my burka and went crazy, she practically dragged me into the house. Now she has gone to search for Jamila with her friends. She told me to stay here.'

'Is my mother okay?'

'She got up earlier but she's asleep now.'

'I must join the search Aisha, before it gets dark.'

Her head dropped, and she started to cry.

'What's wrong? Talk to me. What happened?'

Aisha cleared her throat, and wiped her eyes. 'My mother told me some terrible news. The baker's wife who saw the demon, also witnessed Jamila walking in the street moments before… Rasheed I'm really scared for her now.'

32

Thursday 29th April

Dulwich, London

HUNTER SCRUBBED CLEAN THE blood and grit embedded in his flesh, but couldn't purify his mind, nor escape the violent events of the last twelve hours. He stepped out of the shower, dried himself and slipped into a clean t-shirt and jeans.

The journey to London had taken a little over three hours. Longer than expected, but Monkton had taken several detours to avoid the road-blocks.

Hunter made coffee and retired to the living room where Monkton was dozing on the sofa. A photograph of Christian gazed at him from the mantelpiece. His brother looked so proud in his uniform. The only person Hunter could really trust. The one person who loved him and Hunter had turned his back.

Pathetic Matthew. Fucking pathetic.

Monkton sat up, and adjusted his glasses. 'What time is it?'

'Six-thirty. I made you coffee.'

Monkton lifted the steaming mug from the table, and nodded at the photograph above the fireplace. 'I didn't know you were a soldier.'

'That's my twin brother.'

'Of course – I should have guessed. What are you going to tell him?'

'Huh?'

'Your brother. I assume you're going to tell him what's been going on?'

Hunter shrugged. 'He probably knows more than I do.'

'What do you mean?'

'Remember I said I had some personal business to sort out? Well, Nina reckons my brother is caught up in all this. I'm hoping he can give me some answers.'

'She's probably lying.'

'I thought so at first, but now I'm not so sure. I haven't spoken to Chris for such a long time, and I haven't got his details. I can't phone the MOD and Nina's gone AWOL, so that just leaves my parents.'

Monkton opened his mouth to speak but stopped himself.

Hunter sensed his unease. 'You're wondering why I can't pick up the phone and call them?'

'I don't like to pry Matt. It's okay if you don't want to talk about it.'

'Truth is I never talk about my family. Seeing my parents will be difficult. I just hope they're still alive, and living in Croydon. I haven't seen them for five years, and haven't spoken to Chris for nearly two. There's been a lot going on in my head, and I can't ignore it any longer.'

'What exactly did Nina say about your brother?'

'Apparently the two of them were an item for a few months. Chris broke it off, and told her she was in danger, don't ask me how or why, but it had something to do with these creatures. Nina reckons Chris is involved with Zarcom...' Hunter heard his own voice waver, and took a moment to collect himself. 'I've let him down Richard.'

'But what was Nina doing in Afghanistan?'

'Working freelance I guess. Probably something to do with the plight of the Afghan women under the Taliban regime - she's into that sort of thing.'

'Sounds a bit vague. She seems more involved if you ask me, I've always thought so.'

'What does it matter? I should know more about my brother's life.'

'She's not telling you everything, that's all I'm saying.'

'That's why I need to hear the story from Chris.'

'Maybe you'll feel better once you've seen your parents. These things are never as bad as they seem.'

Hunter raised his eyes. 'Easier said than done though Richard. Truth is I've got no choice. It's time to confront the past. I'm concerned about Nina though. I've tried calling her numerous times but only get her voice mail. That's unlike her, especially under the circumstances. 'We've got some time before our meeting with Professor Grealish. We could drive over to Nina's flat and check if she's there. I'll get her address from Tony at the office.'

'At this time of the morning?'

'Tony's a good bloke, he'll help us.'

Hunter dialed Tony Vichelli's cell phone and the fat guy picked up on the fifth ring. 'Early for you Matt. What was it - another all-nighter?'

'Yeah, very funny Tony. Listen I need a favour. I want you to dig out Nina's address for me ASAP.'

'ASAP meaning…?

'The next half hour. I wouldn't ask but it's urgent.'

'Fuck me, have you seen the time? I'm not due in the office for a couple of hours.'

'I know. Believe me Tony I need your help.'

'The favours are stacking up Matt. I hear Bryant wants you roasting on a spit. What's going on?'

'I'll tell you later. Please, I need that address.'

'Give me an hour.'

'Half hour Tony, that's all I have.'

'It's a fucking liberty Hunter. Forty-five minutes, and you owe me lunch.'

'No problem.' Hunter replaced the receiver and glanced at Monkton. 'Let's hope he comes up with something.'

'Sounds like a wild goose chase if you ask me. If Nina's at home, why doesn't she pick up the phone? '

'She might be in trouble Richard, and no one else is going to help.'

33

TONY VICHELLI CAME BACK with Nina's address: Flat 3, 55 Angel Street, north London. They arrived just after eight - a quiet road lined with saplings and chock-full of parked cars. Most of the houses were impressive Victorian buildings converted into flats, but number 55 was a boxy cheerless construction, built in the 1970's.

'So what's the plan?' Monkton said.

'Try the buzzer, if she doesn't answer we'll question the neighbours. Not much of a plan I know, but we're not exactly awash with options.' He pressed the button for flat three. No reply. After four attempts he switched to flat four. The intercom crackled and a female voice answered.

'Oh hi.' Hunter tried to sound upbeat, 'I need to speak to Miss Siketi in flat three, but there's no response. Do you know where I can get hold of her?'

A pause. 'Who?'

'Siketi. Nina Siketi.'

'Never heard of her.'

Hunter glanced at the address and read it aloud.

'That's this building,' the woman said. 'What's your friend's name again?'

'Nina Siketi. This is an impromptu visit but… she said she lives at flat three.'

'You're mistaken. You must have the wrong house.'

Hunter sensed he was losing her, and spoke quickly. 'She's a brunette, late twenties, shoulder length hair, usually tied back, about five one, five two… not one for make-up.'

'And who are you?'

'Matthew Hunter, a colleague of Miss Siketi's. I have ID.'

'No, I'm not coming down.' The woman sounded uneasy, and had every right to be - alone in her flat, this was London after all.

Hunter tried to reassure her. 'I'm on the level. I think my friend might be in trouble.'

A brief pause, before she said, 'The person you describe sounds like Miss Standwick but I haven't seen her for a while. I'm not sure of her first name.'

'Standwick?'

Hunter's surprised tone seemed to frighten the girl. 'I've got to go now,' she said. 'Please leave, or I'll call the police.' She cut the connection.

Hunter stared at the intercom feeling utterly confused.

'So what next?' Monkton said.

'We'll wait until someone enters the building and execute Plan B. Oh, and we need a bunch of flowers.'

'I hope plan B turns out better than plan A Matthew because I've got to tell you, that wasn't great.'

Hunter sighed. 'I'll get us inside Richard, trust me.'

Twenty minutes later, two nurses strolled towards the apartment block. One was Asian, the other blonde. Hunter loitered at the kerb while Monkton stayed out of sight in the Jeep. The women wandered down the path, laughing and chatting. At the door, the Asian girl fished her keys out of her bag.

Hunter toyed absently with the flowers he'd bought at a corner shop a few minutes earlier. He poked his head through the Jeep window. 'Time for Plan B Richard.'

Monkton groaned and climbed out looking bored and tired. Hunter urged him to hurry. Together they raced across the road, and reached the path as the Asian woman pushed open the door.

'Just in time!' Hunter announced, striding purposefully down the path.

The woman turned and regarded him with a bemused expression.

'We're here for Miss Standwick in flat three. She's not well, and can't make it down the stairs.' Hunter breezed past her, and Monkton bustled in behind.

She eyed them warily. 'Nothing serious I hope?'

Hunter shook his head, 'Probably just a dose of the snuffles.'

'Because we can help her - we're both qualified.' She watched Hunter closely, smiled, and stepped back. 'We'll leave you guys to it. I wish my boyfriend surprised me with flowers, Nina's a lucky girl. Let us know if you need anything.'

Hunter grinned. *Nina.* She said *Nina.* 'I'll drop in some flowers for you next time I pass,' he said. The woman's eyes fizzed flirtatiously. She slinked down the hall, and shot him a glance before she disappeared into her apartment with her friend.

Hunter beamed at Monkton. 'The secret's in the charm.'

Monkton rolled his eyes. 'I'm in awe. Now what?'

'Follow me.' Hunter bounded upstairs to the first landing, put down the flowers and studied the lock to Nina's apartment.

'Try the door,' Monkton whispered.

Hunter gave him a withering look. 'Best leave this to me Richard. Just keep a lookout.' He fished his keys out of his pocket and began straightening the key-ring into a picking tool.

Monkton peered over his shoulder. 'You sure that's going to work?'

'Unless you've got any better ideas?' Hunter grunted as he tried to manipulate the metal with his fingers.

Monkton inspected the lock, gave the door a firm shove and watched it swing open. 'Job done,' he said, 'not even locked.'

Hunter felt a chill of anxiety. 'Be careful Richard. This doesn't look good.'

They walked through the hall, past a kitchenette on the right, and into a sparsely furnished living room. There were no signs of a struggle, but the air was stale, and the curtains were still drawn. A solitary mug, drained of its contents, sat on the coffee table.

Hunter pointed to the bedroom door. 'Search in there Richard – pick up anything that might help find her.'

Monkton disappeared into the bedroom while Hunter examined the wall-unit next to the TV. The top two shelves contained a collection of framed photos, and miniature pigs. The girl on the intercom had lied - Nina Siketi definitely lived here. She appeared in every photo.

The other shelves were filled with books. Hunter ran his finger along the spines: Advanced Genetics, The Truth about Dolly, The Human Genome Demystified, DNA Research in Medicine. Close to thirty titles, concerning genetic engineering.

She's obsessed.

On the bottom shelf he found a couple of unusual titles - Advanced Weapons of the 21st Century; Satellite Defence Systems, Making Star wars a Reality.

Perhaps she had a guy living with her? It certainly seemed a male orientated library. He also found a collection of phrasebooks in Pashto, dictionaries, and road maps of Afghanistan. Hunter rechecked the photographs. In two of them, Nina was dressed in combat uniform standing in a desert terrain as a group of soldiers patrolled in the background.

So she had indeed been working with British troops. Perhaps she had told the truth about meeting Christian. Hunter cringed at the thought, felt sick just contemplating it.

Monkton entered the room clutching a thick folder. 'Matt, you need to read this.' He passed him the papers.

Hunter dropped into the sofa, and pulled out a wedge of documents from the file. The first was a copy of an email addressed to someone called Miss N. Standwick, flight instructions from Brize Norton, but no destination specified.

Next, a request from the same N. Standwick for a consignment of uniforms: destination Kandahar. *Uniforms?*

Hunter glanced up at Monkton. 'Nina must share this flat with another girl, this Standwick or whatever her name is.'

Monkton shook his head, 'Keep looking Matt, there's more to it.'

Hunter sifted through the paperwork, and uncovered more emails and meaningless correspondence before he found three photocopies of a passport, Nina's photo on each one. He checked the name beside the picture, and there it was. Not Siketi, but Standwick. *Nina Standwick.*

'Christ Richard, who is this woman?'

'Obviously not who she says she is.'

'Where did you find these?'

'Good old fashioned detective work. Under her bed. But you haven't got to the juicy stuff yet, take a look at the photographs.'

Hunter rifled through and picked out half dozen digital photographs printed on A4. A picture of two soldiers on foot patrol set against a background of rocks and scrubland. It looked like Afghanistan but there was no sign of Nina. He switched to the next photo and gasped with revulsion. A heap of mutilated bodies, limbs broken or missing, heads twisted, eyes frozen in terror. Blood everywhere.

Al-Qaeda terrorists maybe?

No. There were children here too, no older than nine or ten judging by the remains. The men had no weapons, and their bodies had been torn apart. These weren't terrorists, they were shepherds. In amongst the human remains, Hunter counted four dead sheep.

'Jesus Richard, this is a slaughter of the innocent. Perhaps that's why Nina was out there. She must have been chasing this injustice...'

'I doubt it. Look at the bodies Matt. You don't need to be a genius to work out what happened to them.'

Hunter flicked to the next photograph and what he saw changed everything. The photographer had panned left along a ridge where two British soldiers stood over the open grave. Neither wore helmets. The shorter man had a scarf wrapped around his face, and posed like a freedom fighter, weapon pointed at the sky.

The taller had short brown hair, bleached slightly by the sun. He held a black rod in one hand, and strapped to his forearm was an arm-guard with a panel that looked similar to a cell phone display. The soldier grinned like a trophy fisherman, standing over his catch. The face seemed darker than Hunter remembered, and the teeth whiter. But then he hadn't seen his brother for two years.

'I'm sorry Matthew.' Monkton spoke softly but Hunter wasn't listening. Chris was out there fighting a war, defending his country. The dead *must* be terrorists. Chris would only kill bad guys. Perhaps this was a mock-up, some sort of sick practical joke.

But up until now, Hunter hadn't noticed the main subject of the picture. The creature rested so peacefully between the two soldiers - a demonic abomination built to kill. The animal lay perfectly still at his brother's feet, raven-black and broad as a grizzly, its head larger than a bison's.

Hunter stared in disbelief. This was the story. The truth. The nightmare.

Nina said Chris tried to put a stop to the project and as a result had placed himself in great danger. Truth was, they were all in trouble and Hunter knew it. 'What the fuck are we into here Richard?'

Monkton looked pale and drawn. 'The question is: what is your brother into? Because I can still walk away, and maybe you could too if weren't for that picture. I'm not sure what it means but I don't think we're going to like it.'

Hunter grimaced. 'I'm going to find out Richard. Whatever it takes, I want to know what Chris is doing in that picture and God help anyone who tries to stop me.'

34

CHRISTIAN FOUND REFUGE OVERNIGHT in the cellar of a deserted house. He barely slept, expecting the Taliban to find him at any moment, but only the occasional murmur of voices had disturbed him late on.

Now the morning sun began to filter through the cracks in the ceiling, creating dusty bars of light in the cellar. Christian needed water. More importantly, he needed a vehicle. He crawled out of the bunker, brushed dirt from his clothes and went searching for a means of escape. The town was silent. Amongst the rubble, he found a band of metal, ideal for breaking into a car. Eventually, he spotted a rusty Russian Volga parked in one of the dusty back roads. Keeping back behind a wall, he scanned for signs of life. A baby cried in a house nearby, but nothing stirred in the street.

Christian limped to the car, crouched at the driver's door, and slid the metal band against the glass. A clunk and the lock released. He climbed behind the wheel, cracked open the ignition casing and hot-wired the engine. The car belched a cloud of black smoke as he rammed into gear and pulled away.

The sound of the engine jolted Rasheed awake. He sat up, ran to the window, and saw a car chugging down the street. The drivers face was obscured, but Rasheed recognized the white hands and bloody knuckles. *The Englishman.*

He dressed quickly, and raced out of the house, followed the trail to the north of town. When he reached the outskirts, his heart sank. The car was already a dot on the horizon. To the west, mist settled over the mountains, and to the east the wilderness extended like a lunar landscape, punctuated by tufts of scrub.

A sound echoed in the mountains, faint but distinguishable. The roar of a large animal.

The suspension creaked and the wheels juddered over the surface craters, as the Volga headed north. Christian checked the fuel gauge – a fraction above empty. He gripped the wheel and eased off the accelerator, had to make the most of what little fuel he had left.

Through the mountain pass, something stirred in his peripheral vision and he slowed down. A figure appeared from behind a rock out to his left - a little girl, three or four years old. She ran in tiny, rapid movements, arms pinned to her sides as she scurried along. Perhaps this was the girl the young Afghans had been trying to tell him about? If so, she was heading in the wrong direction - away from Qatif.

Christian didn't have time to get involved. The temptation to stamp on the accelerator overwhelmed him, but he couldn't keep his eyes off the child. He stopped the car.

He watched her trip and fall among the rocks. As she started to cry, he put the car into gear, and spun off the road towards her.

35

The London Institute of Biology

Stratford, East London,

MONKTON INSISTED ON DRIVING across London, despite Hunter's appeals to take the tube. They left Nina's apartment at 9:15 and arrived at the science institute an hour later. Monkton steered into the car park and snagged the last space.

A fresh breeze greeted Hunter when he climbed out of the Jeep. The questions he had prepared to ask Grealish had been swept away. Instead, he thought about his brother. He peered through the glass doors into empty foyer as Monkton pressed the intercom. A man in his fifties hurried down the spiral steps and into reception. He was about five-six, unkempt brown hair, and a frayed check shirt beneath his unbuttoned lab coat.

He pulled open the door. 'Welcome Richard, please come in.'

Monkton stepped inside and made the introductions.

Grealish shook Hunter's hand vigorously. 'So you're the journalist. I hear Richard's got you chasing mysterious beasts around the countryside.'

Hunter smiled uncomfortably. 'We're working on a project together.'

'So I understand. Please, follow me. We'll go up to my office and talk.' Grealish beckoned them through the foyer, and up the spiral stairs to his office.

They sat around an oval desk and the Professor began chatting about Monkton's deceased uncle. It turned out Colin Grealish and Robin Monkton had both attended Leeds University, and the two men had become lifelong friends.

Hunter had a lot on his mind, Chris, his parents and Nina. *Yes Nina.* He coughed and fidgeted until Monkton eventually raised the subject they had come here to discuss.

Monkton lifted a plastic bag onto the desk. 'Here are the samples Professor. We hoped for a quick turnaround on the results.'

Grealish looked taken aback. 'I know you're desperate for answers Richard, but I won't have anything for you until next week at the earliest.'

'We haven't got that long,' Hunter said. 'We need them in the next few days. Sooner if you can.'

'I'm afraid that's impossible.'

Monkton butted in. 'Matthew's right. This is urgent.'

Grealish tilted his head, removed his spectacles, and rubbed his eyes. 'To be honest Richard, I didn't invite you here to discuss lab results.' He glanced at each of the men in turn. 'You're both in danger, and I strongly advise you to stop what you're doing now. Go home and get on with your lives. Nothing good will come of this crusade you seem intent on pursuing.'

'What are you talking about?' Hunter said.

Grealish slipped his glasses back on and cleared his throat. 'Richard told me about the mutilated horse and the creatures you encountered at the horse sanctuary. But I know far more about this subject than you realize Mr. Hunter.' He turned to Monkton. 'You also mentioned Zarcom Research.'

Monkton nodded. 'We believe there's a link.'

'We know there is,' Hunter put in.

The Professor eyed Hunter gravely. 'Yes I'm afraid you could be right.'

Hunter was astounded. At last a bit of honesty. He leaned forward. 'Go on Professor, we're listening.'

Grealish folded his arms, and relaxed back in his chair. 'I worked for Zarcom for two years. The problem is gentlemen; you are now entering the realms of national security. I was forced to sign the official secrets act before I set foot in the labs. Simply discussing this with you puts me in a very sticky situation. They could shut down the Institute, put a halt to the work I'm doing here, and might even arrest me.'

Hunter glared at him. 'You're stalling Professor. You must know innocent people are dying. You have to help us put a stop to it.'

Grealish's face reddened. 'What are you talking about? Nobody's dead Mr. Hunter.'

Hunter felt his anger rise and this guy pushed all the wrong buttons. 'The story has been all over the damn news,' he snapped.

Monkton intervened, and explained what happened in Tunbridge Wells. 'We stood right in the middle of it Professor. The media reported a terrorist attack but I swear it wasn't. The army fired a missile at the creatures from a helicopter. They blasted a crater right in the town square. The whole thing's a cover-up.'

Grealish paled, ran his fingers through his tousled hair. 'Impossible. No sane government would sanction firing missiles into its own people. It's a ludicrous notion.'

'Perhaps the government doesn't know,' Hunter replied. 'The cover up might be as much for their benefit as ours. We need the DNA results to prove these things exist.'

'And then what?'

Hunter started to shake. 'I intend to expose these bastards and help my brother.'

'Your brother?'

'I believe he's involved. He's on tour in Afghanistan but I've lost contact with him.' He resisted showing Grealish the photograph of Chris.

The Professor leaned in. 'When was he born?'

'Nineteen eighty-two. What's that got to do with anything?'

Grealish stared at the ceiling, and took a deep breath. 'This is worse than I imagined. If you're brother is involved Mr. Hunter, then they already know you're here. Look, I'll tell you what I can but you're not going to like it.'

'Don't compromise yourself Professor,' Monkton said. 'We can sort this out ourselves.'

'But you must understand what you're up against Richard - powerful people who will stop at nothing to protect their secrets. I want to help because of your Uncle Robin.'

'I don't understand.'

'I'm sorry Richard, but I'm pretty sure the car crash that killed Robin was no accident. He loved chasing conspiracy theories, and broadcast his beliefs on radio. He was investigating Zarcom before he died.'

Hunter saw Monkton struggling to cope with the enormity of this revelation, and spoke for him. 'You're saying Richard's uncle was murdered?'

Grealish ignored the question and placed his hand on Monkton's arm. 'I couldn't help him Richard. But I can help you, and I will, I promise.'

Monkton suddenly stood up and went for the door, hesitated, and slumped back into his seat. Staring through reddened eyes, he said, 'Start from the beginning Professor. Leave nothing out.'

Grealish closed his eyes and nodded remorsefully, wiped his mouth with a handkerchief and started to speak.

'In 1979 Zarcom Research won a contract to develop advanced bio-genetic weapons for the US military. This involved crossing DNA from different animals to create a beast that could be used in warfare. The programme became known as The Darwin Project. After two decades of failure, the US ditched the project, but the British invited Modjarrad over here to continue his work.

'I joined Zarcom in 2002. By this time the technology had reached an advanced stage. They had engineered animals that survived beyond birth, although the results still proved unpredictable. For every 600 embryos, only one made it through gestation. Even then, one in three was still-born. When I left the company two years later, they had produced a small group of healthy infants and had started to clone them.

'Anyway, I left all that behind, until last year when Robin made contact with me. He started asking questions about Zarcom and a week later he was dead. I'm sorry Richard, truly I am.'

Monkton replied with surprising calmness. 'I understand Professor. At least you're doing the right thing now.'

'I hope so Richard, I really do.'

'So what was your role within Zarcom?' Hunter asked.

'I led a small team. Our remit was to integrate the satellite tracking technology and radio transponders into the animals' neuron systems. We fitted every animal with a microchip that emitted and received electronic signals. The device was implanted in the creatures' nervous systems. We developed a technique to fuse transponders into the nerve endings without killing the animals. I could have stayed on but the whole thing rested uneasy with me. I didn't become a biologist to create war machines, biological or otherwise. I had answered the call to serve my country and that was enough. More than enough.'

'Serve your country? Is that what you call it?'

'I'm sorry if my work offends you Mr. Hunter.'

Hunter snorted dismissively and changed the subject. 'Why are you so interested in my brother's age?'

Grealish rested back in his chair. 'He's in the military?'

'Yes.'

'Then he could be a handler, an elite soldier trained to control the animals. Robin was investigating this very subject before his death. You see, when Cyrus Modjarrad started the Darwin project, he struggled to find the right people to work with the animals. Then he encountered the SAS during the Iranian embassy siege in 1980. I take it, you know what happened?'

'Yes, saving the hostages brought the SAS to the World's attention.'

'Quite. And among the hostages was one Cyrus Modjarrad. You can imagine the uproar in the corridors of power. Modjarrad had access to military secrets. Thankfully none of the terrorists recognized him. You can understand the increased urgency with which our government acted. They had to get him out of there.'

'Where are you going with this Professor?'

'Seeing the SAS in action gave Modjarrad an idea. He wanted them in on his project. Of course men of that quality are like gold dust, there just aren't enough to go around. That's why he started a secondary project to run in tandem with Darwin.'

'What kind of project?'

'Modjarrad paid volunteers from elite forces such as the SAS for sperm donations. He then introduced a human breeding programme using artificial insemination techniques with a view to breeding a platoon of super-soldiers. At the age of ten, each resulting child was implanted with a microchip similar to those we later used on the creatures. The children were predominantly raised by families with military connections, some in this country, and some in the US. The chosen few - those that fitted the profile - were drafted into the army. I could be wrong about your brother Mr. Hunter, but if he's involved in this, then the chances are, he's a handler. The programme started in eighty-one. All of the children were born the following year. You said he was born in nineteen eighty-two?'

Hunter felt sick as the nightmare unfolded - the demons had finally caught up. 'Yes... we both were.'

36

'AND YOU'RE SURE THE soldier was driving the car?'

Rasheed nodded. 'What have we done Aisha? How are we going to find Jamila now?'

'My mother has organized another search party. Her friends are meeting here later, perhaps we should join them.'

'No. I need to speak to the Englishman again. He's the only person who knows anything. We must go after him.'

His eyes shifted to the door as it creaked open, and his mother shuffled in. She steadied herself against the jamb.

'Rasheed. Tell me we where my baby Jamila is. Please tell me she is safe.'

'God will protect her Mother. Don't worry, I promise we'll find her.'

Nura closed her eyes. 'I pray that you do. You are the man of this family now. Please bring my daughter back to me.'

Rasheed helped his mother back to bed. 'I'll find her for you, I swear.'

Her pale lips twisted into a smile and he kissed her cheek.

Aisha urged him to hurry. 'I have an idea.' She tugged his shirt. 'Quick, come with me.' She bolted out of the room and into the street.

'Where are you going?' he called after her.

'To steal a horse.'

'What?'

She didn't stop to explain. They ran through the dusty streets all the way to the southern edge of town. Aisha stopped in front of a ramshackle building, and guided Rasheed round the back. Sweating, and gasping for breath, he followed her into a large shed, the door of which lay shattered on the ground.

Once inside, she shook her head and groaned. 'He's not here.'

'Who?'

'Samir. My friend's horse.'

'Huh? Don't tell me you were expecting to find a horse in this old place? It's not big enough to house a chicken. It doesn't even have a door.'

Aisha sat wearily on the floor and crossed her legs. 'Laila must have taken him out to ride.'

'Then we'll have to search on foot. Come on, we're wasting time.' Rasheed turned to leave, but something on the ground caught his eye.

Aisha gazed up at him. 'What's wrong?'

'Look under the straw. There are dark patches everywhere.'

Aisha stood up, and looked down at the ground. 'Oh god. I hope that's not what I think it is.'

An elderly voice spoke softly from the open doorway – the hunched figure of Mullah Ahmed. 'Come on you two. You must leave here. Yesterday I helped Laila clean the stable but we couldn't remove all of the stains.'

'Is it blood?' Aisha gasped.

'Yes. I'm sorry. Samir is dead.' Mullah Ahmed shook his head mournfully. 'This town is no longer safe. These beasts come and go as they please.'

Rasheed said, 'We can't find my sister. She might...'

'I know all about Jamila. The women are searching the town, and the men are scouring the desert. Someone will find her.'

Rasheed glanced at the blood stains, and a shiver went through him.

Mullah Ahmed rested a hand on his shoulder. 'Be brave young Rasheed, have faith in the Almighty. Everything will be revealed to us in the course of time. Pray and be patient.'

'We can help search the town,' Aisha said. 'We mustn't give up.'

The women were only a couple of blocks away, around thirty of them picking through the empty buildings. So many homes in Qatif were unoccupied, many reduced to rubble. Rasheed trampled across the heaps of broken masonry, calling out his sister's name. He felt sure the exercise was futile, but had to remain hopeful no matter how bleak the prospects.

His father once told him: "A true Muslim isn't afraid of death - not like these westerners. They have no faith and only worship their possessions."

But many Afghans had no possessions, not even their homes. Even before the foreigners arrived, Afghan culture had already regressed. The Taliban regime, arcane and ruthless in its doctrine, had outlawed television, western clothes, female education, and many other 'luxuries.' Indeed, for women, the regime had proved particularly oppressive. Hopefully that would change in his sister's lifetime.

Jamila where are you? God help me – where are you?

Christian pulled off the road, and instantly regretted his actions. The desert terrain was strewn with rocks that threatened to tear the underside of the Volga apart. He stopped, and got out to walk. The little girl sat on a rock, sobbing quietly. She didn't move as Christian hobbled towards her, but when he picked her up, she started to squeal and kick.

'All right sweetheart. Let's get you home.'

What am I saying? I can't risk taking her back to Qatif.

The roar of a huge beast echoed through the mountain pass: the sound of a chimera. Christian knew it was homing in on the child. *Easy prey.*

The girl shivered in his arms, her face pinched, and smudged with dirt. Christian ran to the car, opened the back door and bundled the girl inside. He jumped into the driver's seat, and glanced back towards the slopes. The beast appeared, running down the mountainside at breathtaking speed.

Christian slammed the car door and wired the ignition. Nothing. He tried again and again, but still got no response. The creature reached the flat ground and powered across the terrain towards them.

Shit, come on! The engine laboured but wouldn't start. The beast unleashed another sickening roar and the girl started to scream.

37

HUNTER HAD NO CHOICE but to talk to his parents. After five years without contact it wasn't going to be easy, but he had to tackle this thing head on. He issued Monkton with directions to Dale Avenue, the street in Croydon where he had grown up as a kid. He only hoped his parents still lived there.

When they arrived, he saw much had changed since his childhood. Many houses were freshly painted, some had new extensions and windows. Despite the renovations the street remained dour in Hunter's mind. He left Monkton waiting in the Jeep, and crossed the road to number 56. His stomach churned, and part of him wanted to head back. At the gate, he heard the TV blaring from the living room. His father always turned it up loud. Hunter reminded himself he was doing this for Christian. Nothing else mattered, he had to see this through.

He pushed the gate and walked down the path. The front door was just as he remembered, a peeling skin of navy blue. Before he could press the doorbell, a shadow passed behind the frosted glass. The latch rattled and the door opened a fraction, clunking against a security chain. Sunken grey eyes peered through the gap.

'Mum, it's me... Matthew.'

Mary Hunter's face twitched, and her eyes widened. Without speaking, she unfastened the chain and opened the door. She stood before him, hunched and frail. Her face sagged beneath a nest of grey hair. Eventually her mouth lifted, and she began to weep.

Hunter wavered as his mother threw her arms around his neck. Stunned, he held her gently, almost guiltily. Her body trembled and she wept into his chest. He released her, and stepped back. Her tear stained face was now filled with wonder. Emotion swept over him, a lifetime of pain washed away by his mother's tears.

'I've prayed for this every day,' she said, holding his face in her gnarled hands.

'I'm sorry mum, I can't stay long.'

'Please. Long enough for tea surely?'

He smiled and nodded. His heart thudded as he followed her into the drab living room, the once bright flowery wallpaper now curled at the edges, the brown carpet, patchy and threadbare.

His mother had to raise her voice to make herself heard above the TV. 'Graham, we have a visitor.'

Hunter's father sat in a shabby armchair with his back to the door, the once thick black hair, now thin and grey.

'Hi Dad.'

Graham Hunter was unmoved, no longer the man with huge biceps, bunched shoulders and a barrel chest. Instead Hunter saw a haggard face, a vulnerable old man, withered and frail. The skin around his eyes was loose, his pallor grey, almost translucent.

What happened to the ill-tempered tyrant he remembered so vividly?

Hunter glanced back at his mother, who shook her head dolefully. 'He's suffering with Alzheimer's. 'Don't worry, I can tell he's pleased to see you.'

His father stared at the TV, bony fingers tapping the sides of his armchair for no apparent reason.

'Come on Graham, say hello to your son. And we don't need the television on do we?'

'Let him watch it Mum.'

'No Matthew, it's rude.' She picked up the remote and switched it off. 'You two can chat while I make tea.' She shuffled out to the kitchen as the picture hissed and faded, but his father remained unmoved, eyes focused dead ahead.

Hunter shifted in his seat watching for a glimmer of recognition on his dad's face but there was none.

'How long has he been like this Mum?'

She popped her head through the doorway. 'Since he was told to stop drinking - about two years ago.' She chuckled and returned to making tea. Moments later she walked in with a tray of biscuits. 'It's wonderful to see you Matthew, we've so much to talk about.' She knelt at the coffee table and started to pour.

Hunter decided to cut through the niceties. 'Mum, I think Chris might be in trouble. I know about Dad's involvement in the SAS and the Darwin Project.'

Her head jerked up. 'Chris in trouble? What are you talking about?'

'I need his details. Has he phoned recently?'

She smiled nervously. 'He sends mail, but rarely phones me these days.' The cup rattled in its saucer as she passed it to him. 'Matthew, I need you to know one thing before you ask any more questions... Please understand that if I could change the past, I would. I know how hard it was for you.'

Hunter saw the pain in his mother's eyes. 'It's okay Mum. I didn't come here to dwell on my childhood. Right now I need to find Chris. We can catch up another time, I promise.'

'But what makes you think he's in danger?'

'He's involved with a project that is somehow linked to Dad's time in the SAS. I need to know what happened.'

She raised her eyes and returned a look of surprise. 'You're father in the SAS? Matthew I'm afraid someone has misinformed you.'

Hunter tensed, sick of all the bullshit. 'In that case there's nothing more to discuss. I need to leave.'

Her eyes pleaded with him. *Don't go.* She got up and walked to the bureau in the corner of the room, opened a drawer and removed a brown envelope. 'Christian sent this for you. It came about a month ago, but don't ask me what it's about.'

Hunter took the packet and read the scribbled message on the front. *Matt, in case you need to reach me. Chris.*

'Mum are you sure you've never heard of the Darwin Project? It's important.'

She shrugged. 'Matthew, you're not making sense.'

So Grealish was wrong... or the bastard had lied. Hunter announced his departure, and promised he would stay in touch. He gave his father a half-hearted clap on the shoulder, and walked to the door.

As he stepped outside, he turned and said, 'I didn't mean to worry you Mum. I'll call you soon.' He tore a page from his notebook, scribbled his number and gave it to her.

Mary Hunter kissed her son's cheek. Hunter stuffed the envelope in his pocket, and started up the path, turned to wave but his mother had gone - the door was already closed.

38

AFTER HOURS OF SEARCHING, Rabia and her friends began to tire as the mid-afternoon sun took its toll. They had covered every building in Qatif. Rasheed watched and listened as Rabia instructed the women to search yet another house.

'But we've already looked in there,' one woman protested.

'So look again.'

Rasheed appreciated the effort, and tried to stay cheerful. Aisha brought him a jug of fresh water.

'Here, you must drink.'

He threw his head back and tipped the vessel, allowing the cool liquid to trickle over his face and into his mouth.

'I'm sorry about everything Rasheed.'

He handed back the jug and wiped his mouth. With every minute that passed, his hope deteriorated. He turned away from Aisha as his emotions threatened to overwhelm him.

She said: 'I prayed for her Rasheed, just like you asked. I begged for a miracle. I love her too you know. I love her so much.'

He tried not to listen. *This is hard Aisha. Please stop.*

He heard her crying, and glanced around, saw the wet streaks coursing down her cheeks. He reached out and touched her hand. 'I know you love her. We have to keep looking.'

Christian tried the ignition again. *Jesus – come on.*

Too late. The creature rammed into the back of the car like a locomotive. Christian jerked forward and his head smashed into the steering wheel. The vehicle rocked, and slewed 90 degrees, sending up a cloud of dust and sand.

Christian glimpsed the beast in his rear view preparing to make another charge. He touched the wires together. Finally the engine sparked, and fired up.

Thank fuck!

He stamped on the accelerator, but the brute crashed into the car again, sending it hurtling across the sand. The child wailed in the back seat as Christian tried to regain control. The wheels spun and the Volga juddered forward but not fast enough.

Again, the beast thundered up behind the car and clipped the rear end. Christian fought with the steering while visibility shrank to zero in the swirling dust.

Still screaming, the little girl scrambled between the front seats and dived into the foot well on the passenger side. Christian rammed his foot to the floor, willing the car to speed up. The chimera roared from somewhere to his right. He glanced out and saw the chimera take an enormous leap. The beast crashed down onto the roof of the car. The windows shattered, showering the interior with glass.

The roof groaned under the weight, as the thing grappled to stay aboard. The little girl curled herself into a ball on the floor. Christian threw a hard left, and heard a thump as the chimera rolled off into the dirt. Again, he plunged his foot to the floor and picked up speed. Useless. The chimera was quickly alongside them, matching the car for pace.

Christian tried to ram the monster, but it veered away. On the second attempt the bumper made contact with the creature's heel as it turned. Suddenly the thing was stumbling off balance, slowing down, staggering.

One hand gripped tight on the wheel, Christian yanked the handbrake and spun the car 180 degrees. He stamped his foot to the floor and accelerated towards the beast. This was his only chance.

The front of the car smashed into the creature's back legs and the impact sent Christian thudding into the steering wheel. The animal bellowed and thrashed its tail as it sank to its haunches and rolled over in the sand.

Christian reversed. Steam rose from the crumpled bonnet, obscuring his vision as he made it back onto the road. He felt the tyres grip the road surface, put the car into drive, and floored the accelerator. The car picked up speed, and Christian sank into his seat with a sigh of relief. The little girl was still curled on the floor, crying, but alive. There was no question now – he was heading back for Qatif.

39

HUNTER WALKED BACK TO the Jeep, uptight and confused. His reunion with his parents had left him bewildered. They were both so frail, especially his father.

Alzheimer's?

A life of fear founded on his father's brutality no longer had a basis to exist. The memories imploded. Erased. Wiped clean. The tyrant was dead, replaced by a feeble old man. *That's all he is*, Hunter thought, *juice in a wrinkled skin.*

He opened the passenger door and climbed in.

'How did it go?' Monkton asked.

'Mum gave me a letter from Chris, but we'll have to go through it at my place. I'm still trying to get my head around all the stuff that Grealish came out with.'

'What did your parents say?'

'They're clueless Richard.' Hunter deliberately omitted his father's illness.

As Monkton turned out of Dale Avenue, Hunter took a final glance back at the street where he'd grown up, relieved to be leaving the place behind at last.

They arrived in Dulwich thirty minutes later. Hunter raced upstairs and checked his apartment for any sign of a break-in. The front door was still intact, and inside everything was in the same shit state he'd left it in earlier.

Monkton removed his coat and dropped into the sofa. Hunter slumped in the armchair and tore open the envelope. Inside: a typed note, a dozen photographs, and a roll of film. He flipped through the snapshots. 'Jesus! I hadn't expected this.'

'What's up?' Monkton asked.

Hunter shook his head. 'I haven't got a clue.' He checked the photos again - obscene images of two naked men engaged in sexual acts. One was fat and middle aged, the other a black haired youth. Hunter didn't recognize either of them at first and hadn't expected to. But when he looked closer, he identified the older guy as Sir Edward Lang, owner of The Daily News and a major shareholder in Zarcom Research.

Hunter stared in disbelief. 'Holy Jesus.'

He passed the photographs to Monkton, and read the accompanying note.

Matt, if you're reading this you're probably looking for me. Don't worry, I can take care of myself but I need your help to nail these bastards. Take the pictures to the following address. Keep the negatives safe. They'll get you what you need. Whatever you do, don't try to call me. Promise me Matt, I mean it. DON'T CALL. Chris.

The address read; *Chiltern Manor, Tenterden, Kent.*

'Well that's as clear as mud.' Hunter gave the letter to Monkton.

The little guy put the snapshots on the coffee table and read the note aloud. He removed his spectacles, wiped the lenses and looked across at Hunter. 'I'd say your brother wants you to blackmail these people for some reason.'

'Possibly, but he could have made the message a bit clearer. Why doesn't he want me to contact him, and how the hell did he get hold of this material anyway? *Jesus.*'

'Are you going to follow it up?'

'What do you think?' Hunter picked up one of the pictures and pointed to the bald man. 'Do you recognize this guy?'

Monkton put on his glasses, and leaned in. 'Thankfully not.'

'That is Sir Edward Lang, owner of the Daily News, the newspaper I work for.'

'Huh?' Monkton frowned, and then his face creased into a smile. He began to laugh - that annoying titter of his. Hunter was too tired to share the joke. He checked his watch - nearly five thirty.

A ring tone chirped. Monkton grabbed his coat, rifled through the pockets, and pulled out his phone. He answered breathlessly. 'Yes this is Richard Monkton...' He listened carefully for a few moments and then picked up a newspaper from the coffee table and began making notes. Eventually he said, 'Okay, I'll be over as soon as I can. It might be a couple of hours.' He ended the call and tore off the page.

'I've got to leave Matthew. Another sighting I'm afraid.'

'Where this time?'

'West Kent. A farmer found several strange markings in one of his fields, and two of his livestock are missing.'

'I'll join you.'

'Are you sure?'

'We're a team Richard. You go, I go.'

The rain glistened like crystal darts beneath the streetlights, while rivers of water gushed under cars and into drains. Hunter stood in the porch waiting for Monkton who was dawdling on the stairs, checking and rechecking his pockets to make sure he had everything. When the little guy finally caught up, Hunter made sure the envelope of film was still secure in his pocket, and then dashed across the street to the Jeep. The rain soaked him before he reached halfway.

At the kerb he turned and called to Monkton. 'Watch it when you come through...'

The little guy had vanished. Hunter called out again, his words muted by the rain clattering on the cars. He wiped his eyes and peered into the gloom. 'Come on Richard, where are you?'

No answer. Ten yards away, a dark shape thrashed in the gutter. Hunter raced back across the road, saw Monkton pinned on the ground beneath a figure in a black trench coat. Monkton struggled against his assailant, his face contorted in pain.

Hunter drove his boot into the side of the attacker's head. The man groaned and flopped to one side, tried to get up, but Hunter wouldn't let him. Another kick to the chin, and the man fell back. This time he stayed down.

Hunter helped Monkton to his feet. 'What the hell happened, Richard?'

The little guy searched frantically for his glasses. Hunter spotted them at the kerbside, picked them up, and wiped the lenses.

'Richard, just tell me you're okay...' Hunter didn't get a chance to finish. A bulldozing rugby tackle sent him crashing to the pavement. Instinctively he rolled to one side and sprang to his feet. Hunched forward, protecting his face with his forearms, Hunter watched the figure lunge at him through the watery haze.

'Behind you Matthew!'

Two of them? But Hunter had to deal with what was in front of him first, take the initiative, and do it now. His opponent flashed a right. Hunter ducked, took the man's lapels in both hands, and butted him in the face. The guy crumpled, his nose split open.

The third assailant joined the attack, and Hunter immediately spotted the man's weak spot. A ponytail.

A fist flew at him. Hunter dodged, feeling the draught of the punch as it skimmed past his cheek. He blocked a second blow, dived forward and snatched the man's ponytail. Dropping to his haunches, Hunter used his bodyweight to drag the man down. He let go, and his opponent staggered backwards, allowing Hunter to move in and finish him with a single punch. Hunter swiveled from his hip, and unleashed a blow to the man's jaw. A sharp crack of bone, and the guy dropped to the ground. As he lay stunned, Hunter sifted through his pockets.

'Who are these people?' Monkton said, voice quivering.

Hunter found the man's wallet. 'Quick let's go, we can ask questions later.'

They scrambled into the Jeep, Monkton gunned the engine, and pulled away as Hunter flipped open the wallet.

'Oh shit!'

'What now?'

Hunter opened his window and tossed the wallet into the street as they sped through the rain.

'Matt. What's wrong?'

Hunter grimaced. 'Secret Service Richard. Those guys were MI5.'

40

THE WINDOWS OF THE Volga were shattered and the interior bejewelled with fragments of glass. The child whimpered in the foot-well. Better than the screaming, Christian thought.

Suddenly, the engine spluttered and the vehicle rolled to a stop.

Christ. Not now, please.

He checked the petrol gauge. Empty. The beast was only a couple of miles back and could make up the ground quickly. Christian kicked open the door and got out, his body still wracked with pain. Trailing behind the car, he noticed a long trickle of petrol stretching up the road. He circled round to the passenger door, opened it, and beckoned the girl out.

'Come on sweetheart, not far to walk.'

He held out his hand, but she only curled herself tighter. Christian tried lifting her but she punched and clawed at his face. He grabbed her arms and pulled her gently. 'Like a bloody eel on steroids,' he muttered.

Finally, he lifted her out and put her down at the roadside, her tiny hand clasped in his. She yanked on his arm, jabbering in defiance. Alien words, but their meaning was clear. *Let me go!*

Christian started along the dusty road. The girl wrenched his arm and bit his hand. He stopped and lifted her up. 'Come on kid. Mum needs to sort you out a bath.'

Curled safely in his arms, the little girl settled down and began to doze.

Christian knew the next hour might be his last. There would be no happy faces waiting in Qatif, only men who wanted to kill him. As the town appeared on the horizon, something came up fast behind him.

His heart sank.

The first pickup overtook him and skidded to a halt at the roadside. A second pulled up behind, both vehicles crammed with Taliban miltia, Christian counted thirteen in all.

Don't let them see you're afraid.

The little girl awoke, rubbed her eyes and stretched. Christian set her down as he watched the Taliban commander climb out of the first truck. The child looked confused. She spotted the Afghan and immediately ran to him, shouting and squealing with pleasure.

His daughter?

The man picked her up and their relationship became clear. Christian only hoped it would buy him some time.

'Where did you find her?' The Afghan's voice remained tinged with hostility.

Christian explained how he had found the girl in the desert. 'The beast came down from the mountains and chased us. It's still out there somewhere.'

The Afghan stooped and whispered in his daughter's ear. She answered in a loud, animated fashion, pointed at Christian and waved her hands. She spoke for an age without taking a breath.

Eventually, the man straightened and strode back to the truck. He ducked into the cab and emerged with two bottles of water; one he gave to the girl, the other he tossed to Christian. When he spoke again, he sounded more at ease.

'The beast is dead. We found the body crippled at the roadside two miles north.' He pointed to the first truck and Christian saw a large mound in the back covered with tarpaulin. The Afghan cocked his head and grinned. 'My daughter tells me you saved her, and for that you have my gratitude. You are still an enemy of the Afghan people, but you have given me something to think about. Your actions may well have saved your life. Before I consider what to do with you, I need to know more about these beasts, and the men that ambushed your patrol.'

But Christian was curious about the child. He asked the Afghan how she got lost in the desert.

'My daughter falls asleep wherever she pleases,' the commander said. 'She went looking for her brother yesterday, and wandered out of town where apparently she found a metal house on wheels. She climbed inside and fell asleep. This morning, she ventured into the desert and lost her way.'

'Must be an old tank?' Christian said.

'Yes, it would seem so.'

There was a definite shift in the mood. The tension eased and some of the rebels were now smiling, albeit warily. Christian wiped sweat from his brow, unscrewed the bottle and gulped it dry. He had bought himself a temporary reprieve, but one word out of place and these men would undoubtedly kill him. He spoke with caution.

'The animals are being reared in the UK, hordes of them destined for places like Afghanistan, and they won't stop coming.'

The Afghan's eyes narrowed. 'Tell me about the men who attacked your patrol. How many were there?'

Christian shrugged. 'They were firing at us from all sides – I'd say, fifteen to twenty. Why?'

'Many people have been tortured and killed by these men. They seek information of your whereabouts. When I find them, I will kill them all. If you help us Englishman, I will let you go free.'

Christian had no choice. The two men had a common enemy and he had to trust that the Afghan. Suddenly, the air crackled with distant gunfire. The sound came from Qatif.

Rasheed heard the rumble of engines and his heart fluttered - the vehicles were approaching from the south, but his father had driven north out of town.

'They're back,' Aisha said. 'Perhaps they've found Jamila.'

Rasheed remained guarded. 'I'm not so sure. I think it might be the British.'

Aisha ran into the street to get a clearer view, but Rasheed stayed put. He glanced at the two blackened tanks in the centre of the square, a constant reminder of the violence around them. To some they served as proof that the foreign invaders were not invincible. The Taliban, although not responsible for the ambush, had claimed responsibility. The attack was seen as a gift from God, but Rasheed felt dark forces were at work.

The engines grew louder, but on this occasion the locals did not venture out to greet the visitors. Aisha shielded her eyes from the sun, and stared at whatever was approaching.

Rasheed called to her. 'Come away from the road Aisha. It's a British patrol, I swear.'

She shook her head. 'No. It is Taliban.'

Two large trucks drove into the square, and pulled up directly outside Rasheed's house. Men spilled out, armed with Kalashnikovs and rocket launchers. These weren't his father's men, indeed their faces were covered with scarves. No words passed between them and they communicated only with nods and hand gestures.

Aisha crossed the road and stood beside one of the trucks, but Rasheed noticed some of the men staring at her.

'Aisha. Let's go home. Please come.'

Too late. Three men broke away from the main group and moved towards her. Two of them grabbed her arms. A third ran up behind Aisha and yanked her hair. She squealed and tried to pull away.

Rasheed's chest tightened. He cried out, first at Aisha and then at the men. 'Leave her alone!' He ran to her, but a powerful hand snatched his arm and pulled him back.

Aisha became frantic. 'Rasheed, what's going on? What are they doing?'

People appeared from their houses, voices raised in panic. Rabia ran out of her front door and screamed as the men dragged her daughter away down the street. One of the militia fired a Kalashnikov into the air and everyone backed off.

Rasheed's arm was held in a firm grip and he couldn't shake free. He glared up at the man's pale blue eyes, his face hidden behind a black scarf. Rasheed struggled hard and managed to snatch the scarf away with his free hand. Just as he thought, the stranger's face was white. A western foreigner dressed in Afghan clothes.

A vicious back-hand whipped across Rasheed's face and sent his head twisting to one side. Blood sprayed from his mouth, and he sank to his knees. He heard Aisha crying. One of her captors kicked open a door on the other side of the square and the three men bundled her inside, closing the door behind them.

'No!' Rasheed yelled, 'please no.'

41

HUNTER COULDN'T REMEMBER THE last time he'd thrown a punch, let alone hit anyone that hard. His shoulders were as stiff as hell and his knuckles throbbed. He gazed into the darkness as Monkton drove along the back roads south towards Maidstone. According to the news, Tunbridge Wells was still a no-go area. The authorities had maintained the pretence of a terrorist attack and the media had swallowed it. No doubt the recriminations and conspiracy theories would surface later.

'So what's the story this time?' Hunter said.

'Story?'

'What's going on at this farm?'

Monkton shrugged. 'The guy just gave me his address, and said they had a couple of cattle missing. He found some strange animal prints in a field, but didn't go into detail.'

Hunter sighed. 'Sounds like bad news to me. Still, at least your name's getting around Richard. You're becoming quite popular.'

'Yes, but for all the wrong reasons.'

'So do you want to talk about it?'

'About what?'

'What Grealish said about your uncle. I can tell you're pissed off, maybe I can help.

'Kind of you, but no – I don't need to talk.'

'Let me know if you do, that's all I'm saying.'

They arrived at Logan's farm just after eight. A figure at the roadside flagged them down with a torch, and Monkton stopped the Jeep. Hunter wound down his window. Through the darkness he could just make out the guy's face - early twenties dressed in a quilted jacket and Wellington boots.

The man flashed the beam into the car. 'Mr. Monkton is it?'

'That's me,' Monkton said, leaning across. 'This is Matt Hunter, a friend of mine.'

'My name's Addie Logan, my dad asked me to call you. You can leave your car here Mr. Monkton, it's perfectly safe.'

Hunter zipped up his jacket and blew into his hands as he trudged across the road. Addie led them through a side gate into a yard at the rear of the property. Hunter was astonished that the cattle-shed was no more than twenty yards from the house. The cows snorted and jostled for position, barely visible in the blackness, but the smell was intolerable.

'My father's too old to be gallivanting across the fields at night, so I'll take you up there myself,' Addie said. 'We've got two cows missing and a busted fence. We found some weird tracks. I don't know what made them, but they ain't hoof prints.'

The words chimed inside Hunter's head. *Weird tracks, a fence near the woods?* Exactly like Faraday's place.

Addie invited them through the back door of the farmhouse into a rustic kitchen, complete with stone floor and oak beams in the ceiling. The smell of stewed beef wafted through the room. Addie's mother, a hefty woman with arms like slabs of dough, stood at the stove stirring broth in a large saucepan. 'Sit yourselves down boys, supper's nearly ready.'

Hunter couldn't imagine anything worse than eating food in such close proximity to heaps of cow shit. He conjured an excuse. 'We've no time Mrs. Logan, we're heading back to London shortly.'

'Not on an empty stomach you're not. The food will only go to waste.' Mrs. Logan ladled generous scoops of broth into three bowls and carried them across to the table on a tray. 'Tuck in boys, there's more if you want it.'

Hunter sat and stared at the bowl of orange liquid loaded with cubes of beef. Reluctantly he started to eat. To his surprise the food tasted good.

After supper, Addie handed out torches as they prepared to leave.

'Tell us about these tracks you found,' Hunter said.

Addie shrugged. 'They don't look like anything in particular. It's as if they've been...'

'Brushed over?'

'Well not exactly. I'd say smudged. But I don't understand why anyone would want to steal a cow?'

The table fell silent. Hunter waited until Mrs. Logan was out of the room before he spoke again. 'Addie. Do you have a gun?'

'What do I need a gun for? And why are you whispering?'

'No reason,' Monkton interjected. 'There's nothing to worry about.'

Addie smiled nervously. 'Okay, then we'd better take a look at the tracks and see what you think.'

The three men shuffled out the kitchen door into the yard and then through a metal gate into the first field. Hunter walked pensively, hunched against the cold, hands in pockets, collar turned up.

Addie's breath billowed in the chill air as he called out to the animals. 'Come-on come-on come-on.' He repeated the words over and over like a mantra.

They skirted the edge of the field, and the ground curved upward in a steep gradient. Hunter felt the pull at the back of his thighs and Monkton began to wheeze. When they finally reached the top of the hill, Hunter shone his torch into the trees. Twigs snapped and leaves rustled. Small animals scurried across the woodland floor to escape the torchlight.

Monkton told everyone to remain still. 'Listen, I think there's something out there.'

Hunter heard the footsteps of a heavy animal and angled his torch in the direction of the sound.

The animal stopped.

'Must be one of the cows,' Addie said, 'nothing else walks that heavy, not round here anyway.'

'That's not strictly true,' Hunter replied.

'What?'

'Nothing Addie. Let's move on and find this break in the fence.'

They turned away and the rustling started again. Hunter's heart pounded, his fingers wrapped tight around the torch as he directed the beam into the darkness. A bulky silhouette moved between the trees and a loud snort resonated in the still air.

Hunter grabbed Addie's coat sleeve and pulled him back from the fence. 'Stay calm and back away slowly.'

The woodland floor heaved and pounded as the animal lumbered towards them. Hunter turned to run, but Addie put an arm out to stop him.

'I don't know what you're afraid of Mr. Hunter but I swear it's only a cow.'

Hunter looked back into the shadows and saw the outline of a cow trot gingerly towards him.

'Come on my darling,' Addie said.

'Oh for Christ's sake.' Hunter glanced at Monkton who returned a grin.

Addie chuckled to himself. 'I don't know what you boys were expecting, but you scared me half to death.'

'False alarm,' Hunter replied.

Addie looked puzzled by the remark but quickly shook it off. 'If you two stay here, I'll climb over and guide her back to the gate.' He cocked one leg over the wire but struggled to maintain his balance in his heavy clothes.

Hunter leaned over the fence and patted the cow's nose while the animal chewed on a clump of grass, not a care in the world.

Another crunch of twigs emerged from the woods.

'Sounds like they're both here,' Addie said. 'I'm sorry to bring you boys all this way for nothing.'

Hunter heard the second cow trot towards the fence, and thrust the torchlight deep into the trees. The animal picked up speed, and crashed through the undergrowth. Hunter shuddered as a deep throated snarl resonated in the blackness. Demonic yellow eyes blazed and a huge beast charged out of the woods.

'Run! Both of you for Christ's sake run!' Hunter shouted.

The cow sagged to the ground with a grief-stricken moan as the predator pounced on its back and clamped its jaws around its neck. The cow's head was ripped clean away with a single jerk.

Addie's leg remained caught on the barbs. Hunter and Monkton worked frantically to free his trousers, while the beast devoured its kill. The farmer thrashed like a skewered fish as he attempted to break free, but his efforts only made things worse.

'Take yours trousers off!' Hunter yelled.

The monster shuffled back into the undergrowth, dragging the cow by its legs. The headless body disappeared into the blackness as if the bushes themselves had sucked it in.

Addie unbuckled his trousers, and pulled them down. Hunter dropped his torch and yanked the guy's Wellingtons off his feet. They managed to pull Addie clear of the fence, leaving his trousers twisted on the wire.

The three of them pelted down the hill together. Addie Logan made a pathetic sight, white legs streaking beneath his bulky coat. With only socks on his feet, he quickly lost ground on the other two. Hunter reached the bottom of the field and opened the gate into the yard

Monkton wasn't far behind. 'It's coming after us!' he yelled.

Hunter stared up the hill. Fifty yards back, he saw Addie slip and fall into the mud.

Hunter waved Monkton through the gate. 'Hurry Richard, get in the house.'

The kitchen door was wide open, and light flooded into the courtyard. Hunter noticed a large mound lying in the shadows but he was more concerned about Addie.

'Keep running Addie, come on!'

The beast closed in. Addie gasped for air, his stubby white legs pounded the turf, his arms wheeled like windmills.

'Don't look back, you can do it.'

Monkton prodded Hunter's arm. 'Matthew, look!'

Hunter glanced over his shoulder at the bundle laying in the yard. In the half-light, he recognized Mrs. Logan, on her back in a lake of blood; head turned towards them, eyes glazed in a death stare. A line of blood leaked from one corner of her mouth. Beneath her chest there was nothing. A few feet away was another body, crippled and bloodied - *Mr. Logan.*

This isn't happening.

A howl echoed from the field. Hunter snapped his head round and saw Addie run for the gate, but his left arm was missing, and blood jetted from the stub. The beast ran alongside him, spat out the severed limb and pounced on the young farmer. Addie collapsed and screamed as the brute tore into him.

Monkton grabbed Hunter's jacket and told him to 'get down.' Hunter didn't argue. He dropped to crouched position behind the gate post.

Two masked figures armed with laser-sighted weapons, burst out of the kitchen door and opened fire into the field. White muzzle-flashes blazed in the darkness and the air shuddered to the sound gunfire.

'Quick. Get to the cow shed,' Hunter said.

Keeping tight to the fence, they scurried to the shed as the shots continued. Hunter ducked under the railing into a forest of bovine legs. The cattle jostled and bellowed, their eyes bulged in terror.

Hunter squeezed through the squirming bodies and stamping hooves. He checked that Monkton was still behind him. The little guy's face and clothes were covered in filth. Hunter was in a similar state. The shooting stopped, but the cows were still frenzied.

A red beam sliced the air above Hunter's head. A laser.

He ducked and shuffled backwards, but slipped on the greasy surface. As he fell, his hand brushed against a cow lying prostrate on the ground. Realization dawned. Hunter stared into the void and his eyes adjusted. He wasn't looking at a whole cow, but the half-eaten remains. Locked onto the rump, monstrous jaws tore at the carpeted flesh. Hunter heard the crunch of bone, caught a whiff of the creatures foul breath. He kicked himself away and scrambled to his feet.

The shed gate opened and the two gunmen began waving the herd into the yard. The animals surged forward and streamed out. At the back of the shed, the beast rose to its feet, and emerged slowly from the shadows. The thing sprang from its hind legs and launched itself onto the backs of the fleeing cattle. The stragglers at the rear buckled and collapsed under the predator's weight.

Instantly, the gunmen opened fire. Cattle stampeded across the yard, and out into the field beyond. The beast continued to charge, despite the barrage of fire.

This was Hunter's only chance of escape. He gripped Monkton's arm, about to turn and run when something caught his eye. He stood, transfixed.

A third masked figure, dressed in black ops gear appeared in the kitchen doorway. Instead of a gun, this man carried a black rod, no more than three feet long. Hunter watched the man stride towards the creature. A bolt of electricity arced from the tip of the rod, crackled through the air and connected with the beast's head. The skull popped like a balloon, and the creature slumped to the ground.

A red beam flashed across Hunter's chest and the tiny dot of a laser hovered over his heart.

They had him.

42

RASHEED HEARD AISHA SCREAM, but was powerless to help her. Breathless and exhausted, his body wilted and he sank to his knees, but the foreigner would not let go of his arm.

Father where are you? Please come and help us.

Across the square, two men dragged Aisha's mother away from the house where her daughter had been taken. 'Who are you?' she cried. 'What are you doing with my baby?'

A line of armed men kept the angry locals at bay. One of the militia approached Rasheed. He removed his turban and the scarf around his face to reveal his fair skin and yellow hair. His accent was strange but he spoke in Pashto. 'If someone tells me what I need to know, the girl will go unharmed.' He gestured to the crowd. 'You can tell these people they are perfectly safe. We just need some information.'

The thug holding Rasheed's arm let go. The boy gasped and tears ran down his cheeks. He heard Nura crying for her daughter.

The man with yellow hair grabbed his shirt. 'You know where the British soldier is don't you?'

Rasheed spluttered out the words. 'He escaped into the desert. I saw him drive out of town this morning.'

'I saw him too,' a voice piped up from the crowd.

Rasheed looked round and saw his father barge his way through. Asad's voice remained calm and authoritative, even in these dire circumstances. 'The soldier stole a car and headed north. If you go now you still might catch him.'

The crowd backed away. A face appeared at a window up to Rasheed's left - one his father's men.

'Very well,' said the foreigner. 'We will see if you are telling the truth. We will keep the girl. If you are lying, then I cannot be held responsible for what happens to her.' He turned and waved at one of the trucks. Six men climbed in the back of the vehicle and two more got in the front. As the truck pulled away, Rasheed sensed a movement to his right. He glanced round to see the man with yellow hair stagger forward and fall face-first into the dirt. A knife protruded from his neck and blood oozed over his white flesh into the dust.

A hand touched Rasheed's shoulder, his father's voice low in his ear. 'Get behind me quick!'

Gunfire erupted from the rooftops, windows, and alleyways. The foreigners crumpled in the street as the locals ran back to their homes. One of Asad's men shepherded Rabia back inside her house, her screams now drowned out by the deafening gunfire. Asad drew a pistol from his belt, and ran for the cover of the remaining truck, yelling at Rasheed to stay close behind.

The first truck stopped at the end of the street. A rocket propelled grenade hurtled down from a nearby rooftop, slammed into the cab and exploded. Three survivors fell out the back, but were quickly mown down by Taliban machine-guns. Asad shot one of the foreigners fleeing back to the house where Aisha had been taken, and this time Rasheed felt no shame at seeing such aggression.

'Aisha is in that house Father. They dragged her inside.'

'I know Rasheed, but you must stay here, and keep down.' Asad picked up a Kalashnikov lying next to one of the dead men, and rattled off several rounds. Only a handful of the foreigners remained alive. Scattered around the square, bodies lay twisted and deformed like pieces of a ghoulish jigsaw puzzle.

But the three men who had abducted Aisha were still inside the house with her. Rasheed sprang from the cover of the stationary truck and sprinted towards the house as bullets whizzed over his head.

'Rasheed no!'

The young Afghan didn't look back. He crashed through the front door and called out to Aisha as he ran from room to room. A noise thudded above his head. Rasheed charged up the stairs. On the landing he saw a body riddled with bullets.

One of the foreigners.

Rasheed called to Aisha again, but still no reply.

Downstairs, the front door burst open and his father shouted up to him. Rasheed's mind was crowded with gruesome thoughts, images he tried desperately to blank out. There was nothing he could do. *God will take care of Aisha and Jamila.*

There were two rooms in front of him. Rasheed pushed the door to his right and stepped through.

Face down on the bed, a body splattered with blood.

Another body lay on the floor at the foot of the bed, punctured with bullet wounds. These were the other two men who had dragged Aisha away. Rasheed hurried back onto the landing and met his father on the stairs.

'Everything is good Rasheed. Allah has made us victorious.'

Rasheed glared at him. 'What do you mean? You are obsessed with fighting. If you had been here all along, then none of this would have happened.'

Asad looked taken aback but showed no sign of anger. Instead, he said, 'I have learned many things today Rasheed. Everyone is safe.'

The boy was speechless. *Is he mad?* But as he stared at his father searching for his next words, he noticed the other door swing open. A face peeked out and for a moment he could only gape in astonishment.

'Aisha…' That's all he could manage. He wrapped his arms around her and held her tight, not wanting to let go.

'Rasheed, I can't breathe,' she said softly.

He stepped back and looked at her face. 'How did you get free – are you hurt?'

Before she could answer, Rasheed saw the man move out of the shadows behind her. He emerged wearing Taliban clothes. Earlier, Rasheed had helped the British soldier change into these garments. Now here he was, his father's enemy; face caked in blood, holding a Kalashnikov assault rifle.

'How can this be?' Rasheed said.

'He saved me,' Aisha replied.

'And he saved Jamila.' Asad put in. 'Today the soldier is our friend.

Christian could see the boy was overjoyed and a feeling of elation rushed through him. He had repaid his debt to the kid and had somehow gotten through this alive.

Earlier, on entering the outskirts of town with the Taliban unit, he heard the girl's screams, but the Taliban fighters wouldn't allow him a weapon. Asad's men took up positions around the square, preparing to attack the mercenaries but no one took notice of the girl. Christian heard her cry out again and broke away from the others as soon as the fighting started. He sneaked around the back of the house, grabbed a knife from the kitchen and crept upstairs. All three men were in the back bedroom with the girl. His footsteps creaked on the landing and the bedroom door flew open.

Christian acted on pure impulse, plunged the knife into the man's stomach as soon as he stepped out and grabbed his Kalashnikov. In a split second he shot the other two men in the room, grabbed the girl and hid her until the fighting was over.

He could see the Taliban commander was pleased. Christian handed him the machine gun as a show of trust. 'Now can I have that radio? I need to make a call.'

The Taliban commander took the weapon and nodded. 'You will have it. But first we need time to clean up the street, and leave this place. Then you can have your radio. Come, you are invited to my house. My wife will want to thank you. It was because of her that my son tended to you when you were sick. I would have had you killed but I would have been wrong.'

Christian glanced at the Afghan boy who returned a beaming smile.

'Friend?' the boy said, and pointed at his chest.

Christian smiled. 'Yes. Friend.'

43

THE MASKED FIGURE STOOD over the dead creature and prodded its broken skull with the tip of his rod. Hunter recognized the device - identical to the one his brother brandished in the photograph. This man also wore a similar armlet, complete with screen and keypad.

'It's okay Matthew. We're on the same side.' The man straightened and pulled off his mask. *Phoenix?*

The two gunmen lowered their weapons and also removed their masks.

Tom Swain and Turk.

'Welcome to the party dude,' Swain said.

Hunter couldn't begin to understand what these men were doing here. He stared at the creature flopped in the yard, its thick black tongue protruding through its huge jaws. Phoenix spoke, but Hunter didn't hear his words, unable to tear his gaze from the beast. Its eyes rolled back, the hide punctured with bullet wounds, but there was a surprising lack of blood. In the gloom, the pelt seemed rough, almost scaly. Hunter gasped at the size of the thing. The tail was longer and thicker at the base than he had realized. The body was around twelve feet long but the tail added another twelve to its overall length.

Hunter caught a lungful of the foul stench and a mouthful of bile surged up from his stomach. He swallowed it, and glanced out to the field where the second creature lay. A few yards behind was the body of Addie Logan, at least what was left of him.

'Gruesome fuckers aren't they? We've been tracking them for some time,' Phoenix said.

Hunter looked round at him. 'Tracking them... how?'

'All in good time Matthew. The bad guys will be here soon and we need to leave before we get caught with our trousers down.'

Swain laughed, a hoarse cackle that reverberated in the still air.

'What's so funny?' Monkton snapped.

Swain pointed at Addie's corpse. 'Irony,' he said.

'For God's sake, you find *that* funny? Who are you people?'

Hunter rested a hand on Monkton's shoulder. 'Ignore him Richard. Unfortunately these guys are the nearest thing we've got to friends right now and we need their help.'

Monkton shot Swain a look of disgust, and started across the yard. Hunter shouted after him. 'Richard! Where are you going?'

'Home,' Monkton replied. He trudged past the Logans and a couple of stray cows before reaching the gate. A burst of gunfire shattered the stillness. Hunter jerked round to see a wisp of smoke trail from the muzzle of Swain's gun.

The American called out, 'Can't let you go Mr. Monkton. We've got a job to do.' He rested the weapon on his hip, a veiled threat. Monkton stopped and turned. The kitchen light glinted on his spectacles, conveying a mean quality to his anger.

Phoenix said, 'Tom's right Mr. Monkton. If you head out on your own I guarantee you'll get picked up within the hour.'

Monkton's eyes flicked angrily between the two men.

'Come on Richard, let's stick together,' Hunter said. 'At least they've got firepower and god knows we need it.'

Phoenix nodded in agreement. 'You need us and we need you. There's a young woman out there on her own somewhere, and we intend to find her.'

'You mean Nina?' Hunter asked.

Phoenix nodded.

'And if we cooperate, you'll tell us everything?'

'Of course.'

Hunter glanced at Monkton who finally responded with a weary nod.

'Good. There's a Lexus parked out front,' Phoenix said. 'We'll give you fresh clothes to change into, but I'll need the keys to your vehicle. We're heading for a secure location Mr. Monkton. Turk will follow us in your Jeep.'

Monkton reluctantly dug out his keys and handed them over. Phoenix led them through the gate to the front of the farmhouse where the Lexus was parked. Swain opened the back and retrieved a couple of boiler suits and a roll of refuse sacks. He handed them each a suit and tore some bags from the roll. 'We don't want you guys stinking the car out do we?'

Hunter and Monkton changed into their new outfits and put their dirty clothes into the bin bags. Hunter discovered an inside pocket where he could hide the picture of his brother along with the lewd photographs Christian had sent him. Swain dumped the bags in the back of the car, and emerged with a couple of blindfolds. 'I'm gonna have to ask you to wear these guys.'

'For god's sake this is ludicrous,' Monkton protested.

'He's got a point Tom. Is this really necessary?' Hunter said.

'Afraid so. I'll explain later, right now we need to get going.'

They climbed into the back of the car and slipped on the masks. Swain got into the drivers seat and started the engine. Phoenix joined them, the Lexus tilted as the big man climbed in. Hunter smelled petrol, and as they pulled away he swore he heard the crackle of fire.

An hour later the car bounced over uneven ground and slowed to a stop. Hunter and Monkton were helped out of the car and led up a stone path. The jingle of keys in a lock, a door opened and Hunter was ushered into the warmth of a carpeted room. Once inside, Phoenix told both men to remove their masks.

Hunter found himself in a cramped hallway. To his left a door opened into a small living room and straight ahead, a set of stairs. Phoenix beckoned through the right door into a dining room where Phoenix offered them each a seat at the table. 'Make yourselves comfortable, I'll make coffee.'

Monkton dropped into a chair, his face was pale and gaunt.

'It's going to be okay Richard,' Hunter said, 'We'll hear what they've got to say before we tell them anything.'

Monkton nodded meekly.

The front door slammed shut and Tom Swain appeared. 'Turk's on stag,' he called out to Phoenix. He glanced down at Hunter. 'Still got that crazy ring tone of yours?'

'No. I changed it.'

'I bet.' The American grinned and playfully punched Hunter's arm. 'I'm only kiddin' with ya. Who gives a shit anyway, that's what I say.' He glanced at Monkton. 'Is your friend okay? He looks like he could do with a couple of espressos.'

Richard Monkton slumped forward and rubbed his eyes. 'I need to sleep,' he murmured.

'Come on buddy there's a sofa in the next room. I'll take you through.' Swain put his arms around Monkton's chest, lifted him up, and helped him out of the room.

Phoenix set a mug of coffee down in front of Hunter and pulled up a chair.

'So what happened to Nina?' Hunter said.

'We don't know. She got picked up, probably by Modjarrad's people but we're not sure. Her car was found abandoned on the outskirts of Tunbridge Wells, the front all smashed in. Modjarrad knows we're out to stop him and is trying to track us down. He'll use Nina to lure us out into the open.'

Swain returned and joined them at the table. Phoenix leaned across to Hunter and said, 'How much do you know about Zarcom?'

'I heard they have a contract to supply the military with these genetic mutants or whatever they are.'

'Chimeras,' Phoenix said, 'nasty fucking things. Great if they worked but they don't. The army conducted live tests in Afghanistan and the damn things killed nearly every villager within a five mile radius, not a single terrorist. The incident was reported but no one ordered a stop to it. As a result the chimeras were sent out again and yet more innocent people died.'

'How do you know all this?'

'Because I've been involved with this project from the start, we all have. We were part of an elite group assigned to work with the animals. It was exciting at first, helping to save lives on the frontline, but the whole thing proved a disaster. These creatures are still wild animals and it doesn't matter what precautions you take, they don't discriminate who or what they kill.'

'Surely someone in government would have realized the dangers. What did they think would happen?'

'Zarcom supposedly introduced safety measures to control the creatures, but when they're fuelled with adrenalin the animals are impossible to handle. The technology itself is quite simple. Spotters on the ground locate the enemy and splash the area with lasers. Each chimera has a chip wired into its nervous system which recognizes the laser signal. An electronic pulse stimulates the chimera's adrenal glands. This makes the animal incredibly aggressive, and once released, it will charge towards the target and kill all the bad guys in its path. That's the theory. The reality is somewhat different.'

'How?'

Phoenix arched his fingers under his chin. 'First, the animals don't like aircraft and get spooked by anything flying over their heads. They veer off course and attack innocent people rather than head for the target. It takes between thirty minutes to an hour before the chimera's metabolism returns to normal, and during that time it hunts and kills without prejudice. Once the animal tires it follows the signal back to its handler. Therein lays the second problem. Every handler controls two chimeras, otherwise known as 'pods.' If the handler is killed, then his signal disappears. The transponders are heat sensitive and if a handler's body temperature drops by two degrees the device simply shuts down, never to work again. This stops the implants getting into the wrong hands. However, unless there is another handler in the vicinity, the chimeras have nothing to follow.'

'I don't understand.'

'The project goes far beyond these creatures Matthew. There were originally twenty soldiers on the assignment, and we discovered a very disturbing truth about the Darwin Project.'

'The human breeding programme?'

Phoenix looked surprised. 'You've heard about it?'

'I've done some research.'

'I see. So you know we were all earmarked for the project from day one? Born and raised for combat, born to be controlled.'

'Yes, but I found it hard to believe at first.'

'I'm afraid it's true. The real problem is the chimeras are still killing innocent people. Your brother filed a report to high command, but everything was hushed up. That left us no choice but to stop the project at source. Through a secret contact, Christian organized a flight home for us via Pakistan and also sorted out this house. He wanted to come with us but feared MI5 or Zarcom would use you to get to him. Now we've now lost contact with your brother and we haven't heard from our unit for over a week.'

'Christ Phoenix, we have to get them out of there.'

'No. His orders were clear - sit tight and wait for him to contact us, no matter what. We're here to watch your back Matthew. Nina decided to bring you in because she reckoned you needed to know what's going on.'

'She got that right. So she's a soldier just like you?'

'Yes, she's part of the programme just like the rest of us.'

'And her name's Standwick, not Siketi.'

'Her real name – yes. She changed it to hide her identity and get a job at that newspaper.'

Perhaps it was exhaustion, or maybe relief that he was still alive, but Hunter felt no anger towards her, disappointment maybe, but no anger. He unzipped the boiler suit, pulled out the photograph of Christian from his pocket, and placed it on the table. 'Tell me what's going on in that photo?'

Phoenix pointed at the black rod in Christian's hand. 'This is an EPD, or Electrical Pulse Distributor, used to control the chimeras. You saw me use it earlier. There are two levels, stun and kill.'

'And what about that gadget on your forearm?'

'It's a satellite receiver.' Phoenix unclipped the device and laid it on the table. 'We use this to track the chimeras. A red triangle on the screen indicates a chimera is in the vicinity.'

'So there any more of these things out there?'

'We're not sure. The tracking device is only as good as the strength of the signal. When the creatures hide underground or venture into dense woodland we instantly lose them. Those last two animals were impossible to hunt down and we had to rely on a different strategy to find them.'

'What strategy?'

'Every handler was fitted with a chip during childhood and like the chimeras, these microchips emit a signal. This shows as a green dot on the tracker screen.'

'So you guys are sending out signals?'

'Not any more. I had my chip removed.' Phoenix turned his head, and pointed to the long scar at the back of his neck. Phoenix glanced at Swain and said, 'Fill in the rest of the details Tom. You know more about this than anyone.'

Swain lit a cigarette and leaned back in his chair. 'This whole mess started back in the States when the CIA initiated the Darwin Project in '79. We needed a solution to get up close to the enemy with minimal losses. Current operations in the Gulf and Afghanistan highlight this problem.'

'I heard all this from Professor Grealish,' Hunter said.

'Who?'

'Never mind. I know the US employed Zarcom to produce a genetically engineered animal that could be used as a weapon.'

'Yes, Zarcom's research was the most advanced at the time. Using animals in combat is nothing new of course, but these things are brutal. They strike with speed, and get into the tightest spots to flush out the enemy. They're huge animals but you wouldn't believe the spaces they can get into. The U.S. quit the programme in 1999 in favour of other projects. The British took over and as a consequence… here we are.'

'So where do you fit into all this?'

'I was born and raised in the States. I joined up at the age of sixteen and was sent over to the UK two years ago to work with Captain Hunter's unit. We underwent an intense SAS training programme, and ten months ago were sent to Afghanistan and formerly introduced to the Darwin Project. That's when we first laid eyes on these creatures. It was cool at first, then we started to see innocent casualties. Chimeras attack anything that moves and have no fear. The laser guidance technology doesn't work. The only thing we can guarantee is they follow the signal from a handler. It's a powerful urge they cannot resist.'

'So you're a handler too?'

'Like Phoenix, I've had my chip removed. It's a dangerous operation. One of the guys was killed in the process. The fucking things are stuck right at the base of the skull.'

'Let me see.'

Swain turned down his collar and twisted round in his seat. There on his neck was a three inch vertical scar.

'So if none of you guys are chipped, then who is? Who have you been tracking?'

Swain looked awkwardly at Phoenix and Hunter sensed he'd hit a nerve. Phoenix looked ill at ease as he answered the question. 'It's you Matthew. You are sending the signal. Just like Chris and the rest of us, you must have been implanted when you were a kid.'

Hunter remembered what Grealish had said about his brother, and here it was: Phoenix had confirmed it was all true. His mother had lied to him.

Hunter buried his head in his hands. 'Great. We've developed a creature that hunts and kills humans. Now you're telling me I have an implant in my head and you've been using me to lure these things out in to the open!'

'I know it's hard to take Matthew but we intend to put a stop to the project and we need you on board.'

'But if we're all part of this project, where do our parents fit in?'

'I was raised in an orphanage in South London and joined the army from there. Others were raised by families with military connections. I guess you fit into the second category.'

Hunter closed his eyes and gripped the edge of the table. Had his mother really lied to him? 'If I'm emitting a signal then surely Zarcom or the security services can track me down,' he said.

'Yes, but don't worry. We've got specialist equipment both inside the house and in the Lexus that blocks out a GPS signal. You're safer with us than out on your own.'

'But I'm not a soldier Phoenix. If I'm chipped why wasn't I drafted into the same unit as you guys?'

'I guess there must have been something about you they didn't like. There's a filtering process, you still have to prove yourself. There are probably other people out there just like you, carrying on their daily lives as if nothing's wrong.'

'Your kidding?'

'I'm just saying it's possible.'

'What about Modjarrad? Tell me what you know about him.'

'He's a loose cannon. We know he's moved his research and gone underground. We think the government has pulled out and shut Zarcom down. MI5 are looking for Modjarrad but it sounds like he's vanished. He'll probably resurface when he's found another buyer for his technology. That means the chimeras could show up anywhere on the globe. Modjarrad was seen courting a Russian delegation only a month ago in London, so we have to find his new facility and stop him.'

'But if MI5 are after him then surely he's got no chance. They must know where he is.'

'If only it were that easy,' Swain butted in. 'We have a list of Modjarrad's backers, rich fuckers who invested a lot of money in Zarcom. We're talking powerful people who aren't about to let their investment slide. They want a return no matter what.'

'What people?'

'I'll show you.' Swain stood up and left the room, returned moments later with a sheet of paper containing a list of at least thirty names including two or three high profile businessmen Hunter recognized. One name however, did stand out - a name he knew only too well, and now he realized what his brother was up to.

Swain dropped his cigarette and crushed it under his boot. 'Some of these people, if not all of them, probably know where the new facility is. We're guessing its underground, hidden from spy satellites. If we could put the frighteners on one of these dudes then we might get a result.'

'I know a way.' Hunter delved into his pocket, pulled out the photographs that Christian had sent him and tossed them on the table. 'Either of you know the fat guy in those pictures?'

Phoenix picked up one of the snapshots and a broad grin stretched across his face. 'Oh yeah, where the hell did you get these?'

'From Chris.'

'Clever,' Phoenix said. 'Sir Edward Lang, married man with three daughters. Now we've got a chance of getting the information we need.'

44

MATTHEW HUNTER STARES AT the ceiling, writhing against the straps that pin him to the table. The room is grey. Everything is grey. But he isn't alone, two figures with their backs turned, talk quietly to one another. One is a woman - a nurse. The other is a man in a white coat - a doctor. Metal objects clink in a dish. The room seems big, as if he sees through the eyes of a child. It must be a dream, but he can't escape it.

The doctor turns. He has a grey beard and an unpleasant smile that seems almost threatening. The nurse leans over with a syringe. Hunter's mind drifts. Images and colours fade.

Now he finds himself in a corridor. A door slams shut behind him. His head is numb, and begins to throb. He sees his mother seated on a plastic chair, handbag resting on her knee. 'Does your head hurt?' she asks.

Matthew's mouth is dry and he struggles to answer. 'What did they do to me Mum?'

She smiles but her eyes are blank. 'You want to be a good boy don't you? You want to be like Christian?'

'What did they do to me Mum?'

She sighs. 'They're making you better. You need this treatment Matthew. If there was any other way ... but there isn't.' Her voice is impatient. He takes his mother's arm and they walk together along the bleak passage.

Hunter awoke and took a moment to recognize his surroundings. He found himself lying on a sofa and realized he was in the living room of the cottage.

Phoenix knocked and walked in with a mug of coffee. 'Breakfast is on,'

Hunter rubbed his eyes. Someone moved upstairs, the boards creaked above his head and the smell of bacon wafted through the open door.

'What the hell happened to me?' Hunter said, taking the mug from Phoenix.

Phoenix laughed. 'One minute you wanted to take on all the bad guys, the next you were out like a light. There's a shower upstairs but no hot water. I threw your clothes in the machine; they're clean but need pressing. That's your job. In the meantime, put your feet up and watch TV.'

Phoenix left the room but Hunter couldn't stand being alone. The dream was still fresh in his mind. He got up, walked through to the dining room and took a seat at the table while he waited for breakfast.

Monkton appeared minutes later bleary-eyed but a lot healthier than he'd looked the previous evening. Phoenix served up bacon, sausage and fried eggs. The smell was wonderful and Hunter tucked in heartily. Monkton merely picked at his food. He seemed distracted. Hardly surprising after what he'd been through and Hunter decided to give him some room so he could come to terms with his emotions. He asked Phoenix the whereabouts of the other two men.

'Turk's patrolling outside and Tom's checking out Lang's place.'

'Not on his own surely?'

'Don't worry, he's just sussing the place out. We've got to plan the route and access points. We also need to make sure the target will be home when we raid the house. Tom is mapping it out, and if all goes well, we'll extract Lang tonight.'

Hunter went upstairs to shower and half an hour later joined Monkton in the living room. Monkton stared morosely at the TV screen. 'I'm sorry Matthew but this is all getting too much. I can't get the vision of Addie and his parents out of my head.'

'I know,' Hunter replied, but thought it best to change the subject. 'It seems what Grealish told us was true. Phoenix said I've got a chip inserted in my head, some sort of transmitter. Zarcom and MI5 can trace the signal which explains why we got jumped at my place.'

Monkton's eyes remained fixed on the TV. 'I wouldn't pay too much attention to anything these people tell you.'

'What do you mean?'

Monkton checked the door behind him was closed and then his gaze rested on Hunter. 'They're up to something. I don't know what, but I think they want to frighten us into believing we need their help. I don't trust them Matt.'

A brief silence followed. Hunter said, 'I had a dream last night. Something that happened to me as a kid, some kind of operation performed on my head. It was so real, it got me thinking about this implant.'

'I'm just saying keep an open mind,' Monkton replied. 'I mean, what do you really know about these people? An implant… some kind of transmitter? It's a bit hard to swallow.'

'But Grealish also mentioned it. You trust him don't you?'

'He didn't specify you Matthew. Just your brother, and that's not proven. Your mother didn't know anything. What about scars? Have you got a scratch on your neck even?'

'No. Not that I can tell.' It was true. Apart from the sporadic pains in his head, Hunter had no evidence that he had anything wrong with him. He considered for a moment, an electrical device small enough to remain hidden under the skin and yet powerful enough to keep going all these years. Did such technology exist? More importantly did it is exist ten or fifteen years ago? But the dream had been so vivid, almost real.

Despite Monkton's reservations, Hunter knew he couldn't destroy Zarcom without help. He didn't have the firepower or the know-how, so he had no choice but to give these guys a chance.

The morning chat show ended and the midday news came on. The headlines rang out:

'Al Qaeda claim responsibility for terrorist attack in Kent.'

More bullshit.

'Foot and mouth discovered at two more farms in Kent.'

Foot and Mouth disease was the last thing Hunter was worried about. But the next headline made him sit up. 'Seven British troops killed and one missing in Afghanistan.'

The hairs on his arms bristled against his sleeves. He leant closer to the screen.

Shit, please don't let it be Chris.

Re-runs of the 'terrorist attack' at Tunbridge Wells flashed up on the screen and of course the newsreader stated that Al Qaeda had claimed responsibility.

Phoenix breezed through the door and stood in the centre of the room as the newsreader continued. 'More cases of Foot and Mouth have been discovered in the South East with a reported six farms now affected.'

'Don't believe a word of it,' Monkton said. 'They want to close down the countryside and deny people access while these creatures are still out there.'

'Shut up I'm trying to listen.' Hunter was shocked how easily he snapped and quickly apologized. Phoenix stepped closer to the TV, eyes fixed on the screen. The newsreader got to the next piece.

'More deaths in Afghanistan. Seven British troops were killed on Monday when their convoy was ambushed in a town eighty miles south of Kandahar.'

Kandahar? Chris is based in Kandahar...

Six faces flashed up on the screen and the names were read out. 'The dead have been named as; Private Patrick Larkins, Corporal James Miller...'

'Oh Christ, the bastards got to them,' Phoenix said, his huge bulk obscuring Hunter's view. When he moved back, Hunter saw another face on the screen and a sharp pain stabbed his chest.

'The missing soldier has been named as Captain Christian Hunter. He is believed to have been captured by Taliban militia, but as yet no ransom note has been issued.'

'Bullshit!' Phoenix yelled. 'It's a trap. They want us out in the open. This isn't Taliban, its Modjarrad.'

Hunter stared at the ceiling, feeling utterly helpless. Tears formed in his eyes.

'We'll get Lang today,' Phoenix said. 'He'll know what they've done with Chris. We'll get the information even if we have to kill him. Then we find Modjarrad and destroy him.'

'I'm coming with you,' Hunter said. 'He's my brother and I ...'

Phoenix raised his hand. 'I know. When Swain returns we'll get started.'

'Get hold of him Phoenix. Get him back here now.'

Swain returned to the cottage in time to join the debate. They sat around the dining table. Monkton made soup but no one was in the mood to eat. The discussion centred on the events in Afghanistan. Hunter felt on edge, devoid of patience. He wanted to kick off the operation right now, get Lang, and find out what he knew about Christian's capture.

Swain spread a map on the dining table, a diagram of Chiltern Hall and the surrounding area. 'I spoke to a local guy who told me there's a party planned at the manor tonight, a black tie event. It starts at eight and goes on until the early hours, so the chances of us being seen are extremely high if we break in.'

Phoenix said, 'The way I see it, we have two choices. We could try to sneak in through the back door but the problem is we're likely to be seen. We'd have to go in all guns blazing. Our second option is through the front door which means tricking our way in.'

'As guests?' Hunter asked.

'No we haven't got the gear to pull that off. But we do have fake police ID'S.'

Swain grinned. 'Lang won't say no to the police, he'll want to keep things sweet.'

'Great,' Hunter said. 'What about me? I'm not just going to sit here waiting for you guys to get back.'

'It's okay Matthew,' Phoenix said. 'We have clothes and fake ID'S stored right here at the cottage. We prepared a load of stuff for your brother in case he joined us. We can sort you out no problem.'

'Okay, but I want to confront Lang. Chris sent me the photos, and I want to put the screws on the bastard.' Hunter glanced round the table for an objection. There was none.

45

PHOENIX SUGGESTED LEAVING THE house at ten and crashing the party in full-swing. The guests would be merry and less likely to pay attention. Hunter and Swain agreed, but the wait proved intolerable. Hunter paced from room to room, clenching and unclenching his fists, his mind plagued by thoughts of his brother's predicament.

Swain and Turk took turns patrolling outside while Monkton remained glued to the TV. Phoenix sat at the dining table polishing his collection of handguns while Hunter watched with interest.

'Ever used a gun?' Phoenix asked, as he stripped down a Beretta.

Hunter shook his head. 'Never had to.' He pulled up a chair and sat down.

Phoenix put down the automatic and picked up a heavy Magnum revolver which he held up to the light. The barrel gleamed icy black. Hunter noted the look of fondness on that planet sized face, but the big man's expression quickly darkened. 'Understand this Matthew. As yet you've done nothing to upset these people. They don't see you as a threat, an opportunity to get to us maybe, but not a threat. All that changes tonight. Once you step inside this man's lair you'll cross a line from which there'll be no going back. You're going to have to threaten this guy, blackmail him, and probably even rough him up. Can you do that?'

'No problem. He knows where my brother is. I'll kill him if I have to.'

Phoenix smirked. 'Remember we're not talking about any guy off the street. This is Edward Lang, a powerful man and knight of the realm. He has contacts and influence, and could easily destroy us.'

'Okay. I'll be careful, but Lang will tell us everything. I'll make sure of it.'

'You can threaten him, and yes maybe even kill him if necessary, but there are others who'll come after you. Lang has people everywhere.'

'I understand.' Hunter picked up a small automatic, and turned it over in his hands. 'Can you show me how to use one of these?'

'Of course. I insist on it.'

The gun training went on for most of the afternoon, conducted in the dining room and Hunter was still working on his firing stance when it got dark. He rehearsed loading the guns and taking aim, checking his stance in the full-length mirror that Phoenix provided. But handling live rounds would be a different matter, as would killing someone in cold blood.

Phoenix placed a stack of clothes on the table, including the suit originally intended for Christian. There was a wallet on top of the pile. Hunter opened it. The ID read: Detective Inspector Andrew Potter. The photograph was Christian wearing a shirt and tie. *What the hell are you doing Chris?* Even now, after all the explanations Hunter was still confounded by the fact his brother was involved.

The suit was navy, exactly the colour Hunter would have chosen. A morbid feeling passed over him, as if he were about to...

No. He had to believe Chris was alive.

They left the cottage just after ten, all three men suited up for the operation. Hunter put on the blindfold. Phoenix helped him from the front door, down the path to the Lexus. Swain gunned the engine and the car ambled down the dirt track towards the road. Hunter hoped Monkton would cope on his own. Turk was with him, but wasn't a particularly sympathetic guy. None of these men were.

Hunter's thoughts turned to the conflict awaiting him at Chiltern Manor. The plan to get inside was straightforward; the problem was what to do after that. He had to get Lang on his own to question him and that wouldn't be easy. He had the photographs and the negatives were stored safely back at the cottage. That would surely be enough to persuade Lang to cooperate.

He could only hope so.

46

RICHARD MONKTON SAT ALONE in the living room while Turk patrolled outside. Monkton had made careful observations of his captors throughout the day. He knew Turk's routine: twenty minutes checking the area outside, and then back inside for half an hour. Not enough time for Monkton to make a run for it, but he could work out a plan of escape.

Hunter could say what he liked, these people were holding him against his will. Monkton didn't trust their motives. They were deserters and that made them dangerous.

Monkton wandered aimlessly from room to room, thinking through his options. There weren't many. For a start, Turk had the keys to his Jeep. He sloped into the living room and collapsed on the sofa, plucked a worn photograph from his wallet – the one taken only hours before his father Colonel Neil Monkton was killed in battle. Funny thing was, it didn't matter how many times Monkton studied the picture, he just couldn't see the resemblance.

His father was dressed in combat fatigues with a red beret set diagonally across his forehead. He sat on a rock with a machine-gun resting across his knee. The backdrop was bleak, a rocky terrain and dark grey sky. The scrawled handwriting on the back of the photograph read: *Mount Tumbledown, Falkland Islands, May 23rd 1982.*

Richard Monkton was born two weeks later in Hastings hospital. His mother, unable to cope with the loss of her husband, vanished from the ward and abandoned her son. That was the story. Monkton had never met his parents. Robin, his father's brother, had rescued him from the hospital and raised him as a single parent. Now he was dead too.

At school, Monkton had been unpopular, and grew up accustomed to living life on the outskirts of society. His father was very different: a tall, powerfully built man with a strong jaw and commanding presence. He was a leader of men, a Colonel in the Parachute Regiment. 'The genes must have skipped a generation,' his uncle used to say.

Monkton slipped the photo back into his wallet and traipsed through the cottage, gripped with anxiety. Perhaps Turk had hidden his keys somewhere in the house? He searched every room, turning out drawers, and cupboards.

He found his cell phone buried in a bedroom drawer but the SIM card had been removed. No sign of his keys. He checked his watch – 10:30 pm. Turk had been gone fifteen minutes and there wasn't much time.

In the dining room, his gaze settled on the black rod lying on the table. Monkton picked it up and tested the weight in his hands, only three inches in diameter and eighteen inches long, but much heavier than he expected. The butt section was twelve inches of rubber, two buttons set into the top of the handle but no indication of their use.

The top section was metallic black. Monkton noticed a third button on the base of the handle. His finger hovered over it for a second, and then slowly pressed it. The shaft hummed and the rod extended until it reached its full length of about three feet. Monkton studied the tapered shaft and noticed the tip seemed to be carbon fibre.

Into the kitchen to find his keys.

Lying on the work surfaces next to the sink he saw the armlet that Phoenix had worn earlier. He picked it up. The screen was twice the size of a mobile phone display, and beneath it, a simple keypad. The green button seemed simple enough. Monkton pressed it and the screen flickered to life. A message appeared: *Searching for valid signal.* He walked to the front door, opened it an inch and listened out.

Still no sign of Turk.

The urge to test the device was hard to resist. Monkton stepped out into the night air and immediately, the screen beeped and came alive - a simple block graphic similar to an in-car GPS. In the centre of the screen, a green dot pulsed. Underneath the dot was a code: 43/009.

Must be Hunter's signal. But why had it appeared? Phoenix said there were cloaking devices inside both the house and the Lexus. Surely Hunter was still in the car? But if this device could pick up his signal then so could MI5.

Monkton had to warn him.

'What the fuck are you doing?' A voice boomed.

Monkton spun around, the rod gripped tightly in his hand. A hooded figure stood behind him, too close to avoid. The tip of the rod whipped across the man's face.

Oh God, Turk!

Monkton watched in horror as Turk stumbled backwards while raising his gun.

'No, don't shoot!' Not thinking, Monkton pressed a button on the grip handle. The rod fizzed in his hand and a bolt of electricity shot from the tip. The lightening fork zapped Turk in the face and knocked him off his feet. The machine-gun flew from his grasp as he crashed down onto his back.

Monkton stared at the wisps of smoke curling from Turk's blackened face, the man's expression rigid with shock.

Oh God what have I done? Jesus help me.

Hands shaking, Monkton dropped the rod like it was molten metal. He backed away from the smouldering body, tried not to look at the man's face but smelled the burning flesh. Turk had his car keys. Monkton closed his eyes, tried not to breathe as he knelt over the man's body and rifled through his pockets. Eventually he found the keys, jumped up and ran to the Jeep without looking back.

The flashing green dot and reminded him that Matthew Hunter was in trouble. Monkton glanced back at the EPD rod nestling in the gravel. The device was lethal but he might need a weapon if he was going to help his friend. Monkton dashed back, picked up the rod and pressed the top button so the device retracted.

Into the Jeep. The engine coughed and spluttered when he turned the key in the ignition. On the fourth attempt, the motor sparked and a cloud of exhaust fumes filled the air.

Monkton rammed into gear and set off down the track, turning left onto the road. The screen cast an eerie glow as the flashing green dot moved across the display. *Strange…* it hadn't moved before. Monkton took a left at the next junction signposted for 'Tenterden.'

At the same time, the dot also changed direction. It seemed to follow him.

Monkton tapped the buttons on the keypad as tried to make sense of it, but his eyes strayed for too long and suddenly the Jeep veered off the road and bounced onto the grass verge. Monkton bounced in his seat as he struggled to regain control. He swerved back across the road, brushed up against the hedgerow, and narrowly avoided a telephone pole before he finally brought the car to a stop.

'For god's sake!' He closed his eyes and gripped the wheel as he took a moment to calm himself. After a few moments, he checked the screen again.

The green dot was now static.

Where are you Matthew? What are you doing?

Then the truth dawned. No, it can't be...

He reached to the back of his head, and ran his finger over the bone at the top of his spine. His fingers moved up to the nape into his hairline. There it was - the tiny lump that had been hidden under his skin since he was a kid. He had always thought of it a simple blemish.

Monkton started the Jeep and pulled away. The green dot mirrored his movements, and he knew the truth.

47

CHILTERN MANOR WAS SITUATED in countryside a mile outside
Tenterden. The house was a beacon, illuminated by dozens of spotlights
buried in the surrounding lawns. Swain pulled up outside the main gates and
a uniformed attendant approached the passenger side.

Phoenix lowered his window. 'Good evening, we're here to see Sir
Edward.'

'Your invitations please sir?'

Phoenix grinned and slipped a couple of neatly folded notes through the
window. The guy snatched the money and buried it in his back pocket but
still refused to budge. 'I still need to see some ID sir. You could be terrorists
for all I know.'

'Indeed.' Phoenix pulled out the fake police ID from his jacket.

The attendant paled and turned to his colleague. 'Okay Howard. Let them
through.'

Howard, a drippy-looking kid wearing an oversized jacket, pressed a
button on his remote control and the gates opened in a smooth arc. The tyres
of the Lexus crunched on the gravel as Swain snaked up the drive towards
the house. Hunter felt his stomach knot as they approached the grand
entrance. A rivulet of sweat ran down his cheek and he became nauseas at the
thought of confronting Lang. He stared out at the neat lawns and rows of
prestige cars parked on the grass: Rollers, Mercs and Limousines.

Lang certainly had enormous wealth and a network of powerful friends.
Hunter just prayed he would keep his nerve and see this thing through.

 Swain parked in front of the broad steps leading up to the mansion
entrance. At the door, a posse of uniformed girls greeted guests as they
arrived. Phoenix opened the passenger door and told Swain to keep the
engine running.

'We won't be long Tom. Make sure you're ready to go when we return.'

Hunter and Phoenix climbed out of the car and mounted the steps where
they mingled with the crowd. The air bristled with animated chatter and Jazz

music blared from somewhere inside the house. Hunter marvelled at the expensive clothes and jewellry around him and felt totally out of place in his 'job interview' suit. He breathed in the smell of expensive fragrances, wondering what it must be like to afford such things.

A girl with red fly-away hair asked for their invitations. Hunter showed his fake ID. 'We're on official police business. We need to see Sir Edward urgently.' Hunter spoke authoritatively but the girl seemed unimpressed.

'Sir Edward is entertaining,' she replied. 'I'm afraid you'll have to call back another time and make an appointment.'

Hunter tried reasoning with her but she wouldn't concede. He was about to push his way past when a voice spoke behind him.

'Is there a problem sir?' The voice had a feminine quality, and yet belonged to a stout middle-aged guy with greased-back hair, dressed in a tuxedo.

Phoenix answered. 'There's no problem Mr....?'

'Farrington. I'm overseeing the guest list.'

'Mr. Farrington, we're on police business and need to speak to Sir Edward in private. We only need five minutes of his time.'

'Please understand gentlemen, Sir Edward has important guests inside, this is quite impossible.'

Phoenix bore down on the man. 'I can assure you, we won't be long.'

Farrington coughed nervously and told the girl to let them through. 'It's alright Tiffany, I'll inform Sir Edward these men are here.'

Hunter didn't wait to be shown inside. He weaved through the bodies and barged into the lobby where women in ball-gowns handed expensive coats to young attendants and men in dinner jackets lit cigars. Hunter strode across to the white doors at the far end.

Phoenix grabbed his arm. 'I'll wait here and keep Farrington at bay while you locate Lang. Have you got the photographs?'

Hunter nodded.

'Good. Get him on his own, and remember if you have to squeeze him, squeeze him hard. Rich fuckers like him don't buckle easily. Take this if he needs persuading.' Phoenix furtively passed him a Beretta and Hunter slipped into his jacket pocket.

'Hurry Matthew, and remember you're still being tracked.'

The doors were opened by a man in a white tuxedo. Hunter walked into a wall of noise, blaring trumpets and crashing drums. He pushed through the dinner jackets and glittering gowns, searching for Sir Edward Lang. A middle-aged woman draped in diamonds, eyed him curiously over a cocktail glass. She raised her voice as he walked past. 'Lost someone?'

Hunter glanced at her and sidled up close to make himself heard. 'I'm looking for the host.'

'Eddie?' The woman swirled an olive in her glass. 'The old devil's probably chatting up the waitresses, perhaps even the waiters, you never can tell with that one.' She smiled and brought the olive seductively to her lips.

'You couldn't point to him could you?'

She flicked a lock of hair over her shoulder and pointed a long finger across the room. 'The boys were in deep conversation when I saw them last. They're over there by the painting.' She sounded bored but her eyes remained fixed on his.

Hunter glanced at the giant painting of a cavalier mounted on the far wall. He thanked her and loosened his tie as he slipped back into the crowd. He spotted a group of men sharing a joke, one of whom fitted Lang's description – stocky, and a bald head dotted with liver spots.

One of the toffs in the group saw Hunter and gave the bald guy a nudge. When the man turned around, Hunter immediately recognized the small eyes set in the pale, pudgy face: Sir Edward Lang; media mogul and the creep in the photographs.

Lang detached himself from his conversation and stormed up to Hunter with a murderous expression. 'What the bloody hell are you doing here Hunter?'

Hunter was thrown by the outburst. *How does he know who I am?* He tried to keep his nerve. 'I need a word in private.'

Lang grabbed his arm. 'Have you any idea how dangerous it is for you to be here? You're putting us both at risk.'

Hunter shrugged. 'This won't wait.'

'For Christ's sake man, it had better be good. Follow me. We'll talk in the study.'

Lang swaggered out into a plush corridor, obviously the worse for wear. At the top of the passage he stopped at a door and groped through his keys.

'Allow me.' Hunter said, snatching them from him. He found the right key, unlocked the door and ushered Lang inside.

'Who the fuck do you think you are? Barging into my home like this and throwing your weight about.' Lang staggered to his desk and poured himself a brandy from a glass decanter. 'Sit yourself down then man.'

Hunter pulled up a chair on the opposite side of the desk.

Lang slugged his drink and slammed the glass on the table. 'Right, you've got two minutes. Make it quick.'

Hunter felt himself tremble as he stared at the arrogant overfed face of Sir Edward Lang and when he spoke, his voice quivered with emotion. 'What happened to my brother?

Lang made an exaggerated gesture of surprise, jutted his chin and his mouth dropped open. 'What? Have you gone mad? What sort of question is that?'

'And the chimeras. Where are they? I know they've been moved. I want to know where Christian is, the whereabouts of the new Zarcom laboratories, and the girl you've taken hostage.'

Lang's brow furrowed as he squinted across the desk. 'You've got to be bloody joking.' He reached into a drawer, pulled out a gun and aimed it across the table. 'You're him. The twin brother. The fucking journalist. I knew you were trouble, and now you're a dead man.'

Lang's aggression only galvanized Hunter's resolve. 'You're not going to shoot me Edward. You're up to your neck in this. Innocent people have been killed and more will die unless Zarcom is stopped. I'm going to offer you a way out. Now, tell me where the new site is.'

'I'll tell you nothing. You're a worm, and a dead one at that.'

Hunter pulled a scroll of paper from his breast pocket and tossed it across the desk. 'That's the entire list of investors, every businessman and government official who has a stake in Zarcom. As you can see your name is right at the top. They are all going down Edward and so are you.'

Lang scanned the page, his expression wilted, and the gun dropped onto the desk from his limp hand. 'I might not kill you,' he said raising his eyes, 'but others will. You know I won't tell you anything. You're wasting your time.'

Hunter rested back in his seat and this time pulled out the envelope containing the lewd photographs from his jacket. 'Discretion is an important consideration for a man in your position Edward. I can be discreet... or not, as the situation demands.' He spread the snapshots on the desk so they faced Lang. 'As you can see, I know about your weakness for the exotic.'

Lang recoiled from the images, eyes bulging with shock. 'You're trying to blackmail me? *Me!*'

'You have a wife and three daughters. I doubt your family would survive the scandal and you certainly won't.'

'Fuck you.'

'Wrong answer Eddie.'

Lang's face bloomed scarlet; the veins in his neck grew fat like slugs. He poured another drink and knocked it back. 'I'll watch them tear you to pieces. You'll rot in your own stink you bastard. Where did you get these?'

Hunter smiled. 'Calm down. You can keep the photos. I still have the negatives of course but hopefully I won't need to use them.'

Lang pulled a handkerchief from his top pocket and wiped his forehead. 'Modjarrad will have both of us killed.'

'We can deal with him. Just tell me where the new site is.'

Lang's expression sagged like a lost child searching for a way out, but Hunter wouldn't let him off the hook.

'I need an answer Edward.'

'Sir Edward to you!' Lang wiped his brow once more. 'Modjarrad has the girl. If I give him to you, do you swear you have the resources to deal with him? Because if you don't; he will kill you, your brother, me and every member of my family. Do you understand?'

'We can finish him. Now get on with it, there isn't much time.'

Lang stood up and walked to the unit behind him, opened a door to reveal a small safe set in the wall. He unlocked it and pulled out a thick file which he tossed onto the desk. 'There you are, now piss off.'

Hunter picked up the file along with Lang's revolver. 'Not that I don't trust a knight of the realm, but I just need to check.'

He leafed through the papers and discovered several maps as well as plans for a twin level construction, seemingly built underground. Hunter unfolded a smaller map which showed the exact location of the facility. As he'd suspected the site was right here in Kent. He snatched up a pen and a clean sheet of paper from Lang's desktop and drew a rough copy. 'This had better be Kosher, Edward.'

'Of course it is. The complex is beneath an old dockyard. There's nothing around for miles, just fields and sea. You've got what you came for, now get out.'

Hunter finished sketching the map. Now, if Phoenix decided to ditch him, he could go it alone. He folded the sheet, slid it into his back pocket, and scooped up the rest of the documents. 'Before I leave, I need to know about my brother.'

'What about him?'

'Don't fuck me about. What has Modjarrad done with him?'

Lang's face twitched into a half smile. 'I'm afraid you'll have to talk to the Taliban about that.'

'You're lying.'

'It's true. Your brother's in the hands of local militia in Afghanistan. Nothing I can do about that now is there?'

Hunter should have felt exhilarated. But Christian's predicament was worse than he had imagined. How the hell was he going to help him now?

Back in the lobby he saw Phoenix engaged in a heated debate with Farrington.

'There you go. Job done,' Phoenix said, leaning into Farrington's face. He turned to Hunter. 'Everything cool?'

'Yeah. Let's go.'

'Wait.' Phoenix put a hand across Hunter's chest as he headed for the door. 'Did you get a map?'

Hunter pulled the file from his jacket and handed it over.

'Excellent.'

They hurried down the steps to the waiting Lexus and jumped in. Swain toed the accelerator, and the tyres churned up the gravel as he sped towards the gates.

Phoenix glanced over his shoulder. 'Don't bother with the mask Matthew, you're one of us now.'

The gates opened and the Lexus skidded out onto the road. Hunter couldn't help think about his brother. He told Phoenix what Lang had said about Christian being taken by the Taliban. Phoenix slammed his hand on the dash and the car fell silent. Hunter stared out through the window. The road signs indicated they were heading along the A28 towards Ashford. Suddenly the car interior illuminated, and a car closed in behind them.

Swain cursed at the rear view. 'Turn your beams off will ya? Jesus.'

Hunter twisted round to take a look.

'Keep down,' Phoenix yelled. He turned to Swain. 'Take the next turn, see if they follow.'

Swain picked up speed but the tail stayed with them. The American took a sharp right. Darkness returned inside the car but seconds later their tail closed up again.

'Shit!' Swain yelled. 'There's another car dead ahead. It's gonna get rough guys, strap yourselves in.' The American turned down a tight lane and crashed through a wooden gate into a field. Hunter gripped his stomach as he jolted in his seat.

Phoenix leaned back, and passed Hunter a gun. 'Don't shoot until we're out and clear of the car. Tom's gonna slow up in a second. Follow my lead and bail out of the left side door. Roll as soon as you hit the dirt and shoot at the lights. Understood?'

A bullet slammed into the boot of the car. A second shattered the window behind Hunter's head and lodged in Swain's headrest, ripping out the stuffing.

'Jesus!' Hunter cried.

'I'm okay,' Swain replied. He killed the lights and hit the brakes. A blast of cold air rushed in as Phoenix kicked opened his door and jumped out. Hunter grimaced and dived out after him; hit the wet earth with a thud, plastering his face and hands with mud.

Swain revved and skidded away, the wheels spewing clumps of grass. The chasing cars closed in, their beams flashed through the darkness. Hunter fumbled with the safety catch while Phoenix stood up and let rip with the assault rifle. Tracers zipped through the night air and ripped into the lead car. Hunter, flat on his stomach, watched the vehicle burst into flames and crash into a fence at the bottom of the field. Phoenix fired at the second car while Swain weaved figure of eights to shake it off.

Hunter neither heard nor saw the incoming fire, but saw the line of holes that appeared in Phoenix's chest. The big man jerked like he'd been zapped with a tazer, stiffened and fell onto his back.

Machine gun fire sparkled from the windows of the chasing car, sparks flashed off the Lexus as the bullets grazed the bodywork. Swain seemed to lose control and the car vanished into a cluster of trees. Hunter heard the crash, saw the pursuing vehicle behind pull up and three men jump out.

Hunter leaned his face into the mud and cursed. *What now?* He heard the drone of another car, glanced up to his left and saw a set of headlights bounce across the field towards him. There was something familiar about the chugging engine. Hunter prayed for a miracle. The Jeep closed in, slowed up next to him, and the door sprang open.

'Get in,' Monkton yelled.

'Richard! Thank Christ.' Hunter grappled the frame of the door and clambered aboard as the vehicle moved off. As he slipped into his seat, he heard gunfire in field behind.

A bloody execution, Hunter thought. Swain wasn't going to make it out of there alive.

Monkton steered through the smashed gate, back onto the road. 'Thank god I found you,' he said.

Hunter felt a hard object against his leg, looked into the foot-well and saw the Electric Pulse Distributor rod. He noticed Monkton was wearing the armlet. 'What do you need that thing for Richard?' Then he saw the green dot pulsing on the screen. 'Christ, is that how you found me?'

'Sorry Matt... at least the thing works.'

'Great.' As if he needed reminding. 'But why did you leave the hideout?'

'After you left, I overheard a conversation... who's the guy with the beard?'

'Turk?'

'That's him. I went upstairs to use the toilet and overheard him talking on the phone, saying something about needing your signal to guide the creatures to a populated area. It seems your rebel friends are no more than terrorists.'

'That can't be right Richard. You've it wrong.'

'Have I? Imagine what it must be like for these people. No family. No future. Society has shunned them, turned them into freaks, and they're probably angry how they've been treated. Didn't you sense the resentment, the anger? Especially Nina. Their plan was to use you to lure the chimeras to a public place and cause maximum damage.'

Hunter was unconvinced. 'Are you sure you heard it right?'

'I admit I didn't hear everything. When Turk was distracted, I managed to sneak up on him and knock him out with that baton down by your feet. That's what gave me the idea to use it to find you. As I said, thank God it works.'

48

MONKTON RACED ALONG THE country lanes to Ashford, ten miles west of Tenterden. When they arrived the streets were deserted and the town eerily quiet. Monkton pulled into an empty retail park so they could plan their next move.

'I've got the location of the new Zarcom facility,' Hunter said. 'It's only a rough map but its good enough.' He pulled the map from his back pocket and flattened it on the dashboard. 'The facility is hidden underground near this thin strip of waterway on the east coast. The guy who gave me the map said it was a derelict wharf.'

Monkton glanced down at the map. 'I know it.' He jabbed his finger at the map. 'The island just off the mainland looks like the Isle of Sheppey. If I'm reading your diagram right, then this cluster of buildings on the mainland represents the Zarcom facility, and just here, further to the right is the Sheppey Bridge.'

'So how far from here?'

'By car - forty minutes.'

They waited until first light before continuing their journey. Monkton drove north along the M20 to junction 7 and took the A249 towards the Isle of Sheppey, about 8 miles east. Just before the bridge he veered left onto a narrow road flanked by overhanging trees.

'There's only one entrance,' Hunter said, 'according to the map you should be able to see a fence on your side about now.'

Monkton slowed the Jeep and stared out into the woodland. 'Nope. Nothing but trees, see for yourself.'

Hunter leaned across and peered out but couldn't see beyond the first line of trees. They continued at a crawl but after a mile, the road finished at a dead end.

'Shit I hope we've got this right.' Hunter took a moment to scrutinize the map. 'It has to be back there somewhere Richard. We'll have to try again.'

It proved tricky maneuvering in the tight space but Monkton eventually managed it. They retraced the route, scouring the woodland for an opening. Hunter glanced down at the verge.

Of course. How could he have missed it? The soil at the roadside was mashed with tyre tracks.

He told Monkton to stop the Jeep and got out to make a closer inspection. The tracks appeared recent, and snaked along both sides of the road, broad imprints made by heavy vehicles. He tried to imagine the scene; dozens of lorries rumbling through the narrow thoroughfare. They probably arrived from Devon overnight at staggered intervals. There were spy satellites to consider, cameras on the roads, and eye witnesses.

The road widened, and Monkton parked on the verge. Hunter approached the driver's window. 'Stay here Richard. I'm going back to see if these tracks lead anywhere. Give me an hour and if I don't show, alert the authorities.'

Monkton bit his lip. 'I'd rather come with you.'

'No. I might need a quick getaway and no offence but this isn't your scene.'

'It isn't yours either.'

Hunter smiled. Monkton was wrong. If this wasn't his scene, why did he feel so exhilarated? He fingered the outline of the gun buried in the breast pocket of his crumpled suit. The weight and power of the weapon made him feel invincible, as if something inside him – something dark – was itching to be unleashed. He was here to sort out business and intended to see it through.

'One hour,' Hunter said. He doubled-back and it wasn't long before he noticed the tracks arc across the road and vanish into the bushes to his right. The road was quiet and they hadn't encountered a single vehicle, yet here was a lattice of tracks disappearing into the trees.

He peered into the tangled barrier of twigs and vines searching for evidence of an entry point. His eyes rested upon a rusty object ten yards behind the screen of foliage. *A gate?* Hunter scooped armfuls of loose vegetation aside to make a path - none of it was rooted. He pushed through and reached a set of iron gates flanked by a crumbling stone wall about seven feet high. If this was Zarcom's facility, there would be security and surveillance beyond this gate. Not that it mattered; they probably knew he was here anyway.

Hunter stooped to examine the padlock, tugged at the chain, and it came free in his hand. The links had been severed and the chain twisted loosely around the bars to make out it was still intact. Undeterred, Hunter shoved the gate and stepped through. He hesitated and scanned the trees for cameras or other surveillance equipment, but saw nothing. Carefully, he trampled across the carpet of foliage. Small animals scurried in the undergrowth and water droplets fell from the canopy splattering the leaves below.

Hunter stumbled out of the trees where a ten foot wire-mesh fence blocked his path. He smelled a faint whiff of the sea and on the other side of the fence saw an expanse of wasteland strewn with rubble. About a hundred yards in, a ramshackle roof nestled in a deep hollow, the walls of the building partly obscured from sight.

No sign of activity. Maybe Lang had tricked him?

Surely he wasn't that stupid? Hunter had negatives of the photographs and could easily expose the slimy bastard…. unless of course, Lang didn't expect him to get this far. Not after the attack last night.

Hunter checked his watch – 7:05. Twenty minutes since he'd left Monkton.

Got to push on.

He skirted the fence, staying back behind the tree line. The dew-soaked ferns dampened his shoes and trousers. Thirty yards further on, he noticed a kink in the fence. No, not a kink - a break in the wire. The mesh had been cut, and pulled back to allow a channel big enough for a man to slide under. *First the gate and now this.*

Hunter considered turning back and contacting the authorities. But who could he trust? *No one.* Besides, if it all went pear shaped, Monkton would call the police. He wriggled under the gap and headed across the wasteland, keeping low. His progress went unchallenged and he reached a clump of bushes about twenty yards from the building. The structure looked like an old warehouse, black walls coated with grime, all the windows smashed. The place exuded decay.

On the far side of the building, the land dipped towards the Swale shoreline about five hundred yards away. The water glinted and rippled in the pale light and Hunter saw a small ferryboat alongside a jetty. He shuddered, and his mind crawled with images of what might lurk beneath his feet, deep underground. He pulled the gun from his jacket, held it double-handed, just as Phoenix had shown him, and edged out from the bushes.

Out in the open, Hunter felt vulnerable and exposed. He sprinted across the cratered earth, tripped and sprawled into the mud. The gun slipped from his grasp and landed with a clunk amongst a pile of broken bricks.

For Christ's sake!

Lying prostrate, he reached out and grabbed the gun, remaining motionless while collected himself. His heartbeat thudded in his head and blood charged through his veins in a torrent. The murmur of voices drifted across the wasteland, seeming to come from inside the warehouse. Hunter got to his feet and brushed himself down, glanced back at the ground where he'd tripped, and his eyes widened as they focused on the contorted knot of broken limbs lying amongst the weeds.

The guard lay on his back, staring at the sky, a deep gash across his throat. Hunter recognized the black uniform and the letter 'Z' embroidered on the breast pocket - Zarcom. His mind reeled as he tried to imagine himself slitting a man's throat in cold blood. *Who could have done this?*

Hunter ran to the building and threw himself against the wall, sucked in deep breaths, and then slid along its length, avoiding the debris underfoot, broken bricks and shards of glass. He reached the corner and heard voices filter through the broken windows above. An engine started up, the throaty murmur of a heavy vehicle. Hunter peered round the corner and saw a lorry rumble along the narrow track that curved down towards the water.

Chains clinked and a metal shutter clattered shut. Hunter rounded the wall and sprinted for the shutter before it closed. 'Hey wait!'

The door halted three feet from the ground and a head appeared under the gap. Hunter threw himself to the dirt and in one movement swung his boot into the man's face, lost his grip on the gun, and rolled under as the shutter crashed down.

Hunter sprang to his feet inside the warehouse and was confronted by a guy in a butcher apron, sporting a tattoo on his left cheek and wielding a meat hook in his right hand. Behind him, the fat guy Hunter had booted in the face, lumbered towards a loading dock. Hunter dodged Face Tattoo and went for the runner, caught up with the fat guy and dived at his legs. Both men rolled to the ground but Hunter got up quickly and aimed a kick at his head.

As he squared up, a stinging pain stabbed into his shoulder. Hunter whirled round as Face Tattoo swung the hook again. He ducked and the hook arced over his head, missing him by an inch. Hunter straightened, and countered with a punch to the man's stomach followed by a powerful uppercut that sent him stumbling onto his back.

Meanwhile, Fat Guy was back on his feet, running up to the loading dock - a concrete platform with two goods lifts that provided access underground. Lined up along the bottom of the platform were around thirty cages stacked with pig carcasses.

Hunter picked up the meat hook but Fat Guy had already dived into one of the lifts and was closing the concertina gate behind him. In desperation, Hunter threw the hook and the projectile clanged against the gate. Fat Guy jumped back with surprise, hit the buttons but the gate wasn't fully closed and the lift didn't budge.

Hunter leapt onto the dock, ripped the gate open and dragged Fat Guy out of the lift. The man raised his hands and began pleading his innocence.

Hunter raised his fist. 'Quiet. You're going to take me on a little tour of the site. Understood?'

A submissive nod. But if Hunter was going to make it any further he needed his gun. He picked up the hook and ordered Fat Guy back to the shutter. As they crossed the warehouse Hunter sensed someone behind him. He spun, just as the tattooed man lunged at him, fists raised. Hunter saw the aggression on the man's face change to one of shock. Eyes wide, he stumbled and fell to the ground. Planted between the man's shoulder blades was a hole, oozing blood.

A voice called out to him. 'Looks like I saved your sorry ass again. How the fuck did you get here Hunter? '

Tom Swain emerged from behind the cages of meat, an Uzi slung over his left shoulder and a silenced pistol in his right hand. Like Hunter, he was still wearing yesterdays clothes.

'Jesus Tom. I thought you were dead.'

'You assumed. Never assume. I bailed out of the car before it hit the trees and managed to salvage these.' Swain pulled a sheaf of papers from his jacket, the plans of the Zarcom facility.

Hunter stared in disbelief. 'But how the hell did you escape?'

'I laid low in the dirt and when those fuckers gathered round to watch the Lexus burn, I took 'em out one by one. Pop, pop, pop.' Swain made a shooting motion with his gun. 'I took their car and drove straight over here. Nice motor too. A black 4X4.'

'What about Phoenix?'

'He didn't make it.' Swain's expression remained impassive. 'My guess is Lang pressed the panic button and got Modjarrad's guys to come after us. It was too clumsy for MI5. What about you? How did you get over here?'

Hunter hesitated. He couldn't tell Swain about Monkton and what happened to Turk, at least not yet. He had to invent something. 'When I saw those bastards shooting at the Lexus I ran back to the road and flagged down a passing car. I made a rough copy of the map back at Lang's place, so I hitched as far as I could and walked the rest.'

Swain frowned. 'So you ran away? No wonder I couldn't find you. I was driving around that field for ages. I suppose I can't blame you. At least you made it over here.'

Hunter quickly changed the subject. 'I take it you killed the guard outside?'

'You saw that one huh? I hid the other three around the perimeter but didn't have time to cover up the last one. I had to sneak in here quick while they were making the meat delivery.'

Swain's shirt and hands were smeared with blood, and Hunter knew he was telling the truth. He was relieved to have the American on board, even if he didn't know his true motives.

49

MONKTON SAT IN THE Jeep staring at the green dot flashing on his forearm, wondering if he was wrong about the signal. There might be another explanation, although he couldn't think of one. The evidence was pretty conclusive. Somewhere beneath the tiny lump on the back of his neck was a microchip buried in his flesh.

It was him all right.

He tapped the buttons beneath the screen, pressing each one in turn. The blue button enlarged the map. With each tap it increased from a two mile radius to five, ten, and then twenty miles, but the terrain became more indistinct. The green button zoomed back in and the black button appeared to do nothing. When he pressed the yellow button however, two specks appeared on screen: red triangles heading north along the banks of the Swale, no more than 500 yards from his position.

No. It can't be.

Monkton started the Jeep and drove with one eye on the shifting triangles. Their movement was sporadic, speeding up, slowing down and stopping before moving off again. He parked the Jeep at the roadside, grabbed the EPD rod and followed the signal on foot. Branches clawed at him as ventured into the trees, snagging his clothes and scratching his hands and face. Twenty yards into the woods he saw a channel where the vegetation had been pushed aside. The creatures had made no attempt to smudge their tracks, the prints were clearly identifiable. They weren't hunting this time… this was something else.

Monkton followed the trail to a high wire fence crowned with coils of razor-wire. One of the sections had been flattened, the poles and concrete bases ripped out of the ground. Monkton extended the EPD rod to its full length and trampled across the broken fence onto the wasteland. When he checked the screen again, the triangles had vanished.

A hundred yards to his right, the Swale oozed past the mud flats. Further up the river he saw a dock, and a couple of rundown buildings. Beyond, partially obscured from view, was a jetty that extended twenty yards out into the water and moored alongside, a small ferry.

Up on the hill to his left, Monkton saw another ramshackle building, and a dirt track leading to the dockside. A white truck came into view, heading down towards the wharf. Monkton stayed low as it drove onto the jetty and boarded the awaiting ferry. The ferry cast off into the main flow and floated upriver.

Monkton skulked down towards the shoreline but the ground was cratered and slowed his progress. He scrambled to the top of river bank and walked north along the shoreline. The chimera tracks were easy to follow sunk several inches deep into the mud. Fifty yards along, the trail diverted down the embankment and vanished into the water.

Monkton had not considered this. The sludge was churned and punctured with prints up to a foot deep, but no sign of the creatures.

The water. They're using the water.

He started across the open landscape. The first building he came to was a large wooden boat house, the exterior rotten and shot with holes. As he got closer, Monkton glimpsed through the cracks in the panels and saw inside. An old fishing boat lay on its side in the centre of the building, surrounded by mounds of junk. The floor was covered with rusty old machinery and smashed up hardcore.

There was a hole at the base of the wall, big enough for a man to crawl under. The ground had been dug away and the markings seemed recent. The soil was wet and there was a faint smell in the air… rancid decay.

A chimera would be far too big to squeeze through a gap that small… wouldn't it?

Monkton returned to the shoreline and found the trail where the creatures had dragged themselves out of the water. Wooden stilts protruded at the waters edge, and the mud around them was scored with tracks. He followed the trail back to the hole in the boat shed.

If the chimeras were able to squeeze through such a tight space then they must be able to elongate their skeletal structure like a rodent or a cat. But this wasn't the only revelation regarding their behaviour. Up to now, the beasts had demonstrated a complete lack of fear. They were audacious to the point of self destruction. But these two animals demonstrated an acute awareness of danger and had employed stealth tactics to sneak across the wasteland unseen, using the water when there was nowhere to hide.

Monkton pushed a button on the grip handle and the EPD rod collapsed to its regular length. He took a deep breath and got on his hands and knees. He had to find out what these creatures were up to. Slowly he crawled under the gap and into the building.

50

HUNTER RAMMED THE BERETTA into Fat Guy's neck. 'You can start by telling us your name.'

'I'll help you. I promise I'll help you.'

Hunter grabbed his collar and pressed the gun harder under his chin.

'Your name?'

'A... Alfred. Please, you're hurting me.'

Hunter relaxed. 'Good. Alfred, where do those lifts lead to?'

'I'll show you.'

'Just tell me.'

'But... but then you'll kill me.'

'Not if you cooperate. Where do they go?'

'Down two levels. Sub-level 1 is where the labs are located. Then sub-level 2 is where...'

'Where the creatures are?'

Alfred nodded.

Swain stepped forward. 'What about security?'

'The corridors on both levels are sectioned off at intervals by steel doors. Guards are stationed at each door. If you let me, I can help you get right inside.'

'Where would they hold someone prisoner?'

'I don't know. I just take in the meat deliveries and send it down to feed the animals.'

'Wrong answer.' Swain leveled the Uzi at Alfred's chest.

'No! Don't shoot. Tell me who you're looking for.'

'A woman,' Hunter said, 'late twenties, dark hair. She probably turned up here a couple of days ago.'

Alfred wiped his sleeve across his forehead. 'I can show you where they might keep her.'

Hunter felt uneasy about taking the man along, but realized they might need him. He glanced at Swain. 'What do the drawings tell us?'

'There's nothing identified as a cell, I already checked. Sub-level 1 is the smaller of the two levels, a network of labs and offices.' Swain unfolded a cross-sectioned diagram and spread it against the wall. 'The lower level has half a dozen intersecting corridors, all connected to this massive room at the far end. It seems more like a cave, maybe eight hundred feet long and over a hundred feet high.'

'Shit. That must be where the chimeras are.'

'It is,' Alfred said. 'There are secure rooms down there used for storage. They would be ideal for keeping someone locked up.'

Swain was still engrossed in the map. Hunter glanced at him and said, 'What about a way in?'

'The lifts are the obvious route. There's also a sloping shaft that leads from the chimera enclosure right up to the surface.'

'That's sounds too dangerous.'

'Agreed. There are a number of ducts and effluent pipes leading out of the complex, but we don't have the time or equipment to attempt that option. The lifts are our best bet. Besides we've got our friend here. I'm sure he'll help us.'

Hunter looked down at the body of the man with a face tattoo. 'Okay, but first one of us is going to have to wear this guy's apron. We can't both go down there dressed in our filthy suits.'

'Be my guest,' Swain said.

Hunter took off his jacket, removed the dead man's soiled apron and put it on. He pointed his gun at Alfred. 'From now on, I'm your new workmate.'

Alfred nodded, and Swain shoved him towards the loading dock. They entered one of the lifts; Hunter closed the gate, and pushed the button for sub-level 2. The car rattled and groaned as it descended. Hunter tensed. There was no telling what awaited them at the bottom.

The lift shuddered to a halt and he slid the shutter across, jabbed his gun into Alfred's ribs, and pushed him into the corridor. The passage was clear, but the stench was overpowering. *Chimeras.*

'This way,' Alfred said pointing left. The corridor was damp and dimly lit, a concrete floor with stone walls and an arched ceiling supported by steel struts. They walked twenty yards, and the passageway dog-legged to the right. Moments later they reached a large steel door. Alfred stopped and whispered to Hunter. 'Tell the Yank to stay out of sight. I can explain your presence but not his.'

Hunter nodded, slipped the gun into the back of his trouser belt, and turned to Swain.

'Yeah, I heard,' Swain said. 'I'll wait back here. If he fucks up I'll be right behind you.' The American stepped back into the shadows.

'I'll pretend you're one of the delivery guys,' Alfred said. 'Leave it to me.'

'You know I'll kill you if you try anything?'

Alfred laughed nervously. 'I know I know. You just want to find your girlfriend.'

They approached the door and Alfred hammered on it with his fist. A spy-hole set at eye level slid open. 'What?' a voice said sharply.

'It's me - Alfred. Stellios asked me to come down and collect some cash. We need extra meat and I have to pay the driver.'

Dark eyes fixed Hunter suspiciously through the hole. 'The first I've heard of it. Let me see your hands, both of you.'

Hunter raised his palms.

'Okay, step inside while I check it out.'

A clunk of metal and the door creaked open. Hunter pushed past Alfred and stepped through first. The guard stood back and aimed a gun at Hunter's head. A second guard stood in the doorway of a small office smoking a cigarette, machine-gun slung casually over his shoulder.

The first guard ordered them to stand up against the wall and called over his shoulder. 'Nick, get Stellios on the phone. Ask him about the extra delivery.'

Nick tutted, squashed his cigarette under his heel and disappeared into the office. Hunter kept half an eye on Alfred, expecting him to blow their cover at any minute. He needed Swain to make his move. The steel door was ajar about ten inches. He glanced through the gap and saw Swain edge along the wall. The American put a finger to his lips.

Alfred fidgeted. *Don't say a word*, Hunter thought. He leaned against the wall, and the gun tucked in his trouser belt pressed against his spine. His fingers moved slowly over the grip handle. He was about to make his move when a searing pain shot through his head.

'Jesus!' Hunter crumpled to his knees clutching the sides of his head. Just like the incident at Tunbridge Wells, the implant was burning a hole into his skull.

'Kill him!' Alfred yelled. 'There are two of them, they've got guns. Kill them both.'

Hunter cowered as the first guard took aim, but there was no shot. The pain began to subside. He looked up, saw the guard stumble backward, blood streaming from his face and a knife buried to the hilt in the man's left eye. The good eye stared back in shock, and a deep gurgle emerged from his open mouth.

Swain ghosted in, aimed the Uzi at the second guard as he emerged from the office. A double-tap and two bloody holes appeared in the man's face, one in the forehead, the second through the throat. The guard crumpled in the doorway.

Hunter got to his feet and grabbed Alfred. 'You little shit. You thought you could...'

Swain pushed Hunter aside, raised the Uzi and put a diagonal line of holes across Alfred's chest, dropping him on the spot.

'Christ Tom! We needed him to show us the way.'

Swain picked up one of the Uzis and passed it to Hunter. 'In future Matt, don't stand there talking about it, just drop the fuckers, otherwise you'll be the one who winds up dead. Take advice from someone who knows.' He gave Hunter a slap on the back. 'Come on, let's finish this thing.'

'Wait,' Hunter pulled him back. 'We'll need their uniforms.'

51

HOWARD GRANT, HEAD OF Zarcom's science team, questioned the wisdom of Modjarrad's future plans for the project. Grant's involvement had never been about money but about proving the doubters wrong. His team had achieved the impossible, merged DNA from different species and created a new animal. The building blocks of life had proved to be nothing more than a puzzle that could be pulled apart and reconstructed. The difficult part was nurturing the animals beyond infancy. If a creature lived six months then its chances of survival improved dramatically. Once they produced a healthy batch of young chimeras, the scientists used cloning techniques to copy the blueprint again and again.

But they hadn't considered the consequences. The creatures were cunning and destructive. People had been killed and the British government wanted the project shelved and all evidence of it destroyed.

So now Modjarrad wanted to sell the technology to another nation. For Grant and the rest of his team, that meant a lifetime working in a bunker in some foreign country. That, or prison. Modjarrad and his backers had committed treason to safeguard their investments and Grant knew the billionaire had made contact with the Russians and Chinese. Several Arab states had also showed an interest.

He had to put a stop to it.

Grant gazed through the window of the control room. From this level, he had a birds-eye view of the chimera enclosure, nearly a hundred feet below. The enclosure was a natural cave, bolstered with steel pylons. The creatures were caged inside a huge corral, packed in tight and they had started scratching and biting one another with increasing regularity. The walls echoed to the howls of these soulless creatures as they lamented their captivity.

Grant felt disgusted with himself. Professional vanity had got the better of him. Having successfully proven what his team could do, now it all seemed like a terrible mistake. These animals should not exist - he had to destroy them.

He glanced around the control room. Four men and two women, hunched over their monitors, dissected information coming back from the chimera corral. Along the back wall, a bank of security monitors dominated that side of the room. Chief of security, Lance Murdoch watched the screens, alongside his subordinate Dan Baxter. Murdoch seemed agitated. The guards stationed outside, in the grounds of the facility had not responded to his calls.

Grant stood at Murdoch's shoulder. 'Is everything okay Lance?'

'Stay out of it Howard, this is my problem.'

'I thought security was everyone's problem. You've got cameras out of action and your people aren't responding. Does Modjarrad know?'

Murdoch turned and glared. 'I said stay of it. I've sent someone out to check the perimeter - now back off.'

Grant realized his chance. With the guards distracted he could sneak down to the strong room and fetch the key to the control panel. Then all he had to do was initiate the termination programme. He had all the codes - tap them into the computer and *whoosh!* The chimera enclosure would turn into a giant incinerator and burn every creature inside.

Nina peered at the light under the door. Her face was swollen, and her body stiff but she wouldn't allow herself to despair - not yet. Hunger and thirst tormented her, but at least her bonds had been removed and her circulation had returned. Footsteps approached outside, voices raised in conversation. She noticed movement under the door. The guards were arguing... or was it someone else? She shuffled across and pressed her ear to the cold metal.

It can't be... An American accent... Swain. Had they captured him too? She heard him say, 'We're taking this woman to a high security facility.'

We? Swain used the word *we*.

'But this is high security.' Nina recognized the voice of one of the guards.

A dull thud as if a body had dropped to the floor. Keys jangled. She cried out excitedly. The lock rattled and the door swung open. She stepped back, shielded her eyes from the light, as two tall silhouettes entered the cell. When her vision adjusted, she stifled a laugh, partly through relief and partly at the comical sight stood before her. Tom Swain and Matthew Hunter appeared in the doorway dressed in ill-fitting uniforms, both their trousers hanging an inch above their muddy shoes.

'Nina?' Hunter ran to her, his face etched with concern. 'Jesus what have they done to you?'

Swain dragged the unconscious guard into the cell, grabbed the man's sidearm and tossed it to her. 'Now let's get the hell out of here.'

'Wait,' Hunter said. 'I hear footsteps.' He peered around the door and then quickly ducked back inside. 'Guards. Three of them.'

Nina seized the initiative and leaned around the doorframe, fired three shots from a crouched position. She stepped back. 'Two down.'

Bullets pinged off the steel door as the remaining guard returned fire. Hunter thrust his arm around the frame and fired blind. Four shots. A groan echoed in the passage, the clunk of a rifle hitting the floor.

'Follow me,' Nina yelled. She ran into the corridor and spun right, heading back for the lifts. Hunter and Swain raced after her. An alarm started up, and a voice-activated intruder alert barked through the loudspeakers in the ceiling.

They reached the steel door. Two half-naked guards lay in a lake of blood. Hunter and Swain ran into the office and swiftly changed back into their clothes while Nina stood guard.

Hunter grabbed two Uzi machine guns from the gun rack and together, the three of them headed for the lifts.

Lance Murdoch stared at the alarm panel. 'Fuck, we've got serious problems here - intruders in sector 3.' He turned to the unshaven Dan Baxter. 'Find Modjarrad. I can't get hold of him on the radio. Tell him we've got two chimeras loose in the facility.'

'What! How did that happen?'

Expressions of horror appeared on every face in the room. The scientists looked at Murdoch and then at each other.

Howard Grant stared at the monitors, most of them were blank. A couple of cameras still worked, including one placed in an empty corridor on sub-level 2. Two chimeras appeared on the screen.

'They're not ours,' Murdoch said.

'What do you mean?' Grant asked.

'They must have got in somehow, look at the state of the filthy bastards. They're not from this brood, the corral is completely secure. They must be survivors from the accident, come back for their friends.'

'But how did they get in?'

Murdoch looked tired, his complexion ashen. 'Our systems are down, they must have bypassed the cameras outside. But the facility was compromised before the chimeras entered the complex.'

'Compromised by whom?'

Murdoch turned back to the screens and pointed at three figures running past one of the cameras.

'Christ! Who are those people?' Grant said.

But Murdoch didn't reply. Both men watched as one of the intruders stopped beneath the camera and looked up into the lens - a woman with an Uzi slung over her shoulder. She raised the gun. A flash of light and the picture disappeared. Murdoch snatched up his radio and called for back-up.

The room ascended into uproar. Grant had to act fast. These people could be Special Forces and he had to be seen to be helping them. To do that, he needed the key to the burners. He swiped himself out and headed for the lift.

The screaming klaxons echoed in the corridor as Nina, Swain and Hunter made for the lifts. They arrived without incident and Hunter reached for the call-button.

Nina grabbed his hand. 'No don't! We don't know what's up there waiting for us. There must be another exit.'

'I've already checked,' Swain yelled. 'This is the quickest way.'

Nina wouldn't have it. 'Guys. They'll shoot us before we even open the doors; we've got to find another way out.'

Hunter stared up at the green arrow above the lift door. The lift was descending. 'There isn't much time. Someone's on their way down.'

Nina ordered them to take up firing positions. Hunter took dead centre, Nina to his left, and Swain to his right. The pulleys groaned and the lift rattled to a halt. When the gate crashed open, Hunter lowered his gun.

A pale, gaunt looking man in a white lab coat cowered in the corner. 'Don't shoot; I'm on your side.'

Hunter stepped into the lift and grabbed him. 'Who are you?'

'Howard Grant, I'm head of the science team here. I'm on my way to destroy the chimeras, but I'm in a hurry. There's a security breach.'

'We know,' Hunter said. 'We're it.'

'Not just you. There are two chimeras prowling on this level; probably got in through the drainage system. They've come back for the rest of the brood. I've got to stop them.'

52

'I SAY WE GO back and destroy the entire horde,' Nina said.

Hunter agreed and asked Howard Grant if he would help them.

'Of course,' Grant replied, 'but your guns are of no use. We need to incinerate the chimera compound and in order to do that I need the security key to switch on the burners.'

'And this key is where?'

'Locked in the strong room. That's where I'm heading now.'

Hunter wondered if he'd missed something. What was wrong with mowing these creatures down with machine guns? The animals were tough to kill but they were trapped inside a caged compound. He looked questioningly at Grant. 'Exactly how many creatures have you got down here?'

The scientist rubbed his chin and stared at the ceiling as he made the calculation. He delivered his verdict with shocking coolness. 'Sixty four infants, less than a year old. That's the second batch. Two hundred embryos, yet to...'

'Jesus! How many adults?'

'I'm getting to that. We're talking animals over two years old... Altogether, there must be one hundred and sixty five.'

Nina gasped and Swain cursed. Hunter glared at the scientist. 'You're saying there are over a hundred and fifty of those things just along the corridor?'

Grant nodded. 'That's why we need to burn them.'

'How the hell did you transport them all here from Devon?' Nina said.

Grant returned a puzzled look. 'We didn't. They've been here all along. For control purposes the MOD restricted us to eight adults at the primary site in Devon but they escaped when we tried to relocate them. Only Zarcom people know about this place.'

Hunter was incredulous. 'So this underground hell-hole has been here all along and the government didn't even know about it?'

'It was constructed three years ago. We moved all the technical equipment across from Devon of course, but that only took a couple of days.'

Hunter shook his head in disbelief. 'So Modjarrad double-crossed the British government?'

'Yes. This is the main holding facility. If that shipment hadn't crashed last weekend, no one would be any the wiser. Modjarrad should have destroyed the eight adults as agreed in the contract, but he didn't want to lose a penny of his investment. He got greedy and the whole thing blew up in his face. Now he plans to continue his work overseas.'

'Then it's down to us to stop him,' Hunter said. 'How far to the strong-room?'

'We can make it there and back in ten minutes.'

'Good. Nina. Tom. Wait here and secure the area. I'll go with this guy. We'll grab the key, head up to the next level and destroy these creatures.'

Cyrus Modjarrad stormed into the control room, slammed his fist on the central consol and stared down into the chimera enclosure. 'Where's Howard Grant?' he yelled.

In the corral the animals were frenzied, sensing two of their own close by. Modjarrad turned his attention to the bank of monitors. 'Why aren't these damn things working Lance? I pay you to take care of security. What are you playing at?'

'We haven't enough men. Only a third of the personnel I originally asked for.' Murdoch stepped back, sucked in a deep breath as Modjarrad pulled out a pistol and aimed it at his face.

Modjarrad cocked his head and watched the droplets of sweat trail down Murdoch's temple. He squeezed the trigger and the Zarcom head of security collapsed in a tangled heap, a crimson hole in his chest. Modjarrad turned to the group of scientists, their eyes averted in terror. 'Now, will somebody tell me where the fuck Howard Grant has got to?'

Matthew Hunter followed Grant to the next intersection amid the unrelenting alarms. He grabbed the scientist and pulled him back against the wall. 'Wait.'

'We're wasting precious time.'

'Quiet.'

Hunter peered into the passage. Further down the corridor came the echo of gunfire and men screaming. 'Hear that?'

The scientist nodded.

'It's coming from the right-hand passage.'

'But we need to go that way.'

'I was afraid you'd say that. How far?'

'Ten or fifteen yards.'

Hunter looked out once more as the passage began to fill with smoke. 'Okay, follow me.' They stepped out of the shadows, and ran to the strong-room. Grant swiped his pass card. The panel beeped and he pushed open the heavy door.

Hunter waited outside, as Grant fiddled with the key box mounted on the wall. He yelled at him to hurry.

Christ – come on.

Grant turned to him and shook his head in dismay. 'The box is empty. Modjarrad must have confiscated the key along with all the files. Everything has gone.'

Something moved in shadows ahead. Hunter scanned the smoke-filled corridor, gun up, ready to fire. A thunderous roar echoed off the walls and his limbs trembled as he fought to maintain his grip on the gun.

Veils of smoke shifted apart as two beasts emerged, stalking shoulder-to-shoulder, heads bowed, sniffing the ground like dogs. They looked up, drool salivating from their open mouths.

None of the science team knew where Howard Grant had gone, but Modjarrad had a good idea. He had prepared for this, guessed that someone would double-cross him if things turned sour. The project was finished and he had to evacuate the facility.

But not before the chimeras were destroyed.

If any of them escaped, his business would suffer, making it difficult to sell the technology. He didn't mind dealing with the Russians, Chinese or even the Iranians. They could afford to pay and protect him. But if the chimeras killed innocent civilians then none of these governments would entertain his project - not for a while at least.

Modjarrad looked at each scientist in turn. 'Our work has suffered major setbacks, and I have no choice but to issue a code red. This facility must be destroyed.'

Everyone gasped and the mutterings began. Modjarrad held up his hand and asked for quiet. 'We still have the technology. Everything we have worked for is backed up, and is completely safe. We have two thousand frozen embryos stored in a secure location. Our work goes on and your pay cheques are safe.'

The disappointment lifted and a renewed sense of eagerness spread through the group. 'Are we going to evacuate now?' one of the scientists asked.

Cyrus Modjarrad stooped over the central console, inserted a key and tapped a password into the computer. He pressed enter before turning back to the group. 'We're on a countdown to destruct in twenty minutes. Follow me to the emergency exit. We'll be taking a flight directly to mainland Europe.'

Tongues of white flame flashed from the muzzle of the Uzi but the two creatures kept coming. The weapon jammed. Hunter dived into the strong-room, pushed Howard Grant back against the wall and pushed the door shut behind him. A huge black limb swiped at the handle and snapped it open.

'They've got us,' Grant whimpered.

Hunter reached for the pistol tucked in his belt. No way out. The room was small; no windows and only one exit. The door crashed against the stone wall and the hinges snapped. Hunter edged back, the pistol wavering in his outstretched hand as Howard Grant cowered behind him.

One of the beasts thrust its enormous head through the doorway, but the gap appeared too small for the animal's broad shoulders. The creature wedged itself in the frame, jaws snapping, its rancid breath filling the room. Hunter aimed at the gaping mouth and fired. The beast snarled, but didn't retreat. The great bulk of its body contracted with the suppleness of a cat and it began to squeeze through the door frame.

Backed into the corner, shielding the scientist, Hunter emptied his automatic as the chimera forced itself through the frame, shaking its head violently. Outside, the second chimera bellowed. Hunter heard a crackle of electricity and another roar went up followed by a heavy thump. The beast in the doorway bellowed and started to withdraw, squashed itself back through the gap until it was out of the room, then wheeled right and disappeared from view.

Hunter hauled Howard Grant to his feet and the two men stumbled out into the passageway. One of the creatures lay dead outside, a hole the size of an orange in the back of its head. Further down the corridor a bedraggled figure pointed a tapered rod at the second creature. The beast reared up and thrust its head forward with a snap of its jaws. The figure nimbly dodged the attack and aimed a tapered rod at the beast's head. A lightening bolt looped through the air. The hair on the creature's body bristled, sparks skipped over its head, and the skull exploded, washing the walls and ceiling with blood. A faint hum as the rod retracted and the figure turned to face them.

Hunter gasped. 'Richard, what the hell are you doing here?'

Richard Monkton stood proudly between the two slain bodies. 'I picked up their signal.' He tapped the control pad on his arm. 'I saw them enter through an outlet pipe near the shoreline and followed them. It led all the way into the complex.'

'Did you contact the police?'

Monkton shook his head. 'I couldn't sit waiting for them to turn up.'

'You saved our lives,' Howard Grant gasped.

Monkton smiled briefly, but his face sagged when the loudspeakers boomed a new alert.

'CODE RED - ALL PERSONNEL MUST EXIT THE BUILDING.'

'What does that mean?' Monkton said.

Grant paled. 'The entire place is going to blow. It sounds like Modjarrad's pulled the plug.'

Tom Swain and Nina Siketi appeared through the smoke. Swain was hobbling slightly, blood ran down his trouser leg.

'They're shutting the place down,' Nina yelled, 'we need another way out.'

Hunter inspected Swain's wound. 'What happened?'

'They're sealing off the exits, we couldn't hold them.' Swain's eyes fixed on Richard Monkton. 'What the fuck are you doing here? Is Turk with you?'

Monkton stuttered to form a reply. 'Uh... no.'

'So where is he?'

Hunter stepped in, knowing he had to cover for his friend. 'Richard saved our lives Tom. Give him a break. It turns out Turk went out on patrol outside the cottage and didn't come back. Richard got worried and found his way over here.'

Swain looked incredulous. 'Found his way how?'

Monkton answered. 'Turk left my car keys in the kitchen. Listen we really ought to get moving.'

Swain's face contorted into a snarl. 'Okay, but I'll be needing some straight answers from you later buddy.'

53

MODJARRAD STARED AT THE corpse of Lance Murdoch, lying in the centre of the control room, wondering what emotion he was supposed to feel. He bristled with impatience. So many things to organize and he had precious little time. He glanced at Murdoch's lieutenant, Dan Baxter. 'You're in charge now Danny, follow my lead and don't let me down.' Modjarrad ordered Baxter and the six scientists out of the room and along the corridor to his office twenty yards further up.

This office was stark in comparison to his other offices in London and New York, but this was a strictly 'hands-on' environment. It did the job. All the discs containing information on the Darwin Project were stored here, locked in steel carry-cases. There were ten cases in all, and Modjarrad ordered his team to spread the load between them.

He showed them to a door located at the rear of the office, punched in a code and the door slid open. The exit led to a narrow passage that stretched five hundred yards underground before widening into a large parking bay.

The scientists followed wearily, lugging the heavy cases as Modjarrad urged them to hurry. They reached another door and Modjarrad once again punched in a four digit code. Inside the bay, three blacked-out BMWs were parked along the left hand wall opposite a metal roller-shutter.

'We'll take two cars,' Modjarrad said, glancing at Baxter. 'I'll drive one and you the other. The keys are in the ignition. Make sure all the cases are accounted for.'

The cases were loaded into the vehicles and Modjarrad explained the exit strategy. 'We drive through the shutter into a passage which leads to the surface a mile outside the complex. There's a helicopter waiting for us, and we'll be airborne in ten minutes.' He studied the faces staring back at him, and knew he couldn't trust any of them. The scientists were rapt in the project and most had been with him since the beginning. But they wouldn't be happy working in a foreign country as fugitives, not unless he made it worth their while.

Modjarrad opened the boot of the first car and lifted out a black leather case. 'If any of you have any doubts about my commitment to you, I have prepared a going away present.'

He laid the case flat on the roof of the BMW, popped the locks, and spun it round to display the contents. 'American dollars. Two hundred thousand for each of you as soon as we touch down.'

A voice piped up from the back of the group - Greg Perryman, the youngest of the team. 'Where are we going Mr. M?'

'I can't divulge that at present,' Modjarrad replied. 'Rest assured the people waiting for us are sympathetic to our cause and very generous. You will all be handsomely rewarded.' *If you're needed.*

Modjarrad knew the rest of his employees, security personnel, administrators, and technicians would follow the standard evacuation procedures. Everyone would head for the dock and leave the area by ferry. They would be on board soon, and in ten minutes Modjarrad would be on the helicopter. Ten minutes, and he would detonate the explosives in the boat's hull, and blow it out the water. With a simple press of a button, there would be no survivors, no one to testify. He snapped the case shut. 'Time to leave. My helicopter is waiting.'

The lifts had been sealed off and Monkton suggested leaving the complex through the effluent pipe where he'd entered earlier. Howard Grant insisted the quickest exit was through the chimera enclosure. Hunter didn't like the sound of either but decided to go with the Zarcom scientist and told him to lead the way.

Guards littered the corridors, their bodies torn apart. Hunter was sick of death but felt almost immune to the horror. They reached another steel door; Grant swiped his pass card and punched in the code. The door opened and they hurried through.

'It stinks down here,' Monkton complained. 'How much further is it?'

Grant said, 'This passage leads to the underground loading bay. From there, a ramp stretches up to the surface. We'll have to pass by the chimera corral but it's perfectly safe.'

They passed through a second security door, and Swain placed a single bullet against the jamb to stop it closing behind them. A quick exit was essential if they needed to double-back.

The corridor narrowed and the light faded to almost complete darkness. Hunter found the stench intolerable. At the end of the passage, he helped Grant heave open the huge door leading to the main chamber.

Hunter stepped through and found himself standing on a wide mezzanine floor, high up in the dome of the cavern. The place was the size of a concert hall, bolstered by steel pylons. Spotlights shone from the ceiling, illuminating the rocky walls. A metal walkway skirted the cave. On the far side of the mezzanine were a door that had been left ajar and a lift shaft. Hunter looked down through the metal grate under his feet and saw the vast cage crammed with chimeras wallowing in their own mess. Some of the creatures paced and snarled while others clawed at the heavy shutter at the far end of the cavern. Up in the wall, ten feet above his head, an oval window about twenty feet in diameter looked down onto the chamber.

'That's the control room,' Grant said. 'The nerve centre of the complex. All the systems are managed from there.'

Hunter was more interested in how they were going to escape with their lives. 'So how do we get out of here?' he said.

Grant pointed to the ground seventy feet below them. Running alongside the chimera enclosure Hunter saw an open passage the width of two cars and at the end a steel shutter. 'That's the exit,' Grant said. 'It's used for large deliveries. If we can make it through, we'll have a clear route straight to the surface.'

Next to the shutter, a second steel door abutted the chimera corral.

'What about the creatures?' Hunter said. 'What happens if that other door opens?'

'It won't. The delivery shutter is opened from the wall-panel next to it, but the chimera exit is operated from the control room. It's perfectly safe to go down there.'

Hunter wasn't convinced. 'So you're saying both doors open up into the same passage?'

'Yes.'

'Christ. Well let's hope you're right and no one opens that second shutter.'

Swain leaned over the railing and peered down into the corral. He looked back and yelled at Grant. 'Hey Professor, did you say these creatures are all clones?'

Grant nodded. 'Yes, and they'll be dead in less than ten minutes. So will we if we don't get a move on.'

Nina started across the gangway towards the lift and Hunter followed. Suddenly a guard appeared in the open doorway, raised his machine gun and opened fire.

Hunter hit the deck. Bullets whizzed past him and ricocheted off the metal structure. He heard Nina scream, looked up, and saw her lying on her stomach staring back at him, horrified. No, not staring at him, she was looking further behind. Hunter turned and saw Swain draped over the railing, blood sliding down his face.

Hunter took up a kneeling position and returned fire. The guard staggered backwards, dropped his gun and collapsed in the doorway. Nina ran over to Swain, lifted the American off the railings and laid him on his back. She bent over and checked his wounds, two bullet holes, one in the arm, and one in the chest.

Hunter grabbed her hand. 'It's no use. He's gone.'

Howard Grant pleaded with them to get moving. 'Please. There's no time.' He pointed down the wall of the cave. 'See those pipes jutting from the base? They're flame throwers, and could go at any second.'

Kneeling over Swain's lifeless body, Nina kissed the man's forehead. A deep rumble echoed through the cave, the sound of grinding metal.

Grant grasped the railing, and stared down into the cavern, terror etched across his face. 'Oh God no!' he gasped.

Nina cried out. 'Jesus Matthew. Look!'

Hunter gazed into the chimera compound. The beasts bellowed and jostled each other. At the far end of the enclosure the steel shutter had started to rise and the creatures were scrabbling through the gap.

'Someone's up in the control room!' Grant cried. 'It's the only way to get that shutter open.'

Hunter watched helplessly as the chimeras began flooding out. He turned to Grant. 'Does the passage lead directly outside?'

'Yes, there's nothing to stop them breaking out. The ramp leads up to a concrete pit inside a warehouse at the waters edge. The walls of the pit are twenty feet high but the chimeras will easily jump out. We'll have to take our chances and follow them. There's a scissor lift for deliveries which we can use to escape but we need to get clear before the place blows'

'But who opened the shutter… Modjarrad?'

Grant pointed over Hunter's shoulder to the control room window. Hunter spun and caught a brief glimpse of a figure before it pulled back. It couldn't be, just couldn't be...

'Where's Richard?' Hunter said. He called out to him, but there was no reply. Monkton had disappeared.

Richard Monkton was determined to destroy Cyrus Modjarrad and all those involved with Zarcom, but he needed hard evidence. The facility was going to be destroyed and Modjarrad would start the project all over again in another country. Monkton couldn't let that happen.

He heard what Grant had said about the control room and reckoned there must be a way to stop the countdown. He looked down at the creatures and remembered what happened at Logan's farm. He remembered his dead uncle. If he was going to stop this, then now was his chance - he had to get to the control room.

He slipped away from the others and doubled back. The route was easy. Signs pointed the way and the place was empty. He hoped to find data discs and files, anything that might hold valuable information. The lifts were out of action but he recalled passing a stairwell on his way into the complex. He found the stairs just along the corridor from the waste room where he'd entered the building.

When he arrived at the control room, the door was locked. He stepped aside, pointed the EPD rod at the lock and blew the mechanism apart, shoved the door and rushed inside. Monkton rifled through the desks, scouring for data, but found nothing. All the computers were smashed. He had to stop the countdown and keep the place intact, then the world could see what Cyrus Modjarrad had been up to.

He directed the EPD rod at the centre of the main console. A rope of blue current blasted a hole in the unit. Electricity fizzed through the panel, smoke rose from the circuitry and the smell of burning filled his nostrils.

Then he heard it. The deep rumble of grinding metal. Monkton stared out the window…

No, please no. What I have I done?

At the far end of the cavern, the steel shutter started to rise. Monkton blasted the console unit again but to no avail. The chimeras were disappearing out of the chamber, and he could do nothing to stop them.

Sparks fizzed from the electric cables along the walls and flames licked the control panel. Monkton heard Nina's voice inside his head, 'he's fucked up hasn't he?'

Yes I have.

Monkton ran back into the corridor and retraced his steps to the waste room. The door was torn from its hinges, rubbish strewn across the floor where the two creatures had burst through earlier. Monkton found the outlet leading to the effluent pipe. The metal cover had been pushed away and beneath it, the duct dropped six feet to join a network of pipes deeper underground. Monkton heard an explosion and felt the ground shake beneath him. He had to move fast.

54

HOWARD GRANT CHECKED HIS watch. 'We've got four minutes. We have to leave *now*.'

Hunter stared at the empty corral and felt Nina's hand on his shoulder. 'It's not over yet,' she said. 'Come on. I need you alive.'

They raced across the gangway towards the lift on the other side of the cavern. Nina reached it first. 'Shit! It's out of action.'

Hunter saw the buttons in the lift had been shot away. Grant showed them to the emergency escape further along the mezzanine. The ladder was a straight seventy foot drop to ground level and Grant wasted no time in starting his descent.

'Two minutes,' he shouted.

They hurried down, Nina yelled at Grant to jump the final ten feet. He managed six. Nina slid the final twenty feet and rolled when she hit the ground. Hunter came down behind her. Twelve feet from the ground he closed his eyes and made a leap for it, jarred his knee when he hit the ground.

Nina helped him up.

'I'm okay. Keep running!' Hunter forced himself on towards the exit. They ran past the chimera corral, Hunter gagged at the stench. An explosion resonated somewhere above them.

'It's started,' Grant screamed. The scientist punched a green button on the wall and the delivery shutter began its ascent. But the mechanism was slow and they waited several seconds for a gap big enough to crawl under.

The ground shook, the control room window exploded behind them. Chunks of glass and masonry fell onto the mezzanine. The pylons groaned and more detonations went off. Sections of the gangway collapsed and the structure started to disintegrate.

Nina and Grant crawled through the gap first, followed by Hunter. Flames shot into the corral behind him and he felt the searing heat on his back as his feet slipped in shit left behind by the creatures.

The ground sloped up in a steep gradient towards the surface. Hunter only hoped that no chimeras were waiting for them at the top.

'We're nearly there,' Grant yelled.

A thunderous tremor rumbled through the passage. The walls ruptured and rocks fell from the ceiling. A chunk of stone struck Howard Grant on the head. He moaned and collapsed to the floor, blood streaming down his face.

Hunter turned and went back.

'Leave him,' Nina cried.

'We need him for Christ sake! What's wrong with you?'

Hunter checked the man's breathing. He was unconscious and his pulse was fading. He tried hauling the scientist to his feet but couldn't find the strength.

Nina relented and ran back to give him a hand. 'We shouldn't be doing this Matt. He'll slow us down.'

'Are you kidding? He can help us nail Modjarrad, and might know something about Chris. Come on, help me.' He ditched the machine gun and took Grant's left arm. Nina supported the man's right arm and together they supported his weight. Up ahead, a shaft of light glinted in the darkness.

Daylight.

At the summit, they found themselves in a concrete bunker, thirty feet long and twenty feet below ground level. Directly above was the empty shell of an old boathouse. No sign of the chimeras.

Hunter eyed the massive hydraulic platform, designed to support an articulated lorry. They stepped onto it and Hunter pressed the button to ascend. The platform rose and shuddered as more explosions went off deep underground. The platform hissed and came to rest at ground level. They staggered towards the opening on the far side of the building, only one exit, and the chimeras had left a clear trail of filth behind them. Hunter stumbled outside and his strength wilted.

The dark waters of the Swale swept past on their right; the surface littered with debris, pieces of wood and clothing. Hunter saw what looked like a cluster of bodies bobbing on the surface. To his left, a dense plume of smoke swirled from the warehouse where he had originally entered the complex. He swallowed the sweet cool air. For once, the grey sky looked beautiful…

He was alive.

'Swain hid the car in a field just outside the boundary,' Nina said. 'We have to get this guy to hospital and the quickest way is to take him ourselves.'

'What about Richard?'

'What about him? I'm sorry Matt. I don't know what he was up to, but he couldn't have made it out alive. You saw that for yourself.'

Hunter shook his head. 'I don't believe it. Why did he do that? So many people will die Nina. These creatures will not stop. They'll find places to hide and...'

'One thing at a time. Let's get this guy to hospital first.'

55

THE TRACKS LEFT BY the chimeras curved northwest across the compound and disappeared into the trees at the perimeter. The earth was churned where the creatures had stampeded and a section of the fence was flattened. They followed the trail across the wasteland. Hunter placed Howard Grant down at the roadside and tore the man's lab coat into strips to make bandages while Nina went in search of the car that Swain had hidden in bushes nearby. Minutes later she drove up in a 4X4 riddled with bullet holes. Hunter hauled the scientist into the back seat and squeezed in beside him.

As Nina pulled away, Hunter suggested making a dash for Maidstone, the nearest town with a hospital.

'Okay, how's he holding up?' she said over her shoulder.

'He's alive but that's all I can tell you,' Hunter replied. He managed to stem the blood flow with the makeshift bandages, but Grant remained unconscious. As Nina turned onto the dual carriageway Hunter changed the subject. 'Phoenix told me about you being a soldier.'

'Old news Hunter. I know he and Swain told you about the Darwin Project. I was involved just as you are.'

'I need to know one thing, it's important.'

'Go on.'

Hunter paused as he considered how to put the question. 'What do you know about our parents? Not just mine, yours, Swain's and all the other handlers.'

No response.

'Nina?'

'I'm driving for God's sake! None of us know who our parents are. I was brought up in a children's home. I have got no family which is why I get so pissed off when I hear people griping about their sad little lives... Oh shit!' She hit the brakes and the car slewed across the road before screeching to a halt. Hunter grappled with Howard Grant as the two men were thrown forward.

Nina slammed her fist on the dash. 'Bloody traffic.'

Hunter straightened and peered out the front windscreen. Two lanes of cars stretched as far as he could see and the opposite carriageway was also jammed. He sighed and sank into his seat. "This is all we need. Can't you swerve round them or something?'

'Better still, why don't I fly over the top?' Nina drummed her fingers on the steering wheel.

Hunter couldn't bring himself to speculate the consequences of the last hour, and supposed she felt the same. How long before the populace found itself confronted with these beasts? Not long. It may have probably already come to that. He prayed the security forces were on the way and on cue, two low flying jet fighters screamed overhead. Seconds later four military helicopters whirred past, following the highway east towards the burning complex.

This section of the road was flanked by woodland. To Hunter's left, a wall of trees formed a barrier at the roadside and on the opposite carriageway, grass sloped down towards the road. The crest of the hill was lined with trees.

Another fighter plane shrieked overhead. Hunter watched the aircraft arc into the sky and heard more helicopters approach. Two Apaches swooped in low and hovered at the top of the embankment up on his right. The treetops billowed in the downwash like a rippling sea. A third Apache arrived to their left. The collective drone of rotor blades was deafening; dust and leaves swirled over the packed highway.

'This is isn't good,' Nina murmured, craning her neck to look up.

People jumped out of their cars, pointed and stared in wonder at the helicopters. Nina opened her door and swivelled to climb out. 'Wait here, I'll find out what's...'

A loud guttural roar pierced the air, audible even amid the clamor of thudding blades. She shrank back and slammed the door shut. 'It can't be,' she gasped.

Hunter saw her hands tremble as she grasped the steering wheel. The roar of a large animal whipped across the highway. People ran to their vehicles and then the screams began. From the edge of the forest, up on the embankment, a huge black shape crashed through the trees, and hurtled down the slope as one of the Apaches veered to stay with it. The speed and agility of the creature astonished Hunter, even now.

Horns blared, people screamed and rotor-blades pounded, the sounds merged to produce a cacophonous wail. Undeterred, the chimera reached the bottom of the hill, and leapt over the crash barrier onto a stationary saloon.

The impact dented the roof and blew out the windows. The monster's head lolled from side to side as the creature surveyed the area. Inside the car, a woman shrank into her seat, and screamed her lungs out. The animal seemed hesitant at first, shifting its gaze along the line of stationary traffic. Then, without warning it leapt from the roof of the saloon and pounced onto a family estate in the next lane. Once again the impact shattered the car's windscreen, and the roof bowed under the animal's weight.

Horns blared and people shouted, everyone united in trying to frighten the thing away as it peered through the smashed windscreen under its feet. The driver, a middle-aged guy in a suit, scrambled between the front seats into the back. The creature thrust a huge paw through the windshield and groped around for him. Hunter heard a faint, almost pathetic, 'help me.' The childlike voice stirred something inside him that he couldn't ignore.

He booted the door open, despite Nina's protests and ran across to the central barrier. 'Here you ugly bastard. Over here.' At that moment he felt no fear, only rage. The creature fixed him with a murderous glare, it inclined its head and shifted position, ready to spring.

'Matt. No!' Nina jumped out of the car and ran to him.

The chimera adjusted its stance. Watching her. Watching him.

I will not run, Hunter thought. His body shivered, but the words repeated themselves over in his mind. He said it aloud through clenched teeth. 'I will not run.'

He heard someone call out, 'Yeah, come on you fucker!' The voice belonged to a trucker stood in front of his cab, brandishing a metal bar. His t-shirt said, 'Vegan men pack more meat.'

'Get back in your truck,' Hunter shouted, but Nina grabbed his arm and pulled him away.

The beast's attention switched to the tough guy. It leapt from the roof of the car and landed deftly in front of the man. Now the steel bar didn't look so menacing. Hunter was powerless. Memories of the balloon seller came flooding back as the beast attacked. He watched the creature dive at the man's shoulders, knock him down, and clamp its great jaws around his head. Hunter turned away. There was so much blood.

Brilliant white flashes danced from the Apache gun pods as they opened fire into the trees at the top of the embankment.

Nina yelled at Hunter. 'Get in the car!' She slipped behind the wheel and beckoned him over, the desperation clear in her eyes.

He ran to the car, climbed in next to her and slammed the door. When he glanced up at the embankment, he saw the woodland come alive. The creatures emerged from the trees like stampeding buffalo, thundering down towards the highway and sending up a chorus of frenzied roars.

One of the Apaches strafed the creatures as they rampaged down the hill while another fired a missile into the forest. The explosion sent up a cloud of earth and splintered wood high into the air. Hunter braced himself, watching the creatures swarm onto the highway and smash through the cars. The horde of hulking bodies buffeted the 4X4 and Hunter felt sure the vehicle would be ripped apart. The windows smashed and the car rocked wildly. He stayed down, forming a shield over Nina as the bedlam continued around them. Finally, the car stopped moving and the last howl faded in the distance.

Hunter sat up and stared out through the broken windscreen. At the top of the hill, the Apaches continued to scan the forest. Then two stragglers limped from the cover of the trees and started down the embankment. The first helicopter opened fire. Shells rained down, churning up the turf. One of the beasts took a hit, and tumbled down the slope. The other kept going and reached the bottom, jumped over the crash barrier and bounded across the highway.

The Apache followed, cannons blazing. Shells tore up the road surface missing the creature as it dodged and weaved. But then the animal's legs collapsed and it rolled into the central barrier. The helicopter cut the beast into ribbons as it lay spread-eagled and helpless.

From the woods to Hunter's left, the air crackled with more heavy gunfire. The sounds receded as the battle shifted south. Smoke billowed into the sky, and dust settled over the wreckage strewn road. Hunter stumbled out to survey the damage. All around him, screams gave way to sobs. Vehicles lay battered and upturned like wreckage washed up on a shoreline.

Nina fell out of the 4X4, coughed and rubbed her eyes while Hunter watched people roam amongst the carnage looking dazed and terrified. A woman sat in the road and rocked herself as a little girl ran past, chased by her hysterical mother. A headless body lay on the ground, the T-shirt slogan now bloody and obscured. 'Vegan men pack m... The rest had been torn away.

Hunter glanced back at the crumpled 4x4. Howard Grant hung out of the back door, arms draped on the road, head upside down, eyes staring back accusingly.

Nina grabbed his arm. 'Matt, I'm sorry. He was probably already dead.'

Hunter gazed at the sky, streaked with vapour trails. 'God, if you're there. If you really are…'He didn't finish.

Thumping rotors echoed from the east as two Chinooks swooped in on their position. The helicopters descended over the highway stirring up swirls of dust and leaves. Ropes dropped from the aircraft and swarms of troops slid down onto the tarmac. Some took up firing positions at the roadside while others distributed medical supplies. A black bundle plummeted from the back of one of the Chinooks. Body bags.

Hunter was tired of running. So what if they detained him? His clothes were filthy and torn, his hands grazed, and his body bruised. He watched Nina wander through the crowd in her blood stained t-shirt and her nest of dry hair. She looked like shit. They both did.

He watched her approach one of the soldiers - an officer. Their conversation was brief and almost instantly Nina turned around and waved at Hunter, an animated gesture accompanied by a huge grin.

She's lost the plot, he thought. He trudged towards her, feeling every ache in his body. She reached out and snatched his hand; tears of happiness streaming down her beaming face. Despite all the horror, she seemed genuinely excited about something.

The soldier's expression remained deadpan. 'I take it you're Mr. Hunter?'

'Yeah.'

'I'm Captain Vincent of Her Majesty's Parachute regiment. I have orders to escort you to a military installation. A Lynx helicopter is on its way to airlift us out of here.'

'What's going on?' Hunter glanced at Nina, who stared back with wide eyes, one hand covering her mouth as if trying to stop herself squealing with excitement.

'What is it?' The words caught in Hunter's throat. He sensed good news. No, some brilliant news. He looked into her eyes, but couldn't bring himself to believe...

Captain Vincent continued. 'You'll be briefed when we reach HQ. In the meantime I have been instructed to inform you that your brother Captain Hunter is back from duty in Afghanistan and is awaiting your arrival.'

56

THE LYNX HELICOPTER SOARED high above the dual carriageway offering a panoramic view of the pitiful scene below – people and cars scattered and crushed where the chimera horde had trampled through. Hunter felt an overwhelming sense of sadness and yet he shivered with nervous excitement at the thought of seeing his brother.

Nina clung tight to his arm like they were newly weds. She hadn't stopped grinning since the news of Christian's return and he noticed she had a perfect smile. Why hadn't he seen that before? Her green eyes, flecked with amber, and the fine bone structure of her cheeks. Perhaps, in his revere he was seeing the world through a utopian haze, and Nina had become an object of beauty and desire?

Maybe I'm drugged, he joked with himself. She grabbed his hand and in that moment he felt an overpowering connection with her. Nina Siketi had come through for him. She was his friend again, and he'd missed her.

Two Hellfire missiles tore into the trees below, snapping them like twigs while four creatures broke clear of the forest and streaked across a field of tall grass, heading south. One of the Apaches swooped in to cut them down.

Captain Vincent regarded Hunter's fearful expression and yelled to make himself heard above the engines. 'Don't worry. We'll annihilate the bastards before they reach the towns.'

Hunter didn't share the soldier's confidence but settled back and tried to block it from his mind, not wanting to spoil the moment. He would be reunited with Christian soon. Tomorrow he might have a different outlook. Tomorrow he would consider all the other issues. He closed his eyes and tried to figure what he was going to say to his brother. Two years, and no contact. Harassed by guilt, he rehearsed his lines silently within the protective walls of his mind.

Minutes later, the helicopter circled over the base and landed in the centre of the parade ground, close to a sprawling complex of flat-roofed buildings. Hunter hoped to see his brother, but instead the landing area was ringed by armed troops. The helicopter settled on the tarmac and the whine of its engines subsided as the blades slowed. Hunter and Nina jumped out, followed by Captain Vincent. From the building across the square, a tall man in a dark overcoat approached, flanked by two burly men in civilian casuals, jeans, and hooded tops. One had a ponytail, and Hunter recognized him as one of the agents who'd jumped him and Monkton in London.

The tall man shook Nina's hand. 'Hello Standwick,' he said. The man spoke with an upper crust accent, late fifties, slim with silver hair, and grey eyes that glinted beneath thick black eyebrows.

'My name's Siketi now. You know that.'

Charles Fenwick, head of MI5, gave a wry smile. 'If you insist.' He turned to Hunter. 'And you must be Matthew Hunter.'

Hunter nodded wearily.

'Your brother's waiting inside,' Fenwick said matter-of-factly, 'you're no doubt itching to see him, but I suggest you get yourself cleaned up first. Captain Vincent's men will show you to your quarters.'

Hunter thanked him.

'Oh don't thank me Mr. Hunter. Your brother is holding onto some valuable information and refuses to share it with us until he sees you. We're in the middle of a crisis and there's a lot to get through.' He paused, and his expression darkened. 'What happened to your friend Monkton?'

'He's dead.' Hunter was too exhausted to issue lengthy explanations.

'Are you sure? The man represents a serious security threat. If you think there's a chance he's still alive, you need to tell us.'

Hunter shrugged. 'I doubt that.'

Fenwick looked unconvinced. He glanced at Vincent, and nodded. 'Get them inside Captain.'

Hunter and Nina fell into step behind Vincent, and two of his men. Fenwick called out to them as they entered the building. 'One thing to bear in mind, while you think things over,' he said. 'Monkton is wanted for murder. We believe he killed a man named Paul Morgan. You probably know him as Turk.'

Hunter and Nina spun around. Fenwick stared icily, hands in his overcoat pockets.

'We found Turk's body at that hideout of yours. Seems he received a lethal bolt of electricity, cooked half his face. I am right in saying Monkton was the last one to leave the hideout aren't I Mr. Hunter?'

Hunter stared back at him, numb with incredulity.

'Don't worry,' Fenwick continued. 'We'll catch up shortly. As I said, there's a lot to go through. I suggest you get changed quickly.'

57

AFTER LEAVING THE FACILITY, Monkton ran back to the Jeep and drove north. It wasn't a conscious decision, he just needed to get away and give himself time to think.

Now he was parked on a hill, overlooking the Bluewater shopping complex near Dartford, Kent. He had a perfect view of the silver domed structure, a huge undercover mall nestling in an excavated chalk pit.

Monkton had always regarded such places as the epicentre of an ignorant society. He watched people filing in, wallets and purses stuffed with credit cards, and watched them filing out, loaded down with armfuls of shopping bags, a behaviour totally alien to him. A voice in his mind interjected. 'Who are you to judge?'

He couldn't shake it. His mind repeated a single word over and over again. *Murderer*. He buried his face in his hands.

'It was an accident,' he cried. The voice fell silent. Monkton slumped despairingly over the steering wheel. 'Richard, what the hell have you done?' His thoughts turned to his father. He pulled out the photograph and stared at it through wet eyes.

I'm sorry father. I tried to be like you. I just wanted to bring Modjarrad down... Please believe me - I had to do something.

The drill sergeant's office was a small room with a polished desk in the centre and a window covered with black tape. Overhead, a single bulb lit the interior with a stark glow. Seated at the desk, Christian looked up as his twin brother knocked and entered the room.

Matthew Hunter froze in the doorway, unable to speak. The two men gazed at each other for what seemed an age. Christian's face was scarred and swollen, his neck swathed in bandages. He lifted himself slowly out of his seat. A crooked smile crossed his lips.

'Close the bloody door then bro.'

Hunter kicked the door shut and the two men met in a back-slapping embrace.

'Chris – thank god. You must tell me everything.'

Christian nodded at the seat opposite. 'Pull up a pew.'

Hunter sat as Christian stared down at his fists clenched on the desk. 'I'm lucky to be here Matt. I met some good people in Afghanistan who helped me even though it meant risking their lives.'

'Well thank god they did. I'll be sure to thank them personally one day.'

Christian smiled weakly, but didn't reply.

Hunter sensed his brother needed a pick-up. 'Nice touch sending me those photographs of Lang.'

Christian frowned. 'Careful what you say bro, they're watching.' He pointed to a spot above the door - a tiny lens, no bigger than a match-head. Then he pulled a pack of cigarettes from his top pocket, shook one free and lit it. 'What photographs?' he said, inhaling deeply.

'The sick ones of Lang and the boy... are you allowed to smoke in here?'

'Who's gonna stop me?' Christian exhaled a column of smoke at the ceiling. 'I don't know what you're talking about Matt. I never sent you anything.'

'You posted them to Mum. She handed me the envelope – it was addressed to me, in your handwriting. In the letter, you told me not to contact you.'

'Matt, I didn't send you a letter, photos, or anything else for that matter. I wouldn't lie to you.'

Hunter shook his head and changed the subject. 'What about your contact - the one who helped Phoenix and the others get back to the UK?'

Christian flicked ash on the floor, and studied the tip of his cigarette. 'I can't tell you much. I received coded text messages, and coded letters containing snippets of information about Zarcom and Modjarrad. I was given a cell phone number to call when I needed help, but could only leave voice messages. When I got a reply, it was always a text, along with a different number to call next time. I can't tell you any more because...' He jabbed his cigarette at the camera.

Hunter was stunned. So who had sent his mother the photographs? Who would want to? Oh Jesus. It couldn't be. He leaned across the table, and spoke in a low voice.

'Chris what do you know about our parents?'

Charles Fenwick sat alone in a small office along the hall, watching the Hunter twins on the monitor on his desk. He picked up the phone and dialed a London number. It rang three times before a female voice answered. 'Hello?'

'Mary its Charles. I need a word.'

'My boys are okay aren't they?'

'Yes, they're both here with me. Look, I'm sending a car round to pick you up. It's time we got this thing cleared up once and for all.'

'Are you sure? I thought you said...'

'I know what I said, but it's time the boys found out the truth. But that's your department; I don't want to get involved. Clear?'

'Of course, thank you Charles. You're doing the right thing.'

Fenwick switched off his phone and stared down at the photograph lying on the desk. He traced his finger over the faces of the two young boys, smiling so happily. A tear threatened to fall. He brushed it away, took a deep breath and slotted the photo into his wallet.

58

CHRISTIAN DROPPED HIS CIGARETTE, and crushed it under his heel of his shoe. 'I'm not sure how much I can tell you about our parents Matt, and now probably isn't a good time.'

A knock on the door, and Charles Fenwick entered. 'Time to go gentlemen, the meeting starts in two minutes. I need you both present.' He loitered impatiently in doorway as the twins rose from their seats and left the room.

The corridor outside was frenzied. Military personnel scuttled back and forth with bundles of paperwork, and passed on urgent messages to their superiors. Tension inside the building stopped just short of panic, but Hunter knew it wouldn't take much to tip the scales.

He filed into the conference room behind Christian and Fenwick. The windows were blacked-out and a large screen had been set up along the far wall in front of a slide projector.

Nina sat at the table, alongside a handful of high-ranking military officers and government officials. She smiled at Matthew and Christian when they walked in, but hers was the only happy face in the room.

Fenwick stood at the head of the table, shirt sleeves rolled up to the elbows, the immaculate silk tie now hanging in a loose knot. He called for quiet, and informed everyone the Home Secretary was en route from London and would arrive in twenty minutes. The Prime Minister had cut short his engagements in France and had boarded a plane at Charles De Gaulle airport.

'This meeting has been called in respect of the current Zarcom crisis,' Fenwick said. 'I am receiving up to the minute reports so we may be disturbed if anything significant develops. Please understand if we're interrupted.'

Collective nods around the table. Fenwick paused to take a sip of water and then continued his address.

'A large number of genetically modified quadrupeds, known as chimeras have escaped from an illegal installation in north Kent. The purpose of this meeting is to gather intelligence, and ensure any counter measures are effective and watertight. I need an assessment of the situation and the recommendations from everyone in this room so I can advise the Prime Minister accordingly. Recriminations can be discussed at a later date. These creatures are loose among the general populace, and we need to eradicate them.'

The room remained silent, every face stared intently at Charles Fenwick.

'A temporary command centre has been set up here at Lydd. It's the perfect location to conduct air reconnaissance, and manage operations. You all know about these creatures but I want to reiterate the point. There are significant casualties on the ground, and the story is out. The world's press is having a field day, and so as of now, the gentleman seated at the back of the room, Matthew Hunter, is the only journalist who will be privy to any information. He is no longer affiliated to a particular publication, so we are expecting an honest and objective view from him. As far as the rest are concerned, there is a total news blackout until we work out an appropriate public relations response.'

He looked at Hunter. 'I hope you appreciate the trust we are placing on you Matthew.'

'I'll do whatever I can to help,' Hunter replied, feeling secretly elated. The story of the decade handed to him on a plate.

'Good.' Fenwick signaled to his assistant David Bentley. 'David, could you run the slides please.'

Bentley stepped forward, tapped the keys on his laptop and the first slide came up on the screen; a map of London, and the south-east counties. Fenwick used his pen to point to a blue circle on the map. 'This circle represents the location of the destroyed Zarcom facility. Fifty years ago, this area was a commercial dock. There is an entire network of tunnels buried deep underground and Zarcom used these to conduct its activities in secret.' He asked Bentley for the next slide, an identical map with two red arrows sprouting from the circle. Fenwick explained the arrows identified the route taken by the chimeras after they escaped.

'According to eye witnesses the creatures headed west across the M2 motorway and then turned north towards London. We headed them off and they retreated south towards Sittingbourne.'

Matthew recognized the spot where he and Nina had encountered the beasts on the highway. A shiver went through him.

'Civilian casualties are high,' Fenwick said. 'The Army has surrounded the area, and is conducting both airborne and ground attacks. We've made a significant impact but the number killed is still unclear at present.'

Fenwick paused at the next slide. This map was littered with small arrows, splayed in every direction. Hunter counted at least fifty.

'We face two major problems gentlemen. The first is shown by the arrows on the screen. The animals have split into smaller groups, making it difficult to destroy them in large numbers. One thing in our favour. The creatures are fitted with transponders so we can track them above ground. However, the next slide shows the current situation as of twelve hundred hours today. Just thirty minutes ago.'

The slide changed - all the arrows had vanished.

'You've got them all?' one of the ministers asked.

Fenwick shook his head. 'No George. We estimate we've halved their number - there are still hundred or so running loose, but we're no longer picking up their signals.'

'Christ! You don't know where they are?'

'No.'

Gasps of shock circulated the room.

Fenwick cleared his throat. 'The second problem is the animals are following a homing signal. Under live conditions a chimera is injected with adrenalin, increasing its urge to attack and kill. Once satiated, the animal returns to the handler, directed by a pulse emitted from a microchip. The frequency works in conjunction with the creatures brain waves and placates them. For security purposes, the chips were implanted beneath the skin of the individual handlers. The devices are extremely sensitive to changes in temperature, and if a chip is extracted or the handler is killed then the mechanism automatically shuts down. This also stops the technology falling into the wrong hands.'

One of the Generals piped up. 'But Captain Hunter sustained an injury and his chip was removed. Who else would they be following?' The General's eyes moved suspiciously to Matthew Hunter. 'Unless...'

Fenwick raised his hand. 'No General. Matthew wasn't part of the programme. He was never chipped.'

Hunter stared in disbelief. He'd seen the green dot on the GPS screen himself –Monkton had showed it to him. Besides, how else had Phoenix tracked him?

The next slide answered his question, and made him sick to his stomach.

The face of Richard Monkton filled the projector screen. Fenwick began speaking but his words were no more than a background drone. Hunter's mind reeled in shock and confusion.

Christian nudged him. 'Are you okay?'

Hunter nodded absently and tried to refocus, his head thudding like a jackhammer.

Fenwick continued his monologue. 'Not every individual selected for the programme was enlisted. Several didn't meet the standard and were left to merge into civilian life. All those concerned are now in protective custody and will remain there until the crisis is resolved.'

'How many people are we talking about?' The Brigadier said.

'A dozen or so. Unfortunately this Monkton character managed to evade us, despite several attempts to bring him in.'

'How the hell did a weakling like that elude MI5?' boomed an angry voice; the minister again.

'A good question,' Fenwick replied.

Hunter squirmed in his seat. Suddenly the pieces all fitted together. MI5 had been tracking Monkton all this time. They wanted to isolate him so the chimeras wouldn't follow his signal. That's why the damned creatures kept turning up everywhere.

All those people killed in Tunbridge Wells.

He hadn't protected Monkton at all - he'd dropped him right in the shit.

'So what do we know about this individual?' one of the Generals asked.

Fenwick confirmed that Monkton was raised by his uncle. His father was listed as Captain Neil Monkton of Her Majesty's Parachute Regiment; killed in action during the Falklands war, and one of the donors selected for the Darwin Project.

'We've identified Monkton's signal, and have reason to believe he knows his predicament. He seems to be running scared,' Fenwick said. 'We've traced him as far as north Kent, but the signal has disappeared. We're scouring the area and hope to have him picked up soon.'

Fenwick tucked his hands behind his back. 'We need help from someone who has worked with these creatures in the laboratories. All Modjarrad's people either escaped or were killed during the destruction of the underground facility.'

Matthew Hunter was only half listening. He was in Richard Monkton's shoes right then, trying to imagine what the guy was thinking. He caught Fenwick's last words and an idea leapt from his lips like a pistol shot. 'Grealish,' he said.

Every head turned. Matthew saw he had struck a chord with Fenwick. A thin smile crept across the man's face. 'Of course.'

'Who the bloody hell is Grealish?' George, the minister demanded

'A prominent scientist from the London Institute of Biology and an ex-Zarcom employee,' Fenwick replied. 'He's our man.'

A rap at the door, and a soldier walked into the room.

'What is it Corporal?' The Brigadier said.

'Bluewater Shopping Centre sir. We've found the fugitive's Jeep.'

A commotion ensued. Fenwick told Nina and Christian to meet him in the parade ground in five minutes and then grabbed Hunter. 'I need a word in private, Matthew. Follow me.' Fenwick slipped on his overcoat, and bustled out of the room.

Hunter followed him to a small office at the end of the corridor. Fenwick ushered him inside the room and closed the door. 'I'm sending you back to London. There's a Lynx waiting outside for you. Don't ask, just do it... please.'

Hunter shrugged. 'Okay, but I'll need a phone to stay in touch.'

'You can borrow my secretary's. It's only for a couple of hours, and then we'll come and get you. You've already helped a great deal and just for the record, none of this is your fault, I can see you've been beating yourself up. It's time to give yourself a break.'

'But...'

'The helicopter will drop you in the grounds of Dulwich College. There's an anxious lady waiting to meet you. I'll be in touch later.'

'Who's the lady?'

Fenwick paused. 'You visited your mother a couple of days ago. She was under strict instructions not to divulge anything for your brother's sake. Now do you understand? Mary will explain everything to you.'

59

COUNTER MEASURES TO NEUTRALIZE the chimera threat were implemented swiftly, and the effects were far reaching. All inbound flights to Gatwick, Heathrow, and London City were diverted, and all outbound flights were grounded. The London orbital motorway, the M25, was closed from the Dartford toll-bridge in Essex, across six junctions clockwise into East Sussex.

To protect the Capital, ground and air defences were posted along a 25 mile stretch of the motorway. The result was a succession of traffic jams that choked every arterial road skirting London.

The M2 and M20 corridors heading south through Kent were shut, train, and bus services cancelled, and reports of a serious terrorist threat were broadcast on every TV channel, and radio station, urging people not to travel.

The military began closing a net around the east coast of Kent, and yet inexplicably lost track of the chimeras. The horde had dispersed, and in doing so, had stretched the army's capacity to the absolute limit. Helicopter gun-ships couldn't track each individual animal. Command HQ lost the signals, the creatures had simply vanished.

Fenwick took the phone call, as the Chinook he was sitting in, swooped over Bluewater shopping centre. He turned to Nina and Christian sitting behind him. 'Sixty three confirmed kills so far.'

Nina tutted. 'Animal or human?'

'Chimeras,' Fenwick replied.

'That still leaves more than eighty unaccounted for.'

'Progress,' Fenwick said. 'That's the way we have to view it at this stage.'

Nina gazed out the window. The saplings at the roadside bustled in the downwash as the Chinook landed on a large expanse of grass in Bluewater's northern sector. The evacuation of the mall was at an advanced stage, but hundreds of cars still queued for the exits.

Monkton's Jeep had been discovered on the roof of the multi-storey on the south side of the centre. The area had been sealed off and police forensics teams were on the scene.

Nina and Christian jumped out the Chinook. Charles Fenwick followed, cell phone glued to his ear. The MI5 chief hung up, and immediately another call came in. He turned to Christian. 'Go to the main entrance, and ask for Robert Lucas, the centre manager. He'll run through the CCTV tapes with you. Monkton's got to be on there somewhere.' Fenwick turned his back, and answered the call.

Christian and Nina hurried towards the main entrance, a magnificent construction of glass domes that exuded a cathedral-like quality. A knot of uniformed guards loitered outside the automatic doors. 'Mr. Lucas is engaged with the police at the moment,' one of the men explained. 'Come inside and help yourself to a coffee while you wait.'

Minutes later, the two of them were sipping lattes in an open area, surrounded by eateries and fast food outlets. Christian stared into his drink, paddling his spoon in the froth. 'What do you know about this guy Monkton?'

Nina shrugged. 'Not much. Matt and I bumped into him a few days ago. He struck me as a creep, but Matt seemed to like him. God knows why.'

Christian raised his eyes. 'But he's one of us.'

Nina rocked back in her chair and laughed. 'He's a reject, a runt who didn't make the grade. He's not like us at all.'

'Is that how you viewed my brother when you met him? A reject?'

Nina registered his look of disgust. These were precious moments, stolen seconds she wanted to savour. Even if the world descended into chaos, something still might evolve between them. Even now. Even here.

'It's a simple enough question,' Christian snapped.

'Damn it Chris, do I have to do this now?'

The glare in his eyes told her she did. 'Okay, Matthew proved me wrong. That doesn't mean I viewed him as one of us.'

'My brother's the bravest guy I know.'

'Chris, I didn't mean to...'

'Listen to me. I was terrified of my father as a child. He was a violent, nasty piece of work, but never laid a finger on me or my mother - just Matthew. And my brother took the blame for everything.

One evening, my father disappeared down the pub while Mum was out working a shift at the local supermarket. Matt and I were alone in the house, so I decided to try some of the old man's sherry. Matt pleaded with me not to, but I couldn't help myself. I drank two glasses and puked all over the carpet.

'Matthew helped me to bed and set about cleaning up the mess. Minutes later there was a key in the front door. Dad had returned home early. I heard him stumble into the hall, cursing and belching. I hid under the blankets while he yelled at Matthew. I remember hearing furniture being thrown around the living room, Matthew begging him to stop...

I later discovered Matthew had pretended it was him who drank the sherry. He even took a swig from the bottle so his breath smelled of alcohol. He took the beating, and all the time I was crying under the bed covers.'

Christian leaned across the table. 'Don't ever accuse my brother of being a wimp, and the same applies to his friends. If Matthew likes this guy Monkton, then he's all right with me. Understood?'

Nina closed her eyes and nodded. She felt like shit, but couldn't help asking the question. 'Why didn't your mother stop it?'

Christian's face turned scarlet. 'The bastard was clever. He punched the body so the bruising wouldn't show, and threatened to kill us if we grassed him up. Of course questions were raised from time to time, but Matt blamed his injuries on rugby and football. Sometimes Dad showed his true colours, and let rip in front of Mum, only to fall on his knees and promise he'd never to do it again. But he did. And before you ask, Matt didn't want mum to know the whole truth in case he turned his anger on her instead. I swear to God, Matthew and my Mum are the only people that mean anything to me. That's who I am Nina.'

'Thanks for pointing that out,' she replied tersely. *But you must know I'm in love with you?*

No, he didn't. Either that or he simply wasn't interested. Christian Hunter was the only man who ever made her cry. She bit her lip, and forced it back. Her thoughts interrupted by the clicking of shoes on the polished floor. A man wearing a navy suit, holding a walkie-talkie strode alongside Charles Fenwick. Both men wore grave expressions.

60

THE HELICOPTER SET DOWN in the grounds of Dulwich College at 2:45 pm. Hunter spent the journey thinking about Monkton, and the balloon kid in Tunbridge Wells. Because of him, the boy's mother was now dead. He should have informed the police from the start - snatched Monkton's camera and handed it over. Then it all might have been avoided.

Something else nagged him. Hunter noticed a flicker of emotion in Fenwick's voice when he spoke his mother's name. He called her *Mary*.

A cab waited in the road outside the college. Hunter didn't notice his mother sitting in the back, until he opened the door. She greeted him with a huge smile. He climbed in beside her, and took her hand. She had obviously been crying and immediately asked about Christian.

'He's bruised but in good spirits,' Hunter said. 'I didn't get a chance to ask him about Afghanistan.'

'At least you're both okay.'

'Yeah… we're okay,' he murmured, unsure whether to believe the sentiment. They continued the journey in silence.

The taxi dropped them outside his flat. Hunter led his mother upstairs to the second floor, opened the door and groaned. The place was a mess, and he had so many questions he didn't know where to start.

She smiled and sat down. 'Matthew, I'm afraid I couldn't tell you everything when you came round to see me yesterday.'

Hunter dropped into the sofa next to her. 'No need to explain Mum. Chris was in danger - Fenwick explained it all to me. Tell me about this package you gave me. It contained some photographs, very disturbing photographs.' He spoke lightheartedly, trying to ease the tension.

She fidgeted uncomfortably with her hands.

'Don't be embarrassed Mum. I figured you got hold of the photos and pretended they were from Chris, and I understand why. I'd love to know what you've been up to.'

She stared at her shoes. 'I've got contacts, people I knew in a previous life so to speak. I asked them for help and they obliged.'

'Previous life?'

'After leaving college I became an administrator for the Ministry of Defence at Aldershot. That's where I met your father - he was a squaddie. After a brief romance we decided to marry and start a family, but I soon discovered we couldn't have children.'

'Huh? But you had us twins.'

'No. You must listen to me. The thought of a life without kids proved intolerable for me - I had to be a mum, no matter what. A year after we married, I was given the opportunity to work with national security. Of course, that meant moving to London. We found a small flat in Croydon and your father left the army to start work as a labourer. But I always had the ache in my heart. Six months into my new job I was assigned to the Darwin Project. I had to identify and compile lists of potential donors as well as families who could raise the kids. I couldn't help myself, and added my own name to the list.'

'Whoah. What are you saying?'

She paused. 'Your father isn't... '

'Isn't what?'

'Your real father.'

'Jesus, I knew it!'

'I'm sorry Matthew.'

'No, no, it's okay. I knew something was going on. I've heard things about the project, but it's still hard to grasp. So who is he? My real dad I mean?'

'For years I wasn't sure, Matthew. I had the list of donors, but I didn't know who your father was until recently.' She reached out and took his hand. 'I know it's a lot to take in.'

'Who is he?'

'I think it best he tells you himself. If he wants to have any kind of relationship with you Matthew, then it needs to come from him. I'm sure he wants to. He's been helping out financially. That's how I paid for the rented cottage to help Christian's friends.'

'So you're the contact whose been helping Chris and the others?'

She nodded.

'What about the implants - why was Chris chipped and not me?'

'I swear I didn't find out the truth until about six months ago. I told Christian everything, and wanted him out of Afghanistan, out of the army. I didn't tell you because you weren't involved, and I didn't want you to worry. I always knew you were both destined for the armed forces but I wasn't told the whole story. None of us were.'

'So how did you find out?'

'Again, from your real father.'

'Did he explain why I wasn't selected for the programme?'

'Each child was chipped at the age of ten, but you had a complication. You were diagnosed with epilepsy which relates to electrical pulses in the brain. Having a microchip inserted could have caused you major problems. Although the medication seemed to cure it, you were still deemed unsuitable for the programme.'

'But I don't recall suffering any seizures.'

'Symptoms vary Matthew. Epilepsy is more normal in children than you might think, there's nothing for you to worry about now.'

'So what were my symptoms at the time? It's important I know.'

She rested her hand on his arm. 'They only surfaced when you were under extreme duress. You suffered temporary memory loss, and sharp head pains. You used to say you felt funny, as if things didn't seem real.'

'Tell me about the head pains.'

'Epilepsy is caused by irregularities in the electrical circuitry of the brain. You suffered from brief spasms but nothing more.'

Hunter remembered the incident at Zarcom a week ago, the guards shooting at him as he cowered in the corridor frozen with fear. The entire scene had unfolded at a slow, dream-like pace.

The incident in the elevator. In a fit of rage he'd punched the wall, but his mind blanked it out.

He remembered the shooting pain in his head when the chimeras had crowded round him in Tunbridge Wells, and then again yesterday in the underground complex. Every time he'd undergone severe stress in the last week, he had the symptoms. He relayed his fears to his mother, and explained the events of the last seven days.

'We must get you to a doctor,' she said.

'Not before I meet my father.'

'Wait for him to come to you Matthew, he will in his own time. I know he's proud of you. He approached me about six months ago, and told me everything about the Darwin Project, and then he started to help Christian and his comrades. You boys mean a lot to him Matthew. Just give him some time son. He'll reveal himself to you soon.'

61

NINA AND CHRISTIAN SEARCHED through a pile security tapes in the Bluewater management suit, and identified Monkton driving into the car park at 12:37 but no sign of him leaving.

Charles Fenwick paced the room, cell phone glued to his ear. Nina noticed he was becoming increasingly uptight and heard him make a sudden outburst: 'The signal turned up twenty miles north! What the hell are you saying man?'

She nudged Christian who was studying the security monitor next to her. 'Something's up,' she whispered.

Fenwick stared at the wall, ashen faced. He murmured something unintelligible, and then closed down his phone.

'What is it?' Nina said.

'Monkton's not here. Command HQ picked up his signal, albeit briefly, but it vanished again. It's pretty clear what he's up to.' Fenwick took a deep breath. 'He's in London, riding around on the underground. Once he resurfaces, and his signal appears, the creatures will head straight for the capital.'

'Christ no.' Nina glanced at Christian hunched forward with his head in his hands.

'We must put all our resources into locating him,' Fenwick said. 'Finding Richard Monkton is now our top priority.'

'When you say "find him" you mean find him and kill him?' Nina said.

Fenwick flipped open his phone and tapped in a numbers. 'I mean, I need to find him and stop the signal… at all costs.'

Matthew Hunter sat pensively, listening to his mother. She said Christian had no idea Matthew wasn't part of the project. She had never told him about the epilepsy, and so he must have assumed that being twins, they were both chipped.

Hunter knew his brother would have been going out of his mind with worry. His cell phone rang and he took the call standing up. It was Nina.

'Matt, if you want to keep Monkton alive, you need to get to him before the security services.'

'What are you talking about?'

'He's in London. He dumped his car at Bluewater and caught a bus into the city. We picked up his signal a few minutes ago.'

'Any news on the chimeras?'

'They're still off the map. Without Monkton's signal, they'll stay undercover but as soon as your friend pokes his head above ground, those bastards will be heading straight for your doorstep.'

'Jesus.' Hunter stared at the ceiling. He needed some time to think this one through. 'Nina I'll have to call you back.' He shut down the call and turned to his mother. 'Mum, I've got to leave for a while. Wait here for me and I'll get Chris to call you. I don't suppose you've spoken to him since he got back?'

She smiled. 'It's okay. I can wait until all this is sorted out. Then perhaps we can all sit down together.'

'Sure we can.' Hunter slipped into the bedroom, put on his leather jacket, grabbed his motorcycle helmet, and bolted for the door.

Richard Monkton had purchased a bike helmet on his way to the Bluewater shopping mall. After parking the Jeep, he put the helmet on, figuring it might mute his signal, and hopped on a bus to Dartford. From there he had caught a train into London. Despite suspicious looks from other passengers, he didn't remove the headgear until he got on the tube at Cannon St. He journeyed underground to Stratford in East London, and walked to the London Institute of Biology.

Professor Grealish was the only man who could help him now. Grealish would know how to remove the chip in Monkton's head and then he might have a chance of starting a new life.

But when he got to the institute, the sight that greeted him sapped any hope from his thoughts. Grealish was being helped into the back of a waiting police car by two policemen. Monkton stood across the street, helpless, as the squad car sped away, lights flashing. Not thinking, he removed his helmet and dropped it into the gutter. Who would help him now?

Hunter raced into central London on his Triumph, had to clear his head, and riding his bike was the best way to shut everything out.

What the hell are you thinking Richard?

Monkton had always followed his uncle's footsteps, and Hunter just prayed he wouldn't do anything stupid. If the creatures did follow his signal into the city, they'd be virtually impossible to exterminate. Countless places to hide and plenty of food meant the security services would have only one option. Eradicate Richard Monkton.

Hunter reached Waterloo Bridge, crossed the Thames, and zipped through Parliament Square, before taking a right turn into a narrow side-street. He pulled over, removed his helmet, and phoned Nina.

'Where do I start looking?' he asked her. 'Is there any more news on Monkton's signal?'

'I'm sorry Matt, I only that he's somewhere in London.'

Hunter sighed, about to finish the call, but Nina stopped him.

'Hold on, don't hang up for a second.'

The line went quiet for a few seconds and then she returned with an animated tone in her voice. 'Matt, we got another trace in East London. It disappeared again, but we think Monkton is back on the tube.'

'East London? Could it be Stratford?'

'Fenwick didn't say. Why - do you know something we don't?'

'I think Richard might have gone to see Professor Grealish at the institute. Has Fenwick tracked the professor down yet?'

'Yes, he's on his way over here. A squad car picked him up five minutes ago, just before we identified Monkton's signal.'

'That's it Nina. Richard went to find the professor, and probably arrived too late.'

'So where would he go now?'

'That's the problem. I haven't a clue.'

A pause, then Nina said, 'Chris wants a quick word with you.'

Christian came on the line, sounding anxious. 'If there's anything I can do Matt, just let me know.'

'Why don't you phone Mum and say 'hello'. She's still stuck at my place.'

'I will Matt, but I'll do it later. At the moment I'm more concerned about you. The whole world is watching events over here, so for Christ's sake be careful.'

Hunter froze. Why hadn't he thought of it before?

'Matt? Matt, are you okay?'

'Chris, you said *the world is watching.*'

'That's right. There's media frenzy but…'

'You're a bloody genius Chris. I've got to go; I'll call you back in ten.' Hunter slipped his phone into his jacket and revved the bike. The BBC World Service, broadcasted from Bush House on the Strand and he guessed Monkton might go there in an effort to grab media attention. His uncle had worked there as a journalist and it seemed the obvious choice.

Where else could Monkton go?

62

EXCITEMENT BUZZED THROUGH THE Command Centre at Lydd. After staring at blank screens for more than two hours, the Communications Systems Operators - CSO's - suddenly had a green dot flashing on their monitors. This time they pinpointed the exact location: Charing Cross station in central London. Monkton was out in the open at last.

Seconds later, a dozen red triangles appeared further south in the Medway area of Kent. The numbers increased across a ten mile stretch of the county, from Rochester in the east across to Maidstone to the west. They roamed in pairs, moving north towards London, not the rampaging surge seen earlier, but a steadier pace - a cautious prowl.

The information was passed to Charles Fenwick. He learned the creatures were skulking close to built-up areas, making an air assault impossible. There couldn't be any more screw-ups like the missile strike on Tunbridge Wells. But the headcount was lower than Fenwick expected - only thirty-eight chimeras remained. He only hoped the figure was accurate.

Worn and disheveled, he paced the room, while Nina and Christian studied the last of the tapes. 'We can't just sit around waiting for the police to apprehend Monkton,' Fenwick said. 'We need a plan. I need something from you two pretty damned fast. You're supposed to be the experts.'

'I've got an idea,' Christian said, 'but it's a huge risk, and depends on keeping Monkton alive.'

Fenwick waved a dismissive hand. 'Impossible. The Prime Minister made his feelings clear: stop those things reaching London no matter what.'

'But if the chimeras are going after the signal, why not use that to our advantage?'

Fenwick sauntered to the window and looked out at the empty car park. Up to now he'd only thought of stopping the signal and killing Monkton seemed the only solution. But without it, the creatures might disappear again, and there were no clues how they were avoiding detection. Fenwick couldn't afford anything less than a total extermination of the entire brood and he had to organize it quickly.

He spun and looked at Christian. 'Okay. What's on your mind?'

Christian Hunter switched off the video monitor and asked Nina to listen in while he explained his plan.

Matthew Hunter threaded through the London traffic, keeping one eye on the sidewalks. He passed BBC Bush House, but saw no sign of Monkton. When he circled the block to make a second pass he noticed a figure barge through the crowds, heading for the BBC building.

Monkton. Thank God.

Hunter swept his bike across the street, and rolled up beside him. The little guy immediately backed away from the kerb. Hunter lifted his visor. 'Richard look at me. I'm begging you, please let me help you.'

'I didn't mean to do it,' Monkton cried, 'they put a chip in my head Matt. A bloody microchip. They killed my uncle. They're all bastards.'

'I know all about it Richard. Let's head back to my place and get this thing straightened out. We'll take the tube - it's safer.' Hunter stopped the bike, took off his helmet and dismounted. He just wanted Monkton underground and out of harms way.

'It's time people understood the truth,' Monkton said.

'I'm your friend remember? Don't run out on me Richard, please.'

Monkton blinked furiously, his eyes now empty hollows, his skin pale and sickly. 'You *were* my friend.'

'I still am. I know how it feels to have your life messed up like this. We can make this right. Just listen to me.'

Tears streamed down Monkton's face. If he disappeared into the crowd, Hunter knew he would never find him again and the authorities' would undoubtedly kill him. He took a tentative pace forward and Monkton took a corresponding step back. A guy in a business suit pushed between them and knocked into Monkton, sending him stumbling backward. The guy strode purposefully down the street, his thoughts clearly elsewhere.

Monkton shouted after him but he didn't bother turn around. 'See what I mean Matthew? Nobody cares. Nobody.'

Hunter didn't have time for this. He lurched forward and caught Monkton by his wrist. The little guy's face reddened as he squirmed and twisted to break free. He sank his teeth into the soft tissue next to Hunter's thumb and Hunter had no choice but to let go.

'Richard, I'm truing to save your life for god's sake.' He watched Monkton dodge the traffic and scamper across the street. Hunter gave chase but the crowds were solid and his friend soon disappeared.

A policeman pushed past and Hunter heard him talking into the radio. The word 'suspect' was used several times.

A commotion started further up the street. Twenty yards ahead, Monkton ducked out of the crowd and sprinted back across the road, chased by two cops as sirens went up in the distance. Hunter turned and ran for his bike, dropped his crash helmet and watched it roll under the wheels of a passing taxi.

No time to stop.

He jumped onto the Triumph, and gunned the engine while Monkton tore up the street, pursued by half-a-dozen police. Hunter accelerated towards him, but Monkton stumbled and the first cop reached out to grab him. Hunter kicked out and caught the officer in the stomach with his boot. A squad car plunged through the parting traffic and screeched to a halt a few yards away.

Hunter pulled up, keeping the revs high. 'Jump on Richard!'

Monkton dithered, as more officers piled out of the squad car, and a crowd of onlookers gathered round. He looked at Hunter pitifully and then jumped on the bike. Uniforms moved in from every angle. Sirens wailed and blue light flashed. Hunter accelerated and broke clear of the police ranks. He arrowed through the heavy traffic, south across Westminster Bridge, pursued by a string of squad cars.

In the back of his mind, Hunter couldn't escape the greater danger. The chimeras were coming, and Richard Monkton was still sending a signal.

Christian's plan was simple: use Monkton's signal to lure the chimeras into an open area so the Apache helicopters could destroy them. The animals would home in on the signal until they were practically stepping on Monkton's feet. Not a foolproof strategy and these particular creatures had never been outside their enclosure so this made them even more unpredictable.

'We've got to try,' Christian insisted.

'But where can we lure them to?' Fenwick said. 'We need to hem them into a large area - somewhere close but away from populated areas.'

'What about the bridge at Dartford?' Nina suggested.

Both men looked at her doubtfully.

'The Queen Elizabeth Bridge; where the M25 crosses the Thames,' she explained. 'If we can lure the chimeras up there, we can trap them and attack then from all sides.'

'It's too risky. You'd have to lure them along the motorway.' Christian said. 'Besides, how do propose to get Monkton up there?'

But Fenwick warmed to the idea. 'She's right, don't worry about Monkton. I'll put out the order to capture him and inform the Prime Minister to ensure his approval. We have got to move fast. Get Matthew on the phone, we might need his help.'

Hunter shot through the back roads and somehow managed to shake off his tail but he knew there would be road blocks on all the major arteries out of the city. His phone buzzed in his pocket.

Monkton tapped his shoulder as he pulled over. 'What's going on Matt?'

'Don't worry - it's only my brother.' Hunter answered the call. 'Hi Chris.'

'Bro where are you?'

'Near Lewisham, heading south. I've got Richard, but the cops are after us.'

'Okay, listen. The police have been instructed to help you. Don't worry about the signal. We've got a plan that relies on the chimeras following it. You need to head for the M25, and the Queen Elizabeth Bridge at Dartford. Make sure Monkton stays with you. We'll be waiting with troops and air support. We want you to lure the fuckers onto the bridge so we can trap them.'

'Where are the chimeras now?'

'Heading for the city, five miles south of the M25. The army is holding back from attacking in case the creatures disperse again. Fortunately they're not stopping to feed this time; they seem more concerned with homing in on Monkton.'

'Tell Fenwick I'm on my way, but try and think up something better than using Richard as bait. He's been used enough and I don't want him hurt.'

'I know.'

'I'm serious Chris. Tell Fenwick to protect us both.' Hunter closed down the phone and slid it into his pocket.

'They want to use me to divert the chimeras away from the city don't they?' Monkton said.

'It's probably the only way Richard.'

'I know. I want this over with. I'll do it.'

Hunter checked his watch - 16:30. He could reach the bridge in twenty minutes, but not long before dark.

63

THE MILITARY SET UP checkpoints along the Kent stretch of the M25 motorway. The first was Checkpoint Zero at the Dartford Crossing. Here, the eastbound section of the highway burrowed under the Thames through two tunnels into Essex and running parallel, the westbound section arced over the river via the Queen Elizabeth II Bridge. The bridge was a huge cable-supported construction, nearly 3,000 yards long - easily big enough to herd the creatures onto.

Nina peered out of the Chinook as they circled the area. The weather had deteriorated. Black clouds loomed to the south and the wind buffeted the aircraft as it came into land. On the Kent side of the crossing, all traffic had been cleared and the motorway was deathly quiet. On the Essex side however, the roads were jammed.

The bridge and tunnels were barricaded with concrete blocks. The chimera horde would have access to the bridge from the western approach and tanks were on standby, waiting to close in behind them and block their escape.

Nina willed for Hunter to arrive. Everything was in place, and ready to go. The tricky part was figuring out how to rescue Hunter and Monkton once they were up on the bridge itself. Fenwick reckoned they had two choices. First, allow the men a clear passage straight across, and through the barricade on the other side. They'd have to move fast, or risk being caught by the chimeras.

The second option was to extract them from the top by helicopter. But with the weather worsening, this idea now seemed impossible.

The Chinook landed close to the toll booths on the western approach to the bridge. Fenwick turned to Nina and Christian, seated behind him. 'We don't have much time. The chimera horde is eight miles west, but they're not behaving as we expected. Reports from Checkpoint 4 suggest the animals won't approach the motorway. They seem wary. I've instructed all units to pull back, and let them through. If we get this wrong, there'll be an open gateway for the creatures to break into the city.'

The rotor blades slowed and the whine of the engine diminished. Fenwick pulled the door open and everyone stepped out. Overhead, the sky darkened and the wind howled down the estuary and blew hard against the bridge. They crossed the tarmac and entered a square flat-roofed building at the side of the motorway, usually reserved for local traffic police. This was now the checkpoint command post. Satellite communication links had been set up inside, and a bank of monitors were being watched by a team of experts including Professor Grealish.

Fenwick singled him out. 'Professor, I'm glad you were able to make it.' They shook hands, and Fenwick introduced Nina and Christian. He asked the scientist for his assessment of the situation.

Grealish leaned over one of the screens and pointed to the display. 'It's not good I'm afraid. If you look here, you can see the chimeras are splitting up.'

Nina stared at the red triangles splayed in a haphazard formation. 'Where are they now exactly?' she said.

Grealish ran his finger across the screen. 'This area is Junction 4, where the M25 intersects the M20. The creatures have been moving north towards this point, staying close to buildings and trees. But they seem reluctant to come onto the motorway itself. I can only guess they feel exposed.'

'Unbelievable,' Fenwick spat. 'This plan is doomed to failure if we can't get them onto the motorway.' He shouted to a young officer, standing on the other side of the room. 'Lieutenant Driscoll?'

'Yes sir.'

'Send word to Field Marshall Gedney. Tell him the units at checkpoint 4 need to back off, they're spooking the creatures. Better still, just ask him to call me.'

'Wait!' Nina said. She bent over one of the screens and stared at the red triangles spreading out. 'They're not just dispersing... they're outflanking our defences.'

'She's right,' Christian said. 'They're not avoiding the checkpoint at all. That looks like a pincer movement to me. They're moving in to attack.'

Fenwick leaned in, and studied the screen. 'Are you telling me these things are intelligent enough to agree a strategy and work as a team? That's impossible.'

'Not impossible Mr. Fenwick,' Grealish said. 'The baseline DNA used to create these animals was taken from lions and for the very reason you're seeing before you. Lions hunt in packs and co-ordinate their tactics to suit any given situation. These creatures are more than capable of working as a team; they were engineered for this very purpose. You'd better warn your people that an attack is imminent.'

64

HUNTER REACHED THE A2 overpass near Woolwich where he was greeted by a cluster of police motorbikes. Here, the single lane A2 merged into a three lane highway heading south to the M25. The first two lanes were gridlocked but the far right lane remained clear. Two motorcycle cops signalled Hunter to follow them onto the slip road and they rode south at speed.

Hunter hoped Monkton would stay strong. This operation had been pieced together at the last minute and its success rested on Monkton - an awful lot for one man to cope with.

After eight miles or so, they reached the M25 intersection at junction 2. Hunter joined the motorway and sped past the police cars and armoured vehicles strung across the A2 carriageway. Scores of armed troops lined the roadside. Hunter raced towards the Dartford Crossing, now less than two miles away.

A helicopter circled overhead as the light faded and storm clouds drifted in from the south. Either side of the carriageway, lights flickered and came to life. No sign of the creatures but in the distance Hunter heard gunfire.

Within minutes, he pulled up in front of the toll booths. The area teemed with troops and heavy armour. *A sign of the times*, Hunter thought, *a disaster recovery plan for everything.*

Security guards confiscated his bike, and two soldiers escorted Hunter and Monkton to the checkpoint command centre. The wind gusted in, blowing dust across the road. Hunter glanced across at the bridge and saw the structure visibly shift.

Christ. That's all we need.

Inside, he was relieved to see Chris and Nina, although they both seemed tense.

Professor Grealish strode up to Monkton and put a consoling arm around his shoulder. 'I heard what happened Richard. Don't blame yourself.'

Hunter jabbed a finger into the professor's chest. 'You're damn right he shouldn't blame himself. It's people like you who should be ashamed.'

Fenwick grabbed Hunter's arm and pulled him away. 'That's enough Matthew. You're not helping the situation.' The MI5 chief turned to Richard Monkton. 'I'm glad you finally saw sense and gave yourself up. I can't pretend you'll get off lightly but helping us will go a long way to aiding your defence in court.'

Hunter glared at Fenwick. 'You don't want to upset this guy. Remember you're asking him to risk his life.'

'Yes, well it might not come to that. At present, the creatures aren't responding. They're not following your signal.' Fenwick gestured at the screen. 'As you can see, the damn things are swarming all over checkpoint 4 and we're taking casualties.'

Hunter glanced at the monitor, a mass of red triangles closing in around junction 4 of the motorway. He counted twenty of them. 'Do these red blips represent the entire brood?'

'I bloody hope so. We picked up thirty eight signals when our friend Monkton walked out into the open. We've destroyed half their number, but God knows how many people are dead.' Fenwick turned to Monkton. 'I hope you can see what you've done.'

'For Christ's sake, give him a break,' Hunter snapped.

'It's okay Matt,' Monkton said. 'He's right. I'm responsible for this.'

'No Richard. You're a victim. The perpetrators are too cowardly to take responsibility. ' Hunter rounded on Fenwick. 'What the hell did you people expect would happen when you created these abominations? This whole thing lies at your door - you and all the others who knew about the project.'

Fenwick appeared taken aback. There was sadness in his eyes, and as the two men held each others gaze, Hunter sensed something else... *No, it can't be.*

Before Hunter could blurt out the words one of the CSO's yelled, 'They've vanished.'

'What?' Fenwick pushed through the huddle of bodies and leaned over the man's shoulder. A single green light appeared on screen indicating Monkton's signal but the red triangles had gone.

'How could they just disappear?' Hunter said.

Fenwick shook his head. 'This is absurd.' He yelled at Lieutenant Driscoll. 'Get on the radio and find out what's going on over there. I need a full report. These creatures can't just be disappearing into thin air.' He turned back to Hunter. 'Okay Matthew. So you want to exonerate your friend? I need Monkton on that bridge. The wind's too strong to airlift you away, so when the time comes, you'll have to exit through the barricade on the other side of the crossing. Understood?'

Hunter shrugged. 'No problem. I'll take the bike. We'll get away easy enough.'

Fenwick called everyone together for a final briefing. 'We have to assume the chimeras are still following Monkton's signal so the plan remains unchanged. Matthew's taking Monkton up onto the bridge to see if we can get a reaction.' He fixed Monkton with a firm stare. 'I hope you're still committed to helping us?'

Monkton said he was.

'Okay. We will all have radio com-links so we can stay in touch but I want someone on the other side of the bridge to ensure you get a clear passage across the barrier - you'll need a fast exit.'

'Count me in,' Christian said. He glanced at his brother. 'I want to be the one watching your back.'

Fenwick looked at Nina. 'I also need someone on this side of the crossing. If anything goes wrong we'll need a Jeep to pick these guys up and drive them to safety. Can you do that?'

'Of course.'

'Good. Take Christian across the bridge, drop him off and come straight back here. I want everyone to stay in radio contact at all times. We can't afford any slip ups.'

The wind howled as rain started to fall, but Hunter didn't care – he just wanted this nightmare finished tonight. He clambered onto his bike and waited for Monkton to join him, neither bothered with helmets. Hunter gave Chris and Nina a thumbs-up, wheeled around and started up the incline of the bridge. The wind got stronger as they ascended, and the rain quickly soaked through their clothes. Hunter fought to stay in control of the bike.

Two Apache helicopters banked and flew north away from the scene. To Hunter's left, millions of lights stretched into the distance - London. To his right lurked the back abyss of the river Thames. He stopped in the centre of the four lane carriageway, his body shaking uncontrollably, partly through cold, but mostly fear.

Nina drove Christian across the bridge to organize the escape plan from the other side. Hunter watched the Jeep hurtle past, his brother grinning at him from the passenger seat.

The two men got off the bike. Too blustery to prop the machine on its stand so Hunter laid it flat on the ground. Monkton looked petrified.

'It's okay Richard, this will all soon be over.'

'Are you trying to reassure me or yourself?' Monkton replied.

'Both of us.' Hunter dug the Com-Link headset out of his pocket and clipped it over his ear. 'Shit, this contraption isn't going to stay on.'

Nina returned, having dropped Christian off. She pulled up alongside Hunter and wound down her window. 'I'll keep you updated from the monitors. Just make sure you keep your headset on.'

Hunter nodded and smiled, trying to stay upbeat. As she drove away, he turned up his collar and stared through the lashing rain. Beyond the toll booths the motorway curved to the left and disappeared out of sight. By the time the chimeras appeared around that bend there wouldn't be much time – only seconds. He had to put his faith in Nina. If she didn't give them enough warning...

Don't even think about it Matt. Let's just get this over with.

65

JAKE ROGERS STARED OUT of his apartment window overlooking the Thames estuary. The murky waters boiled and undulated with increasing severity as the wind whipped across the surface. Above, black clouds crossed the dark sky and rain began to fall. A raft of debris floated along the river, heading upstream with the tide. Most of the crap down there was broken pieces wood and old clothing.

Why would anyone dump all that stuff in the river? Perhaps a boat had capsized? Jake hated how people mistreated the environment.

He shrugged. Despite the state of the river, Jake was happy with his new flat, high up in the exclusive apartment block. On a clear day, the view was stunning and his friends were impressed. They came round every Saturday evening, quaffed a few beers, and then went down the pub to pick up women.

But not tonight.

Tonight, Jake had invited a couple of girls over for drinks, conquests from a previous weekend. He just about remembered their names - Vicky and Sue - but couldn't remember who was who.

He switched on the TV while they waited for Andy to turn up. Sky news came on but Jake wasn't listening, there were other things on his mind.

'Have you heard the news,' one of the girls said, perched on the edge of the sofa. She was the shorter of the two – Vicky probably. 'They reckon, there a whole load of wild animals escaped from one of the zoos in Kent. Howlett's I think.'

'Yes I heard that,' the second girl confirmed.

Jake laughed. 'Wild animals? Probably just a couple of deer or something.' He shook his head, and took a swig of beer as he stared out at the river.

'No. Listen.' Vicky said. 'They reckon there are lions and all sorts on the loose. You must have seen the helicopters searching for them.'

Yes. Jake was aware of the activity in the sky. He'd seen the fighter jets too. Perhaps the girls had a point.

'Not only that,' Vicky added. 'But there's a major security alert in London. My sister phoned earlier and said there's a terrorist threat or something. They're practically shutting off the roads. It's chaos.'

Jake shook his head in disbelief. *Where's Andy got to?* He was bored with these two, and wanted a decent conversation, not to mention a curry. He knocked back his beer, and gazed out the window – saw a strange shape bob in the water. He squinted through the rain and again he saw it, but in a different part of the river this time.

'Girls, what do you make of this?' he said without turning round. 'They're popping up everywhere!'

The two girls joined him at the window and peered out. Jake pointed to the centre of the river. 'Look. Right there. It's weird. There are lots of them, rising out of the water and ducking back down again.'

'Oh wow!' the shorter girl said. 'Perhaps they're dolphins.'

Jake shook his head. 'Can't be. They're too... scaly looking. And they've got tails. Long tails like a... Shit those things can't be real!'

The girls stared in silence for a few seconds. Then the realization struck. Suddenly the taller girl dropped her glass, vodka and ice cubes all over the carpet. She put her hand to her mouth and screamed.

66

NINA CLIMBED OUT OF the Jeep and ran into the command post. The chimeras had reappeared at checkpoint 4 and launched another attack. Human casualties were high, but according to the monitors, no more than a dozen animals remained alive.

Fenwick ordered the radio operator to contact Matthew Hunter. 'Let him know the creatures have re-emerged. Tell him to stand by. ' His phone rang, and he turned away to take the call.

Arms folded, Nina studied one of the monitors. 'At least we'll destroy them all before they reach the motorway.'

Professor Grealish disagreed. 'I'm not so sure. We're getting odd blips on the screens that I can't decipher. I don't like it.'

'Have you told Fenwick?'

Grealish shook his head. 'He's busy on the phone. I don't want to say anything until I'm sure. The point is, we're relying on satellite technology and there's a storm approaching. The signals may become distorted.'

'Show me.'

Grealish leaned across to the monitor and pointed to an area to the right of the screen. Nina recognized the horizontal line in the centre, the M25, and she identified the Dartford Crossing. Grealish pinpointed an area about half a mile due south.

'I don't see anything,' she said.

'It appears every minute or so. Watch.'

Nina kept her eyes fixed on the screen. A scattering of red blotches appeared briefly and then vanished. 'Shit! That's the Thames.'

'Exactly,' Grealish said, 'that's the estuary.'

Nina shouted across to Fenwick, who was still talking into his cell phone.

He put his hand over the mouthpiece and looked up. 'What is it?'

'Get Matthew off the bridge. The chimeras are swimming up the Thames. Look. Watch that screen.' Nina jabbed a finger at the monitor. Fenwick rushed over, and sure enough, seconds later the red blotches appeared, closer to the bridge this time.

'That's not possible,' Fenwick gasped. He glanced pensively at Grealish. 'Professor, you said the baseline DNA was extracted from lions. What other animals did they use?'

'They introduced a number of species, a bit of a concoction. They needed a tough hide that would be difficult to penetrate.'

'What animals Professor?'

'The most significant was crocodile DNA, Estuarine crocs to be exact. They grow up to twenty feet in length and swim in salt water.'

Nina stared at the ceiling. 'Fuck. All this time, they've been hiding under the water. We've got to get Matthew off the bridge, the chimeras are virtually on top of him.'

The signals strengthened. A red triangle flashed on the screen, followed by another, then another, until swarms of them appeared clustered together.

Nina scrambled for the radio handset. 'Matt, this is Nina do you read? Over.'

Hunter answered immediately. 'Loud and clear. Over.'

'Matt get out of there now. Don't go over to the east bank, just come straight back to the command post. Over'

'What's the problem?'

'The chimeras. They're beneath you. They've been using the river, that's why we couldn't track them. They must be able to stay underwater for long periods. Listen, if I'm right, they're coming up out of the water right now, and might even be climbing up the bridge itself...'

Nina faltered, hearing the sound of machine-gun fire crackle over the radio. She dropped the handset, and sprinted for the door.

67

FROM THE EAST BANK of the Thames, Christian stood at the riverside and stared out into the darkness as the wind funneled downriver, chopping up waves on the surface. Rafts of debris floated in with the tide and he saw something break water around mid-stream, a dark shape – a seal maybe? Another swell appeared, across the far bank this time.

He called Colonel Henderson on the com-link and asked for the searchlights to scour the far side. Two powerful beams flashed across the swirling currents and Christian saw the full extent of the driftwood and debris coming upriver – masses of it. The beams swept across to the two huge pillars supporting the bridge on the opposite bank. Christian stumbled back in shock, snatched up his binoculars and homed in.

'Oh Jesus!'

A large black shape scuttled up the wide concrete support like a cockroach might climb a table leg. Suddenly, they appeared en masse - swarms of the things emerging from the depths, dripping water as they dragged themselves out of the current. They crowded around the pillars and climbed up in single file.

Christian reported the sighting to central command and the order was given to shoot on sight. The 50-cal machine-guns dug in along the river bank opened up in a blaze of fire. The beasts made easy targets; at least half a dozen dropped and splashed into the murky water below. The others quickly edged around the other side of the struts, out of sight and out of reach of the bullets.

Christian looked up at the underside of the bridge, looming above him, fifteen storey's high, four pillars so smooth it seemed impossible that these huge creatures could scale them so easily. He scanned the top of the bridge with his binoculars, saw the creatures clamber over the railings onto the bridge itself.

Oh God, Matthew!

Fumbling with his headset, Christian tried to contact his brother but got no answer. He turned and ran across the road to one of the parked military

Jeeps. He grabbed the driver. 'Hand me your weapon soldier. I need you to get me onto that bridge!'

Hunter hauled his motorbike upright as the sound of gunfire pierced the night air. He jumped on and kick-started the engine, yelling at Monkton. 'Quick, get on the bike Richard. We're leaving.'

Monkton stared past Hunter's shoulder. 'I don't believe it,' he gasped.

A chorus of roars went up. Through the lashing rain he saw two dark shapes clamber over the side railings onto the bridge. *Jesus, they're here!* Hunter circled the bike to face the toll booths. 'Richard, for Christ's sake get on.'

More chimeras poured over the railings and leapt onto the carriageway. They kept coming - twenty, thirty, forty, spreading out across the road and moving straight for him.

Back at the command post, the multitude of red triangles increased significantly. Fenwick ordered the armoured units into position, ready to attack.

'I'm going up there,' Nina told him.

To her astonishment Fenwick didn't argue. He ordered Driscoll to prepare a Jeep and provide them with guns.

Outside the rain sheeted down and the wind whipped around her ears. Nina got in behind the wheel of the Jeep, while Fenwick jumped into the passenger seat. She started the engine and rammed the gears.

'We need those helicopters back here,' she yelled, 'where the hell are they?'

'They had to withdraw. The wind's too strong; they'd be no good in this,' Fenwick replied.

Nina floored the accelerator. The Jeep sped up the slope of the bridge and now she saw the chimeras for herself, swarms of them leaping over the sides, surrounding Hunter and Monkton at the summit. The tanks moved into position behind her, ready to follow her up, but it was all too late, they couldn't attack now.

'What the hell are we gonna do?' Nina said. 'We can't shoot the damn things with Matthew up there.'

Fenwick clenched his fists. 'I know. We'll have to fetch them off. Get as close as you can.'

Nina rammed her foot to the floor, and the Jeep catapulted forward. She glanced at Fenwick, shocked to see a tear fall from his eye.

Monkton grabbed Hunter's arm and steadied himself as he climbed onto the back of the bike. Hunter revved, but had nowhere to go. The chimeras formed a line across the highway, at least thirty blocking his path down to the toll booths and another group was creeping up from the rear.

The bridge swayed in the wind. Two lines of tanks approached and leading from the front was Nina in the Jeep. *What's she playing at?*

Hunter heard a shout behind him. A burst of gunfire. He wheeled the bike around and saw Christian race towards him, firing into the chimeras. 'Chris, for Christ's sake go back!'

His brother ignored him. Christian Hunter was now the focus of the horde's attention. The chimeras, sixty or more, turned away from Hunter and charged at Christian.

68

HUNTER TWISTED THE THROTTLE and accelerated towards his brother while Christian sprayed bullets into the oncoming chimeras. Hunter weaved between the hulking bodies, Monkton hanging on behind. He raced through the front ranks and overtook them all as Christian fumbled for a spare magazine. Hunter hit the brakes and the wheels slipped on the greasy surface. He steered to avoid Chris but the back-end slid out and Monkton toppled off the back, crashed onto the asphalt screaming in agony.

Holding the bike at a thirty degree angle, Hunter pushed himself away and let the Triumph go. It skimmed across the road surface and slammed into the railings at the edge of the bridge. Lying dazed on the wet road as the rain poured down, he tried to gather his senses, looked up and saw his brother running to him, as the creatures homed in only a few yards behind.

'Matthew! Get close to Monkton, he's our only chance,' Christian yelled.

Soaked and bewildered, Matthew Hunter got to his feet, gasping for breath. Monkton lay on the ground holding his leg, face contorted in pain. Christian caught up, turned and fired into the advancing horde.

The creatures were virtually on top of them. Collectively, they slowed to walking pace. Matthew and Christian backed off and managed to reach Monkton as the chimeras crowded around them in a circle.

Christian emptied his magazine into one of the creatures. The animal buckled and collapsed but the rest kept coming, a calm air of assurance about them as if they sensed victory. The last bullet left the chamber and Christian threw his gun to the ground. The chimeras stopped only yards away, but didn't attack. They seemed curious, docile even, as if all aggression had been drained out of them.

'Stay calm guys,' Christian said. 'This might be okay. They've locked onto Monkton's signal. The frequency has a calming effect that stops them attacking handlers.'

Hunter couldn't move, or avert his eyes from the beasts - every inch of his body jangled with fear. Thirty yards away, the tanks stopped and aimed their cannons, ready to fire.

'No sudden movements guys,' Christian said. 'These things will become agitated if we don't demonstrate who we are. Who Monkton is.'

Hunter's jaw shuddered as he spoke. 'Why? What are they expecting?'

'I'm not sure. The signal lulls them when they get in close to the source, but I've never worked with more than two animals at any one time. I've got no idea how an entire horde of the bastards will react. We need to distract them and get ourselves out of the firing line of those tanks.'

Monkton, writhed on the ground, face red and running with sweat. 'I think I busted my knee,' he groaned.

Christian turned to Matthew. 'Where's your com-link?'

Hunter felt his pockets but found nothing. He looked back and saw it lying in the centre of the bridge, ten yards away. 'Chris, I'm not attempting to get that back.'

'I'll get it. I know what I'm doing. We'll contact Fenwick and tell him to send the choppers in no matter what. That will scare the damn things off.'

Nina stopped the Jeep halfway up the slope, and she and Fenwick jumped out to assess the situation.

'The chimeras aren't attacking at the moment, but they will,' Fenwick said peering through his binoculars. 'Looks like Monkton's sustained an injury.'

Nina zeroed in on the centre of the bridge through her 'binos.' 'There's another solution, but it's risky.'

'What?'

'Get those helicopters back.'

Fenwick dismissed the idea. 'Even if weather permitted I couldn't do it. The animals would only disperse and we'd be back to square one. We need to stop them now, and this thing finishes here tonight, no matter what.' He lowered his binoculars and radioed the command post. 'Make sure the tanks follow us onto the bridge. I want the infantry close behind. This is going to get bloody.' He glanced at Nina. 'Okay, I've seen enough. Let's get up there and help them before its too late.'

Nina rammed her foot to the floor; the car jerked forward and they sped towards the summit.

69

SCUFFLES BROKE OUT BETWEEN the creatures – they growled and butted one another.

So many of the damn things, Hunter thought. Sixty, seventy, maybe more: a grotesque gathering of heaving bodies with powerful tails that swished behind their demonic frames.

'This isn't good,' Christian said. 'Forget the com-link. We'll have to make a run for it.'

'But Richard's injured.'

'For God's sake go!' Monkton yelled. 'Get out of here, both of you, while there's still a chance.'

Hunter wouldn't have it. 'No way. We've been together from the beginning. You stay, I stay.'

'It doesn't matter anyway,' Christian put in. 'I'm afraid we're too late.'

The creatures inched closer, until those at the front were only feet away. Richard Monkton howled with pain. The signal from his microchip no longer pacified the creatures and their expressions turned hostile - identical to the behaviour Hunter had witnessed in Tunbridge Wells a few days earlier.

One creature reared up and bellowed a gut-wrenching roar. Hunter crouched next to Monkton, squeezing his eyes shut, sensing the jaws coming down onto him.

Suddenly, gunfire erupted from both sides of the bridge. Bullets zipped through the air. Hunter looked up and saw the beast crash to the ground, its underbelly ripped open. The chimeras at the rear of the horde broke away and charged towards the eastern side of the bridge. Hunter saw the barricades had already been moved aside and swarms of troops across, followed by armoured support.

A larger group of maybe fifty animals turned and raced down towards the toll booths, on the west bank of the river. Hunter saw Nina speeding up the incline in the Jeep, heading right into the advancing pack.

Behind her, a line of tanks lay in wait. Nina weaved through the chimeras as they swarmed around her. One veered straight into her path. She swerved but the creature cracked its tail into the windscreen, and shattered the glass. Hunter saw her terrified expression as she fought to stay in control.

'Jesus Nina – look out!' His words were lost in the clamour of gunfire and howling beasts.

A second creature charged the Jeep, rammed the vehicle broadside, and sent it spinning like a carousel. Grotesque silhouettes sprang out of the gloom, illuminated by the reeling lights. The Jeep toppled onto its side, and fizzed across the road surface, cutting up sparks.

Hunter screamed into the rain. 'Nina!' He saw her body motionless inside the wreckage. A sickening roar bellowed in his ear. The chimera snapped its jaws inches from his face. Suddenly, an arc of electricity zipped through the air. Hunter ducked. The rope of blue light connected with the creature's skull, crackled and the head exploded.

Richard Monkton sat up against the railings, the EPD rod clutched in one hand. 'Take it,' he said. 'The top button means kill.'

'Matt, behind you!' Christian yelled.

A second beast charged in. Hunter held the rod in two hands, and pressed the top button on the grip handle. The shaft vibrated and a bolt of electricity crackled from the tip. The effect on the chimera was devastating. It reared up and collapsed as its skull split open.

Christian broke away and sprinted across to help Nina. Hunter could only watch as the fighting continued. A group of chimeras charged at the tanks but as they swarmed over the turrets they were cut down by the troops advancing at the rear. The beasts seemed to be running blindly now, hurling themselves into a wall of heavy fire.

A Chieftain tank bulldozed into one of the injured creatures and crushed it against the metal railings. Another flattened one of the beasts under its tracks as it lay panting in the centre of the road.

Nina crawled out the window of the upturned Jeep. Christian tried to help her, but they were both caught in the crossfire. Hunter pushed got up and ran to his brother, keeping low as bullets whizzed past his head. Nina's face was streaked with blood, and her legs unsteady. Christian helped her stand. Hunter tensed, expecting another attack, but then noticed the creatures were starting to disperse.

Further up the length of the bridge the soldiers marched through the dead and dying beasts, finishing them off with head shots. Carcasses lay strewn across the four lanes. None were left standing.

'Matt… You okay?' Christian's voice sounded shaky.

Hunter dropped the rod to his side and stumbled towards him. 'We've done it,' he said. 'I can't believe it – we killed the lot of them.'

Christian's face twitched but he didn't smile. Matthew followed his brother's gaze to the body lying within the wreckage of the Jeep. His heart sank. Charles Fenwick lay inside, covered in glass and blood. Hunter bent down and peered in, saw Fenwick was still breathing. He turned and yelled at Christian. 'Get a medic!'

Fenwick muttered something. Hunter leaned in closer and spoke to him as calmly as his sense of shock would allow. 'Just hold on, help is on the way.'

Fenwick shook his head weakly, taking shallow breaths, tried to speak but managed little more than a croak.

Hunter crawled through the broken glass on his hands and knees, reached out and grabbed Fenwick's arm as he lay at a crooked angle on what used to be the roof of the Jeep – now the floor. 'Father we did it,' he said softly. 'It's over. They're all dead.'

Fenwick jerked and his body went into spasm. 'Not over. You must find Swain, he's the key.'

'But Swain's dead. I thought you knew that?'

'No Son, not dead,' Fenwick insisted. 'Find him. Not much time...' His head slumped to one side, his eyes fluttered and closed. Charles Fenwick was gone.

70

HUNTER WATCHED THE AMBULANCE drive away from the bridge and was overcome by a wave of sadness. Charles Fenwick, his true father was dead. But this wasn't the intense pain associated with losing a loved one, more a deep loneliness, a longing that left him empty inside. Maybe the real hurt would come later? He had never known the man - that was the shame of it, the reason for the dull ache inside his chest.

But the battle plan had worked and the chimera horde had been destroyed. Some of the creatures had leapt off the bridge during the attack only to be slaughtered by the machine guns positioned along the river. The Army had taken surprisingly few casualties. Hunter counted only four bodies. Armed with heavy weapons the troops were able to cut the chimeras down in large numbers.

Despite their success, Hunter felt something missing.

What did Fenwick mean about Swain? He said it wasn't over.

Hunter's thoughts were interrupted by a hand on his shoulder.

'I'm sorry Matt,' Christian said, 'I would have told you about Fenwick sooner or later, but I couldn't say anything until all this was done with.'

Matthew sighed and nodded. 'How long have you known?'

'Not long. The truth is if it wasn't for Fenwick we'd all be dead. His hands were tied to a large extent. He told Mum what was going on at Zarcom and trusted us to finish it. The man put his neck on the line for us Matt.'

'Yeah. More than Graham ever did.' The name sounded strange spoken out loud. Graham Hunter had always been 'Dad.' But Matthew couldn't bring himself to call him that any longer – even if he *was* dying from Alzheimer's.

'So now you know the truth,' Christian said. 'Come on. Let's give Mum a call. We can meet up and talk this through. It's going to work out okay Matt, I promise.'

Hunter heard a yelp of pain. He turned and saw two medics helping Monkton onto a stretcher. Walking alongside, holding his hand with a deep expression of concern on her face was Nina.

But somehow this thing didn't feel like it had ended. Fenwick had insisted Swain still had something to do with this. But what? More to the point – how? The American was dead.

Matthew shrugged it off - he needed a beer. Somewhere inside him, he felt the pieces of his soul knitting back together. As for the story...

He'd write that in his own good time. It was his story after all.

Epilogue

2 miles outside Lille, France

20:56 local time

THE HELICOPTER SWOOPED LOW over the airfield as it prepared to land. From the cockpit, Cyrus Modjarrad watched the landing lights rise up to meet him and congratulated himself on a job well done. The chopper set down with a gentle bump.

Home and dry.

Modjarrad ordered his team to stay onboard while he went out to greet his hosts. Darkness had set in, but he could still make out the silhouettes of three hangers on the airfield perimeter and a silver Mercedes speeding across the deserted tarmac to meet him. As the drone of the helicopter dissolved he jumped out and strode towards the car. The Mercedes pulled up a few feet in front of him and three men got out.

'Good to see you Mr. Modjarrad.' The man's accent was American and he wore a thick moustache.

'I trust you've arranged transport out of here?' Modjarrad replied. 'I've brought my science team in case you needed them.'

'Yeah we need them,' the American said. 'That's why we're meeting you here.'

A strange reply, but Modjarrad brushed it aside. 'The data you asked for is in a secure location and I'd like to keep it that way for now - let's call it insurance. I don't want a nasty accident before I settle into my new role.'

The American smiled but said nothing.

'I take it the deals still on?' Modjarrad said.

'There has been a slight change of plan,' the American replied. 'I'm afraid we can't accept you back on the programme Cyrus.'

Modjarrad was stunned into silence, but his fury was quick to surface. 'I knew you bastards would double-cross me. You don't get the technology if you can't stick to our agreement.'

The American grinned. 'It's not the technology we're after. Just your people. You see Cyrus, we always thought your project was a good idea. We just stumbled on something better that's all. Perhaps you'd like me to share it with you.' He ordered one of his men to open the back passenger door.

Modjarrad thought about using the gun tucked in his breast pocket, but didn't get a chance. The two heavies drew their automatics and took aim as a tall figure emerged from the back seat of the Mercedes. There was something familiar about the stranger but Modjarrad couldn't place him. 'Is this some kind of joke?' he said, 'Who is this guy?'

'I'm surprised you don't recognize him Cyrus. You could say he was an original part of your Darwin Project.'

Modjarrad squinted. Yes, he recognized the man now; the lanky framework and spiked up hair. How could this be?

'You escaped,' Modjarrad gasped. 'I saw you inside the facility on the camera monitors. How did you get out alive?'

The tall man stared vacantly as if he hadn't heard.

Modjarrad stepped forward, waved his hand in front of the man's eyes but got no response. 'What have you done to him? He's brain dead.'

'This is the future,' the agent said.

The helicopter cut its engines and the blades slowed to a stop. Modjarrad turned and saw his team being led out at gunpoint to a van parked behind the chopper. He spun and glared at the American. 'Enough of this. I have the backing of powerful men; I will have you thrown out of your precious agency.'

'You're missing the point Cyrus. I want to give you a demonstration.' The agent turned to the tall man, whose gaze remained locked on something invisible in the distance. He stood perfectly still and erect, barely seeming to breathe.

The agent barked an order: 'Swain T 81. Command alpha.'

The words and numbers meant nothing to Modjarrad. The name did however. *Swain - Tom Swain. What the hell have they done to him? He looks drugged.*

As the agent delivered his strange instructions, Swain's face took on a sudden look of realization like his senses had finally kicked in. His eyes widened, he took a deep breath as his chest expanded. Weird sounds accompanied his movements as if his joints were snapping. Swain's eyes bulged like they were being squashed out of his skull. The muscles in his face tightened and his entire body began to shake.

Modjarrad backed away.

The veins in Swain's neck thickened, his jaw widened and elongated until his mouth gaped horribly. An unusual sound seeped from his throat. A strange kind of hiss.

'My God, this man isn't human!' Overwhelmed with dread, Modjarrad reached for his gun and instantly one of the agents shot him in the leg. Modjarrad howled, and fell clutching his knee, blood oozing between his fingers.

Another howl drifted out across the tarmac. Not from Modjarrad but from Tom Swain. His eyes were black and bulging. The veins in his temple were thick like telephone cables. His face stretched and his mouth drooped to expose dozens of razor sharp teeth. The human teeth were still discernable at the front of the gums, but these were a deception, Swain's gums were mere flaps of skin. The real internal structure of his mouth began to take shape - a deep cavern with small teeth stretching all the way down his throat. His hands ballooned in size; black needle-sharp claws where his nails should be. Swain bent over Modjarrad who lay pleading and squealing on the ground.

'What is this? What have you done?' Modjarrad yelled.

The three agents looked down at him. The man with the moustache smiled. 'So you've met Tom Swain. This is his clone. With a few minor changes to the programme we were able to create an obedient chimera, one based on human DNA. This guy takes orders and sees them through without question. That's the good news. The bad news is I've just ordered him to kill you.'

'No. Please no!'

The jaws came down with amazing speed and clamped around Modjarrad's face. He felt his skull crack as he gurgled a final gasp of pain.

Acknowledgments

My thanks go to the following people, all of whom have helped to make this book possible.

Editors: Hazel and Bob Lucas.

Proofreader: Don Cousins.

Artwork: Lewis Tolentino.

Support: The Nordic book club – including Pej, Nicola and Nicole.

Inspiration: My children. Matthew for keeping me practical, Becky for keeping me grounded and Hannah (the little girl who never stopped believing) for keeping me positive.

And finally, for her faith and total support, my wife, Rowena. I love you.

Thank You.